GIRLS ON FILM

CELEBRITY NOVELLAS

JOSIE BAKER

EXPOSED PUBLISHING

Girls on Film novellas:
Little Blonde Lies
Body Double
Skyclad

By Josie Baker
Copyright © 2020 Josie Baker

Cover design and page formatting
by Exposed Publishing

FOREWORD

I hope you enjoy these three novellas, a tantalising glimpse behind the scenes and into the rarefied world of movie, tv and stage celebrities, with an international sporting star / playboy thrown in for fun.

I've never been a celebrity myself, but I have rubbed shoulders with a few…

ACKNOWLEDGMENTS

Heartfelt love and gratitude to my support group Writers not Waiters for their encouragement and support, especially Ree Thornton, Dana Mitchell and Elsa Holland for their patience and priceless advice.

Show me a hero and I will write you a tragedy
F. Scott Fitzgerald

LITTLE BLONDE LIES

AN ENEMIES TO LOVERS ROMANCE

CHAPTER ONE

ANYA'S PATH took her past the fountain where she'd always stopped as a child, the water falling sweetly in a shower of sparkling drops. In those days she'd thrown a coin to a wish for something she'd thought she couldn't live without, a doll or some other trifle. Today she straightened her back and hurried past with only a longing glance for simpler times, her wish too grim for the cheerful fountain. No amount of coins would bring her sister back.

Her phone buzzed in her bag. Anya fished it out, grateful for the distraction from the dark path her thoughts and emotions were heading down.

"Anya Stein," she said, pretending not to recognize the number.

"Munchkin! It's me, Joana."

"Joana who?" Anya's attempt at joviality was rewarded with a deep chuckle that softened the sharp edges of her grief. With a genuine smile she stepped onto one of the many bridges that spanned the tranquil canals of her Portuguese hometown.

"*Megera*," her best friend growled, the familiar banter grounding Anya for the first time since she'd arrived. She'd felt disorientated this morning, as if the train had delivered her to an alternate universe, where grueling rehearsal and performance schedules were no longer her concern. Compared to the familiar grey skies and pollution of London, Aveiro welcomed her with the bright blue of the pristine water and clear skies.

"It's been ages! What's it like to be home?"

"A relief." Anya paused at the center of the bridge, balanced between the historic and contemporary town, and tipped her head back to take a lungful of fresh air. After five years based in London, it was a novelty to move amongst the brightly dressed, meandering tourists admiring historic buildings and brightly painted *moliceiros*. The local boats, similar in shape but larger than a Venetian gondola, bobbed lazily where they were secured on the canal sides, or chugged along purposefully with their cargo of sightseers. "I always forget how much I miss this place. Not having to rush… and being warm. One day I'll come back for good." If she made that promise out loud, maybe she would make it happen, but right now she had only a month to get her head straight so she could tackle her dream role.

"The sooner the better. I don't know how you put up with that hideous English weather." Joana's voice was adamant. Her priority was fun and family and had never understood Anya's single-minded ambition.

"Joana…" Anya had to stifle her frustration, but it was impossible to ignore the truth of her friend's words. In blatant contrast to London smog, the only thing hanging heavy in morning air of the seaside town was the promise of coming summer.

Joana didn't wait for Anya to defend her choice but continued with her usual reasoning. "The move may have been good for your career, but I sometimes think those endless grey skies have sucked the joy out of my old friend. Why don't you come home? You're alone over there…"

"It's not the weather." Anya interrupted, pain slashing her chest. "You know how devastating it was. I finally track down my half-sister," her throat tightened, "only to lose her." And what made it even worse, she'd only learnt of her death by reading it in the news.

… crime scene investigation has so far failed to identify if the incident was an accident or intentional…

Her sister, a law student and part-time Uber driver, drink driving? Not if she'd been in her right mind. There was no way she would have risked her job *and* her career.

The words, stark black on the white screen, and the photo of her wrecked VW Golf, were permanently etched in her mind. Months had passed and it still felt like yesterday.

"I know it's hard for you to understand, with all of your siblings and cousins and extended family, but she was the only blood relative I had. The only one I wanted in my life." The knot of anger, loss and resentment twisted tighter, deeper. "I never had the chance to get to know her, let alone to experience what it feels like to have family I share genetics with."

A respectful pause. "So, you're still not keen on your mum?" Joana's voice was a gentle prod to mend impossible bridges.

"The woman who gave me away?" Anya wished she'd never met the woman who'd kept one daughter but discarded the other like her life was worth less. "And now refuses to tell me anything about my biological father, except that he's dead?

No. I'll stick with the small family of un-relations I have, thanks." Her adopted parents; foster brother, Tomas; and only friend, Joana, were so much more than she'd hoped for after two failed placements with foster families by age eight.

Family. Glancing across the cobblestoned street, Anya proudly picked out the blue and white tiled building of Tomas's *pastelaria.* The pastry café 'Sweet Tomas' took up the ground floor of the prime two-story commercial site, his private apartment the second floor. Popular with tourists and locals alike, during business hours it was constantly alight with conversation and the delicious scents of pastries and coffee.

"Where are you?" Joana's question brought her back from daydreams of playing waitress and pastry chef during her month's break. As well as being fun it was her best chance of spending time with her foster-brother, now he had a new lover to monopolize his spare time.

"On the Rialto." Anya automatically used one of the names they'd given the romantically arched footbridge. The town had been their playground, and the girl's favorite game had been playing the parts of Shakespeare's most tragic characters.

"Still playing Juliet?" Joana asked with a sly edge to her voice, deliberately muddling their preferred roles.

"She was always *your* favorite." Anya had preferred the darker, unredeemable characters.

"You didn't mind playing Romeo. Which reminds me, you've come back at the right time. Enfin Studios is here filming the third season of *KingMaker* down by the lagoon. There are so many muscular male actors and extras around, I've never been so glad to be hetero. We're a bit light on female extras, though. If you weren't home for a rest, I'd try to bribe you into signing on for the month."

"Yeah, I heard the film industry in Portugal is picking up." Anya replied absently while gripping the wood of the handrail, hard. If the cast and crew of *KingMaker* were here in Aveiro, then Ethan Cox would be too. Her breath caught. What were the chances that she would come home now to recharge, when the man she'd fantasized about meeting was here? Fate had handed her an opportunity, all she needed to do was work out what to do with it.

"You also heard that our very own lagoon, beaches and wetlands are going to be admired by the world?"

"No. I hadn't heard." Anya flushed with guilt. She'd been so tied up with her own concerns, what else had she missed? "But I can see you're still the region's fiercest advocate."

"Of course. The studio has invested big bucks to build sets on ten acres of unused farming and woodland south of town. There's talk of more series being filmed there too. It's good for business *and* tourism. It also means I don't need to travel so often for work."

The blast from a conch shell horn drew her attention down to an open-topped boat gliding toward her. Her gaze absently skimmed over the crowded deck, the comfort of habit soothing her agitation. Guessing the origin of the tourists had been another of her childhood amusements.

"*KingMaker*. Isn't that the show with Ethan Cox playing the lead?" Anya held her breath, waiting for confirmation. From this distance she could just make out the relaxed expressions of one couple, his arm wrapped around her shoulder, tucking her close to his body. *French?* A family, two young children bickering, parents looking away from each other, expressions frustrated and tired. *American?*

"The sexy Viking lord who charms his way into the beds of nuns and noblewomen?" Joana's husky voice gave away her admiration for the actor. "That's the one."

Her heart already racing with excitement, Anya's attention snagged on a man wearing a black beanie and dark sunglasses. She stiffened with surprise. *It couldn't be.*

From her place high on the bridge, she couldn't gauge his height, but despite the disguise, Anya would recognize him anywhere. She had studied him so closely she knew the shape of his face - his square jaw, high cheekbones and straight nose - and that dark moustache-goatee combination.

Ethan Cox. She wasn't surprised he would avoid being recognized after his highly publicized string of run-ins with the media.

The controversial star of *KingMaker* gazed down into water, deep in thought, rather than up at the historic buildings that lined the canal, glowing in spring sunshine. As his boat edged closer, she could make out his strong body and erect posture, his wide shoulders and deep chest.

Anya's lips stretched in an approximation of happiness. Despite the amount of time she'd spent studying his industry and public profiles, if they ever met, he wouldn't know *her* from Eve. As a Shakespearean stage actress, her career took her in a different orbit to his world of mainstream entertainment. Which suited her perfectly.

"I gotta go, but that streaming tv show - you don't need to bribe me. I want to work as an extra while I'm here. But don't give them my stage CV. I'm just a local girl looking for a few weeks work."

"Really?" Joana said cautiously and paused, as if suspecting a joke. "Okaaay. I'll contact the talent manager. Where are you staying? I'll call by after work and let you know."

"Thanks, *galinha*. Tomas is bunking in with his new boyfriend so I can stay in his apartment above the café. Come for dinner." Anya ended the call and dropped the phone in her bag without taking her eyes off the star of *KingMaker*.

Before the boat reached the bridge, it turned down the side canal. Anya followed Ethan with her gaze. She wasn't sure what she expected to see in his profile – a cruel set to his mouth or shoulders – but all she could discern beneath his disguise was an air of preoccupation.

In that instant, he turned and looked up at where she stood. A jagged current flew beneath her skin. *He was staring directly at her.* Heart hammering in her chest, she acted on impulse and lifted her arm to wave a languid invitation and, keeping her gaze locked on her prey, she turned to walk in the direction of *Sweet Tomas*. Ethan's head turned, following her movement as she wove through the crowd, until his boat disappeared between rows of pastel colored buildings.

His nearness fueled the rage that constantly simmered in Anya's chest, but the acid taste in her mouth held a hint of sweetness. *Revenge.*

CHAPTER TWO

IT SEEMED as if the girl had been perfectly placed on the bridge to distract him, her red beret like a flash of hope. Even from a distance she'd radiated an almost tangible energy, a promise of something not yet hoped for. In response, the fatigue that dogged him ebbed, as if she'd been sent to lift his spirits and distract him from the torture of imagining Heidi's panic, her struggle in the suffocating, freezing water as the Serpentine stole her life. The pictures he'd created over the past months rarely let him rest.

Ethan pushed his way through the crowd of passengers and jumped off at the next stop, long strides taking him to where he'd seen otherworldly creature. He didn't plan what he would do if he found her, but looking for the girl in the red beret would be as good a diversion as any until the car came to pick him and his luggage up in an hour.

Scanning the crowds, he made his way to the bridge. *No red beret.*

He continued on into the town square, searching the crowds of tourists and shoppers, expecting to find the girl from the bridge with every flash of red. But his search was in vain, as if she were a sprite, returned to her watery home in the nearby lagoon. Or had his subconscious conjured her to distract him?

Anxious not to be late but determined to search every cafe and shop he passed; Ethan turned in the direction of his hotel. Before he left the square, he raised his gaze and took one sweeping glance around - and froze mid-turn at the flash of red glimpsed through an open window. There she was, stepping out onto the Juliet balcony of a blue and white tiled building. A café.

He fought the urge to fist pump the air. He'd found her. She *was* real.

The girl raised her slim arm and waved again, beckoning him with a graceful curl of her fingers.

Without thinking what he'd do when he got to her, Ethan strode between outdoor tables of diners indulging in cakes and pastries, tea and coffee, too absorbed in their pleasures to spare him more than a passing glance. Inside, he paused and orientated himself, sweet and bitter aromas and the hum of many conversations filling his senses. He thanked technology for his self-adjusting sunglasses that allowed him to remain anonymous as he glanced around, searching for a way up to her.

Vintage glass cabinets lined the walls as he made his way over the wooden floor, through tables and chairs to a staircase along the rear brick wall. With each creak of the steps beneath his feet, doubt set in. Even if the girl *could* distract him, it would only be for a short time. Any reprieve he found - he didn't deserve.

Thinking he would emerge into an upstairs dining area; Ethan was shocked to find himself in a private living space. A large, unmade bed. A table for two. And there she was, standing in front of open French doors that lead out to the balcony he'd seen from below. With the sunlight pouring in behind her, she was no more than silhouette of a girl.

"Hello," he said, standing on the landing, hands hanging awkwardly at his sides. *What was he doing here, chasing a stranger into her home?*

"Hi," she replied in a soft, warm voice as she moved toward him, stepping out of the light from the window. The red beret crowned a clearer version of the face he'd glimpsed on the bridge, a navy sundress accentuating the paleness of her slim, bare arms.

She was smaller than she'd seemed then, her head would barely reach his chest. A flurry of impressions crashed over him. Pale elfin face. Large, pale-blue eyes. Long eyelashes. Lush, pink lips. The inviting scent of vanilla. The warmth of her fingers as she reached out to take his hand. Ethan swayed and, with a tug, the sprite pulled him into the room. He submitted to her direction, following her to the window where she turned to him. He fidgeted as her incisive gaze started an investigation from his chest, tilting up to graze his chin, sliding over his cheeks. Would she recognise him?

Finally, her curious gaze met his, and even through his shades, something sparked between them. Attraction? Mutual need? As if under her spell, he was unable to look away, unable to move. It was as if her cool blue eyes had pierced his heart, seeing his guilt and promising atonement. The traces of tension he hadn't realised he still held melted away. Even before Heidi's death, anxiety had kept him on a razor edge. For the first time in nearly a year, he relaxed.

He took off the glasses, and when there was no 'I know who you are' spark in her eyes, he took off his beanie. The cool air on his head was a relief after the heat of the sun on the black wool, as was the lack of recognition. Even without his disguise, he was anonymous here.

His soul cried out for forgetfulness, and for a dizzy moment he imagined he could kiss her. But it had been too long since the last time his lips had tasted another's. He knew if he started, it would be difficult to stop, and he had to be ready for his driver. If he tasted her, he would need time to savour everything the sweet sprite had to offer.

"Who are you?" If she lived up here, she must own or manage the patisserie. A pastry chef? He wanted to know more, like what she did for work. More importantly, what she did for fun.

"Who do you want me to be?" she replied in her charming Portuguese accent.

"I would like you to be my date on Sunday."

"Then that's what I shall be."

Her smile ignited a spark of hope in his chest. "I need to go, but I will meet you here, at 10am Sunday?" He smiled and ignored the instinct that told him it was a bad idea.

"I'll be waiting for you." She raised herself on her toes and kissed him, the sweet vanilla scent of her wrapping him in the embrace her body withheld. In the warm soft press of her lips he glimpsed bliss, of satisfaction long denied. The tantalising promise of pleasure threatened to make him forget his priorities, but she pulled away, leaving her taste lingering on his tongue. Floral, with the tang of honey. He yearned for more but forced himself to turn and leave.

Priority.

There was only one, the career he had sacrificed so much for, the dedication to being professional.

Professional?

He'd been insane to ask her out. He should ignore his dick and tell her he'd made a mistake.

Ethan stopped on the top step and turned.

Dragging his gaze from the unmade bed, he tried to think rationally and not imagine how he wanted to spend the rest of the day. Ulrich the Viking had other ideas and fought to take control, hungry to feel the silken skin of her breasts against his palms, a sweet nipple between his fingertips… And he didn't even know her name.

"What is your name?" The question emerged in Ulrich's diction and Ethan cursed the downside of method acting. The sprite had got under his skin and tapped into the creativity he used to become one with his character.

"Anya. And what is yours?" She tilted her head.

Ethan let go of the breath he was holding. That she had asked proved she really didn't know who he was. Everyone in the small regional town might be aware of the filming happening nearby, but it didn't mean everyone was interested.

"Ethan," he replied with a relieved smile, convincing himself his reputation would be safe with her. "I'll see you on Sunday."

ANYA SPENT the day hanging out at the *pastelaria* with Tomas and, as promised, Joana called by after work.

"Look at you! You're pale as a ghost. You need to get that gorgeous body out in the sun." It was the first time they'd seen each other in a couple of months and Joana, lean and tanned, enclosed her friend in a hug.

"Sure Jo. One day." Laying in the sun for hours wasn't Anya's idea of relaxing. It still puzzled her that they'd been friends since the day they met in detention at primary school, despite the differences in their temperaments. Even visually they were opposites, but with Joana's height and dark hair and Anya's petite paleness, they were the perfect foil for each other's individual beauty.

When Stefan, Tomas' new lover, arrived they sat down at the table Tomas had set in front of the open front doors. With the lights off except the candles lighting on the table, no passing tourist could mistake that they were open for business. Gypsy jazz played softly in the background as they feasted on fresh seafood and salad and chilled, crisp white wine.

"It's nice of you to vacate your apartment for Anya to stay." Joana looked knowingly at Tomas over the rim of her wine glass.

"I know she likes to have her own space." He grinned mischievously at Stefan. "And I'll take any excuse to bunk in with my boy for a few weeks."

"A few weeks? I thought you'd moved in judging by all the stuff you brought over." Stefan smiled indulgently. When they hurried off as soon as they'd finished dessert, Anya wondered if Tomas would ever move back to his apartment.

With the boys gone, Joana handed her a DVD case with a wink. "You might want to see what you're in for."

Anya glanced at the cover – season one of *Kingmaker*.

"Does this mean they want me?" Anya tensed with anticipation. Even though she had no plan except to exploit any opportunity that came her way, at least she would be doing something constructive.

"How could they not? But are you sure you want to spend your holidays working?"

"Being an extra isn't work." As well as they knew each other - and Joana was the only one apart from Tomas who really *knew* Anya - if she confessed why she was keen to work on *KingMaker*, she wasn't certain her best friend *or* her half-brother would understand. "And you know I can't do nothing. It's either this or get Tomas to teach me how to make *ovos moles*."

Joana pulled a face. "I've tasted your culinary efforts. I'd like to spare the town from your attempts at our iconic pastry."

Anya laughed but quickly sobered. "Thank you for not saying anything to Tomas about the job. I didn't want to mention anything until I knew. I came here to spend time with him."

"You'll still see him. You'll have the weekends off, and they have a bus to bring the extras back into town every night. Although I think I'd rather be one of the actors and stay at the camp they've setup on location. Imagine what goes on out there." Joana was almost panting at the thought.

"Unfortunately, Tomas seems to be fully occupied at night."

"Perfect! We can go out hunting together. You sure you don't want to hit the clubs now?"

"I'm not up for it just yet. On the weekend?"

"I'll hold you to that. We could watch the first season of *KingMaker* instead?"

"I've seen both seasons already." Anya tried to hand the DVDs back to Joana. She'd watched every episode with her half-sister, sitting side-by side on her sofa while eating take-out.

Joana held up her hands, palms out, refusing to take the case. "I cannot believe you don't want to drool over Ethan Cox and

Liam Byrne. Are you sure you're still breathing?" She placed two fingers against Anya's neck as if searching for a pulse. "Last time I saw you there'd been no horizontal action in your life, and I can see by that guilty look, there hasn't been any since."

Anya shrugged. "I often go for weeks without even thinking about sex. Difficult for a nymphomaniac like you to fathom, but it makes life simpler."

"Your libido has only two settings – full off or full on." Joana shook her head in disbelief.

"And yours only has one." Anya replied with a raised eyebrow. Unlike her best friend, Anya's urge to take a lover didn't happen often, but when it hit, it was as consuming as a fire raging in her blood. One that inevitably burnt out within days. "I'm sure it's for the best. Relationships are hard work. The men I go for always let me down and career success is so much more satisfying."

"I see you as Sleeping Beauty, pale and still, waiting for a prince with the magic…"

"Kiss." Anya finished for her friend with a fond grin.

"Speaking of getting some, I'm hooking up with a barman from Luxe when he finishes his shift at 2am. I should go get a few hours' sleep before then."

After they cleared away the dishes and stacked the dishwasher, Joana hugged her good-bye. "I worry about you. You shouldn't take sex so seriously. Think of it as a bodily need, like eating."

"If that were the case, I'd be bulimic."

"Understandable if you were living with all these pastries on a permanent basis. Maybe that's how Tomas manages to stay so slim – or lots of exercise." Joana giggled and turned for the back door. "I'll text you the address of where to meet the studio bus that will take you out to the set Wednesday morning. I hope you like early starts."

Anya locked up after her friend and took the rest of the Riesling upstairs. She hesitated before inserting disc one into Tomas's DVD player. Watching the series again would be like reliving the fleeting time she had with her sister.

She turned off the lights and settled on the big bed with the remote. Shivering at the memory of Ethan's gaze when he'd been here, drawn like a magnet to these rumpled sheets, she pulled up the blanket and hit 'play'. And there he was, the glorious Ulrich on the flatscreen, stepping out of the lake in all his glistening glory. Anya squirmed at the oddness of watching the man she'd just met in person, right here, naked on Tomas's TV. Most surprising was the rare yet familiar tension flaring low in her abdomen. The last time that spark had been lit, she'd been lured from sexual hibernation by her leading man. Even though she'd known he would disappoint, and then she would have to continue working with him, she'd not been able to control the rare but sudden impulse.

Now it seemed Ethan Cox was stirring her blood. She'd heard that lust sometimes went hand-in-hand with anger, but she'd never experienced it herself. She hoped her fickle libido would work to her advantage this once, rather than hindering her not-yet-formed plans. The last thing she needed was another complication.

Anya hugged her knees to her chest and studied her target in a way she wouldn't be able to in the flesh. Even with long hair and fake scars, she could clearly see the man she'd just met in his on-screen character. There had been glimpses of Ulrich when he'd come to find her. Like his character, his so-expressive eyes had broadcast his thoughts and desires.

It had been obvious Ethan Cox wanted her, and if she wished it, their date would end in this bed.

Anya laughed, a sound without humor. She would find a way to use his desire against him.

CHAPTER THREE

WITH MUD and fake gore from the fight scene caking his costume, Ethan filed into the feasting hall with his fellow actors, leaving the dead and dying to pack up for the day. The other guys horsed around as they took their places for the scene where the victorious warriors quenched their appetites. Ethan smiled at their antics.

Most of the actors were young guys from the city who were behaving as if they were away on school camp. Ethan couldn't blame them their high spirits, he felt the influence of the clear air and open spaces too, but he was also constantly aware of the responsibility of being the lead actor. If the production fell behind schedule, or if they had to retake key scenes, it would cost the studio and reflect badly on him.

He played his part without thinking, merely a face in the crowd for the feast scene, until the brush of an extra's hand against his sent a bolt of lust through him. Out of nowhere, that single light touch had his skin tingling and every sense awakened to the woman who had innocently touched him. He looked up in surprise and caught the profile of the dirty and disfigured serving wench as she turned away, leaving a hint of vanilla in her wake.

He tried to hide his reaction to her touch and mentally kicked himself. He'd been thinking too much of Anya, her pale, elfin face and hot little body. The smell of vanilla had reminded him of her, and his suddenly overactive libido projected his desire onto the extra. She'd been dressed and made-up to appear dowdy and unkempt, but he sensed the grace of her movements beneath her cowering and servile attitude.

For the rest of the scene he struggled to remember his few lines, did his best to ignore the girl with the matted, brown hair, but his body seemed to instinctively know where she was amongst the revellers and servants milling around the dim wooden hall, even when she was outside his line of vision. When one of his fellow warriors carried her off to rape her at the end of the scene, it took all his discipline to stay seated and not deck him.

"It's a wrap. See you all on Monday." The director called out and strode off to speak to the editor.

Ethan slipped away and stalked back to the make-up trailer; fists clenched at his side. In the sanctuary of his cubicle, he slumped in his seat. Having his hair extensions removed before his day off was the sign for his body to relax, but he shouldn't be this exhausted, barely halfway through the seasons shooting.

"Looks like you'll sleep well tonight," observed Josie, his hair and makeup guru, her dreadlocks brushing his arm as she struggled with a particularly stubborn section of hair. Assigned to him since episode one, she'd witnessed his struggle to find reasons to keep going after Heidi's death. Her sympathetic ear and encouragement had kept him sane when the world seemed to make no sense.

"I hope so." Saturday, the last day of the working week, would normally be his best chance at sleep, but he already knew it wouldn't be the case tonight. Was it the move from the hotel to the tent village, the change of location from town to the isolated wasteland, or the girl in the red beret? All he'd been able to think about was how desperately he wanted to get away from the crowds, to feel her arms wrapped tight around his ribs and her breasts pressed against his back as they shared the rush of speed and freedom. He hoped she'd be okay with the bike he'd hired.

At last, the day of their date was only a matter of hours away, after the week had seemed to spin out endlessly. The hours spent sitting still in makeup had been the hardest. He'd been too wound up to flick through a magazine or cruise the web, so he'd spent the time researching and planning their date. At least it had taken his mind off Heidi.

"Any plans?" Josie knew him well enough to expect a 'no' and liked him enough to hope an invitation would be forthcoming.

"Actually, I do. I have a date," he said gently, his gaze apologetic as it met hers in the mirror.

"I thought you seemed distracted this week." Josie dipped her head and avoided his eyes. "A local girl, I'm guessing. There hasn't been a whisper of it in the tent village."

"Yeah. A girl I met the morning we moved here from town. Her name's Anya." It gave him pleasure to speak her name aloud, despite a twinge of guilt. Even though he'd never given her reason to expect more than platonic friendship, he still felt the responsibility of Josie's expectations.

"I'm glad for you. I was starting to worry. All work and no play, you know..." Josie gave his reflection a tight but understanding smile.

Yeah, he knew. It had been so long since he'd had sex, the thought of it was staring to mess with his head. Today was a case in point. Maybe he should have tried to start dating earlier. If the urge was merely an itch to be scratched, it would be safer, and easier to keep quiet, to hook up with someone on-set. Anyone but Josie. She was perfect for him, understood his work and lifestyle, but he felt nothing but friendship for her.

And he had committed to Sunday with Anya. He would not disrespect her by chasing after some bedraggled extra.

"Aren't you worried the media will make a big deal of it?"

Sometimes Ethan wondered if Josie could see into his mind.

"I'm hoping to avoid any photos, gossip, or news articles." More than anything he needed to keep his reputation spotless after the media had painted him as a womanizer before Heidi's death, and the cause of it after the accident.

"Good luck with that."

"It shouldn't be difficult." He shrugged. "It's only one date." One date he hoped would lead to sex. The incident with the serving wench had proven he needed to get whatever 'this' was out of his system. But he would have to make it clear to Anya that he couldn't do anything other than casual. If she was good with that, they could have some horizontal - or vertical - fun. It would be safe it he kept it brief, discreet, and non-committal.

And he really did hope she agreed to have sex with him. *Then* he could get back to focussing all his attention on work, and maybe start to let go of his guilt over Heidi.

You don't deserve it, the voice in his head reminded him.

A stinging punch to his upper arm diverted Ethan's thoughts from spiralling. He looked up at his co-star who was dressed in a crisply ironed shirt and slim tailored pants.

"Look at you, with that frown on your face when every woman on set wants to get into your pants." Liam Byrne grinned down at him.

"I am here to work. You know that. No distractions." Ethan looked around and found Josie gone. Had she said good-bye? *Had he?* Ethan scrubbed his hands over his scalp. Everyone else had already cleared out, eager to get the bus into town.

"You *look* pretty distracted. That extra must have caught up with you." Liam smirked.

"Which extra?" An uneasy feeling unfurled in his gut.

"Little blonde thing. She looks like she'd be a wild ride. Seemed very determined to find out what type you usually go for and how *easy* you are." Liam shrugged to imply it didn't bother him she was more interested in Ethan rather than him. With his rugged good looks and Irish accent, Liam had no trouble finding his own enthusiastic bed partners.

Ethan exhaled in relief even as his chest tightened with disappointment. *Not the brown-haired wench then.*

"What did you tell her?"

"The boring truth. You're a saint. She seemed disappointed. And by the look on your face I'm guessing this won't be the week you're going to prove me wrong."

ANYA WATCHED Ethan disappear into the trailer next to the one allocated to the extras and huffed with frustration. She went inside and sat to wait while the clips that held her wig in place were removed, watching the other extras mill around without urgency, removing their makeup, switching costumes for their civvies. The next bus back to town wasn't due to leave for half an hour and everyone had tomorrow off. She envied their light spirits, heightened by the promise of a night without the restriction of an early start the next day.

But Anya wasn't relaxed. What she'd thought would be as easy as asking the right person the right questions, had turned out to be a lesson in frustration. She had subtly questioned everyone she came into contact with but hadn't dug up anything she could leak to the media. From cast and crew alike, she'd heard only praise for Ethan's work ethic and respect for his professionalism.

But there had to be something. He'd followed *her*, a stranger on the street, when they'd first met in town; and his physical reaction to the serving wench had been obvious. She'd felt the intensity of his attention for the rest of the scene. Surely there were others he'd flirted with. Surely, he'd screwed at least one of them. But there was no proof, no witnesses.

She straightened in her seat and stared at reflection with resolve as the heavy wig was lifted from her scalp. She would have to create the dirt herself, and her first opportunity would be on their date tomorrow.

The door swung open and the talent manager, Phillipe, entered with a waft of salty ocean air, reminding her she was never far from the sea in Aveiro. The room buzzed at the presence of the man who held the promise of career opportunities in his hands. Phillipe looked around the room, his gaze locking on Anya before he headed in her direction. A flick of his head dismissed the hairdresser and he folded his tall, thin frame onto her vacated stool.

"Great work today Anya." He smiled at her in the mirror. Every conversation in the room hushed, all ears pricked for gossip.

"Thank you," she replied and turned to face him. She hadn't expected him to be the type to take the time to praise an extra, or to find out her name.

"I was pleasantly surprised when I found out who you are. I can see this might be fun compared to the high-brow gigs you usually do."

"It has been fun, so far."

"I know you signed up for non-speaking work, but I have something juicier for you if you're interested?"

"What did you have in mind?" Anya asked cautiously. Could Fate be offering her another opportunity?

"The actress we had lined up for a guest role dislocated her shoulder water-skiing. We have a back-up on location who already knows the lines, but she's not you."

"The thing is, I'm here on holiday, and only for a few weeks." And taking on a speaking role would mean not returning to the apartment above the *pastelaria* every night. Less time to spend with Tomas.

"What if I said that would work?" Philippe tented his hands in front of his mouth and gave her a hopeful look.

"Even if I wanted to, I don't think I can. I have an exclusivity agreement with the production company I'm contracted to. There might be a way around it, but I'd have to talk to my agent, *if I wanted to.*" And she might want to if she didn't get what she needed tomorrow. Living on location in the same camp as the actors would give her access to a lot of what happened behind the scenes.

"I understand. I'll have the part delivered to where you're staying. If you like it, talk to your agent." Philippe straightened on the stool and prepared to stand, a surge of hurried whispers amongst the extras accompanying the movement. "And Anya? You'd be doing us a huge favour."

"Okay. I'll take a look." Anya shrugged and willed herself not to get excited. *Yet.* If Fate was on her side, the part might be the perfect opportunity for revenge.

"Let me know by Monday morning. The costumer has an office in town. She can do the fittings and adjustments while you learn your lines. You could be on-set Tuesday. With your experience, we should be able to squeeze it all in before you go back to London."

He turned at the door before stepping outside. "You don't have a problem with nude scenes, do you?"

CHAPTER FOUR

ANYA WAS grateful for the Sunday morning-tea rush at the *pastelaria*. She busied herself taking and delivering orders and clearing tables, trying to escape the flutter of nerves shadowing her every thought. It was a relief when the roar of an approaching engine announced the inevitable. The air seemed to vibrate with the sound, filling her with excitement, the blood in her veins pounding with anticipation. She didn't need to look at the old wooden clock on the wall to know it was 10am. To know it was him.

Rushing outside with a tray of pastries and espressos, Anya deposited the order in front of an elderly American couple and paused to admire the sleek black motorcycle that slowed to a stop out front. The firm, denim-clad thighs and muscular shoulders of the rider confirmed it was, indeed, her date. The surge of desire that coursed through her body, making her skin tingle with the urge to touch and be touched, was a double-edged weapon, but she was committed to seeing this through.

Would today bring her an opportunity to give the media proof they were right about Ethan Cox?

Anya waved to Ethan and rushed inside, tore her apron off and grabbed her leather backpack from Tomas's office. "I'm off," she said, giving her brother a peck on the cheek. He leaned out the office door to get a look at her date through the front windows.

"I can see why you were so secretive about your plans for today, Sis. If you'd told me you were going for a ride with a hot man dressed in leather, I might have locked you away and gone in your place."

"I won't tell Stefan you said that."

"Maybe you should – he might follow your date's example." He gave her a light shove in the small of her back. "Now, go. I don't want to see you until you've had a thorough ravishing, okay? You are way too tense for your own good."

Anya turned and paused. "Do I have your permission to bring him back here?"

"Please do. And make sure you introduce me to your sexy mystery man."

"Oh, don't worry, I intend to." Tomas kept up with all the gossip and would certainly recognise Ethan when she brought him back here. Anya was relying on his business-sense to get material evidence of a visit from the controversial star. No doubt Ethan's image would be plastered over social media by the end of the day, and she would make sure he had an anonymous girl attached to his lips.

Anya took a bracing breath and stepped outside. Ethan stood by the bike, holding a red helmet with a leather jacket draped over his arm. He'd flipped his visor up but kept his sunglasses on. *Incognito.* Despite her hatred for the man, his air of mystery enflamed her body's traitorous response. She wouldn't need to act the part of an amorous date; she would just need to make sure she stayed in her local girl persona.

"You don't mind if we ride?" he asked, lifting the jacket in invitation.

"Mind? I can't wait. It has been an age since I've been on a motorcycle." She said as she shrugged into the unworn leather.

Ethan handed her the helmet and watched her slide it over her short hair. "You're blonde. I couldn't tell the other day, under the beret."

"Disappointed?" she asked, lifting her chin as he reached to fasten her chin strap. His knuckles brushed her neck and she shivered.

"Not at all. I just assumed with your dark eyelashes and eyebrows…"

His mouth was so close she could see the cleft in the centre of his lower lip. She stifled the urge to run her fingertip − or her tongue − over the soft fullness… and follow the crease inside. Instead she dragged her eyes to his. "Maybe, I dye it?" Anya said, and with a raised eyebrow flipped her visor down.

Ethan flipped his down over a grin and a sweet ache pulsed low in Anya's abdomen at the implication he intended to find out. She watched as he gracefully straddled the bike, kicked the stand up and turned to her.

When she was sure she had his attention, Anya gathered the hem of her light cotton dress and swung her bare leg over the seat behind him, sliding forward so her pelvis tucked in behind his.

"As much as I appreciate the view, I should have thought to bring leather pants for you."

"No need. I prefer to ride like this. I love the feel of leather on bare skin." The sun-warmed leather tingled on Anya's inner thighs as she leant forward, shaping her body to his broad back and wrapping her arms around his waist. "Don't tell me where we're going. Surprise me." It was enough of a novelty not to have plans for the day, she could enjoy the indulgence *and* be ready to take hold of any opportunity to expose him.

"I'll do my best." Ethan laughed and started the bike, pulling smoothly into the traffic to ride slowly through the cobbled streets.

The combination of having a man and the throb of a powerful engine between her legs made her yearn for release, and Anya tried to suppress her growing arousal by studying the details of the historic buildings they passed, as if Ethan were the guide and she the visitor.

Once they joined the highway west, Ethan opened the throttle and the engine roared beneath them like a dangerous beast. Anya's pulse accelerated with their speed and for the first time in years she had the urge to laugh with joy. Instead she clung tighter and contained her exhilaration.

They turned north before they reached the roundabout that would have taken them either north to Barra or south to Coast Nova and beyond. Anya's natural curiosity was satisfied when Ethan pulled into the carpark for the platform ferry that would take them across to Sao Jacinto and the narrow spit of land between the lagoon and the ocean.

The deep blue of the Atlantic, uninterrupted by discernible waves, called to them across the canal. Anya fought a dip of disappointment. Unless they stopped at a café, there would be little chance of being seen together in the sparsely populated nature reserve on the other side.

Resigning herself to Fate, Anya breathed in the diesel and salt-laden air with relish as they crossed. The beaches here were known not only for the soft sand, but also the rollers that pummelled the coastline. It seemed today was one of the rare times the ocean showed its benevolence, as if welcoming her home.

On land again, Ethan led them in a slow, graceful dance through the narrow streets, and Anya relaxed her body to abandon herself to the feeling of being one with man and machine.

"Glad you came?" Ethan asked over his shoulder.

"Very," Anya said and pressed her lips closed to stop herself admitting how glad she was to be here, back in the place she still thought of as home. She wished she could visit more often, even though her foster parents no longer lived here. *Keep your guard up, Anya.*

There was no chance for conversation as they sped north along the lagoon, the scent of sun warmed leather and Ethan's cologne filling her nostrils. Not until they slowed at the outskirts of the township of Torreira. "I miss the thrill of being on two wheels and at the mercy of the elements," she admitted, unable to keep her delight fully contained. "Although this is quite different to the scooter my brother used to taxi me around on."

"Let me re-acquaint you," Ethan said and opened the throttle when they'd cleared the town, showing Anya just how different a beast the BMW was, the power of the engine throbbing between her thighs and sending vibrations through her body.

For a short time, Anya abandoned herself to the thrill of moving as one with Ethan as they leant into curves, sharing the joy of flying down dips and over rises at high speed.

Snapshots of their surroundings washed over her, the vibrant blue of the sky soaring above, a green blur of bushland on their left, sunlight on the still water flashing passed on their right.

Too soon, Ethan slowed the bike and turned down a narrow road, where holiday homes and farmhouses gave way to tall pines either side. Reality seeped in with the decrease in speed, and Anya leant back, putting some distance between her body and his, angry with herself for taking pleasure in being with this man.

The road narrowed further and before it turned to sand, Ethan pulled over to the side. The deep blue of the ocean was visible where the trees ended.

Anya loosened her hold, physically missing the feel of his muscular body but relieved to put some distance between them.

Ethan killed the engine and Anya slid off. Before she'd finished stretching her legs, he was in front of her. Too close, but she couldn't move away from the strong hands reaching for her neck. She held her breath as he unbuckled the strap of her helmet, the tiny hairs on the backs of his fingers sending shivers of desire over her skin. She lifted her helmet off, watching the play of a smile on his lips as he removed his own. He held out his hand for her helmet and hung them both from the handlebars.

"How did I do?" Ethan turned back to her with his sunglasses in his hand and she had to look away from the teasing expression that crinkled the corners of his chocolate brown eyes and tied her insides in knots. "Is this a good place for a picnic?"

"I've actually never been to this beach, but it looks perfect." The breeze tickled the damp skin of her face and teased her hair. She glanced around, taking in the beauty. Not another soul in sight, azure ocean stretching to the horizon, seabirds drifting in the air or chattering to each other on the sand. No witnesses, no need to remember why they were here. "Sometimes it takes a visitor to find the true beauty of a place." Anya said. She was surprised Ethan had found such a secluded spot. She'd rarely ventured this far herself, even when she lived here.

"I'm glad you approve." He grinned. "If you'll excuse me a moment, I'll organise the food?" Ethan asked and held up his phone. At her nod, he typed a quick message then slipped it in his helmet. "So the hotel knows where to deliver."

"I'm impressed."

"With my logistical planning?"

"That, and I like the way you ride," she said with a playful smile she couldn't restrain.

"We do move well together," he replied, the caress of his voice inferring they should try out the theory in a more intimate situation. "In fact, that was one of the most enjoyable rides I've been on."

Anya's breathing quickened. "You *ride* often?" She teased him back.

"Not as often as I'd like." He seemed to withdraw; his teasing tone diluted. "I have a Ducati at home. I don't have room at my place so she's currently living in the lounge room at my brother's place."

"Where is home?" Anya had noticed there was barely a trace of Ulrich in his speech today, allowing his native accent to show through, an unusual combination peppered with American 'r's.

"Hamburg is where I grew up, but my mother was originally from New York. I travel a lot for work and don't get to ride as often as I'd like, so I thought I'd hire one." He spread his palm on the surface of the petrol tank. The gesture reminded her of a lover's caress.

"Good choice then. The coast of Portugal is a great place for riding, at this time of the year anyway. Winter will be too wet if you're planning to be here then."

"I won't be, but you're right, the weather is perfect now. Warm enough to swim in fact. Did you bring a swimsuit?" One corner of his mouth quirked up.

Anya's stomach flipped and her nipples tightened, rubbing against the lace of her bra. "I didn't, but that won't stop me swimming. It's rare for conditions to be this calm. I'm not going to miss the chance." Lord, she needed to cool down after that ride. Lucky she was wearing her best underwear.

"I didn't bring swimmers either. I wasn't sure it would be warm enough, but I hoped." The grin was Ulrich's, promising pleasure - if one dared to participate.

Was he testing her, to see how far she'd go? He might be a cheating womanizer, but the dare roused her competitive nature, and she retaliated by stepping out of her sandals, and gathering the hem of her sundress. She raised an eyebrow at him as she slowly lifted it higher.

Ethan grinned and pulled the hem of his t-shirt upward, revealing taut abs and bunching pecs. "Challenge accepted," he said before the fabric covered his face.

Anya swayed, light-headed, blood surging at the sight of his torso stretched almost bare before her, the patch of dark hair on his chest narrowing as it travelled south and disappeared beneath the waistband his jeans.

Breathe, she told herself, turning away from the hungry look in his eyes when his head emerged from the fabric, hair mussed. Anya wanted to cry with frustration. If only she could abandon herself to the rare attraction.

"Let's do it!" he said, hands reaching for his fly.

Anya's insides clenched. As a fellow German, she suspected he'd have no compunction about swimming naked. Instead of watching him unbutton and step out of his jeans, she turned and ran over the hot sand.

"Chicken," he called after her, and his footfalls in the sand soon followed.

The shock of cool water on her sun-warmed skin returned her senses and she waded through the shallows. When she heard him splashing behind her, she dove in, swimming underwater until her flesh cooled.

Surfacing, she turned, treading water, to find him free styling toward her, his strokes devouring the distance between them.

Switching to breaststroke, he approached slowly, a slight smile on his lips, eyes intense.

"I thought you were a water-sprite when I first saw you. Now I'm convinced. And from what you've said of the conditions today, it seems you even have the mighty Atlantic under your spell."

"And what if I am?" Anya shivered, her body aching for him to reach her, to reach *for* her.

"I'm not sure. Will you send me to my death if I touch you?"

The suggestion sent a jolt of shock through her muscles. *Could she?* Even if she was strong enough to overpower him, did his crime deserve such a reprisal?

Finding he could touch the bottom, Ethan stood before her. He placed his hands on her waist.

Anya sighed and stopped treading water. She relaxed in his grip, anticipating the meeting of their bodies. As intimately acquainted as she'd become with his back, his front was still a shock when their hips drifted together. His breath warm on her wet face, his pecs brushing her erect nipples, his stomach cool against hers… and the bulge in his shorts nestled gently into the cleft at the top of her thighs. Regret and relief warred in her gut at the brush of wet fabric. *Not naked.*

"No scales, so I might be safe," he said as he slid his hands over her hips and pulled her to him more firmly, eyes closing in pleasure.

More than anything she'd wanted in a long time, she wanted to share that pleasure. Ignoring the fact there were no witnesses, Anya convinced herself she was playing to script when she slid her hands over his shoulders, up his neck and pulled his mouth to hers. She crushed his lips beneath hers and he responded in kind, the day's anticipation expressed in the pressure of their kiss. She felt weightless… yet anchored to him.

A speed boat raced by in the distance. The drone of the engine and crash of the hull against the waves momentarily lifted the spell wrapping seductive arms around them. Ethan pulled away, gasping. Breathing ragged, he opened his eyes, the befuddlement there revealing his enchantment.

Exhilaration surged like a drug through Anya's veins and she let instinct take over. From the smooth, salty skin of his neck, she sucked his earlobe into her mouth, savouring the taste of his skin and her power over him.

He groaned and pulled her close again, the hard muscles of his thighs pressing against hers.

The sound of his pleasure sparked a rush of warmth to her sex, a the insistent nudge of his erection sparking a tingling awareness, accompanied by the urgent need to have him inside her.

A warning reverberated like a shock in her skull.

She wanted him. She wanted to make love to Ethan Cox. *Desperately.*

Pushing on his chest, Anya launched away from him.

"Sorry," she said and turned in the water, swimming back to the shallows then wading to the beach. As much as her desire was absolute when she was possessed, she had never wanted a man *this* much. The one man she could not lose control over.

Fighting tears of frustration, Anya stomped over the hot sand toward his bike, welcoming the burn. She reached for a towel, folded neatly on top of an insulated hamper and picnic basket that had been delivered while they were swimming.

Shaking out the towel, Anya spread it on the sand, and stretched out in the sun to dry. She took slow, deep breaths and let the sound of lazy waves lapping at the sand and the warm caress of the sun soothe her until she could think clearly again.

Ethan had planned today carefully. If Anya had believed in happy-ever-afters, this would be how they started. But she was not naive. These were the signs of a practised *séducteur*, and she would exploit any opportunity to prove it to the world.

Think of today as an acting job. Enjoy your physical response to him, but disassociate, she told herself. Two birds, one stone. Pleasure and revenge. She would return to London calm and ready for the biggest challenge of her career so far.

A few minutes later, Anya heard the splash of Ethan approaching and sat up.

And there he was, the man who could give her what she needed, wading out of the ocean, wet skin glistening. With the sun at full strength and reflecting off the sand and ocean, it could have been Ulrich striding toward her. But where the gloriously naked Ulrich's modesty was protected by a camera angle that would appease the censors, Ethan wore boxers. A flimsy costume, wet as they were, clinging to his hips and leaving little to the imagination.

Sinking into her role of Anya the *pastelaria* owner, she admired the beyond-perfect physique of the man striding toward her, the sun on his damp flesh accentuating the firmness of shoulders, arms, chest and stomach. Her gaze dropped to the tense and relax of the muscles of his thighs and calves, then his feet as they came to a stop beside her towel. Droplets of water landed in the sand beside her.

She looked up slowly and blinked. "I got a little overwhelmed. I'm okay now. It's your own fault. You shouldn't be so sexy."

"Ditto," he said with a smile and held out his hand. Anya placed her palm in his and he lifted her easily to her feet.

"I'm glad you slowed things down. I wanted to talk to you before things went that far."

"Oh?" *Damn it.* Was he going to tell her they couldn't? Was he in another relationship already? From what she'd heard, that wouldn't stop him screwing her.

"It might help me concentrate if you put this on." He smiled gently and handed her dress, then turned to retrieve the hampers while she slipped it on.

Once her bra and panties were covered again, she sat, watching him unpack and arrange assorted salads and antipasto onto the picnic towel he'd laid out. Despite her concern over what he was about to say, her stomach grumbled. "You planned all this - for me?"

"I wanted to impress you." He added a plate of sliced fruit and a basket of bread to the feast and sat back on his heels.

"But?" she prompted him, wanting to know what she was dealing with.

"Anya, you are gorgeous and special and funny. But…" he said and lifted a bottle of rose and a glass, a question in the quirk of one eyebrow.

"Yes please."

He poured a glass of the wine and handed it to her, then poured his own and sat beside her.

"To pleasure," he toasted, and Anya relaxed at the desire evident in his glance. She had a feeling she knew what the 'but' was. It was common in their profession and she had multiple weapons to combat it.

"To pleasure," she agreed, and lifted her glass to touch his. She sipped, the cool liquid a shock in the heat of her mouth, the dry fruitiness teasing her thirst. She licked her top lip and when his gaze followed the movement of her tongue, she knew she would succeed.

"I like you, *really* like you, and I want to be clear now in case you really like me too. But my work comes first. I've had relationships before, but they don't work. In my experience, no matter how much they say they do, most people don't understand when their partners have demanding careers. The hours, the commitment, the travel all add pressure that most relationships can't withstand. I can't love lightly, and I'm not ready to risk being hurt again. I won't risk getting emotionally attached to someone right now."

Anya took a sip of wine, suppressing the urge to scoff. *He'd been hurt.* What did he know the pain of losing something – someone - irreplaceable, so soon after finding it. He'd proven he put little value in emotional attachments. Specifically, the one he'd had with her sister.

Through the orange flare of rage, Anya clearly remembered the first time she'd seen him.

She'd been at home, with her sister, both of them melting at the beauty of him, at his wit, humour and sensitivity.

"He's really like that," Heidi had gushed, and for a moment jealousy crashed like a sledgehammer through her tightly built defences. Her sister, the daughter her mother had kept. Her sister, with a gorgeous man to love her.

With sheer force of will Anya smothered the guilt of her remembered jealousy and struggled back into the role of Anya the flirtatious and carefree *pastelaria* owner.

"I understand." Anya the assured him. "I like you too, and find you very attractive, but I'm not looking for a relationship either. Thank you for respecting me enough to be honest though. I suggest we enjoy the rest of today."

"Agreed. To pleasure." Ethan toasted again a wide smile and refilled her wine glass.

"To pleasure," Anya seconded.

Delicious anticipation added to the flavors of their meal, and they ate with the knowledge they would each get what they desired.

CHAPTER FIVE

THE SUN WAS LOSING its heat by the time they'd packed up the remains of the picnic.

Ethan picked up his jeans and turned his back, slipping off his salt-crusted shorts and pulling his jeans on. He struggled to button up his jeans without damaging himself with the distraction of the almost physical caress of her gaze on his butt.

"Any plans for the rest of the day?" Anya voice was warm honey, dripping invitation.

When he turned back to her, pulling his t-shirt on, he was struck by her luminosity. In the bright sun her cropped hair shone like a halo and her pale, flawless skin glowed.

"I have hopes, but nothing concrete until 6am tomorrow." He craved her brightness, wanted her closer. Her smile and the mischief sparkling in her eyes assured him she was just as eager.

"We should make the most of our time until then." She uncurled lithely from the sand and helped him fold up the blanket, her lack of curiosity about where he needed to be in the morning – in fact about why he was in Aveiro at all sprouted a seed of unease in his gut.

Could she be *so* casual that she wasn't curious?

THE RIDE back was a exquisite form of torture – the contrast of Anya's warm body pressed against his back and the more than occasional cool gust plucking at his nipples added to the day's foreplay. As eager as he was to continue in private, Ethan had to concentrate on sticking to the speed limit as they rode back to town. He dearly wanted to hear and feel the engine roar in acknowledgement of his growing urgency.

But the gradual return to civilisation began to unravel the intimate cocoon their time together had woven, and the afternoon-tea crowd that greeted them at the *pastelaria* came as a shock after their afternoon of freedom. Ethan parked the bike and hesitated at the sight of the outdoor tables, almost filled to capacity, before taking his helmet off.

"Is there a more private entrance?" he asked.

Anya glanced at him, a flash of impatience tightening her face as she handed him her helmet. *Impatient,* Ethan smiled with satisfaction, his own returning with the thought. But when she took a deep breath and tucked both hands into the pockets of her jacket her body language did not communicate impatient lust.

He followed her down the quiet alley beside the building and waited while she unlocked the door with unease crawling up his spine, walked through as she held it open and found himself at the bottom of the internal stairs. Wincing as the door slammed behind him, he let out a relieved breath when the noise barely registered over the clamour of a busy café at full capacity. He followed the water sprite up the stairs and into her private sanctuary, relieved to avoid the crowds and their camera phones, Twitter and Instagram uploads. He still couldn't believe he had blundered in here a few days earlier. But look where his unthinking impulse had led him. To an afternoon of escape with the otherworldly creature who had given him a few hours of forgetfulness. And promised even more.

He slid closed the Japanese style screen that gave the room visual privacy and felt tension drain from his shoulders. Here, there was no chance of them being seen, the clinking of plates and waves of conversation below loud enough to cover any noise less than a scream. Whatever happened between them here, was between them alone.

Pleasure was important, but his career trumped all.

IRRITATION RIPPLED beneath her skin as Anya led Ethan up the stairs and out of sight of the patrons of *Sweet Tomas*. Half her plan – to expose Ethan's true nature to the world – was off the table. So, she would have to make the other half worthwhile by immersing herself in the pleasures of the flesh.

At the top of the stairs, Anya paused to slip off her sandals and caught sight of the large envelope on the desk. It hadn't been there when she'd left that morning, must be the part Phillipe said he would send over. She hurried over to slide it into the drawer while Ethan's attention was taken closing the room partition.

She turned just as Ethan's gaze swung to find her. "Can I get you something to drink?" She smiled in genuine invitation, eager to focus on the physical sensations that would free her from thought and emotion for a few hours.

"All I want to taste is you." He strode to her, not stopping until their bodies touched.

Anya held her breath as he raised his hands and slowly cupped her face in his palms. Every nerve ending in her body lit up in anticipation of the touch of his lips, and the dance of pleasure they were embarking on.

Lowering his mouth to hers, Ethan kissed her, gently, sweetly, then eased her lips apart and touched his tongue to hers.

She melted against him, desire flooding her body with impatient heat. Keeping the connection, she stepped back, forcing him to step forward to keep their lips touching. She stepped back again, and again, until the backs of her thighs met the mattress. Ever so slowly, to ensure his lips could follow hers, she sat on the bed.

He followed until his hands found the mattress.

Anya scooted back, drawing him along with her, and lay back beneath him.

"Anya," he said, voice soft as silk as he supported himself above her, elbows either side of her ribs, knees between hers, pelvis lightly pressing into hers. "I haven't been able to get the memory of this bed out of my head all week. I hoped to see it again – with you in it."

"And here we are…" His gorgeous body hovering above her, his lips so close, she abandoned any thought other than quenching the need for physical fulfilment. She tipped her head back and offered herself to him.

His warm breath caressed her neck, his fingers at the neckline of her dress. One, two, three buttons undone, and he folded the fabric gently away from her bra. Supporting himself on one elbow, he stroked the lace covering one breast with his fingertips, then slid the backs of his fingers across the other.

Anya shuddered with anticipation, her nipples tightening, yearning for the touch of skin on skin.

He lowered his head and trailed moist warmth with his lips across the swell of her breast, light and teasing along the edge of the lace, sending ripples of pleasure over her body.

Anya arched against his mouth, begging for more. And he obliged, trailing searing kisses to her collarbone, teasing the skin of her neck. She tilted her head back further, and he accepted the invitation to explore the sensitive area beneath her ear. When Ethan positioned his body so his erection pressed more firmly against her sex, waves of anticipation rolled over her body.

"Yes," Anya breathed and tilted her hips to rub against him, trying to satisfy the throbbing need radiating out from her sex.

The pressure of his lips increased, his heated kisses alternating with a light scrape of his teeth on her flesh, making Anya shiver.

She undulated beneath him, needing to feel all of him, harder, closer.

Ethan lifted his mouth and stared down at her, pupils large, breath shallow and fast. "May I make love to you?"

"I'm pretty sure you are already." Anya raised herself to her elbows, looking down at their hips, fused together in a need for fulfilment, then smiled up into his face.

He grinned back and tilted to rest on one elbow, slowly unbuttoning the rest of her dress with one hand and watching as bare flesh was revealed. He gently folded one side of the dress away, then the other, as if unwrapping a precious package. Anya was used to be admired on stage, and in the bedroom, but Ethan's reverence magnified her arousal.

His gaze ignited a yearning for his caress, the length of her slim legs to her feet, then back up to her panties. The pressure of his attention rested on the mound of her sex, and her clit throbbed for him.

"I think it's only fair that we both undress." She said in a lust-roughened voice, looking pointedly down at his crotch and the bulge straining the denim.

"Your wish…" he said and rolled back off one side of the bed. He toed out of his deck shoes, unbuttoned his jeans and peeled them down his firm thighs. Stepping out of his jeans, he was gloriously naked, his erection bobbing slightly before stilling at attention. *Delicious.* Anya wanted to explore every perfect inch of his body with her hands and her mouth. *After* her roaring need was pacified.

For a moment, Ulrich stood before her. His long hair may have been shorn but his unfettered expression matched the untamed moustache and goatee. "Your turn," he commanded, voice low.

Even though Ethan thought he was in control, the glimpses of the Viking lord suggested that Anya held the power. Thrilling with the knowledge that she brought out his primitive side, Anya obediently slid her arms from the sleeves of her dress as she sat upright. Reaching back, she unhooked her bra and shrugged out of it. She threw it to the other side of the bed and rested back on her elbows, breasts exposed to his hungry gaze, nipples calling out for his touch.

"You are gorgeous." He lifted one knee to the bed and leant forward to cup her breast, his thumb rubbing agonisingly slow over her nipple.

Anya arched back, desperate for him to squeeze, to roll, to use his lips and teeth.

Reading her need, he pinched his fingers together and pulled lightly.

Anya gasped, her hips lifting in response to the sudden surge of desire. She reached around his hips and pulled him fully onto the bed so he could lower his head and take her other nipple in his mouth. "Touch me." She needed his hand between her legs while his tongue stroked her nipple. It had been too long since she'd had a man in her bed and her body was greedy for pleasure.

He cupped her mound in his hand, and she groaned, her clit throbbing for release.

Reaching between his legs, Anya cupped his testicles and squeezed gently. When a low growl rumbled up from his chest, she dragged her fingers upward, to the base of his shaft, gripping him firmly. With slow strokes, she caressed him until a bead of moisture crowned the tip of cock. "Do you have a condom?" Anya gasped, fighting her need to have him inside her and putting her last sensible thought to good use.

Giving her nipple a last tug with his lips, Ethan reluctantly released her, then stepped back off the bed to pick up his jeans. He searched one pocket, then the other, then the back pockets with increasing urgency. He looked at her with dismay. "It must have fallen out at the beach."

Anya raised her eyebrow as she sagged with frustration. "It? Just one?"

"One *strip*," he smirked. "Do you have any?"

Where would Tomas keep his condoms? In the bathroom cabinet, or close at hand for situations like this. Anya tilted her head at the bedside drawer, hoping she was right. She admired the tense and release of Ethan's butt cheeks and the nod of his beautiful cock as he strode around the bed.

He pulled open the drawer, pushed something aside and stared inside for a moment. One side of his mouth lifted in amusement as he looked up at her.

"What is it? Are they the wrong size?" Or maybe Tomas had taken them with him to Stefan's. Anya's stomach clenched at the possibility of a forced raincheck.

"No, just not my colour." He lifted a shiny pink bundle, and then spread it between his hands. Moulded, bubble-gum-coloured latex in the shape of an erect penis and testicles lent more than a touch of kink to the situation.

"Oh, um that was a joke from one of the girls." Anya felt herself growing hot with embarrassment, mortified to find out more than she wanted to about her foster brother's sexual interests.

Ethan lowered it to his crotch and Anya was almost tempted to suggest he put it on. The thought of him wearing fitted latex while he fucked her made her squirm with impatience. Luckily for her future peace of mind, he put Tomas's toy back into the drawer and lifted out a box of condoms.

"Are you sure about that?" Ethan smirked and held up the box. Ultra-ribbed with ticklers.

"Will they be okay?" Anya asked, smiling at his laughter but hesitant for him to search the drawer any further. There was only so much she could take responsibility for.

"I'm game," he said with a wide smile and pulled a packet from the box. "At least I now have a good idea of what you like." He slid onto the bed beside her, ripping open the wrapper and placing the condom on the sheet beside his hip. "But maybe you should tell me what else you like." He said and stretched out on his side, his head resting on the hand of one bent arm, his eyes teasing.

Too close, her mind cautioned. The banter between them was too easy, too erotic… too damned addictive. She needed to keep it impersonal, purely physical.

"*Like?* I *want* to see you buried to the hilt in my pussy."

"That, my dear, will be my pleasure." Ethan surged up to hover over Anya. He kissed her on the mouth, slow and deep, before working his way down her body, deviating to lick and tug one nipple, then the other, and settling between her legs. His breath was hot and moist as he gently slid her white lace panties down her thighs. Her sex, exposed and engorged for him, throbbed with need.

She gasped out as he ran his tongue between the lips of her sex and stopped to circle her clit. "There'll be time for dessert later." She wanted to feel that glorious cock inside her. Now.

"A lady who know what she wants. I am at your command." Kneeling, Ethan took hold of his cock in one hand and expertly rolled the condom down.

For a moment her mind expanded outward and Anya pictured the crowded *pastelaria* just below where patrons went pursued their innocent indulgences, oblivious to the fact she and Ethan were exploring the basest pleasures of the flesh, right above their heads. The thought fuelled the flame of her need, and every laugh and clink of cutlery ratcheted up her urgency.

Anya watched him hungrily, opening her legs for him. Her sex dampened for the first taste of him, her hands clenched with the urge to reach for him and speed his entrance.

AT THE SIGHT of Anya opening her legs to welcome him, the sounds of conversations and chairs scraping from downstairs faded away so all he could hear was his blood pumping in his veins, his breath rasping with excitement, the low hum of his water sprite's arousal drawing him close. The sweet smell of pastries and coffee was drowned by the delicious scent of her arousal. Ethan couldn't help smiling at the sight of her. He paused to admire the pleasing folds of her sex, temptingly moist and plump, inviting him to explore the terrain of her with his tongue.

"So, you *don't* die your hair," he said and lowered himself over her so he could watch his cock slide into her nest of almost white pubic hair. He groaned, torn between agony and ecstasy, the sight reminding him of the last time he'd done this. Heidi on top, pale and blonde, riding him hard, like she wanted to punish him, while tears ran down her cheeks. He banished her ghost with a silent *'Good-bye, my love.'*

"No, I tint my eyebrows." Anya ground out as she lifted her hips to meet his thrust, inviting him deeper and grounding him in the exquisite moment. With her.

His eyes locked on hers, fringed with dark lashes and framed by fine dark eyebrows, and he lost himself in the girl beneath him. He fought the urge to rush into the glorious oblivion he knew waited for him, and kept his thrusts slow and controlled.

Her eyelids fluttered, then closed as her breaths shallowed and quickened.

He knew by the pink flush spreading across her breasts and the tightness of her pussy around him, that she was close. "Anya," he called softly, trying to infiltrate her world without shocking her out of her pleasure. His body was full to bursting with the need to climax and he wanted her with him, wanted to ride the waves of pleasure together.

Her eyelids lifted drowsily; her gaze turned inward.

"Look at me, water sprite." He saw recognition pull her from the thrall of her private pleasure. He saw her try to block him out, but it was too late. She'd already opened her eyes. As the vessel of his desire shattered into shards of ecstasy, he recognised in her eyes a moment of panic, then a flare of joy and ecstasy as her sex clenched around his cock. He thrust hard and deep inside her as the force of his own climax hit him like a tidal wave, the surge of pleasure reverberating through him as her sex gripped and squeezed the seed out of him, her writhing movements drawing out his climax, pleasure shooting so deep it ricocheted between them.

She pulled him close, their lips clashing in a kiss of desperation. With a stifled cry of completion, she clenched her eyes closed, forcing the wetness he'd glimpsed there to escape as tears from beneath her lids.

He rolled beside her and cradled her in his arms, uncertain, while she stifled her sobs.

"Did I hurt you?" he asked, sure he hadn't. *Was it his fault? Was there some flaw in him that made him hurt the women he tried to please?*

She shook her head. "It's nothing."

As much as he wanted to know if they were tears of emotion, he was afraid to look too closely at his own response. So, he lay silent, holding her, and ignored the ache of regret that he would not return to her bed again. It could only lead to pain. Already, he suspected what they'd shared had been more than they'd agreed on.

Once she had calmed, he pulled the sheets up and drowsed beside her until Anya's weight shifted on the mattress beside him. He opened his eyes, trying to orientate himself in time and space. Except for the moonlight flooding in, it was dark.

Apart from the click and groan of ovens cooling downstairs, it was quiet. The café was closed, the patrons departed.

Anya slid out of bed, silent, and he followed, at a loss for what to say. He wanted to ask to see her again but knew he couldn't. He wanted to stay longer but knew he shouldn't.

They dressed in silence.

ETHAN CAUGHT her hand as she headed for the stairs, the fluffy socks she'd slipped on noiseless on the wooden floor.

She turned and, wrapping her arms around his back, pressed herself against him in a brief embrace, resting her head on his chest for a fleeting moment. She sensed his reluctance to leave, but there was still a chance the aborted part of her plan might succeed after all. His defences were down and there was a chance there were witnesses in the square outside.

As they navigated the stairs in the dark the clock began to strike, the chimes accompanying their cautious steps to the front doors, the darkness lit only by a waning moon. The lock clicked as Anya unlocked one side of the glass doors. The chimes stopped and Anya's shoulders drooped. Eleven pm on a Sunday night. She stepped outside into the cool, still air and glanced around the town square, not surprised to find it deserted.

This wasn't London. Not one person to recognise the famous Ethan Cox and his bed ruffled partner. Not one person with a camera to record the lover's farewell. In that moment, she almost didn't care. She felt almost buoyant with something light and new she didn't want to identify, her need for revenge banked to a warm glow in her chest.

Ethan caught Anya's hand and pulled her to him, lowering his mouth to hers. She met his lips with an eagerness to savour one last sip of forgetfulness. He kissed her back fiercely, as though preparing to plunge beneath the surface of the lagoon and couldn't breathe without their lips touching. Too soon his kiss softened to jaw aching sweetness, ripe with longing and regret, and he pulled away. With gentle hands he cradled her face, head bowed so their foreheads touched.

Anya stepped away, breaking the connection, turmoil and disgust lashing at her. How could she want more of this man who had destroyed the sense of family she had only just started to build?

"I wish I could see you again." The flatness of his voice made it clear it was a desire he would not satisfy.

"Is there someone else?" Anya asked, stalling, looking for a way to get what she needed. A replay at a time and place there would be witnesses. Somewhere he couldn't hide.

"No. There hasn't been for a long time." His eyes were sad and serious. "But I can't do this again."

She admired his willpower and did her best to match it.

"I suppose this is good-bye." She reached up on tiptoe and kissed him with just enough passion to challenge his resolve, but not enough that he would give in and follow her back upstairs. She wasn't strong enough yet, hadn't recovered from the shock of unexpected connection. She needed to think and come up with a plan. One that was guaranteed to work. "Pity we never made it to dessert." She dragged her fingertips down his chest and slipped back inside before he caught her hand.

UPSTAIRS, Anya flicked on the bedside lamp and pulled the envelope out of the desk drawer. She sat on the rumpled sheets that smelt of recent and rampant sex, and read the part Philippe had sent over.

Luring Ethan to bed had got her nothing except a mind-blowing orgasm - a performance he was determined not to repeat - and proof he was not leading a celibate existence. But as a supporting character on *KingMaker*, Anya would be staying in the actors' village at least five days of the week until her part was wrapped. Whatever dirt there was to find, she had a better chance of unearthing it as a member of the inner circle of cast and crew. And if she still couldn't find any, she would make it.

"Perfect." She whispered to herself, a flutter of excitement after reading the first scene. Playing the part of Vivienne, the pagan sorceress, was her answer. Success might still possible, if she had the balls to grasp the opportunity.

An hour later, Anya placed the pages down on the bed with a triumphant sigh. She'd never acted for the screen before, but it shouldn't be too hard to tone down her gestures and facial expressions into a more natural form of acting. And there wasn't much dialogue for her to memorise, most of the communication was physical.

Her concern was for the part itself. As the sorceress, the scenes she'd share with Ethan would test the resolve of a saint. Tonight, for the first time she'd felt a connection with the man attached to the body parts which had given her sexual pleasure. When she'd opened her eyes to him at that most vulnerable moment, it was as if their souls connected. Only for justice would she risk the danger of a repeat performance.

Even though it was after midnight, she dialled her manager. Maurice would be awake. Even if he wasn't, he wouldn't object to his star client disturbing his sleep.

Briefly, Anya explained that she planned to accept a bit part in the streaming tv series.

"My advice is not to do it. You are in the middle of your contract with the production company, and if they decide to take offense at you moonlighting like this, it's within their rights to take action. They're not likely to fire you, but they can make you pay in other ways."

"Don't worry, I won't give them grounds for objecting. No-one will recognise me on screen with the costume and make-up. I'll specify in the agreement with Enfin Studios that they use my birth name in the credits. It's only a small role, Vivienne only appears in three episodes." Anyone who recognised her on-set would know her as Anya Stein. None of the actors or crew had any reason to link her with the name Forsyth until the season screened and the credits rolled, and by then the damage would be done.

"It's your decision Anya, but rehearsals for *The Merchant of Venice* start in six weeks. You said yourself, this is the pinnacle of your career, the reason you tied yourself to a contract for five years and agreed to take on parts you wouldn't have normally accepted. I don't understand why you would risk it now."

But this isn't for me. It's for Heidi.

CHAPTER SIX

IT WAS LATE on Monday afternoon when Anya made her way back to the studio in town where the costume maker worked, her bag packed for a few days on location. Almost before she'd had a chance to change back into her clothes after trying her new wardrobe on, a driver in a town car arrived to collect her and her costumes. They drove south to where the production company had built the sets representing various villages, feasting halls and churches, battlegrounds and huts.

Phillipe met her at the admin tent and took her to meet her tent-mate.

"Mary, you'll show Anya around, won't you?"

"Of course!" When black haired Mary from Brixton realised who her new roomy was, tears filled her eyes. "Anything I can do for you, just say the word," she whispered as she embraced her fellow actress in an over-zealous hug.

The girls had worked together on *A Midsummer Night's Dream* a few years back. A month into the season Anya had found Mary sobbing in the ladies room, having just been diagnosed with a serious STD, contracted from the latest of a string of cheating bed partners. Anya had been uncertain what to do, unused to women other than Joana confiding in her, but Mary had been almost delirious with anger and shame. When Anya realised she could help without getting emotionally involved, she'd been happy to cover for Mary during her treatment and recovery, visiting her every day and reporting the progression of her 'flu' to theatre management. In fact, Anya had enjoyed the challenge – and her success. Not a whisper of the truth had spread. After that Mary had been a frequent visitor to her dressing room. They'd seen little of each other since the show ended, especially after Mary started chasing roles for the screen in the hope of bigger jobs.

"I'm just on my way to the mess tent if you'd like to come with. I'll introduce you to the people you should know."

Anya declined, preferring to lay low until she was expected on-set in the morning. She hoped the element of surprise would turn her luck and give her the advantage she needed. Once Ethan knew she was here she would start digging, but until then, she had Mary to interrogate.

"Thanks, but I think I'll unpack and prepare for tomorrow."

"Would you like me to bring something back for you?"

"That would be amazing. Thanks. I can't wait to hear all your news."

MARY HURRIED down the path to the mess tent in the fading daylight. She hugged her arms in the quickly cooling air. She'd been so excited she'd forgotten to put on a jumper.

It took her less than ten minutes to organise a six-pack of beers and two bowls of lamb curry with rice. When she stepped back inside the tent she'd moved into earlier in the week, she still couldn't believe her luck.

Anya had unpacked her luggage and was sliding her bags under the vacant double bed. The share tents allocated to minor actors, although far from luxurious, were generous in size and comfortable, with a private bathroom. Now Anya was here, it felt homely.

The girls sat cross-legged on their beds to eat and catch up on what they'd been doing since they'd last worked together.

"You've been on-set since the beginning of the season?" Anya asked.

Mary nodded and drained the last of the beer from her bottle. The move from the stage to small screen had been exciting at first, but she missed the stage – and London. She reached for another beer, offering one to Anya, who shook her head.

"What's the goss. Anything I need to know?" In the theatre, arriving into an established cast could be awkward. Sort of like moving schools part way through the year, with webs of politics and relationships already well-established.

"There are some good people on-set, only a few rotters you should steer away from, although knowing you, you'll keep to yourself." Mary was pleased to be Anya's personal guide and would enjoy the kudos that came with bunking in with the new kid, who was also a renowned stage actress.

"Any decent guys worth hooking up with?" Mary was surprised, not by the question, but the fact she'd asked. Anya wasn't the girly-friend type, not known for hanging out or gossiping with the girls. Mary had been lucky in her personal misfortune to be the only person she knew to be invited into Anya's limited circle of familiarity, but everyone who had worked with Anya Stein was familiar with her no-nonsense approach to romance. She was the epitome of the ice queen until someone caught her interest, then a short-lived but torrid affair would ensue for a week or two before the subject of her attention was left abandoned and reeling.

Once Mary recovered her composure, she put her matchmaking skills to work, sorting through the cast and crew for a man worthy of her idol. "The best of them all - and strangely the only guy who hasn't hooked up with anyone - is Ethan Cox." Mary hoped she wasn't wrong. She'd been so tied up with yet another disastrous hook-up to take much notice of anyone else. But the lead actor was friendliness itself with all the girls. As far as she knew he'd shown no more than a kindly interest in anyone.

"I've heard he's a player," Anya asked, fiddling with the lip of her beer bottle, her voice casual.

"Yeah, I've heard the rumours in the media, but I've never seen it. Maybe he's sneakier than the others, but I've not heard even a whisper of anything since I've been here, which is unusual on location. Not like Liam Byrne. Keep away from that one, he'll screw anything without a dick." Mary grimaced and took a swig of beer to wash the sour taste out of her mouth.

"I guess Ethan has to be super careful after all the talk that he was responsible for his girlfriend's death." Anya finished the last of her beer and stood to clear the bowls, her bland expression not matching the interest in her gaze.

So Anya was on the hunt. Watch out Ethan.

"Yeah, there was talk he cheated on her and she killed herself over him. A 'serial cheater' *sources close to the victim* called him. He doesn't seem like the type, but he *is* a celebrity. You really need to find a guy out of the industry if you want to be able to trust him. Even then, who knows."

Mary hugged her pillow tight, wishing she followed her own advice.

"Thanks for the heads up. I'll check out the deal with Ethan. He's certainly built for pleasure." Anya winked, but seemed disappointed.

Unsettled by the reminder of her latest relationship failure, Mary pulled out her phone and held it out for Anya, who scrawled through photos of the cheating bastard in various stages of undress, with different women, in public places. One, taken through a window, of Liam sitting in a chair straddled by a woman with a nun's costume bunched around her waist, a bench of stage make-up and hair styling equipment behind them.

"Most of the cast were filming when I took that," Mary muttered, furious he'd treated her like trash and disgusted with herself for being fooled yet again.

"So, you're speaking from experience about Liam being a player?" Anya scrolled through the photos, showing more interest than Mary would expect. It was nice to be able to talk to someone who cared. Mary wondered what it was about herself that interested Anya enough to treat her different than the rest.

"Yeah, when I first started on the series. Then I realised he was shagging at least three others *that I knew of.* So I decided to find out just how many. He's married you know? I could shaft him like he shafted me, with just one of these photos."

Mary looked over Anya's shoulder, placing a hand on her back. The next photo showed Liam humping a girl in a caterer's uniform between two skip bins, surrounded by rubbish; the next of him with one of the set crew against the rough-hewn timber wall of one of the huts. "That last one was just yesterday."

"What a bastard." Anya shook her head and looked up with a thoughtful expression. "I might have a favour to ask…"

"Anything. You know that." Mary stood taller, thrilled that she *had* asked.

POOR MARY, she always seemed to fall for the slimeballs. Anya handed the phone back, a rough plan forming. "You must be stealthy to get photos like that." If Ethan was getting up to the same as Liam, he was being much more careful about it. Which left her no choice. If Mary hadn't heard anything, it was unlikely anyone else had. And visual proof was so much more powerful than rumours and gossip.

"Not really. Wrong place at the right time. And there's no skill involved in taking the shots. The bastard was so focussed on getting off he wouldn't have noticed a fire alarm."

"I can see that. Well, I'm for bed. Its good to see you Mary. If I have to share a room, I'm glad it's with you." Anya excused herself and went to change and brush her teeth.

When she closed her eyes that night, it was with the promise of justice warming her bed.

It shouldn't be difficult to seduce Ethan once he found out she was an actress, someone he thought wouldn't be a threat to his career. Someone who would understand his lifestyle if a fling grew into something more, and he had seemed to wish there was more when they'd said good-bye. He'd want to be discreet, of course, which was fine by Anya. Up to a point. She needed to stay anonymous to protect her career, at the same time as shining a spotlight on his womanising.

Strategically taken 'happy snaps' would drag the scandal with Heidi back into focus and there'd be little doubt he was guilty of what her sister had accused him of − affairs with multiple women - fans, fellow actors, *random women he met on the street.*

Soon she would have hard evidence Ethan Cox was responsible for Heidi's death.

Anya slept well, until Mary's whimpering in her sleep woke her. After half an hour of trying to ignore it, Anya crawled out of her warm bed. She knew from experience with Tomas as a child, there was only one thing that would soothe her back into quiet sleep.

Wrapping her blanket around herself, she lay carefully beside Mary and stroked her hair until they both fell into a deep sleep.

ETHAN SLOUCHED IN HIS SEAT, gripped by an unfamiliar lethargy, and watched the cast and crew hanging out in the mess tent, joking around and winding down after the first work day of a long week to come. Someone was playing some old 90's grunge and he suddenly felt the urge to go back to his tent and play some comfort music.

"Come for a beer, man," Liam clapped him on the back on his way to the bar.

"Not tonight, mate. I'm beat."

"Must have been some day off you had. Where did you disappear to? Don't bother answering unless it involved a woman." After a pause he grinned. "Didn't think so. Tomorrow − you, me, your shout. No excuses." Liam called over his shoulder as he made a beeline for one of the prosthetic make-up artists who was leaning over the bar, her pert ass lifted high.

Ethan shook his head, wishing his on-screen right-hand man wasn't such a jerk. If he'd told Liam about Anya, or his reaction to the extra, he wouldn't have shut up about it.

His gaze surfed his co-workers as he gathered the enthusiasm to stand, not expecting to see the girl who had caught his attention. He had been interested to see if he still reacted to her after his day with Anya, but he hadn't seen her on-set all day. As one of the extras she'd be on the bus back to town by now anyway. Ethan hoped she was okay but was glad for the lack of distraction. He was still having trouble keeping his mind on the job, which was a problem in itself. He had never thought of acting as 'work' before.

Instead of being in the moment and playing each scene as he'd rehearsed until he *was* Ulrich, he'd stayed stubbornly Ethan. And the scene playing on repeat in his head was the one where he was naked with Anya. He couldn't stop remembering her nipples hard as unripe berries in his mouth; her tiny, toned body shuddering beneath him, then dozing sweetly in his arms.

Goddamnit. What was wrong with him? Could he not sleep with a girl without getting attached? He'd managed to avoid any record of the one-day affair, not a whisper in the media of what would sully his painfully protected reputation, but he didn't kid himself that he'd get away with it again. Those dodgy bastards would take any hint of a flirtation and turn it into a sordid scandal.

Remembering the insinuations that he'd betrayed his girlfriend, that he'd done something to push her to drink and drive, turned the lamb curry he'd eaten to cement in his gut. Sure, things had been bad between them in the end, but he'd been trying to find a way to work things out. He could never have intentionally hurt Heidi.

Ethan sighed and looked around at his colleagues. Here he was, surrounded by his fellow actors, relaxing, flirting and fucking like they were on holiday in Ibiza. He hadn't felt so isolated since the night the police had called him about the accident. The night his plan to get Heidi help died with her.

Not one of the cast or crew had the stench of scandal chasing them, although Liam probably wasn't far off. In many ways, he envied their freedom, but being the lead meant he had more to occupy his thoughts, less time to think about Heidi. He had more responsibility and on-screen time than any of them, and he preferred it that way.

"See you tomorrow," Ethan said to anyone who tried to divert him as he made his way through the crowd of co-workers who were gradually getting louder and more boisterous. If he could get away from the sexual currents swirling through every common area, he might stop wishing *she* was here. If he ran through his scenes for the next day, over and over, maybe he could keep his mind out of Anya's bed.

One of the cameramen stopped him just as he reached the open flaps of the entrance. "You ready for the sex scenes mate? You know, I love my job, but sometimes I wish I was you."

"Just another scene. But Andrew, if you ever want to swap one day, give me a shout." Ethan slapped him on the shoulder and tried to dodge around him as he swayed.

The cameraman reached out and grabbed his arm before he was out of reach. "Actually, I don't think so. Now I think about it, it must be bloody hard," Andrew laughed, and Ethan almost got drunk on the whisky fumes. He'd have a mighty hang-over tomorrow. Ethan shook his head. The cameraman was normally 100% professional – and married. Obviously, this place was getting to him too.

"I don't know how you manage it. Pretending to fuck with people watching, trying not to get turned on. And if you get off on being watched, it must be even harder. *Har har*, get it?"

Ethan pried the drunk man's fingers off his bicep and stepped back. "I'll do my best to forget this conversation when we film the first sex scene tomorrow."

Great. Now he'd be worried he'd be thinking about Anya while he was dry-humping Rowena. The actress had come onto him when they'd met briefly at the wrap party last year, the last thing he needed was her thinking he had a thing for her. But it didn't matter who he did the sex scene with, it was going to be a challenge to not remember the monumental orgasm he'd had with Anya.

Fuck! As much as his cock urged him to, he would not contact her. She'd been a moment of weakness, but his reputation, his career, were more important than anything now.

He took his shoes off and walked around the dark camp, the still-warm sand under his feet and sounds of night insects draining his agitation. By the time he got back to his tent, he was so tired he went straight to bed, but as soon as he closed his eyes, visions of Anya kept him awake. *Curse her, she'd bewitched him.* Even though he didn't deserve the oblivion he'd found in her body, he would have sacrificed a week's worth of sleep for the opportunity to spend the dark hours coaxing those little grunts and moans from her.

Instead of reaching for his cock and pretending it was her hand, he turned on the light and reached for his guitar, his one comfort of home portable enough to keep with him when he was away working. He let himself be carried away on his favourite tunes until his eyelids drooped with fatigue, but she was still waiting to sabotage his sleep when he turned off the light.

CHAPTER SEVEN

AFTER MAKEUP and a quick stop at the mess tent, Ethan made his way around the tent village, taking a little used path. He was glad for a few minutes of relative quiet, and the distraction of birdlife that populated the sand dunes that marked the east boundary of the site. He got up early so he could get through make-up before the rush and used the extra time afterward to walk this way, using the brackish breeze and distant rumble of the Atlantic to clear his mind.

He was halfway through his take-away coffee when he arrived at the low-ceilinged wood hut that would be the set for the morning. "Hi. Good morning. How's it going?" He pushed through the soundproof flap and made his way through the crowd of familiar bodies, mainly crew, greeting everyone he passed. "How are you feeling, mate?" He slapped the hung-over cameraman on the back and stepped back when he heard him groan. "That bad, hey?"

Andrew nodded carefully and turned a pale shade of green.

Everyone – except Andrew - was relaxed, mingling comfortably in the space, except two newcomers. The witch and her attendant. But the witch was smaller than he remembered Rowena being.

He'd seen the attendant on-set before, recognised the red-haired girl from a swamp scene a couple of weeks earlier. She'd had her bright hair mostly covered with a wimple, but he recognised the multitude of freckles, so dense there was hardly any pale skin showing between. The other girl barely came up to Red's shoulder. With her cascade of heavy black hair and voluminous cloak, he couldn't make out her figure, but the way she moved her head and gestured with her delicate hands as she talked seemed familiar. Someone he'd worked with before?

As he paused on the edge of the set to finish his coffee and pull a mint out of his pocket, she turned side on. He studied her with interest. Newbie's face was covered with tattoos, almost as dense as Red's freckles, but the curve of her cheek and nose were familiar. He took a step toward her, his body drawn as if by a magnetised force, but when she turned around, Ethan froze. All the air squeezed out of his lungs.

The width of the set was between them, but there was no mistaking the pale blue eyes, fringed with dark lashes and framed by dark eyebrows, all the more striking surrounded by a mane of black hair. *Not palest blonde.*

Ethan's head spun and he sucked in breaths.

How could this actress have Anya's eyes? Anya's mouth?

Holy shit. How could Anya *be here* when she ran a bakery in town? She never said anything about acting.

Get a grip. Ethan took deep breaths, tried to slow his thudding heart, tried to think logically. *She could be a relative of Anya's.* He reached out to stop a passing assistant. "Where is Rowena?" His voice came out as a croak. "Rowena Simms, the actress playing the witch?" He really needed to get some sleep. He was so tired he must have started to hallucinate. He'd been thinking about Anya so much that he'd imagined her features on a stranger. On the next break, he'd go to the medical tent and get some sleeping pills.

"Didn't you hear, she dislocated her shoulder?"

"No." He'd been too caught up in his own head to listen to gossip. "Who is the new actress?"

"Anya Stein. She's big on stage in London."

Anya Stein. "Yeah, I've heard of her." She was a star of the stage, but Ethan had never seen her work. Obviously, he'd never seen a photo of her either. His head started pounding, but he fought against the feeling his life was veering out of control. The new actress couldn't be *his* Anya. She had the same Christian name, but his Anya was Portuguese, not British.

"Apparently, she's from around here originally, back for a few weeks on a break. A local girl made it big. She started last week as an extra. That's how they knew to ask her."

Fuck! It *was* her. And she'd had been working as an extra. Laughter bubbled up and Ethan almost choked on the irony. *An extra wearing a tangled brown wig.*

Anya, an actress. She would play the role of the sorceress who bewitched his Ulrich. Ethan had fallen under Anya's spell, now it was his character's turn. Ethan had vowed to never see the water sprite again, but here she was, on *his* set, haunting and taunting him.

Anya was an *actress*.

Every atom of his being wanted to confront her, to force her to acknowledge her lies, but not in front of witnesses. At that moment she chose to turn and look directly at him. Her eyes registered barely a flicker of recognition as she strode toward him. He shrunk away from her but forced himself to take her offered hand, almost half the size of his, cool against his sweaty, her grip firm against his wilted.

"Ethan Cox? A pleasure to meet you. I've heard good things about your work." Her voice held no familiarity, just professionalism, her gaze expectant.

"Ah, thanks? You too…"

"Anya," she offered.

"Anya." He repeated, voice firm. He could do this. If it weren't for her eyes - and her voice – and her lips – he could almost convince himself she was a stranger.

It was a relatively short scene, the initial meeting, but for the first time in his career, Ethan struggled to remember his lines and because of him, it took twice as long as it should have to wrap. Anya acted as if they'd never met, treating him with detached friendliness while they played their parts, which made him doubt himself even more. Had he lost his mind completely, conjured her here in his delirium, or imagined a connection that had never been there?

Finally, the scene was over. He was about to turn away, to put some space between them so he could process, when she whispered just loud enough that he could be sure he hadn't imagined it. "Good to see you again, Ethan."

He stared at her, bewildered. "I wish I could say the same." He glanced around at the multitude of crew on the edge of hearing distance. "We need to talk. Later. In private."

He strode off to the medical tent. Fuck sleeping tablets, he needed Valium. Especially for the next scene he had coming up with the witch. The semi-nude sex scene.

IT HAD ALREADY BEEN a long day for Ethan when he next found himself close to Anya again. He'd seen her in the dining tent at lunch time, but she'd been sitting in a corner, deep in conversation with one of Liam's women. Two black haired beauties, heads bent together conspiratorially.

The nurse had declined his request for Valium, giving him a pack of chamomile tea and valerian tablets. The chamomile made him sleepy, but his nerves were still as ragged as the fake scar on his right pec. He'd been in makeup for an hour while they applied the evidence of Ulrich's past wounds, the scars he needed only when he had to appear on-screen naked. Bathing… or fucking.

Every muscle in his body tensed as he ducked through the low doorway and stepped into the low-ceilinged set, built to resemble a hut built in 9th century Britain. Even without unnecessary staff, the skeleton crew for the sex scene were still too many. The noodles Ethan had choked down at lunch seemed to crawl in his stomach. Ulrich had a healthy sex life last season, but this was the first time Ethan felt nervous.

Even though the camera lighting hadn't been turned on yet, Ethan knew where Anya was without looking for her. When he allowed his gaze to rest on her a shock of recognition shot through him. No matter how much he'd tried to convince himself otherwise, she was still *his* Anya - the water sprite he'd swum with then drowned in - beneath the long black hair and intricate tattoos.

The cloak and modest gown she'd worn earlier was gone, replaced with nothing but a terry bathrobe and sheep-skin boots. Ethan's spirit plummeted as his cock stirred, and he knew the day was about to get very long indeed. Heaven help him when she took off the robe. He should have asked the nurse for anti-erection drugs, if such a thing existed.

There was no point trying to distract himself by getting into Ulrich's head, that would only make things worse. Instead he worked through a series of complex mathematical problems in his mind until he felt detached from his physical urges, adjusted the front of his trews and slipped off his robe. His one consolation was that this first intimate scene would be filmed from the waist up. Tomorrow, the only concession to modesty would be flesh coloured G-strings, Anya's with fake 'fur'. If he could get through this scene without embarrassing himself, surely he'd manage that too? And if they could talk before then, in private, they could discuss this like adults and come to an understanding.

He turned to face away while she undressed. Light flooded the set as the camera lights were turned on, and Ethan waited for the initial lighting checks to be completed before he turned and assumed Ulrich's posture and the blank facial expression the scene called for. The Viking lord determined to resist the witch. After the final lighting checks were done, Ethan returned to his start position and took deep breaths while he waited for the director to yell 'action'. Heart pounding, Ethan strode toward Anya, keeping his eyes trained on her face, which was difficult when the swirls of tattoos extended down her neck and drew his eyes to their path over her breasts and around her nipples.

When he grasped her bare upper arms to show her that he *could* resist, Ethan knew there would be no need to retake the first of the sequence of scenes in this battle of wills. He wouldn't have to act Ulrich's struggle against the witch who would use any means to coerce the Viking to impregnate her with his superior warrior seed.

"I'll curse you, Viking. I'll un-man you in bed *and* in battle if you don't give me your seed." Vivienne crooned to Ulrich, who struggled to stand strong against the allure of the naked witch, her threat mirroring Ethan's own struggle to remain professional in the face of his reaction to the actress.

"I will take you when and if I want you, sorceress." The set was silent except the panting battle of wills when Ethan lowered his face and crushed her mouth with his. Need roared through his veins. He almost forgot the crew standing so close, watching every move, almost steered her backward to the bed, almost dropped his mouth to her bare breasts so he could lick and suck her berry-firm nipples while he tore at the beige sarong tied at her waist.

It was no challenge to Ethan's talent as an actor to communicate his character's hard-fought control, but he drew encouragement from Ulrich's victory; that he could walk away from her physical and magical charms.

A film of perspiration coated his torso as the temperature on-set rose steadily, more than could be attributed to the heat of the lights. Ethan couldn't stop his body's instinctive reaction to her, but he didn't lose control. He was able to hide his erection from the multiple camera angles, but he couldn't hide from her.

Thankfully, Anya lent him a sliver of sanity. It was not his one-time lover he kissed; she'd locked herself away and given him a stranger's lips. He could see why she was one of the most sought-after actresses in her field. He could learn from her professionalism.

Between takes her looks were private yet clinical, as if she were judging his reactions in case she needed to go into damage control. Was his tenuous hold on his urges obvious to everyone else on set?

Between takes he kept a respectful distance from Anya's naked torso, desperately trying to ignore her breasts, nipples erect and taunting him. Before they finished the scene, he risked getting close enough to whisper, "When can we talk? Will you come to my tent?"

Anya nodded; her expression bland so no-one suspected anything but a professional discussion.

"Mine is the one at the end of the path, furthest from the dining tent. 11pm?"

She looked down, adjusting her sarong. He thought her lips curved in a satisfied smile as she answered, under her breath. "I'll find it. It will be the biggest one."

ETHAN PACED AROUND HIS TENT, desperate for an explanation but dreading the truth. How wrong had he been? If she'd been working onset as an extra when they'd hooked up, she'd known who he was. Had she been acting all along?

He stopped still at the sound of three light knocks on the tent frame. Anya slipped through the canvas door, dressed head to toe in black, her face free of tattoos, only the fringe of her pale blonde hair visible beneath the hood of her sweatshirt. He held on to his frustration as she glanced around the large room, taking in the king size bed, lounge and desk/dining table that would be more suited to furnishing a hip boutique hotel, rather than a tent village for actors in a historic drama. Her eyes locked on his guitar, leaning beside the bed.

"You play." Her voice was flat but her eyes swirled with hurt. She looked like she wanted to pick up the instrument.

"I do. You?" So strange to see his pale, vanilla scented water sprite here, on location. She'd looked and acted so different today to the Anya he thought he knew; he had almost convinced himself it wasn't her but a doppelgänger.

But his Anya was here now. And she'd lied.

Turning to face him, she straightened her spine. "A little. Someone I cared for told me how special it feels when a lover sings to you."

"Why didn't you tell me you were an actor?" Ethan couldn't make small talk while all he could think of was *why?*.

"It's not like I deliberately kept it from you, I just didn't tell you." She said with a shrug. "A little white lie."

"A blonde lie." He raised an eyebrow and glanced at her hair. Short, perfect for changes of identity, on-stage and in her personal life. She was an actress through and through. "What are you doing? I found out you're only back for a few weeks on holiday. That usually means not working."

"As you said, I'm back on holiday and thought it would be fun to do some work as an extra. Then they begged me to fill in for Rowena, which just happened to coincide with you telling me you wouldn't see me again because I wasn't an actress." She put her hands on her hips and raised her chin, challenge flashing in her ice-blue eyes. "I thought we might have a few more nights together if you knew I *am* an actress." She waved her hand in an arc in front of her in a parody of a stage gesture, presenting the facts.

"Why didn't you tell me who you are when we met?" Ethan scratched at his goatee, unconvinced.

"Maybe I wanted to try on being an ordinary girl for once." She shrugged and dropped her hands to her sides.

"What about when I told you I couldn't see you again because I didn't think you would understand my lifestyle? You do. You could have told me then." Ethan's voice softened. He understood the desire to have the freedom of anonymity, to live and love without being judged by strangers every minute.

"I didn't say anything then because *I* don't want complications."

"Right. Okay." He walked across to the desk and gripped the back of the chair; his head bowed. Her reasoning made sense. She'd taken advantage of being anonymous in a country where she wasn't widely recognised for her work - something he would love to be able to do himself - and used his rule against non-actresses to get the casual sex she wanted.

The muscles of his shoulder tensed beneath the touch of her hand. "It doesn't mean we can't enjoy each other until I leave."

Ethan turned and searched her face.

She smiled, warm and inviting, so different to the almost clinical way she'd looked at him today. Who *was* Anya, really? Could he risk getting involved with her - in even a casual way?

Ethan groaned, torn. She'd come here tonight, discreetly; and helped him today. If they had an affair and kept it quiet, which she was obviously happy to do, he could have more of the woman he craved, *and* it would be less torturous to pretend to make love to her on set. His career was all he cared about now, apart from his family, and he was prepared to do whatever was needed to protect it.

Even so, a feeling in his gut warned him not to trust her.

ETHAN REACHED out a hand to cup her cheek and Anya drew a deep breath, elated by her success. It had been a close call when he'd found out she'd lied to him. Only helping him on-set had got him back on side.

Her body swayed toward him, and when his thumb stroked down her cheek and across her bottom lip, her abdomen clenched in anticipation of lust fulfilled. She sucked his thumb into her mouth with a moan and rubbed her tongue over the pad. When he lowered his head and added his lips to the recipe, Anya closed her eyes and reminded herself no matter how intensely she came alive when she was in his arms, or how her veins ran with fire at the touch of his lips; she was still acting a part. This feeling was always temporary, and even if by some miracle it lasted more than a week, it was something she would never hope for with *this* man. So, she embraced her physical need and pushed aside the longing to belong that was growing alongside it.

But just as she reconciled her body's reaction to him as part of her role of vengeful sister, he pulled away.

Anya opened her eyes and stared at the beautiful features that disguised the monster responsible for her sister's death. He was frowning.

"You should leave. I need to think," he said, his voice tired.

"How will you go working together tomorrow?" Anya asked, frustrated that success was slipping from her grasp.

"The full sex scene? I'll manage." The tightness of his jaw belied the surety of his words.

"You struggled to concentrate today and the scene took twice as long as it should have to film. I need to be back in London in two weeks." Anya tried to reason with him calmly. "Should I tell them we can't work together?" It was a mark of desperation that she would openly question his professionalism.

When he shook his head, Anya took a deep breath and held her frustration. He was forcing her to convince him. Mary was outside, ready. She couldn't miss this chance. "I can help."

"Like you did today? I meant to thank you for that." He smiled ruefully.

Anya reached between them and stroked his cock through his cargo pants. "I meant like this." Her legs felt weak with the need to feel him moving inside her, but she had a very slim chance of making this happen.

"Christ, Anya. Don't tempt me." Ethan stretched behind him and gripped the chair back – to stop himself from reaching for her, or a subconscious consent?

Telling herself it wasn't a 'no', she knelt in front of him and he didn't put his hands out to stop her. She looked up into his tense face, and although his eyes pleaded for her to stop, his expression also begged her to continue. Anya exhaled with the triumph of knowing he was defenceless against her will, the power translating into a surge of lust.

She unzipped his cargo pants and his cock sprung free, silken skin brushing her cheek. That he'd chosen to go commando, whether deliberate or subconscious, implied his intentions had been carnal when he'd dressed. Before he could stop her, she took him into her mouth and ran her tongue over the exquisitely smooth head. With a grunt, he leant back against the chair.

When she took as much of him as she could in her mouth, until he nudged the back of her throat, she felt his knees soften with his will. Imagining she was sheathing his erection with her pussy, rather than her lips and tongue, tension built low in her abdomen and her clit throbbed in time with the slide of her mouth on his shaft. With each stroke she paused to take a breath, then took his penis deep in her mouth again.

"I haven't been able to think of anything but you naked… seeing my cock buried to the hilt in that delicious nest of blonde curls." His breathless voice held a note of wonder, his words making her sex clench with arousal. "I've tried everything I can to not imagine fucking you again." Anya squeezed her thighs together to try satisfy the need that swelled with his words. She longed to shove her hand between her legs and bring herself to climax with him… but Mary was watching.

When Ethan's hips started moving of their own accord, Anya took him deeper still and sucked him hard and fast until his cum spurted down her throat. Juices flooded her sex in a rush of power and triumph.

"Anya," Ethan gasped out, his cock jerking in her mouth as she milked his pleasure.

When he was still, Anya looked up at him and wiped her lips, smiling as she stood. "That should help for tomorrow." She touched his cheek, then started to pull away.

He placed his hands on her hips, urging her close with his touch and begging her with his eyes. "I'd like to do the same for you. I want the feel of your clit under my tongue. I want to taste you again, the sweet cream when you cum. I didn't think I'd get the chance again."

"No. Thanks for the offer, but I'll look after myself." As much craved release, she wouldn't do anything that would tip the balance of power in his favour. She'd got what she came for – proof of a casual affair.

"So that's it?" Ethan's frown showed his confusion and disappointment.

"That's it. See you on set." Anya would have thought rejecting him would be more satisfying than it was, and her victory was unexpectedly anti-climactic.

WITH THE TENSION of unsatisfied arousal screaming in her blood, Anya took a walk around the sandy paths of the tent village to calm down before facing Mary. The sky was a dark ceiling, pressing down on her, the almost-full moon a searchlight on her struggle for calm. As much as she yearned for Ethan's tongue on her clit, Anya wouldn't not abide a witness to her weakness. She had proven her strength, resisted the physical pull. She wouldn't have to go through that again. It was over. Mary would have the photos she needed.

The photos. Mary would want to show her as soon as she got back to the tent. There was no way she could look at them now, in the state she was in. Not until she'd calmed down. After having Ethan come in her mouth while her sex clenched and cried out for him, her body craved release.

Slipping into the nearest change room, Anya left the light off and locked the door. It took barely a minute to reach her first orgasm, with the memory of how she'd turned his rejection into victory. She'd set the stage for Mary to take photos of the man who had cheated on her sister, being blown by an anonymous woman in a black hoodie, the images that would see Ethan get what he deserved. Her second orgasm was accompanied by the memory of the smooth feel of cock sliding in and out of her mouth, the taste of him – the taste of success – still fresh on her tongue.

But Mary wasn't excited when Anya returned to their tent. She found her roommate sitting on the end of her bed with her head in her hands, her long black hair spilling over her face.

When she heard Anya, she raised her head with a look of regret.

"What's wrong? Couldn't you do it?"

"I'm so sorry. Not because I didn't want to! Security came past, and by the time it was clear to come back, you'd already gone."

"Fuck." Anya pushed the hood back and scrubbed her fingers through her hair, trying to silence the roar of frustration in her head. She glanced at Mary and her look of distress helped her to ignore it. "It's okay. We can try again."

"Really?" Mary jumped to her feet and squeezed Anya's hand, a hopeful look lighting her face. "I guess if security have a schedule, we know what time to avoid next time?"

"Okay. Yes. Good plan. We'll try again tomorrow night." Anya told herself the surge of excitement she felt at the thought was only a response to the challenge of getting Ethan to invite her to his tent again.

CHAPTER EIGHT

ETHAN WOKE FROM A DEEP SLEEP, wishing he wasn't alone in the big bed, craving Anya's compact, naked body beside him. He'd been weak to let her do what she did to him last night, but missing her this morning had reminded him of something he'd lost sight of since the trouble began with Heidi.

He'd almost forgotten how it had been those first months of their relationship. They'd been some of the best of his life. He'd had his work, and her to come home to. Until he'd had to leave to work on location in Scotland.

Ethan pushed himself out of bed, hoping the movement would banish the memories of the tantrums and accusations, of Heidi's decline into jealousy and insecurity. He reached for the script he kept by the bed and glanced at the scenes for the day. Reading the stage cues for the sex scene between Ulrich and Vivienne succeeded in distracting him, but also reminded him of his other concern. His growing feelings for Anya.

He threw on the cargo pants he'd thrown over a chair last night before he'd collapsed into a deep sleep. The anticipation that had unfurled in his gut while reading the description of what he'd be doing to Anya today, bloomed at the memory of having the pants pushed down around his ankles and Anya's hot little mouth wrapped around his cock.

But there was more than sexual chemistry between them. Their day at the beach had been like a holiday for him. Even without the scorching sex, just being with her made him feel like he didn't have a care in the world. That was before she turned up on set and things got complicated. *But had they?*

Anya was an actress. She understood the demands and obligations of his career.

And he wanted a relationship again, to give meaning to all the hard work. He hadn't realized how empty his life had become. His career was built on fantasies and he wanted the reality of waking up with same woman whenever their schedules allowed, a partner who would stand beside him, not accuse him. Someone to care if he'd had a good day, to be on his side when he hadn't, would be there for the small things and the large, the good and the bad. And he wanted a family, with children one day. He *didn't* want to be a successful but lonely actor.

Ethan slipped on a t-shirt and his deck shoes and made his way to breakfast, feeling confident about being able to perform professionally with Anya on the scene. And more positive about spending time with her. He hoped he'd see her in the mess tent, but when she wasn't there realized she'd already be in makeup. Those tattoos must take hours to apply.

He hoped she'd agree to see him tonight. He would suggest they spend the rest of her time here getting to know each other, discreetly. Then if they both wanted more, he would happily face the media storm with her beside him. If she wanted to, especially after he explained how he'd let his last girlfriend down.

"You look like you slept well." Josie observed when he dropped into the makeup chair and looked up at her reflection with a smile. He imagined Anya in the next trailer, and the lucky artist who was applying the tattoos to her soft white skin… her round breasts.

"Earth to Ethan," Josie said with a sigh. "You did say the date went well. I'm guessing by your goofy look you're planning on seeing her again?"

"Yeah, I think so." He wanted so much to share this brand-new feeling of hope and happiness with someone, but not with Josie. Not with anyone until he'd had 'the talk' with Anya.

Ethan channeled his previous self from a fortnight earlier and managed to keep his expression neutral while he had his scars applied and hair extensions checked, but his mind kept wandering to the trailer next door.

THIS TIME, when they met on-set, Ethan let his eyes wander over Anya's nakedness, following the swirling lines that decorated her delicious body. He couldn't help smiling at the black bush of fake pubic hair stuck on the front of her G-string, and the thought that he might have his face buried in the blonde curls beneath later tonight had him salivating with anticipation.

Giving in to the witch turned out to be easier than he'd anticipated. Faking sexual intimacy was the part of acting he found the most difficult, but he already knew Anya's body and her responses. After last night, the scenes they filmed seemed more like a sweet, long session of foreplay than work.

"Will you come to my tent tonight?" Ethan breathed in her ear as he curled over her body, on her hands and knees beneath him. Doggy-style wasn't his favorite position but pretending to dominate the actress triggered a surge of primitive power in him that neutralized his helpless craving for her.

* * *

"HOW COULD I refuse such a romantic offer?"

"Just to talk." That might be what his mouth was saying but the rigid cock pressed against her sex was telling a different story. Anya had to stop herself squirming against him, excitement racing through her as she imagined there was no G-string between them, that Ethan would thrust his cock inside her while the crew watched, the camera filming the act as a reality rather than a charade. She'd have to remember this position for next time – and there would have to be a next time. It was perfect, no danger of looking into his eyes at her most vulnerable moment.

"Okay," she panted under her breath as he pretended to collapse on top of her, the warrior both conqueror of, and conquered by, the witch beneath him. "But earlier than last night. I have an early start tomorrow."

"Whenever you can make it." His voice purred seduction into her ear.

Oh yeah, she had him hooked alright. He might plan to talk, but he wanted more than that. She was tempted to exercise her power and make him wait, but the roaring need in her veins wouldn't allow it. Last night, while she'd lain awake waiting for sleep, she'd decided to give into that need – for the sake of the photos. It would only last a week, which would give her and Mary plenty of photo opportunities. And before she'd drifted off, Anya had a brilliant idea how to thoroughly damn him, without exposing herself.

"MARY." Anya called through the bathroom door. "I'm leaving now."

Her roommate popped her head out, brushing her teeth. When she saw what Anya was wearing, she darted back in to spit the toothpaste and popped back out. "Role-playing? Kinky!"

"It's the perfect disguise, and after eight hours of foreplay dressed like this, he won't be able to say no." Anya looked down at the cloak of her costume. Borrowing it had been easy, but convincing Liz in makeup that she wanted to keep the wig and makeup on to play a joke on one of the crew would have been a challenge if she weren't a consummate actress. If Mary took the photos from behind, all that would be recorded would be long black hair.

"Doesn't matter what you wear, there's no way he could refuse you. But after hours of pretend fucking, I'd better get myself outside his window fast."

"I think you're right. Let's hope security stick to the same schedule as last night."

"You know, we're a pretty good team." Mary took a shy step toward her.

Anya turned to pick up a strip of condoms and slipped them into the inner pocket of her cloak. There was no way lack of condoms would stop her tonight. "That we are. Thanks Mary. I really appreciate your help with this, and for trusting my motives." She gave Mary's shoulder a quick squeeze, hoping she'd continue to follow orders without question. Anya could confide in her, but it was easier to let her think keeping a memento of her conquests was just one of Anya's unusual sexual habits. Like role-playing and giving head to random actors.

Anya pulled the cloak tighter around her body, ready to step outside, and grimaced at the rub of the rough fabric of her costume against her nipples. The day had been torture. She'd been close to orgasm numerous times, all the kissing and fondling and simulated sex.

When she was finally alone, she'd been tempted to take the edge off herself, but Anya wanted Ethan's cock inside her when *this* orgasm came.

ETHAN THOUGHT the moment would never come when she slipped through the tent entrance. Initially, he thought she'd borrowed the cape from wardrobe to move through the night unnoticed, but when she dropped the hood and revealed Ulrich's witch, all the blood rushed to his cock. After a day of making love to her character without release, he had developed an unhealthy obsession for the tattooed sorceress.

"What was it you wanted to talk about?" She walked to the window and looked out into the deepening dark.

"I've thought a lot about what you said. It's obvious there's a very strong attraction between us." He started carefully, feeling her out before he decided where to start – with his history or the arrangement he had in mind.

"Glad you noticed." Anya turned back to him with a smirk.

"I agree that it would help on-set if we worked off our sexual urges in private. But we need to be discreet. I'm sure you know about my last girlfriend, the media implying her death was suicide, that it was because I'd been cheating on her." Ethan watched Anya carefully for her reaction.

Her face was perfectly blank, and expressionless, just a flicker of her eyelids confirmed she'd heard him. "Yes, I know the story. There's no need to explain." Her voice was surprisingly brusque. "I'm in, and I also want to keep it discreet. So, if we're agreed, can we stop talking? You've been teasing me with that gorgeous cock all day. The girls, and most of the guys, couldn't keep their eyes off it. Now it's all mine." Her impatience didn't seem completely sincere, but her possessiveness sent a thrill shivering through him, and when Anya's hands poked out from inside the cloak to separate the fabric, revealing a flash of naked flesh, he forgot what else he'd intended to say. "Get over here, witch."

She strutted over to where he stood, a glimpse of bare leg showing with every step. "I thought some role-playing would be fun. Lucky you, you can have us both. Actress and sorceress." She slid her hands beneath his t-shirt, running teasing fingertips over his abs, making him shudder with desire, and lightly bit his nipple through the fabric, bringing his cock to full attention.

"Christ, Anya. After today I'll have trouble enough hanging on. Take it easy on a guy, would you?" He slipped his hand beneath the heavy cascade of the wig, caressing the back of her neck as he lowered his lips to hers. The kiss was meant to slow things down, but it only ignited the barely contained passion between them.

She pulled away, panting. "Why would I take it easy when all I can think about is you finishing what you started today?" While pinning him with her intense blue gaze, she undid the ribbon tie at her throat and dropped the cloak to the floor, a strip of condoms dangling from her fingers. "All the time the camera was rolling I was imagining you were truly inside me."

It had only been a matter of days since they're night, but her absolute nakedness stunned him, the make-up tattoos lending and otherworldly mystique to her toned body, her pale skin heating his blood like the hottest part of a flame.

At the sight of his sorceress naked and offering herself to him with no witnesses to perform for, the Viking in him roared in response. He couldn't get his t-shirt over his head quickly enough, and when he did, he found Anya on her knees on the sofa. Fuck, this girl really was a sorceress, reading his mind and his moods.

Ethan stepped hurriedly out of his shorts, nearly tripping as he hurried to take his position behind her.

Anya looked over her shoulder. "What are you waiting for?" She asked with a frown.

"Protection…" He looked up from having rolled the sheath over his cock and groaned at the sight of Anya naked but for the wig cascading all down her back to her butt. She'd bent over the back of the sofa, her rounded ass before him at cock height, legs spread, sex open - pink and moist and calling to him.

"Fuck," he ground out and entered her. He thought he would slide in slowly, but she was so wet he pushed in right to the hilt. After that, he had no chance of slowing until he found the completion he craved.

Anya's grunts and guttural moans assured him he wasn't alone in his desperation. She reached around to claw at his butt, urging him deeper and faster, and then she was clawing at him from the inside too, her pussy gripping him as if she wanted to own him.

The full impact of the pleasure when it hit him stole all sound and vision from his world. There was only the pulsing ecstasy exploding through his body emanating from where he'd impaled the woman who had teased and tortured him since they met.

His cock still hard, he continued to thrust inside her. He was man, warrior, and he had conquered the witch. She had succumbed to him. He held the power, the instrument he used to stake his claim on her – the vanquished – still drawing whimpers and ripples of pleasure from her.

Gradually, pleasure and rigidity subsided, and he pulled out of her. He wrapped the used condom in a tissue and threw it in the waste basket while Anya undraped herself from the back of the sofa.

"Do I need to remind you we had an agreement?" He asked her as he gathered her to his chest, supporting her unsteadiness. He ran his hands down her back and cupped her butt, lowering his cheek to hers.

"And what was that?"

"I get to taste you tonight."

"Oh, you will. Get on the bed. On your back."

Ethan sat on the bed, gladly giving up his power to be the submissive, if it meant he'd get a mouth-full of her pussy. He pulled himself backward, eyes locked on the witch at the end of his bed. So strange to have her here in his tent, tattoos covering her face and breasts, black hair cascading down her back, but with Anya's almost white curls between her legs.

"Lay down." She ordered, and he obeyed. He would get his wish by letting her think she was in charge.

She crawled onto the bed, up and over his body, looking just like the predatory sorceress she played during the day. When she reached the headboard, she stopped and propped her forearms on it, the perfect position for those sweet curls to tickle his nose. He pulled her hips down, so he had a face full of her sex and nuzzled until her lips opened for him.

He used his flattened tongue in long, slow strokes upward, over and over, awakening the nerve endings over a wide surface area. First, he felt her body relax with the pleasure of his caresses, but he soon felt her concentrating on the jolt of anticipated pleasure each time his tongue flicked the dense cluster of nerve endings.

As the flesh beneath his tongue grew more engorged, he knew his slow movements had become more of a tease. Their initial urgency had been slaked, now he wanted to savor their hours together. But she began to squirm impatiently, the occasional contact with her clitoris no longer often enough. Her movements told him she wanted more, faster, concentrated on the swollen nub of her pleasure, and his body responded to her arousal. Breath quickening, he groaned against her moist flesh, needing her straddling him, riding him like the beast he wanted to be; but determined to draw out her pleasure until she panted his name.

Using the tip of his tongue he brushed across and around her clit, faster. With his fingers he caressed the skin just inside her entrance, then further inside, along the dense, warm and wet front wall.

As she edged closer to orgasm, he tried to think of his action as a mathematical equation to distract his own mounting arousal. He focused on maintaining a consistent speed, until he felt her start to cum. Increasing the pressure of his fingers and tongue, assaulting her pleasure zone from both sides, he didn't slow but rode the waves of pleasure until they subsided, then quickly built again until she was pulsing against his lips for a second time, crying out with her release.

Slowly, unsteadily, she crawled down his body.

"I hope you have a condom ready to go. I need you inside me now," she demanded and rested on his thighs, her sex moist and hot against his balls.

He pulled a packet from under the pillow. "I wasn't going to let a missing condom slow things down tonight." He winked as he rolled it over his rigid penis. "I've stashed these all around the tent. All yours my lady." Ethan spread his hands face up beside his hips, offering himself for her enjoyment.

"Thank you, Viking lord," she said with a grin and dropped herself onto his erection. He gasped at the suddenness of pussy around his shaft, but she didn't allow him time to prepare himself.

She folded her legs, so she squatted over him and leant back, resting on her hands, so his cock was pressed up against the front wall of her pussy. At that angle, her vigorous thrusts created a friction that must have brought maximum sensation for her, but also gave him the most beautiful view he'd ever seen. He knees spread, her swollen sex swallowing his cock hungrily, her breasts thrust high as she arched back, her chest and neck flushed with arousal. Her eyes closed and lips parted. Lucky for his tenuous control she came quickly. Her movements slowed, and she collapsed forward onto him, still moving but slowly, dreamily, sliding down and up in a way that calmed his urgency but maintained pleasure.

He was determined to get her to look at him this time. When she'd come while their eyes were locked above the cafe that night, it had been an accelerant to his climax. He'd felt their connection in his soul as well as his body. He wanted that again, wanted her to be fully with him when they climaxed together.

As her movements became jerky and her neck flushed pink, he called to her. "Water sprite." But she would not open her eyes for him. They climaxed together, but alone.

When she recovered enough to stand, she pulled out of his warm arms and slid from the bed, reaching for her cloak.

"You won't stay? If you leave before five you won't be seen. I'll set the alarm."

"No. I can't sleep like this. I need to get back and get this wig on its holder before I do any more damage. And I need to wash this off." His gaze followed the movement of her hands over the tattoos on her breasts and damn it, his cock stirred again. How is it possible? She *must* be a sorceress.

CHAPTER NINE

ANYA MISSED the enclosed comfort of the indoor scenes. The smell of horses and pollen from the nearby crops on the air was unsettling and unfamiliar, having lived only by the seaside or city. Filming outside left her feeling at once exposed and strangely free, like a field trip at school.

When they finished the last scene before lunch, Ethan hurried back to the tent setup for the cast and Anya followed, hanging back, needing space. She couldn't stop the slide show playing in her mind, the photos of Ethan thrusting into an anonymous woman from behind, the same mysterious woman kneeling over his face and taking her pleasure from his tongue, then riding him mercilessly in pursuit of yet another orgasm. The need to have him again grew with each replay. The added frisson of both having the action recorded for viewing, knowing she was the woman who had – and would again – experience pleasure at his expense, made the whole affair surreal.

For once Ethan hurried ahead and reached the tent to meet a dark-haired woman, not much taller than Anya, and two children who seemed to be aged around ten years old, who rushed to meet him. Anya slowed to take in the scene.

"Happy birthday, bro." The woman threw her arms around his chest and squeezed hard. Ethan pretended to wince, while wrapping his arms around her back.

"Shhh!" he said, even though Anya and a few of the crew were close enough to hear. "And it's not until tomorrow." He let her go and slung his arms around the shoulders of the boy and girl who had attached themselves to each of his canvas-clad thighs.

Anya exhaled, relieved they hadn't been filming a sex-scene today.

"I know, but we won't be here to say it in person tomorrow." She rubbed the shoulder of the girl whose hair reflected that of both her mother and her uncle, the same thick, dark hair as Ethan's. They both stood beaming up at their famous uncle.

"No, because you'll be shopping in Lisbon. I guess I better wish you happy birthday now, too. Although you won't be getting your present until I see you Saturday night."

"Okay then grumpy. You didn't need to buy me anything though. Spending the weekend with you and the kids is all I want for my birthday."

"That's a relief. It will save me trying to shop before I meet you at the hotel. I'm not sure what the gift selection is like at the train station." He joked, ruffling the boy's hair.

Ethan's sister reached up and pinched his cheek, a fond look on her face. Apart from having the same dark auburn hair, for paternal twins they were quite different in appearance, although they seemed to share a similar temperament and sense of humor.

Ethan turned and found Anya standing just inside the tent, half turned away, wanting to give them privacy but drawn by the family scene.

"Hey guys, this is my sister, Lissa, and her kids Jules and Toby," Ethan called out a general introduction to any nearby cast and crew, careful not to single out Anya.

His family smiled and responded to the welcomes, then moved to where Anya hovered near the entrance.

"It certainly is a pleasure to meet you," Lissa said and Anya sucked in a breath, thinking Ethan had mentioned her to his sister.

Lissa slanted a look at Ethan, catching him in the act of raising his eyebrows in a show of innocence at Anya.

"I saw you in *The Tempest*. Your portrayal of Ariel was intriguing." She smirked knowingly between Anya to Ethan, picking up their silent conversation. "Surprisingly androgynous considering your obvious femininity. I wouldn't have recognized you as the same actress if Ethan hadn't introduced us."

Lissa, Jules and Toby stayed to have lunch with Ethan and watch the rest of the day's filming. Anya ate with some of the extras she recognized from when she played the serving wench, but she watched Ethan and his family surreptitiously.

His niece and nephew were playful and curious yet respectful, and Anya was envious of the family weekend they would soon share in Lisbon. She wished she could be there, to see first-hand what it was like to be part of an extended family. *This* family. To get to know Lissa and find out what Ethan was like growing up. She would never have a sister-in-law, probably never have nieces or nephews either. Not that she resented

Tomas's lifestyle choice, but on top of being adopted, it left her with no chance to be part of a large family.

Feeling low, Anya said a quick good-bye when it was time to get back to work and made her way to the stables ahead of Ethan.

"Your sister seems nice. And your niece and nephew."

"Lissa is a sweetheart, and a great mom. Jules and Toby? Yeah, they're good kids. I hope mine turn out like them."

Anya sucked in a breath as the news knocked the wind out of her. "You want kids?" She'd never thought of it herself, just as she didn't expect any other actor did. Generally, with the people she worked with, she thought of their families as a hypothetical part of a distant life, only around on opening night.

She didn't dislike children, she'd just never had much to do with them. And she'd never met a guy she would consider living with, let alone having a family with. But if she ever did, having children with a man she loved would give her the family she'd never experienced. An ingrained feeling of belonging. Something she was not destined to have.

"I didn't realize until recently, but yeah, I do. And not in the distant future." He looked at her with a softness she'd not seen before.

Ethan would make a good father, she realized. Now he'd mentioned it, Anya could imagine him with kids. Smaller versions of him, with his dark hair, his fine features and sincerity. His goodness. *Damn, where was the lying bastard her sister had described?* She still hadn't seen him and was starting to wonder if he even existed.

ANYA FELT UNCHARACTERISTICALLY uncertain when she slipped into Ethan's tent later that night, but was gratified by the lift of his eyebrows when she shrugged off her black hoodie.

"So that's what you were doing while I was being sliced to pieces by a Viking sword after we finished at the stables." He said as he gracefully rose from the sofa where he'd been plucking the chords of a ballad. The words hovered just outside of her grasp, but she remembered loving the song when it had been popular a decade earlier.

"What do you think? Does it suit me?" she asked as she ran her fingers through her short hair, now bronze. She'd never had red hair before. Nicole, the actress playing the witch's attendant, inspired her with the gorgeous colour of her corkscrew locks. The perfect disguise, and the colour would wash out within a week.

"Everything suits you. You're a chameleon." Ethan met her in the middle of the tent and tilted his head down for a lingering kiss.

"I missed our foreplay today," Anya teased.

"I did not. I was glad for a day without having to act like we're making love, while pretending I didn't wish we were alone so I really could. It is much easier - and the weather is perfect - for filming outside."

"I admit it was nice to be in the fresh air and sunshine. A luxury when you live in London. But I'm not looking forward to spending most of tomorrow in a saddle."

"You don't like horses?"

"I like them fine, but I haven't ridden since I was a girl." She steered him to the sofa and urged him to sit, climbing into his lap. "Maybe I can practice on you."

"I definitely recommend it. Now shut up and kiss me."

SATED, but not exhausted, Anya extricated herself from the cradle of Ethan's arm and crawled on top of him, stretching out so her feet rested against his calf muscles. A day's worth of pent-up hunger for each other had taken them from a satisfying session on the couch to another on the bed.

Laying her head on the cushion of one side of his chest, Anya traced patterns in the small patch of dark hair in the valley between his pecs, occasionally venturing out to circle his nipple in a teasing caress.

Ethan's cock stirred against her inner thigh in response and she wondered if they'd used all of the condoms he'd had stashed, and what she would do if they had. Risk pregnancy? Anya lifted her head, his proof of his stamina nudging the thought out of her mind.

"I don't have a birthday present for you. Even if I'd known, there are no shops nearby." Anya shrugged, the movement lifting her breasts, the suction of their wet skin pulling at her nipples.

"That's fine. Having you here is the only present I would ask for." He smoothed the damp hair off her forehead and gazed into her eyes. He opened his mouth and drew a breath to speak.

Anya leant forward and covered his lips with a brief but deep kiss. More disturbing than the thought of what he might say, was what she realized she *wanted* him to say. Something like, *can I see you when your part is over?*

"Only for a little while longer, I need to get back to my tent." She said when kiss had erased the twinge of concern. Anya arched back, the movement pressing her sex against his cock. One more round and she'd have to go, or she'd be too tired to do her job properly tomorrow. Makeup and lighting couldn't hide a bad performance.

Supporting her weight with her hands on his chest, she raised her knees either side of his hips and lowered herself onto his erection, gasping as she devoured his entire naked length, her still-swollen clit bumping against him.

He groaned at the shock of flesh against flesh with no barrier, and up to pull her into his embrace, constricting her movements to a rocking of hips.

"Happy birthday for tomorrow," she whispered against his chest.

<hr>

MARY WAS STILL AWAKE, catching up with the industry gossip on the internet when Anya tried to sneak back into their tent. Mary was in a pensive mood - one of Mary's exes was photographed leaving the hotel where his leading lady was staying. And one of Anya's old flings just got divorced - again.

"I thought you'd be asleep by now," Anya said casually as she secured the door flap.

"I waited up for you. I didn't realize you were going to do an encore, or I would have stayed longer too." What reason had Anya to stay? They'd agreed Mary wouldn't hang around in case security came by.

"No need. I'm sure you got what we need." Anya picked up her sleep shorts and singlet and disappeared into the bathroom.

While Anya got ready for bed, Mary scrolled through the pictures she'd taken that night. She'd got the ones Anya wanted, the ones where you could only make out that it was Ethan, and it was clear what he was doing, but the woman always had her face hidden. The ones she'd taken for herself, had already been saved to the Cloud, and deleted from her phone.

Mary logged out of her Cloud account as Anya emerged from the bathroom, and sat up, cross-legged, ready to show her the photos she'd asked for.

"Good night." Anya slipped into her bed and turned off her lamp.

"You don't want to see the photos?" Mary asked, crestfallen. She'd thought Anya would be excited, and grateful.

"Could you send them to me?" Anya asked, her voice already slurring with sleep.

"Sure." Mary replied and slapped her phone on the bed beside her.

"Thanks love. I owe you big time."

I'll look forward to collecting.

Mary turned off her light and waited until Anya's breaths were slow and deep before she got off her own bed. The breeze from the window ruffled her sheer, short nightie and tickled her pubic hair.

After the first night of waking up from her regular nightmare with Anya stroking her hair, Mary craved that comfort every night. Waking up next to Anya had been like waking up in heaven.

Slowly and carefully, Mary inserted herself into Anya's bed and eased her body against the other girl.

The first time Mary had slipped into her bed, Anya had woken with a start. When Mary explained she'd had a bad nightmare, Anya had sleepily wrapped her arms around her and gone back to sleep.

The next night Anya wasn't surprised by her presence and accepted her embrace without waking.

Mary hadn't had the nightmare that night. Instead she had a wonderful dream.

CHAPTER TEN

ETHAN'S TENT. Friday 10pm

"I don't know how they found out it was my birthday," Ethan groaned as Anya and Mary steered him to his tent. Anya should have been glowing with triumph. She'd managed a coup. When she'd leaked that it was Ethan's birthday and set the wheels in motion for a party, she never imagined how much it would benefit her cause.

Ethan had drunk so many shots that he forgot to be discreet. He'd allowed himself to be seen leaving with the two girls. As they wove along the path back to his tent, Anya imagined a future where, when the photos Mary had taken were seen by the world, people might assume when they saw him with a black haired girl that it was Mary straddling Ethan's face, then being fucked from behind. Mary's reputation alone would ruin him. Could she allow Mary to take the fall for her? Was it really worth it to drag Ethan's name through the mud?

"Thanks love. I'll take it from here," Anya smiled at her roommate as Ethan flopped back on the bed. She nodded her head toward the door with a twinge of remorse. The photos they could setup with him in this state were almost endless, but she just didn't have the heart to setup Ethan tonight. It was his birthday, after all, and the thought of revenge had lost its luster. She was no bunny-boiler. Maybe Ethan had suffered from Heidi's death too?

Mary raised an eyebrow and pulled out her phone, holding it up with a question in her eyes.

Anya shook her head. "Not tonight."

"But we could set up some wild shots. He's virtually comatose." Mary's excitement held a hint of irritation.

"I think we have what we need already. Thank you. Sleep well."

"Sure. Then why don't you come with? I have a bottle of Cointreau I've been saving for a special occasion." Mary crossed her arms and issued her challenge.

"Sounds good. I'll be there soon." Anya gave her a tight smile. What was wrong with Mary tonight? Maybe she had PMS.

When Mary had huffed and flounced out the door, Anya turned back to Ethan and carefully undressed the unconscious lead actor. Luckily, he wasn't as out of it as Mary thought. He obeyed Anya's commands, eyes closed, when she told him to sit up, lift his hips.

Anya took the opportunity to study and explore his body as she never had when he was awake, so he wouldn't take her fascination with the beauty of his form as anything but a superficial admiration. She circled one perfect nipple with a fingertip until it tightened beneath her gaze, then trailed the fingers of both hands over his tight abs, watching his hips rock slightly. The things she could do, the way she could touch him... She flicked a glance up to his face, relaxed and gorgeous in his oblivion, and turned away, searching for the anger that had driven her into this relationship.

She reminded herself that he'd ruined her chances of having a small but real flesh and blood family, but all she felt was sadness at the loss of her sister.

Anya wandered over to the guitar Ethan had played for Heidi. Her sister had told her he'd somehow guessed her favorite songs, or maybe they were his favorites too. They were Anya's now.

She sat down and started playing, remembering the conflicted look as Heidi played the original songs on her iPod on the nights they'd managed to find time to get together. There had been joy and pain mingled there as she'd listened, often with her eyes closed, and something else, a desperation, obsession. At the time Anya had wondered how one would contain a love that powerful, if, over time, it might be worse than no love at all.

Tears slid over Anya's cheeks as she played. She could have been taking the photos that would prove the rumors about Ethan were true. But she really wasn't that person.

She put the guitar back in its place and bent over his sleeping form. Sensing her, Ethan lifted a hand to her cheek and urged her head down, pressing her cheek against his. He smelt of warm male and beer fumes and... Ethan. Anya knew a moment of uncertainty at the path she'd taken. No matter what he'd done to make Heidi drive off that bridge, he wasn't that man when he was with *her*. She'd never seen him flirt. He was friendly but distant with other women – not at all like he was with her in private. Unless he was seeing someone else secretly, as he was her, but between the work and his time with Anya, there was little time. He needed *some* sleep.

"Stay?" he whispered. She was tempted, but she worried she might fall asleep and she would be seen leaving. Whatever was between them had already gone on longer than necessary. It might never be a good time to end it. No matter how many times they made love, the fire he'd started in her only seemed to burn hotter.

"I'll see you on-set," Anya said, and kissed his cheek before pulling away.

"Tomorrow night?" He struggled upright, supporting himself on his elbows.

"I'm heading back to town tonight. I'll be back Monday morning." She pulled the hood of her sweatshirt over her hair and looked out the window, as if expecting someone to be watching. Why did she suddenly feel guilty?

"I'll come back from Lisbon Sunday. We could do something. A picnic?" His expression was hopeful, and her traitorous body urged her to agree.

"No, not Sunday. I want to spend some time with my brother and best friend. I've hardly seen them."

"You have a brother here? I thought your family moved away when you did." His frown showed he was starting to piece together the few facts about her life she'd let slip.

Anya squirmed. Until now she'd been careful to avoid talking about anything outside of work – and sex.

"Ah. He owns the bakery." He said, his face relaxing with the satisfaction of working it out and collapsed back on the bed. He was snoring before she slipped out into the night.

WHEN ANYA finally got back to the tent Mary was still awake, sitting on the edge of her bed with her back to the door. A half empty bottle of Cointreau stood uncapped on her bedside table, the drawer gaping open below. Mary's head was angled to study something in her lap. Anya secured the door flap quickly so she could have a look at their night's work on Mary's phone.

She stepped behind her roommate, glancing over her shoulder and froze, stunned to see the velvet box Mary was holding, open to reveal an emerald pendant.

Mary's head whipped around, eyes wide with shock. She snapped the lid shut.

"Can I see that?' Anya held out her hand.

For a moment Mary looked as if she would refuse, but she handed it over, lowering her eyes to the bed beside her.

Inside the jewelry case Anya found exactly what she thought she'd seen. It was a distinctive design; one she'd admired, despite Alec giving it to her on their second date. Nestled on the black velvet was a beautiful pendant, the beaten gold arrow that pierced the heart-shaped gem curved to hook around the delicate gold chain.

"The stone of Venus, for my goddess of love and beauty," Alec had crooned as he'd fastened the chain around Anya's neck. Too quickly he'd assumed the role of doting lover, had made it clear he thought Cupid had found his mark. Alec had been so sickeningly enamored that Anya worried a diamond ring might be his next gift to her, which was enough to fast-track the expiry date of their relationship.

When she'd ended the fling three days later, Alec had been so horrid Anya assumed he must have taken the gift back when it went missing from her dressing room. But when they ran into each other at the premiere of her next show he'd demanded it back. If she'd had it, she would have gladly complied, to get rid of anything that linked them. When she said as much, he vehemently denied taking it. He accused her of lying.

But neither of them had lied. Mary had the pendant all along.

"You spent a lot of time in my dressing room during *Midsummer Night's Dream*." Anya said.

"Um. Yes. That's true. I'm sorry." Mary's words stumbled around, crashing into each other. "I completely forgot I had it… found it after the show finished. I meant to contact you…"

Anya held up her hand to stop the slurred excuses. They both knew they were lies. Even if Mary had forgotten she had it, why had she packed it to bring with her on location? And she must have unpacked it to place it in its current home in her bedside drawer.

Anya slipped the jewelry case into her pocket and picked up her sleep shorts and singlet, heading to the bathroom to shower and think. "No harm done," she forced herself to say, worried about how much she'd trusted Mary with. "It's been returned now."

———

MARY PRETENDED to be asleep when Anya emerged from the bathroom.

After drinking uncounted shots of Cointreau by herself, waiting for Anya to join her, she'd given up and gone to sleep. But the nightmare had come, the shadow monster who had visited her sleep for years, leaning over her where she lay paralyzed in her bed, terrified as it convulsed and moaned and tugged at her sheets.

Panicked and alone, Mary had lain there, willing her heart to slow, the light on to banish the shadows.

She'd reached for the pendant, a reminder of those days of friendship in London she'd cherished. A reminder of the growing closeness she and Anya shared in this room. Mary was certain what they had now was more than friendship. So why had Anya stayed with Ethan, alone, rather than coming back to their tent?

Why had she been upset about the pendant? The heart meant so much to Mary, but Anya had only worn it once. That slobbering Alec hadn't kept Anya's interest for long, she'd dumped him faster than most.

And she'd wanted to tell Anya about the epiphany she'd had that morning. She'd woken from a dream of them both naked, with pleasure pulsing between her legs. With a wonder at the sense of belonging she felt in that moment, and Anya's small, warm body curled behind hers, Mary was suddenly aware of the mistakes she'd been making. Over and over she'd ignorantly hooked up with the wrong person. But the problem wasn't the men she'd chosen.

It was *men*.

The solution was Anya, and Mary wanted to be her solution too. Once she pointed out to her roommate that the reason she never kept a man around for long was because she should be with a woman – with her – they could both be happy, and satisfied.

Mary had always felt a closeness to the small blonde woman, a protective fondness and obviously, by the way she trusted her, Anya felt the same way. Despite the prickly way she treated the other actors, Anya had befriended *her*. And then last night, after Mary had slipped into her bed, she'd moved seductively against Mary in her sleep, and when she'd caressed her nipples through the thin fabric of her t-shirt, Anya had moaned and squirmed with pleasure.

Mary slid out of bed, anticipation building in her lower abdomen as she slipped her nightdress off and dropped it on the floor. The thought of lying next to Anya naked made her tingle with impatience, and she shivered with pleasure at the caress of Anya's sheets against her bare skin.

Anya didn't stir, her breaths continuing deep and rhythmic as Mary pressed herself along her back, curving her thighs up to spoon her lover. She anchored their bodies together by sliding her hand over Anya's ribs and pulling her pelvis close to Anya's buttocks. Anya's top had ridden up, leaving her stomach naked and Mary held her breath, treasuring the feel of silken skin beneath her fingers. Anya stretched beneath her touch, like a pleasure-seeking cat, and Mary took the opportunity to slip her other hand beneath Anya's ribs and cup her breast. She weighed the small globe in her palm, teasing out the moment she first touched her naked nipple, pressing against Anya's buttocks and building her own pleasure with touch and anticipation. That first brush of her fingertips over the tight bud of Anya's nipple sent a dart of pleasure through Mary's body, and the moan that escaped Anya's lips almost did her in.

They had so many pleasures to look forward to, but not until Anya was finished with *him*. They would grow something special and precious together, something not muddied by whatever it was Anya needed to do to him.

Until then, she would take small pleasures while her lover slept, to making the waiting easier. Little tastes of what they had to look forward to. Tomorrow night she would slip her hand into Anya's panties and search out the moist heat between her legs. Gently and patiently she would give her pleasure while she slept. And once Anya's business was done with Ethan, and Mary had her all to herself, she would make Anya cry out her name as she came under her mouth.

For now, just the thought of it was enough to push Mary over the edge. She thrust her pelvis against Anya, who squirmed with the pleasure Mary was inflicting on her nipples. But the name that fell from Anya's lips was not hers.

"Ethan," she whispered, her voice hoarse with sleep and ecstasy.

Mary rolled away from Anya, disappointment and distress reverberating through her, but desperate to finish. She thrust her fingers between her legs, rubbing her clit viciously and gasping with release and grief, her eyes squeezed shut. Once the spasms of pleasure subsided, she opened her eyes to check she hadn't disturbed Anya, and found her room-mate standing beside the bed staring at her with shock. Disgust flared as their eyes met and Anya turned away to gather up her clothes from the night before and locked herself in the bathroom. Mary squeezed her eyelids shut and curled in a ball on her side.

She listened to the shower, and Anya brushing her teeth, cringing when she heard the door unlock. Mary stayed still, hoping for the smallest touch, hoping Anya had forgiven her rash behavior and give her a chance to make it up to her.

But her footsteps hurried past her bed, only pausing at the door.

"We'll talk when I get back on Monday." Anya's voice was soft yet sharp with ice. "I think we should ask to be allocated new room-mates."

<hr>

ANYA STARED out the window at the blur of native scrub, the aching blue of the ocean in the distance, the brightness of the spring day barely beginning to fade into twilight. The other actors taking the bus back to town were talking and laughing as if they'd been let out on school break. Tonight, they would stay up late and celebrate their day of release from long days with early starts. Tomorrow they could sleep in.

Anya tried to loosen up, breathing in the sharp tang of weed floating forward from the back of the bus, along with the throb of reggae. But she couldn't get her head around what had happened with Mary. She acknowledged they shared a connection after the STD incident, Anya playing the role of both confidant and conspirator. But she couldn't imagine how Mary had got the idea she was interested in her physically. The girl had watched her fucking someone else, after all.

Anya had no experience with rape, but waking up with her top pulled up and her nipples tingling from being pinched and pulled, Mary naked and masturbating beside her, gave her a taste of the violation the victim might feel.

Joana had been excited when her best friend called and suggested they go out dancing for their promised night out. Anya wanted to forget until Monday. Forget Mary and forget Ethan. Forget *everything*.

With the help of a good dose of vodka and a few hours of dancing with Joana, Anya managed to numb the unease she wasn't ready to analyze. She whirled until she felt light-headed, giggling as her skirt flapped around her legs. And when a couple of cute guys joined them, and proved they knew how to move, Anya tipsily wondered if they would move just as well horizontally.

When the girls emerged from a trip to the bathroom and their dance partners were very obviously waiting, eager for their return, Joana raised a questioning eyebrow at Anya.

The four had naturally split into couples on the dancefloor, Joana marking out her preference for the cuter, brown haired sportsman. Anya knew she couldn't take blondie to the room above the *pastelaria*. She would not take him to the bed where she'd first found pleasure with Ethan. She couldn't completely banish him from her thoughts, but she could try to avoid reminders of him.

"You have room at your place?" Anya asked, not used to sharing her sex life with anyone but her bedpartner.

"A spare bedroom. Or I have a king size bed. I'm sure we could all fit." Joana smiled impishly.

The guys approached, staking their interest. "Can we buy you girls a drink?"

"I have plenty to drink back at my place." Joana said and tilted her head.

"Let's go." They both grinned at the ease of their conquest.

Anya tried to get in the mood with the blond in the back seat of the Uber on the way to Joana's. She straddled him, but he felt wrong. He didn't kiss right. The feel of the bulge in his trousers didn't turn her on. She slid off and was the first out the door when they pulled up outside Joana's apartment. Bracing herself, she breathed in the night-moist air, and tilted her head back to look at the stars, not quite as bright here as on location. Dropping her gaze to the Joana's apartment building, gleaming white amongst the shadows of the surrounding shrubbery, she knew she couldn't do it.

"Wait," she said to the driver before he could drive off. She turned to Joana with an apologetic look. "Sorry, I can't."

"Not in the mood?" Blondie asked, hands on hips.

"Sorry. It's been a huge week. Can I give you a lift home?"

He took a step back to the car, but Joana stopped him with a hand on his arm. "Or you could stay."

His head whipped around, and he grinned when he realized what she was suggesting.

"Sure, I don't mind sharing. You, Troy?"

"I don't mind sharing either, you or her." Troy joked.

Anya gave Joana a hug and whispered, "are you okay with this?"

"It was my idea, wasn't it? I had a feeling the night would end this way. Don't feel bad, more for me." Joana grinned and patted her friend's butt. "You weren't fooling me kid; I knew this mystery guy was serious."

Anya didn't justify the remark with an answer.

"Your loss, sweet-pea." Blondie said over his shoulder as he followed Joana and his friend to the entrance of Joana's apartment block, leaving Anya alone on the street, quiet at this late hour except for the Uber driver waiting for her.

I doubt it.

ANYA SLIPPED ALONE in the bed above the *pastelaria* thinking of the afternoon Ethan joined her here. She pulled out the bright pink latex cock and testicles and smiled at the memory of the look on Ethan's face. She would have liked to tell him about Tomas, about her foster parents, her biological mother. It hadn't occurred to her then, but if she had the time again, would she now?

She dropped the latex cock back into the drawer and shut it with a thud, confused by the realization that was surfacing with the clarity of distance.

A beautiful, innocent girl had died.

But had Heidi's death really been Ethan's fault?

CHAPTER ELEVEN

ANYA WOKE IN HEAVEN, to the smell of fresh baking, and the homely clatter of pastry chefs busy creating delicious delicacies before dawn. She didn't open her eyes until sunlight glowed through her eyelids, enjoying the feeling of being still and quiet, yet part of something purposeful. Throwing on one of Tomas's silk robes, Anya stepped through the door she'd left open onto the Juliet balcony.

She looked down, remembering seeing Ethan searching for her, remembering how her grief had flared into anger and resentment knowing he was there looking for her. A stranger. Proof that he had gone chasing other women when he was supposed to be true to Heidi.

A fine cloud of mist hovered over the canal and seabirds swooped low, looking for breakfast.

The only people in sight at this time of the morning were couriers bringing orders from the fish and produce markets.

Once she'd showered and dressed and indulged in too many mouthfuls of heaven, she went in search of Tomas. He was in his office as usual, sipping his usual cup of *lapsang souchong*. He stood when he saw her and gave her a hug. "You'd never make it as a pastry chef. Sleeping in and eating all the produce." He shook his head with a fond smile.

"I make a much better actress, so I'll pretend I'm a good waitress today." Anya said as she pulled an apron over her head.

"Thanks, Sis. With two off sick we could use the extra set of hands today. I'll be out as soon as I sort out the dairy order for tomorrow."

Anya happily spent the morning feeling useful and too busy to think about anything but her current order. A sense of peace she'd never known suffused her with warmth, and she drifted through the day free of the poisonous emotions that had plagued her since Heidi's death.

Even during the lull after lunch but before afternoon tea, she managed to avoid thinking about the past – or the future. Until the sound of an approaching motorbike broke through the murmur of the early afternoon tea crowd.

Ethan. Anya's pulse skipped then raced, and she stood still behind the counter, torn between wanting to hide from how she would react to seeing him, and racing outside to find out.

When the engine stopped outside, Anya raced to the front window to look out, her heart still racing with dread and anticipation. And there he was. Ethan Cox, sexy as hell, dismounting with a grace that stole her breath. She wasn't the only one admiring his legs, clad in tight denim, as he swung his leg over the seat, the bulge of muscles beneath his tight t-shirt as he removed his leather jacket and helmet. But what the other observers didn't see was where Ulrich finished and Ethan the man began. Anya saw the real Ethan, the intelligent and thoughtful man beneath. Everyone else saw the Viking lord from tv, striding toward the *pastelaria*, sans hair extensions;

or the celebrity with no sunglasses or beanie hiding his familiar face.

Shit!

Anya held her breath as he stepped inside. He stopped in the doorway for everyone to see. Ethan Cox was in the building. Anya gasped and his gaze flew to her. His smile was radiant, making her heart clench, and freezing her in place. He strode over to her, took her gently by the waist and bent to kiss her cheek.

"What are you doing?" Anya hissed. "People can see you. They can see us. They might take photos."

"Then let's give them something to look at." He cupped her cheek. "I missed you. I hope you don't mind me coming here."

Anya was too slow to step back, too stunned to feel his touch again and the way it made everything around her faded to insignificance to realize the mistake they were about to make. When his lips covered hers, the yearning she'd felt for him before escalated beyond everything else, crowding out all other thoughts. She clung to his neck, pulling his mouth so his lips ground against hers. Like a drowning woman she opened her mouth and invited his tongue to plunder her.

The shrill alarm of a wolf-whistle cut through the haze of desire and brought her back to the room with a jolt. Anya pulled away, her eyes flying open as she stumbled away from him, releasing her hold on his neck. She glanced around. Most of the crowded café weren't even bothering not to stare. Many were whispering, and she knew they're saying *"isn't that Ethan Cox? He's the Viking lord from* KingMaker?*"*

Anya glanced at Ethan, who was smiling down at her. He seemed to be enjoying the attention as if he were playing the male lead in Romeo and Juliet. She grabbed for his hand and, turning, she hurried to the back of the room, her head pounding with panic. This was exactly what she didn't want – her name, her identity, linked to his. Ethan Cox and his dead ex-girlfriend's half-sister.

She focused straight ahead as she dragged him up the stairs that would get them away from the crowd. When she reached the landing, she turned and stopped him with the flats of her palms against his chest. "What do you think you're doing? Are you crazy?"

"I don't care anymore who knows," he said, with wonder lighting his face.

"I do."

"Well, maybe you shouldn't have dragged me upstairs like that. Their cameras might not reach us, but their imaginations will fill in the blanks." He smirked and slipped his arm around her back, pulling her body close. Despite the differences in height and body shape, their bodies fitted perfectly together, locking in like pieces of a jigsaw. She sagged against him, sick of fighting her reaction to him.

"You're right. We might as well enjoy what they've all assumed we're doing up here." The damage was done and there was no undoing it. It didn't matter what the crowd thought or imagined; the proof of their kiss was recorded for the world to see.

One last time. Anya promised herself and she pressed her cheek against his chest and inhaled the faint scent of perspiration and leather hovering beneath his signature cologne.

"How was dinner with your sister?" She asked, wanting to pause in this instant, before they started the dance that would be their last.

"Good, although I have no idea what we ate." The rumble of his chest beneath her ear simultaneously soothed and excited her.

"She didn't mind you leaving early?"

"She told me to leave and take my body to wherever my mind was."

Dread twisted in Anya's gut. Ethan was talking like a man who wanted a relationship. She needed to distract him before he said something they'd both regret.

"And I hope you brought your own condoms this time." She joked and leant back to look up at his face.

"I quite liked Tomas's ticklers – you didn't?" He pulled a strip out of his back pocket with a grin.

Anya pulled away from him but held his hand. "I've been running around all morning, and I'm kind of sweaty. What do you say to a bath?" Anya pushed open the door to reveal a large freestanding bath placed centrally in front of a large window overlooking a walled garden of blossoming citrus trees.

"Nice view," Ethan said but it was Anya he was studying intently, as if she were the only woman in his world.

She bent to insert the plug, hoping to hide the flare of need that heated her skin.

"Even better," he growled. "You know how to bring the Viking out in a man."

Anya started the water running and picked up two bottles of bath foam, turning to hold them out to him. "Which would your inner Viking prefer? Lavender or jasmine?"

"You. The first time we met I remember thinking you smelt of vanilla. I want that, all over me." He cradled Anya's face gently in his hands and looked deeply into her eyes.

She tilted her mouth up for his kiss and closed her eyes to hide the vulnerability she couldn't let him find.

His lips moved against hers, gentle yet insistent, his tongue nudging them apart. Anya kissed him back, trying to lock the memory of this feeling away to savor later, when she was alone. Every touch and caress was bitter-sweet.

The water of the bath cradled and supported the lovers, the sunlight streaming through the window caressing them as they moved together in the slow rhythm of savored passion. Completion was not the goal, but the experience of touch and taste and exploration.

When the climax of their lovemaking approached, Ethan called to her in a low voice. "Water sprite."

Anya knew what she was doing when she opened her eyes. She selfishly wanted this one last time, even if it destroyed her. Or maybe that's why she did it – to ensure her ruin. The adoration she found triggered the beginning of her orgasm and, drugged by pleasure, she abandoned herself to the connection. There was no-one else, no crowded café below, no set and location to be at tomorrow, no life back in London, waiting for her to return. There was only this room, this bath - this man and her.

As the waves of pleasure washed through her and tears joined the moisture from the bath on her cheeks, she knew for a certainty she had lost. She'd done the one thing she should never have done.

She had let herself fall in love with him.

ANYA WOKE IN THE DARK, alone in the bed. It was quiet downstairs, everyone gone.

Suddenly awake, she looked around for Ethan, hoping and not hoping he'd left so she wouldn't have to say good-bye. She found him crouched on the window seat.

Climbing out of bed, she pulled on a robe and picked a throw rug to drape over his shoulders. He placed his hand on top of hers and held it against his shoulder. In the light from the square she could see the tracks of tears on his face.

"I shouldn't be this happy." His voice held the opposite – pain and sadness.

"Why not?" Anya asked, not sure if she wanted to hear him say it.

"My last girlfriend. She was intelligent, caring, beautiful. I loved her. I killed her."

Anya stopped breathing and felt as if she'd turned to ice. She'd almost convinced herself it wasn't true. But here he was, admitting it. The rage she'd thought she was rid of came roaring back with a vengeance. She pulled her trembling hand out from under his, crossing her arms so she didn't lash out at him. At least he was already suffering for it. And she had the evidence to make him suffer so much more. She would ruin the one thing he loved more than anything. She would do her damnedest to take his career from him.

"What happened?" Anya asked through stiff, cold lips. She would hear his confession in full.

"I wasn't interested in anyone else. I only wanted her, the vibrant girl I met ice skating in Hyde Park. But she changed, she became jealous and possessive, accusing me of cheating on her, even though I gave her full access to my phone and email. She accused me of having accounts I wasn't showing her." Ethan still didn't move but stared out at nothing through the window.

Anger welled up in Anya's chest. Even if hadn't cheated on her, he didn't stop her from getting behind the wheel when she was in no state to drive. "So, what did you do? Let her get in her car and drive when you knew she'd been drinking and wasn't in her right mind?"

"No!" He sobbed. "I wasn't there. She must have finished the bottle of vodka we'd started together the weekend before and got in her car to come looking for me. She probably thought she'd catch me in the act."

Ethan pulled his arms up, leaning his elbows on his knees and grabbing at his hair with clawed fingers. "She could have found me. I was only a few minutes away, visiting her professor who I'd organized to meet with. He was as concerned about Heidi's state of mind as I was. We were deciding on a plan to get her help, to make things better. But I never got the chance."

"What happened?" Anya already knew the answer but needed to hear him to say it.

"She crashed her car and died."

Anya's stomach dropped and the floor tilted. She staggered back to the bed and sat, curled into herself. Everything she'd believed since she'd first contacted her half-sister was wrong. "You were trying to help her." Ethan had been trying to help Heidi.

"It wasn't enough. Me being secretive about meeting with her professor to work out what help was available, just made her more certain I was cheating."

"But you didn't."

"No. Never. There was only her."

Enveloped in a fog of shock, Anya vaguely registered Ethan standing. He'd loved her, not played around.

"Not that it mattered. *It wasn't enough.*" He repeated the words like a mantra.

"Please, don't say that."

Ethan shrugged; the movement labored as if he held the weight of Heidi's dead body on his shoulders. "It's true. I sure as hell don't deserve someone as beautiful, smart and talented as you."

His agony snapped Anya out of her shock. She looked up at the shell of Ethan Cox. He was not the man she thought he was. The broken man, shoulders hunched, eyes red and face puffy from crying, was more beautiful to her than ever.

But Anya? She was the worst kind of person, worse even than she'd believed Ethan to be. Ugly and bitter inside a chameleon shell. She'd messed up. She should have seen through the preconceptions built by Heidi's warped view of reality.

The realization of just what she'd lost hit her like the sky falling. *Ethan was her perfect man.* Talented and thoughtful, her growing passion for him was something she'd never experienced before... and may never again. And he wanted children. She never realized before she met him that she did too. She wanted to give hers the childhood and loving family she'd missed out on.

But she'd blown it with her toxic plan for revenge. He'd let her in, trusted her and she'd betrayed him. If he knew what she'd planned, that she'd slept with him to set him up and ruin his career, he would hate her as much as she'd hated him when they first met.

Even though she deserved his hatred, welcomed it even, he was already so broken, she was worried what knowing would do to him. He didn't deserve that. She wanted to protect him from her poison.

"You should go," she said numbly and stood to pick up his clothes where they were scattered on the floor of the bathroom. "You're right. We should end this now." She had to get him to leave, couldn't bear for him to be close and remind her of the horrid things she'd done to him, to Mary, and the worse things she'd planned to do to this beautiful, suffering soul. She couldn't let him punish himself any longer. "But you shouldn't blame yourself. It wasn't your fault."

Instead of watching him pull his clothes over his nakedness, she went into the bathroom and locked the door to stop herself from doing anything – or saying anything – to make him stay with her.

CHAPTER TWELVE

"SORRY PHILLIPE. I have a family emergency. I need to get back to London today. Any chance we can film the rest of the scenes later?" Anya didn't have to act to make the lie convincing. She felt as if she'd had the worst possible news.

"Well, we're actually ahead of schedule. We had budgeted time based on a less experienced actress. We've filmed the most important scenes, anything else that we can't do without, we can film in a studio in London."

"Good. I'll wait to hear from you then. I'll do what I can to work around your schedule." At least she wasn't letting the production down.

"Hey, Anya? I just want you to know, I really appreciate you stepping up like you did. It worked out really well for us. I hope your emergency resolves itself."

ETHAN BARELY APPLIED the brakes as he entered the airport zone, racing along the drop-off zone, helmet off, searching the pavement, entrance doors and as far as he could see inside the departure area. When he asked the talent manager why the scenes for the day had been changed, and why Anya wasn't in any of them, he'd been told she'd had to return to London. A family emergency.

Or could she not stand to be near him after he'd bared his soul to her?

It would be the worst kind of irony if that were the case. Baring his soul had been cathartic for Ethan, had helped him see clearly. Explaining it to Anya helped to see the situation from a different perspective, not one warped by grief and self-blame.

In their short time together, she had made him question whether he really was the monster he'd believed he was, and now he knew. And he needed to see her, to tell her he loved her.

He'd jumped on his bike, desperate to catch her.

Was he too late though? Had she already gone?

His heart clenched at the sight of faded copper-colored hair and he decelerated as quickly as he dared. Yanking on the brakes, he squealed to a stop behind a vintage Peugeot with its trunk lid open.

A slim, dark haired man spun around at the sound of the strangled roar of the braking motorbike, and for a moment Ethan's jealousy eclipsed all other thoughts. Until he realized the attractive man next to Anya must be her foster brother Tomas. The pastry chef.

The small amount of colour in Anya's pale skin fled at the sight of him, and the dark shadows under her eyes made Ethan feel a tug of guilt. He'd suspected her of running away because of him, but what if there really was a family emergency?

If that were the case, though, why wasn't Tomas going with her?

"Ethan. What are you doing here?" Anya asked in a resigned voice.

"I needed to know you were okay. I did a lot of thinking last night and I realized there is more to life than my career. I'd forgotten that. With you, I can hope for happiness too."

Tomas put a questioning hand on Anya's arm, and she nodded. *It's okay.* She kissed his cheek and tilted her head to the car. He nodded, shot Ethan a searching look and opened the driver's side door. But didn't drive away.

"It's impossible." Anya stated, her voice flat with defeat, *or dislike?*

"There's no family emergency, is there?" He was such an idiot, spilling his dirty secrets and throwing away his chance to start again before he'd even realized it was within his grasp. Scaring her away. He should have waited, got it straight in his head before he talked to her about Heidi and how much he loved her. "You can't stand to work with me anymore."

"It's not that." Anya tugged on her hair and glanced inside, as if she wanted to run.

"I can't let you go without knowing *why* it's impossible. I didn't cheat on Heidi like the world seems to believe. I swear it."

"I believe you. It's not that."

"Tell me then. Why?" Ethan threw his arms out, exasperated.

"Good-bye, Ethan." Anya turned away, her face tight, eyes red-rimmed as if she was fighting back tears.

He couldn't let her go. He had to make her understand they were perfect together.

Anya bent to pick up her backpack. She turned to step onto the pavement and took the handle of her suitcase.

"I love you." He blurted out.

Her head swung around; eyes wide as they locked on his. In that moment, there was no mistaking that she cared for him too.

"You wouldn't if you knew the truth." She rested her backpack on her suitcase. "If I told you what I've done, you would never forgive me. I can't bear to see the way you would look at me if you knew why I slept with you."

"You have to tell me. You can't leave me knowing nothing!"

"I'm Heidi's half-sister. I blamed you for her death and wanted to ruin you for it."

Ethan reeled back on his heels, as if she'd tackled him physically. He stared at the small woman as if he'd never met her, while he tried to process her words. All he came up with was that the girl he'd been making love to these last weeks was related to the woman he'd shared his life with. Heidi's half-sister. Beautiful, funny Heidi and tormented, terrifying Heidi. He looked at the woman standing in front of him, shoulders slumped, and couldn't comprehend how she had concealed the amount of anger and hatred that could drive her to have sex with the man she blamed for her sister's death. *Who was she?* Not the girl he thought he knew.

Anya handed him her phone and he looked at the screen. Acid flared in his stomach at what he saw. A woman with long dark hair bent over while he fucked her from behind. A red-haired girl straddling his naked body, her face hidden but his – and his pleasure – plain for all to see. All Anya, but it looked like different women. All along she'd been setting him up.

Numbness spread through his body as he flicked through photos that would fan the flames of the inferno that would devour his career and leave his reputation in ashes.

He shoved the phone back at her before his unfeeling fingers dropped it, his hand shaking but his actor-trained voice steady. "Delete them."

Anya nodded and, head bowed, deleted every one of them while he watched, arms crossed and rigid with fury.

"Good-bye, Ethan," she muttered, her head still bowed, not able to look at the disgust she knew she would find in his expression. "I *am* sorry."

She shouldered her backpack and wheeled her suitcase through the sliding glass doors. Ethan stumbled back to his bike and swung his leg over. He didn't start the bike. His brain and body refuse to co-operate.

Heidi's sister…

AGONY THROBBED in Anya's chest as if her heart had been torn out of her body and was dying a slow death on the bitumen of the drop-off lane at Ethan's feet. It was beyond hoping that he would pick it up and care for it, rather than crushing it beneath his boot. She'd lied to him when they first met, told him whatever she needed to get close to him, had planned to throw him to the lions and give the media proof that would paint him as a lying cheat.

So here she was, alone again, the way she would be forever. Her one chance at a real relationship was beyond any hope of repair. At least he knew the truth now and the photos were gone. And he'd forgiven himself.

Before she could throw her phone in the bin in disgust, it rang. For an irrational moment, she thought it might be Ethan. Her heart flew up to her throat with the hope that he was calling to say he didn't care what she'd done, that he loved her enough to forgive her.

But the screen told her it was Mary. Her body flooded with cold disappointment – and dread. Just the person she needed to talk to, but the last person she wanted to.

"Why didn't you tell me you were going back to London?" Even through the numbness, Anya could make out the anger behind Mary's hurt tone.

"I'm sorry Mary, family emergency. Look, would you be a love and delete those photos I asked you to take?"

"Sure." A pause vibrating with anger. "No problem. When are you coming back?"

"I'm not."

CHAPTER THIRTEEN

THE ANNIVERSARY of Heidi's death.

Anya placed an arrangement of white roses on the grave of Heidi Forsyth. She had so many regrets, but, thanks to a multitude of sessions with a psychologist, Anya was no longer angry. Her main regret was that she hadn't sought help to confront her issues sooner.

Before she'd met Ethan Cox.

She still felt sorry for herself, especially when she thought of all the years she and Heidi could have had getting to know each other as sisters. Most of all Anya felt sorry for her half-sister. If she'd had psychiatric help, she might still be alive and happy now, sharing her life with the man she'd loved.

After everything that had happened, Anya had come to accept that no-one was to blame for Heidi being in a box under the soil of a London cemetery. Except Heidi. The acceptance had finally brought her peace.

Anya sensed Ethan's presence before she saw him. It was as if her thoughts had conjured him, and she almost expected him to fade to nothing before he reached her.

"Ethan," she whispered as he stopped beside her, so close his elbow almost brushed her upper arm. She exhaled beneath the weight of realizing she still loved him with a fierceness that had only grown since she last saw him.

He knelt at the foot of the grave and placed a huge bouquet of irises and delphinium on the slab below where Anya had used the vase to hold her offering of white roses.

"Anya. How are you?" He didn't look up and his voice was neutral.

"I'm fine." She managed to say while fighting every fiber of her being that longed to throw herself to her knees beside him. "I heard you were called to testify at the inquest." Anya said, lacking anything more neutral to say.

"I was, as well as Heidi's professor Paul Williams. An independent psychologist ruled Heidi was schizophrenic."

"Yes, I heard that." She hadn't gone, hadn't wanted to watch Ethan struggle with his ghosts, or see his look of hatred if he'd noticed her there. "I'm glad that you have irrefutable proof that her death wasn't your fault."

"I still regret not getting her help earlier." He bowed his head and she longed to reach down and run her fingers through his newly cut hair.

"You couldn't have known, just as I didn't know. We all could have done things differently. You may have had her in your life longer, but she was still my sister, my blood. I'd only just found her when her death stole her from me. I don't expect you to…" Her courage failed her before she could ask him to forgive her.

"You still have your mother." He said gruffly and stood, not looking at her.

"Yes, I do. When I heard the ruling on Heidi, I saw a psychologist, scared that our shared genetics might mean I needed help too. You probably think so after what I did in Portugal. Dr McLaren helped me work through why I did what I did. She's still helping me with my issues with my mother."

"It must have been hard for you when those photos came out." He turned to look at her but there was no sympathy in his expression, no satisfaction either. The kind and thoughtful Ethan she'd got to know in Portugal was gone. Ethan Cox, actor, was standing by his ex-girlfriend's grave. Anya was just an inconvenient annoyance.

"No more than I deserved. And I'm truly sorry for that. I asked Mary to delete the photos, I swear."

"Then how did the press get hold of them? And who the hell is Mary, anyway? The girl you were bunking with? Some stranger you asked to take photos of us fucking?"

"She was no stranger. We've known each other for years, we worked together on the stage before she moved into TV. She owed me a favor. I just didn't realize she had feelings for me. I didn't realize she took photos other than the ones I asked her too. Photos for herself. Photos she kept when I asked her to delete them."

"Of course not, you were so determined to ruin me that nothing else mattered. You walked over everyone and used a vulnerable woman to do your dirty work. I'm not surprised it turned out this way." The weight of his disgust bowed Anya's head and she searched the grass beneath her boots for the strength not to burst into tears. "At least there was no harm done as far as my career goes. Thankfully the world is ignorant of the fact that you're Heidi's half-sister, and the public didn't have a problem with me taking a lover after an acceptable period of mourning and celibacy. If anything, it made me a saint in the eyes of the public, especially when the court ruling was announced. The publicity actually gave my career a boost." His voice was a little less harsh. "What about yours? I heard you were fired from *The Merchant of Venice?*"

Anya cringed at the memory. Her dream job, the production set in 1930's London allowing the traditional male role of Shylock to be played by a diminutive woman. "The publicity was a disaster. When the production company found out I'd worked on *KingMaker*, they fired me for breach of contract. Shakespearean audiences prefer their dramas on-stage, not off. But it's what I deserved. I paid the price I wanted you to pay."

Anya took a deep breath to calm her nerves before she offered him the ultimate weapon to wound her. She had to do it, or she would never be able to move forward. "I don't expect you to forgive me. But will you accept my apology? Don't answer now. Think about it. I'll be at the little café opposite the station for the next hour if you decide to join me for a drink. I completely understand if you don't show and I'll never bother you again."

Anya turned and walked toward the entrance. She didn't say good-bye. She hoped it wasn't. For an hour she sat in that café and watched the condensation on her glass of Riesling gather while the contents turned warm, then she walked to her Mini Cooper, parked down a nearby laneway.

She drove at higher than her usual speed, weaving in and out of traffic as if she hoped to find an end like Heidi's, while tears splashed the backs of her hands.

It was definite. She had screwed up her one chance to find happiness and a life partner. She'd lost her soulmate, the one man who could keep her interest and share her love of acting.

She sped in through the wooden gate into the cobblestoned courtyard of the old mechanic's workshop before it was properly open, scraping the front bumper on the edge as the car slid sideways. She turned the engine off and dropped her head on the steering wheel, listening to her heaving breaths until the sound of an engine rumbling closer broke through her misery. Cautiously, she lifted her head and glanced in the rear-vision mirror as a black motorbike drove into the courtyard behind her.

With hope flaring in her chest, Anya stepped out of the car and turned to watch Ethan jump his Ducati onto its center stand.

He pulled the full-face helmet off and smiled at her look of astonishment. "I never thought I'd see the day I'd get the better of the self-possessed Anya." The warmth in his voice was as intoxicating as the scent of fresh-baked bread to a starving woman.

"I thought I'd never see you again." How was it that he was here, in her courtyard, when he'd just made it crystal clear he was disgusted by what she'd done?

"Neither did I, but when it came down to it, I couldn't let you drive out of my life like that."

"No?" So why was he here, to start again, or so he could throw more accusations at her? "Would you like to come inside?" Anya asked cautiously, her stomach twisted in knots.

"That's why I'm here." He said, voice neutral.

Whatever his reason for being there, just knowing he wasn't out of her life forever, the slimmest flicker of a chance was better than a lifetime of Christmases in one day.

The glass windows of her two-level flat soared over them as Anya led him to the entrance and unlocked the old iron door. She led him into the compact combined kitchen living/dining area, and he scanned the room, tilting his head back to gaze up into the open space of the second floor where the bedroom and bathroom nestled on the mezzanine.

"Nice place," Ethan commented, admiration evident on his face as he took in the old exposed brickwork juxtaposed with modern touches in the kitchen and furniture. "Industrial chic?"

"It is. Most visitors don't appreciate the quirkiness of the layout and decor," but Anya liked that the space that was dominated by the courtyard, giving her a feeling of freedom and isolation in the midst of one of the busiest cities on earth.

"I think it's homey… non-pretentious." He wandered over to her vintage Gibson guitar where it had made its home on her favorite Finn Juhl armchair. He plucked a few chords, looking thoughtful and a bit sad.

"Thanks. Can I get you a drink?" Anya said, wanting to pull his thoughts away from the dead woman who'd both brought them together and then come between them.

"Yes, thanks." Ethan turned his head, his back still to her, and sent her a smoldering look from beneath his brow. "Whatever will taste good on your lips."

Anya's pulse stuttered, then raced. She busied herself getting two bottles of pear cider from the fridge to hide the sudden flush of her face. Was he planning to kiss her, or toy with her?

When she turned back, he'd joined her in the kitchen. Anya handed him one of the opened bottles and gathered up the scripts she'd left scattered over the dining table. "Sorry about the mess. I didn't dare to hope you would come back here. I didn't want to jinx it by tidying up."

Ethan shrugged as if the state of their surroundings were irrelevant. "And I'm sorry about turning up like this after not meeting you where you suggested. I'd been so angry with you for so long, it took a while to process. When the photos came out, I was furious. You promised you'd deleted them. If I'd thought about it at the time, I would have questioned why you would leak such revealing photos of *yourself* to the media. I probably would have assumed you were after the publicity." The inflection on the last word sounded like a question.

"Funny you should say that. I was offered a ridiculous amount of money for a kiss-and-tell confession. Imagine what they would have paid for the whole story, the one with Heidi linking us. They could have based a TV drama on it. But I just wanted the whole thing to be over so I could try to resuscitate my career."

"It makes sense now, but it took seeing you drive away to sink in. I realized I would lose you. I can't lose you too." The anguish in his gaze stripped her soul bare.

"So, friends?" Anya asked, wanting - but not daring - to hope for anything more. She leant her butt against the edge of the kitchen counter, trying to look casual.

"I don't think I can do that." Ethan took a long swig of his cider and placed the bottle on the island bench.

"What – be friends?" Anya felt a healthy anger building. Dr McLaren said anger wasn't unhealthy, but what you chose to do with it could be. *The best way to deal with anger is with honesty.* She put her bottle down and braced her hands on the edge of the counter beside her hips, looking at him over her shoulder. "If you can't forgive me, why did you come? To torture me?" He stepped closer, side-on to her body, his thigh nudging hers.

"No. I can't just be your friend. Friends don't experiment with pink latex in the bedroom."

Letting go of the counter, Anya glanced up at him through her eyelashes. Her breath caught at the look in his eyes, a promise that what they'd shared in Aveiro was just the beginning.

Turning, she braced her hands against his hard abs. "Do you mean…"

"Your apartment has the perfect space for my Ducati." He lifted one side of his mouth in a mischievous grin.

And with the bike would come the man. Anya stood on her tiptoes and pressed her body along his. "Your Ducati is welcome here anytime."

His head, and his voice, lowered with Ulrich's primal power. "And am *I* welcome here anytime?"

"Viking lords as well." Anya replied breathlessly, her chest expanding with the joy of having him so close after she'd spent so long trying not to remember the feel of his big, hard… body.

"Good, because I want to be *so* much more than friends. Starting with you and me and this kitchen counter." Ethan hooked his hands behind her thighs and lifted her to sit on the bench. He stepped between her knees, spreading them wide, and pulled her forward so her thighs wrapped around his hips.

Smiling, unable to resist Ulrich - or Ethan - Anya slid her hands over his shoulders and gripped the back of his neck.

"And Ethan Cox is welcome any*where*, any*time*." Anya crossed her ankles behind him and pulled his pelvis closer, so the bulge of his arousal nestled against her sex. And moaned at desire flared through her. The fire had been banked too long. It would take no more than a spark to set her ablaze.

Pressing her body against him, she urged his head down and lifted her face, impatient for the inferno. But Ethan's lips when they found hers were moist and cool from the cider, his body an anchor for her urges, a haven to calm to her turmoil.

Anya had never tasted love before, hadn't expected it to be as sweet as pear cider. She drank deeply. With Ethan holding her, she had no fear of drowning.

the end

BODY DOUBLE

A CELEBRITY BOSS ROMANCE

CHAPTER ONE

"HOLY COW!" Keira muttered and shook her head in disbelief. She glanced up at Jude, the glaring blue Californian sky outside the window the perfect backdrop for her agent's white suit and immaculate, straightened blond hair. "This is some gig, but I'm not sure I understand. You're offering me an assignment that involves a weekend at a six-star island resort in Mexico with a 'mystery' celebrity—and it's an *acting* job?"

"Don't look at me like I'm pimping you out," Jude replied, frowning. "I assure you the job is above-board. Legal have done a thorough check on the date and location details, and the job is legit."

"Okay, so spill. Who is the client?"

Jude pushed her frameless, designer glasses higher on her nose. "Aryan Nadar."

"Aryan Nadar, the hottest guy in the media right now?" Keira asked, her breath quickening at the prospect of rubbing shoulders—but no other part of her anatomy—with the gorgeous, ex-star cricketer for India. "Not NadarTec?" His family's company was famous for the right reasons. NadarTec was *the* international industrial tech and robotics company, where as Aryan Nadar was most recently famous for being one of the most lusted-after bachelors on the planet. These days he was no longer sportsman or bachelor.

"The client is the man himself. Lucky you." Jude raised an eyebrow, obviously envious.

For good reason, and until a month ago, Keira would have jumped at the opportunity to do more than admire Aryan's brooding, athletic beauty from a distance, which she did whenever he graced the pages a gossip magazine or on TV. Opportunities for ogling came thick and fast since injury had forced him to give up his place on the Indian cricket team and he'd become the media's favorite bad-boy.

"Um. He's about to get married." Keira narrowed her eyes at her agent. The assignment seemed more questionable by the minute, but what was it her horoscope had said this morning? *'Embrace an unusual opportunity, it may yield rewards beyond expectation'.*

"He is, so your virtue is safe." Jude agreed with a sigh.

Keira wasn't so sure. With Aryan's reputation, she wouldn't be surprised if he would be open to having a fling. But for Keira, nothing was more important than proving she could make it as an actress. Even sampling the delights Aryan's Victoria Secret model ex-girlfriend had shared in a tell-all interview. She would not risk her professional reputation, even for someone as hot Aryan. Especially now he was engaged.

"Right. Well that's a relief," she said with a sigh. The timing really sucked. Her fantasies would stay exactly that.

Jude glanced at her slyly and smirked, tapping a beige shellacked nail on the desk. "Although… the terms of the confidentiality agreement you are about to sign would protect if you ignored the agency policy against engaging in sexual relations with a client. Unfortunately though, if you did, I must not hear about it."

Keira cringed at Jude's implication that she had permission to behave immorally. "Don't worry, you know me. Professional to the letter. Now, tell me more. About the assignment, I mean." She trusted her agent professionally, even though she didn't agree with her morals.

"The basics are outlined in the contract, and if you accept the job you will be briefed on the details when you're in transit. It's your decision, but the fee alone will make your toes curl."

Keira arched an eyebrow and glanced at the figure on the cover letter of the contract Jude slid over the desk toward her.

"Shivers. You weren't kidding." Even though her father had blocked her access to the family expense account, Keira wasn't exactly desperate for the money, but... "A paycheck like this will give me the breathing space to focus on going after high-profile jobs. I wouldn't have to accept all those small, dead-end jobs just to keep the bills paid." She didn't need to tell Jude she *was* desperate for the exposure a job like this would provide. Exposure indicated success, and success would prove she had made the right decision.

"And stick it to dear daddy," Jude added, as if he'd read Keira's mind.

"Of course." Keira grinned. Her father had made it clear he didn't believe she could make it as an actor, and would soon come begging for her place in the family company. The prospect of validation—and proving him wrong—filled her with warm satisfaction. "I live for the day the high and mighty William Fox has to eat humble pie."

She picked up the paperwork and flipped over the cover letter. Most confidentiality agreements came down to pretty much the same thing... *don't gossip about what happens behind the scenes or repeat anything she might learn about the client.* Keira skimmed over the wording. The agreement was longer than usual, but it had a stamp to show the legal department had vetted and approved it. If Aryan was organizing the assignment and not an employee, the job was probably for some top-secret product launch for his family's International tech company. Now, *that* would make her a household face.

"What the hey," Keira shrugged and fished the Montblanc pen her mother had given her for her last birthday from her handbag. Even discounting the intriguing horoscope for Aries this morning, no matter what the job entailed she couldn't resist the opportunity to meet the 'it' guy of the moment, the man every woman with a pulse lusted after.

"Aryan is gorgeous," Jude sighed as she watched her client sign the agreement.

Keira glanced up and caught the predatory look on her agent's face. Knowing her penchant for celebrity lovers, Aryan's engagement wouldn't have stopped Jude. The more unattainable, the bigger the prize.

"He is attractive, yes." Keira kept her tone noncommittal, even as a recent image of Aryan in dress shorts and polo shirt flashed across her mind. She subtly used the contract to fan the heat from her cheeks. Everything about Aryan Nadar was hot—his dusky skin... the designer beard on his strong jaw... his elegant, straight nose... the way his dark hair waved seductively back from his forehead, just long enough to caress his collar. All a sure sign meeting him would most likely shatter her fantasy. "And he knows it. Celebrities, models, actors, the rich—they're all the same." Keira shrugged off her self-indulgent crush, certain he would prove to be the same as every other handsome man she'd ever met.

"You do know you are part of that equation, right?" Jude grinned.

"More than most people would know," Keira replied with a sigh. Jude was the only person at the agency who knew Keira's family were one of the most powerful yet secretive in LA. She slid the papers back across the desk. "Now, spill it. Tell me what you can about the job—in a nutshell."

"You look like Chloe Thompson. You'll be playing her for the weekend." Jude's level blue gaze pinned Keira to her seat.

"Are you kidding?" Keira tried to picture the girl who, a month earlier, had broken hearts all over America when Aryan announced their engagement. A regular girl who had worked at Walmart before the shock announcement. No one expected the celebrity playboy to give up his bachelorhood for the likes of Chloe Thompson. She was just one of so many other slim, beautiful twenty-somethings. "Is that it?"

Jude nodded.

"I guess we do look a little alike," Keira admitted. Around the same height and figure, similar length blonde hair, although Keira generally wore hers up in an attempt to avoid being pigeonholed.

With her resemblance to Chloe in mind, the possibilities unfurled in Keira's imagination. It could be for a joke—a very expensive one. Aryan's twin, Ravi, could pass for his brother if you didn't look too closely, and with Keira as Chloe's look-alike, it could be a double-vision scenario.

Or… maybe Chloe was unwell, and Aryan needed a stand-in.

Or… perhaps they wanted her and Ravi to play decoys while Aryan and Chloe sneaked off somewhere secret. *To elope?*

Keira stood and paced to the door and back to Jude's desk, excitement making her fidgety. Being a decoy for the celebrity wedding of the year would put Keira firmly in the spotlight once the world found out. Whatever the job entailed; it had to be good for her career.

"Don't look at me like that." Jude smirked and held up her hands, palms up as if to contain Keira's excitement from infecting the composed calm of her all-white office.

"Like what?"

Jude took her glasses off, folded them, then placed them on the table as she leant back in her white leather office chair. "Like you're an addict, and I've just offered you hit."

"It sounds like this could be my big break." Just saying it out loud made her pulse race.

"I thought you'd be excited," Jude leant back in her chair with a self-satisfied smirk.

"Spot on. What do I need to do?"

"Should be easy for you. For three days and two nights you will act like Chloe Thompson. You will *be* Chloe Thompson."

"Do you know why?" Keira took a swig from her water bottle to ease her suddenly dry mouth.

"You'll have to ask the man himself. *When. You. Meet. Him.*" If Jude was trying to hide her envy, she failed miserably. Keira could almost see the tinge of green beneath her agent's California tan.

Standing, she handed Keira a charge card and an iPad. "There's $15,000 credit on here to buy yourself some appropriately expensive bikinis and resort wear. Aryan's publicist has compiled a look-book so you can match Chloe's style. On Friday morning you'll have your hair cut like hers and get some tips on how she wears her makeup. Meanwhile, you need to study as much footage of Chloe you can get your hands on. Make the world believe you *are* her."

"Thanks Jude." Keira took the card and iPad, her skin prickling with anticipation. "I'll keep you posted." This was her chance to justify her career choice—with the bonus of wardrobe expenses. It might only be for a weekend, but this was why she had given up her privileged lifestyle and her family—to follow her dream and build a career that enabled her to *become* someone else. Although normally that someone would be a fictional character.

"Better start calling me Chloe." Keira gave Jude a grin and turned to leave. She no longer saw the sterile white office, already caught up in visions of golden sands, waving palm trees and a half-naked ex-cricketer.

CHAPTER TWO

KEIRA'S DECISION TO trust in her horoscope was confirmed when the hair salon she was directed to was the same high-end salon her mother, and many celebrities, frequented. Then, when the limo that collected her was accessorized by a guy who looked like he'd just switched an NFL uniform for fitted black trousers and fitted, V-neck shirt that molded to his bulging muscles, she knew she'd won the jackpot. Just like an A-list actor, she had a security escort. This was the break she'd been pounding the pavement hoping for, the reason she'd accepted all those anonymous walk-on parts and cheesy tv ads.

"Keira? Nice to meet you. I'm Zac, Aryan's head of security. I'll be escorting you to the airport and will be on-hand during the weekend if you have any concerns." He held out a hand the size of a bear paw for her to shake.

"Hi Zac." She carefully placed her hand in his, but his grip was gentler than she expected. "Nice to meet you. What sort of concerns might I have?"

"There won't be any, but my job is to expect the unexpected. You have the glasses and gloves?" He crossed his arms across his broad, muscular chest.

Keira patted her version of Chloe's 'signature' Kelly bag.

"I'm not expecting any paps, but just in case, please put them on."

She was tempted to ask Zac why a stand-in was needed for Chloe, but suspected direct questioning wouldn't work with him. Instead, Keira took the Prada cat-eyes from their case and slid them into position on her nose, then fished out the short, red gloves. "What are these for?" Keira ventured as she slid her hands into the satin soft leather she'd carefully selected to match her new vintage 1950's sundress. Even though it was cool for April, it definitely was not glove weather.

"So no-one will notice the missing engagement ring," Zac explained, not offering any more information.

Ah. The famous Asscher cut champagne diamond. What she wouldn't give to get a close look at the diamond with the clarity worthy of such an unforgiving cut. In a colour that perfectly suited Chloe's–and Keira's–hazel eyes.

"I'm going to wear gloves all weekend?" Keira asked, sure that would attract more questions at a tropical resort than being seen without Chloe's engagement ring.

"No. There will be a ring for you to wear," Zac said without further explanation and indicated they should make their way to the front of the salon.

"Considering the amount of press coverage your employer gets, I wouldn't have thought avoiding publicity part of your job description." Keira observed, fishing for information. If keeping Aryan out of the gossip pages was Zac's job, it seemed he wasn't very good at it.

Zac grimaced, but still managed to look approachably handsome. He wasn't Keira's type (i.e. not an athletically built, dark haired, olive skinned ex-cricketer) but she could see some girls would drool over him. "The paparazzi are like a force of nature. Avoiding publicity is like trying to dog-paddle in a tsunami."

"I wondered if maybe he enjoyed the attention," Keira pressed, sensing he was letting down his guard.

"He did when he was famous for being the best at cricket…"

"But not so much now he's famous for gambling and womanising?"

Zac pinned her with a serious stare but didn't answer. "Let's go," he said and pushed open the wrought-iron front door, not the 'secret' back door her mother used to avoid being seen.

She adopted Chloe's loose-limbed posture, knowing little more than she had before. She'd been right—she would get next to nothing out of Zac. She would bet half her fee he was a Taurus. Doggedly loyal and protective.

Taking a deep breath, Keira stepped outside but the only camera in the vicinity was an iPhone, held by a tourist snapping anyone who looked like they might be a celebrity. Even so, Zac stood across the pavement, his bulk shielding her as he ushered her into the back of the black town car.

Keira relaxed back into the leather seat as Zac walked around to the front passenger door. *So, this is what it feels like.* Her mother, who had paid dearly for her affair and eventual marriage to the king of Industrial R&D in the US, was obsessive about avoiding the media, and as a result, Keira had never needed to worry. Which suited her fine—she didn't want to be recognised on the street for being the kid of a powerful and influential family—or for *pretending* to be someone famous.

If she was going to be recognised, she wanted it to be for her talent as an actor.

As soon as Zac squeezed into the passenger seat, the driver sped away.

"Where are we going?"

"Airstrip. Long Beach."

"Nice." Of course, nothing but a private jet for Aryan Nadar.

Forty minutes and two glossy magazines later, Zac's phone beeped for the twentieth time as the car arced to a smooth stop, a short distance from a small, sleek jet. Currents of excitement zapped through Keira's body. She was about to meet Aryan Nadar in person. Or would it be Ravi?

"Good timing. We've just been cleared by immigration," he said as he pocketed the phone. "We're good to go."

"My bags?"

"Were collected from your agency as arranged and are already on-board." Zac looked around at the distant cyclone fence and nodded at the smattering of people pressed against the barrier, craning for a glimpse of whoever was inside the limo. "Glasses on, gloves on. It's show-time." He gave her an encouraging smile over his shoulder.

As she slipped the gloves and cat-eye sunglasses back on, Keira focused on picturing Chloe stepping out of the car, as charmingly awkward as a young gazelle in her stilettos.

Zac unfolded himself from the passenger seat and stepped over to open her door, his large body shielding her from the cameras outside of the fence.

Keira *was* Chloe when she stepped out onto the tarmac, her walk enthusiastic but not entirely confident as she made her way to the boarding stairs.

And there he was, standing at the open door of the jet for all the world—through the telescopic lenses of jostling cameras—to see. Aryan Nadar, casually sexy in tailored trousers, with his crisp shirt unbuttoned at the neck to allow a glimpse of dark chest hair, and the cuffs rolled up to expose muscled forearms.

Keira's step faltered. *Holy Macanoli.* If she were to picture what her ideal man would like like, she would see Aryan Nadar. To look at, he ticked every one of her boxes.

Even from this distance it obviously was not Aryan's twin, Ravi, waiting to meet her. This man's shoulders were held straight and proud, not rolled slightly forward; his head held with an arrogant lift, not thrust forward in a way that indicated a belligerent and argumentative disposition. Aryan's posture was that of an elite sportsman, and radiated confidence. As if he owned the world but didn't particularly care. As if, with a fat pay check, he owned her.

Arrogant.

Just like her father.

Every fibre of her being rebelled. She would correct any misconceptions she could be controlled by money, post-haste, as she had with her father. She would do her job to perfection, but he would get nothing else from her, despite the way her body reacted to the sight of him.

Aryan's gaze clung to her every step, a warm, sexy smile on his face. It was a smile for Chloe, but Keira's skin still tingled with the potency of it. Could she keep her cool for a whole three days in the face of his physical allure, *and* resist trying to take him down a peg or two? For her career, yes she could.

When she took a small, lady-like step at the bottom of the stairs, Aryan's almost imperceptible frown reminded her to take more generous, loose-limbed Chloe steps. *What's wrong with you girl, get your head in the game.*

At the top of the stairs, Aryan took hold of her elbow, drawing her body against his.

"Welcome aboard," he said in a clipped tone, the coolness in his beautifully accented voice belying the warmth of his body language.

Physical awareness flooded her senses, devastating her thought process. Every instinct cried out to move closer, to explore the landscape of his muscled shoulders, the smooth tanned skin and toned waist and butt she seen so much of, but never felt. Here he was, so close she could make out his pupils, only slightly darker than his irises, and the faintest shadow of stubble on his clenched jaw. So close she could smell the trace of linen-fresh detergent from his shirt and the product he'd used to tame the wave in his hair.

Suddenly short of breath and lightheaded at her primitive response to his touch, she swayed and might have lost her balance if he hadn't slipped his hand around her waist. A shockwave of sensation radiated from the point of contact, making her gasp. *If this was what it felt like to be touched by him…*

"Smile like you're in love with me," he insisted under his breath.

His command was like a slap, bringing Keira back to reality so fast she had to fight her instinct to step away from him. She was here to work and he was just another gorgeous, conceited man. She forced her mouth to stretch into a convincing smile, determined not to let him get the better of her again.

Keira concentrated on regulating her breathing, slow and deep, but it was a struggle. *Be professional.* But he was so close she could feel the significant heat of his body, searing through the fabric of her dress, his bicep against hers, his chest millimetres from her breasts. Given the proximity, she could see his eyes didn't reflect the smile on his lips.

Not impressed with my performance? Challenge accepted.

"Hello sweetheart." Keira stretched to full height and swayed close, so her breasts brushed his chest, her smile teasing as she parted her lips slightly, just as she'd seen Chloe do in photos.

"Actually it's 'Bunny'," Aryan corrected in a monotone as he slanted his head like a predator intent on the kill.

Hilarity bubbled up her throat at the ridiculousness of the nickname, and a hiccup escaped. "Bunny?"

His eyes narrowed and she felt his body tense.

"We need to kiss for the cameras," he ground out between clenched teeth, his mouth pulled wide into what should have been a smile.

Through narrowed eyes, his gaze dropped to her mouth and he slid his hand down her back, pulling her closer.

Time slowed as his mouth dipped to hers, but it was still too fast for Keira to brace for the impact of his kiss. The shock of his lips on hers tipped her head back, parting her lips and tugging her into his vortex. She gasped, inhaling his breath, sweet with mint, and melted against him, her tongue seeking his. Her body was liquid fire, every nerve ending tingling where he pressed against her, and he was no soft rabbit. Despite his retirement from the pitch, he was solid as granite, his ribs and chest rock-hard.

Dangerous.

By sheer force of will, Keira pulled back.

He released her from the kiss with a sharp inhale and put some space between their bodies, but kept his cheek close to hers. "Careful," he whispered, his breath brushing her neck as he lifted his head.

CHAPTER THREE

CAREFUL OF WHAT? Ruining the farce or losing control? Keira pressed her shaking hands against her thighs to hide her response to his kiss and his words, her turmoil a stark contrast to his cool-and-contained manner. The kiss had seared her to the bone, how could it not have burnt him too?

Aryan's night dark eyes were distant as he steered her inside, past two leather lounges set along either wall. He'd dropped the charade. The cameras had had their show.

Once they were well out of view of observers, he released her with a frown. "What the hell was that?"

"A kiss between lovers? Isn't that what engaged couples do?" Keira asked, hiding her confusion behind an innocent expression as a crew member locked the door behind them, then made his way to the front of the plane.

Aryan waited until the door to the cockpit was closed before he spoke. "You went too far. I'm paying you to follow instructions."

"For one, I haven't yet received full instructions. And, as far as I'm concerned, I'm here to do a job. I wasn't briefed on how I should respond to your kiss. Tongue or no tongue, lip nibbling, teeth? And, by the way, I'm an actor, not an escort." The cheek of him—*he'd kissed her* then pulled *her* up for responding to him! Well, that wouldn't happen again. She crossed her arms and lifted her chin to show him if he could remain unaffected, so could she. He was paying her to *act*, but she would not *feel*.

"Yes, I'm aware of that. I hired you to act like Chloe, and it's imperative that you follow my lead in public." He crossed his arms across his chest, straining his shirt across his chest. It was buttoned to the point that would be conservative on any other man, but on Aryan the movement exposed enough tanned, muscular chest to be distracting. "Do not improvise."

Heaven help her, it was going to be a very long weekend. "It might help if I had all the necessary instructions before the fact," she said defensively as Zac emerged from the door at the rear of the plane, a waft of savoury food following in his wake.

Keira's stomach growled loudly and Aryan raised an eyebrow.

"I'm human. I get hungry." She shrugged. She might be a good actor, but she couldn't hide *every* hunger from him. Hopefully at least the important ones.

"You've met Zac." Aryan squeezed his body-guard's shoulder as he stepped past them and headed for the six luxurious leather recliners at the front of the plane.

"I have. He was both helpful and friendly." Keira said pettishly, then squirmed at her childish reaction.

"That he is. Speaking of helpful, would you organise some snacks?" he asked Zac before he had a chance to take a seat.

Zac nodded and turned around to obey.

Aryan gestured for Keira to claim one of the large leather seats and slid gracefully into one on the other side of the aisle. "The flight will take a few hours. There are books and magazines if you like that sort of thing, or let Zac know if you need anything else and he'll organise it with the crew."

She cursed him for that low, smooth voice; soft as silk but commanding and seductively British-accented.

"Keira wants more details. Will you fill her in please?" Aryan asked Zac as he returned to the cabin, then flipped open his laptop with a focus that indicated that would be the extent of his conversation for the duration of the flight.

Zac perched on the arm of the sofa nearest Keira's seat. "You'll be wanting to know what the job entails."

"No sheep, Sherlock." Keira used sarcasm to cover her flash of fury. "The boss too busy to dirty his hands with the details?" She cursed her anger getting the better of her. Not five minutes earlier she had sworn to herself she wouldn't let him get under her skin.

"It's a sensitive issue. Aryan thought it would be better for me to brief you." Zac glanced at Aryan then pulled out a small, red leather box. He held it out to Keira and flipped the lid. The light refracting off the famous engagement ring hit her square in the eyes.

The stone was even more brilliant in person, and when combined with the elegant setting it was the most beautiful she'd seen, which was saying something considering the primary pursuit of her mother's friends was to out-compete each other in everything, jewellery in particular. She was no expert, but no replica could be that impressive. It was the real deal.

Zac leant forward and held the box out for Keira to take. "Your job is to act like Aryan's fiancé."

She looked at the ring, then back to Zac's face. "Yes, I get that, but for what purpose?" *Why was the ring here and not with Chloe?*

"So that the media and the public think you're her."

"But I'm obviously *not* Chloe. I assume there will be people where we're going? Won't they see I'm not her?"

"Where we're going, no-one knows Chloe well enough to tell the difference. It's a private island and the other guests have been vetted, although it's not likely that anyone who can afford to go there would be on close terms with a girl who worked at Walmart until recently."

"What about paparazzi?"

"They'll only be able get close enough to show the world Aryan and Chloe are together." Zac shrugged and leant back. "They won't be able to distinguish that you're not her."

"Okay then, so why is she not here?"

Aryan looked up from his laptop and pinned Keira with an impatient glance. "You ask a lot of questions." He sighed and closed his laptop. "If you must know, she couldn't make it, but she's approved for you to stand in for the weekend and wear her ring. All you have to do is act like you're on honeymoon."

His condescendingly patient tone made Keira want to tell him to shove his job. Instead, she gave him an abrupt nod. "Okay. Thank you." *I can see why she brushed you off for the weekend.*

"You don't need to like me or be happy to be here. You are an actor. Your job is to make the viewer believe. If you're as good as your agent assures me you are, you'll manage. Yes?" Aryan raised one eyebrow and waited for her response.

Keira took a deep breath. "Yes."

"Good. As Zac said, any photos taken will be from long distance. We just have to act like lovers, whenever there might be a photographer around."

Pulling off her gloves, she slipped the ring on her finger. The band fit perfectly in the air-conditioned plane, but she envisioned it would be a firm fit in the humid Mexican heat. Which was for the best. There would be little chance it would fall off, even though she would be constantly aware of the unfamiliar and very expensive weight.

"There can't be any doubt that Chloe is with me this weekend, and that she and I are happy and committed," Aryan continued. "Speaking of which, I assume you read the confidentiality agreement and have told no-one where you are going and what you will be doing this weekend?"

"Of course." Keira's stomach tensed. She knew the job required her discretion and had told her cousins she would be away at a spa for the weekend, knowing they would assume she was going no further than the Napa Valley. She had hoped she would at least be able to use the Nadar name on her list of referees though. "Just to clarify, will I able to list this job on my CV?" Her voice sounded reed-thin to her own ears. What was the point in being here if she couldn't use it to boost her career?

Aryan stared at her and sighed. "You did read the contract you signed? It clearly stated you cannot include this assignment on your CV. Do you have a problem with that? After all, I am paying you more than the usual fee for three days."

"Yes, I'm well aware of that, but I didn't take the job for the money. I'm a professional; of course any high profile work should go into my CV." Keira heard the emotional throb in her tone and clamped her lips shut before she revealed any more. If she was angry at herself for being so dazzled by the opportunity that she hadn't read every word of that bloody agreement she would not allow him to see it.

"Normally, yes, but this is a private commission." Aryan's tone was non-negotiable.

It wouldn't be easy, but athletes didn't have the market on determination cornered. Sure, other opportunities might come along, but she was here now and she would do whatever she could to convince him to allow it.

"I'll go check the ETA." Zac stood and quietly left the cabin, closing the door after him.

Aryan didn't say any more until he was out of earshot. "Okay. Look, I'm sorry." He slipped his laptop into the compartment beside his seat. "I know this is unusual. I'm sorry it's not what you expected. What if I set something up for you after this? Ever done Bollywood?"

The way he leant forward and the almost friendly look in his eyes softened Keira's frustration–slightly. The compassion in his British-Indian accent made her wonder if there was more to the arrogant jerk than he wanted people to know.

"Thank you for the offer, but it won't count if I don't get the job on my own merits."

He laughed, his mouth curving up in a real but cynical smile, the corners of his eyes crinkling.

"What's so funny?"

"That's not how the entertainment business works, and you know it."

She slumped back in the seat and stared out the window at the wispy clouds beneath them.

"Sorry to have to remind you, *sweetheart*." His grin made him seem a completely different man to the one she'd first encountered. Of course, he *was* a Gemini.

The hostess entered the cabin. "May I offer you brunch?"

Keira gratefully accepted and Aryan nodded that he would join her.

The prosciutto, asparagus and brie frittata was delicious, the side salad fresh and enhanced with a light dressing. Her first sip of champagne was like heaven and Keira started to enjoy the idea of going away for the weekend in the company of an attractive—albeit off limits—man.

"So, where exactly are we going?"

"*Cielo en el Sol.*"

Praise the gods of luxury and good food! *Cielo en el Sol* was one of the most exclusive and sought-after locations for the rich and famous. A private island off the coast of Mexico.

"And what do we do when we get there?"

"In public we pretend to be engaged and in love. You tell me— what do a couple in love do on a weekend away?"

Keira widened her eyes at him. "I would have thought you'd have that covered. You're the one who's engaged." Personally, she'd never met anyone she wanted to date for more than a month, let alone commit to for a lifetime. But her body knew the answer. The way her pulse took off in response to his raised eyebrow, the tingles his lowered voice sent over her flesh, she was all too aware of what she wanted to do with him. Except that she was a professional doing her job, not some groupie to be dazzled by an incredibly sexy celebrity.

"I'd like to hear your ideas," he said with the tiniest quirk of his lips.

Blasted Gemini.

Aryan might be paying for her time—which was all he would be getting—but it didn't mean she couldn't retaliate and toy with him a little.

Keira tilted her head back, and, pretending to think, trailed her fingertips down her throat. Her feather touch slid over the swell of her breast, hand hovering as she sucked her bottom lip and dropped her gaze to his. Releasing her lip, she leant forward and replied in a breathy voice. "Make love, go swimming, make love, have cocktails. Have dinner, make love with our eyes until we can get back to our room and make love with our bodies." She shrugged casually and sat back.

"Sounds like a romantic nymphomaniacs idea of love." His gaze dropped to his wine glass, his fingers stroking the stem.

"Oh. Does it? It's what *I* would want to do." Keira lowered her voice to a purr.

Aryan glanced up, eyes glittering, and she knew she'd reached him. His laptop beeped but he didn't break eye contact, didn't lean down to retrieve it.

Keira raised an eyebrow and tilted her head. "But then, we're not engaged, are we?"

The laptop beeped again.

"And it sounds like you have business to attend to."

Aryan frowned, then glanced down at his laptop as if he'd forgotten it was there.

CHAPTER FOUR

BLINDING blue sky and turquoise ocean flashed outside Keira's window as the jet landed. In a matter of hours, she was in a different world. A world far away from her West Hollywood apartment and the constant struggle to prove herself. Even the air when they descended the steps to the tarmac felt different, clear of smog and heavy with humidity, the sun brighter, colours more intense.

The general manager of the resort, the epitome of an English gentleman down to his grey silk cravat and polished brogues, strode forward to greet them. "Benedict Stacey. Welcome to heaven," he said and led them to a luxury golf buggy and drove them in the direction of the tiled rooves they could see far below, scattered at the sand's edge around a picture perfect bay.

"Anything you want, we can accommodate. Scuba diving, spa treatments, a private beach, water skiing... *anything*," he said pointedly, as they stopped outside a sprawling Mexican villa complete with white-washed exterior, and a path leading to a bougainvillea festooned patio.

The distant hum of a helicopter grew to a clamour, circling low, the glint of a camera lens visible through the open main door. Aryan glanced from the helicopter to Keira, pulled her close and kissed her.

At the feel of his lips on hers, she instinctively responded, kissing him back with a feeling not dissimilar to flying down the slopes at Aspen. Just as her body melted against his, the noise of the blades faded and Aryan took his mouth from hers, his eyes on the retreating aircraft. He dropped his hands.

Keira fumed—mostly at herself. The guy was paying her to be a body double for his fiancé, and she was reacting to him like they were *actually* a couple.

"Please accept my apology for the intrusion." Benedict bowed his head. "Be assured we take security and privacy on the island very seriously and have forbidden any non-essential air traffic for the rest of the weekend. It is unfortunate the wedding scheduled for earlier today was delayed, but the last of the outside staff brought in for the event have departed now." Holding out his arm, the GM directed them to the front door. "As promised, there are no professional photographers or journalists on the island and every member of my staff has had thorough security and background checks."

"Thank you for your diligence, but you can't personally control the actions of every person on the island—or in the air. There's always a smart ass who thinks they can snap a money shot." Aryan clapped the GM on the shoulder. "That's why my head of security will be with us at all times. I expect you will allow him full access back of house during our stay."

"Yes, of course."

Keira followed Aryan inside, with Zac bringing up the rear, as Benedict personally showed them around the open-plan living area and luxury kitchen. Limestone floors stretched to floor-to-ceiling windows, open wide to let in the tropical scented, sultry breeze, with a view over a plunge pool to the white sand and sparkling sea.

Once the GM had left, Zac checked out every room thoroughly, including his own adjoining room and ensuite. He popped his head through the doorway into the living area. "All clear." He nodded and turned back to his room.

"Zac, why don't you stay with Keira and organize a late lunch? She might have some more questions about her role. I'm going to take a shower," Aryan said pointedly, his voice terse. At Zac's nod, he turned and wheeled his suitcase into the main bedroom, on the opposite side of the living area to Zac's.

Keira flopped down on one of the linen upholstered armchairs and fiddled with the ring, already lodged firmly on her finger with the heat, and wondered about the sleeping arrangements. The villa had two bedrooms…

"He's not normally like this," Zac said as he strode past her, his voice raised over the sudden, insistent beat of Nirvana, throbbing and distorted through the closed bedroom door.

"So, what's his story? I would expect someone with so much money and fame, and about to get married, would be more relaxed." Keira picked up the small pile of glossy magazines and sat back, pretending to be as interested in the rarefied contents as she was in Aryan's moods.

"He's usually pretty chilled, but he's under a lot of pressure right now." Zac sprawled on the lounge with a view over the lap pool, stretching his beefy arms out on the soft back. "When I tell you, you'll understand and it will make the weekend easier for everyone. Confidentially of course."

"Of course. Isn't everything?" she said, the magazines forgotten on her lap. "But won't Aryan mind?"

"He's hardly going to fire me," he said, with a raised eyebrow that Keira wasn't sure how to interpret. "No, he planned to tell you–I'm not sure why he hasn't. He and Chloe had an argument and she backed out of the romantic getaway he'd planned for this weekend."

"But why didn't he just cancel? It's not like he can't afford the cancellation fee. It couldn't be that much more than what he's paying me to be here. Or come by himself and say it's rehabilitation for his injury. Are his publicists useless?"

"Well, that's the thing, and you'll need to know this so you're aware of what is riding on your performance. The argument couldn't have happened at a worse time. His dad is ill, and at the next board meeting he's going to announce who will take over as CEO of NadarTec. Aryan has spent the last six months doing everything right so his father will consider him for the role. He's stopped gambling and is working hard in the company, stopped dating and got engaged. Aryan needs it to look like everything is perfect, at least until his father makes his announcement at the next board meeting. So much so, he is going to offer a bonus, to double your fee, if you convince the world you *are* Chloe this weekend."

Double the fee. Holy guacamole! That would give her enough to put a healthy deposit on her own apartment. Something larger than the shoebox that was currently all she could afford. Now that would be tangible evidence she had made the right decision–and an 'f-you' to her father. Keira schooled her voice to stay even. "To be clear, it's not a bonus for sexual favors."

"Do you know of any time Aryan and Chloe had sex in public?" Zac asked without a twitch of a smile.

"No."

"Well, there's your answer. And I wouldn't advise you to even think of having sex with Aryan. I know how attractive he is to women, but it would be a big mistake."

"You're acting like I would even consider it." She glared at Zac at the same time she berated herself. Under different circumstances she *would* consider it, but she wasn't much of an actress if she was that transparent. "But I take your point and assure you I have no intention of being unprofessional."

ARYAN BOWED his head under the blast of cold water. The sharp streams from the massage head beating into his scalp couldn't blast the memory of how he had instinctively reacted to Keira. The way she'd responded when he kissed her, then challenged him, making him question his motives and ethics. Like the music, a beautiful but confusing mess—of soft woman and jagged attitude.

God she was infuriating, questioning everything and demanding answers he wasn't able to give. Still, he couldn't help respecting a woman with fire in her belly. He had been raised by one after all.

Unfortunately Keira was just what he didn't need right now, a distraction. One that could cost him dearly. Why did the best candidate to stand-in for Chloe have to be the first woman he'd met in years who made his pulse race, *and* command his respect?

It would have been so much easier if he'd stuck to the plan and told her what he and Zac had decided. But when it came down to it, he hadn't been able to look into her trusting hazel eyes and lie. Thank god Zac would do it for him.

Taking the soap that smelt of summer and tropical gardens, Aryan lathered his underarms and chest, and let the suds slide down his belly so he could lather his package.

Funny that he'd hired Keira because she looked like Chloe, when close up they actually looked nothing alike. Her eyes reflected an inherent honesty, where Chloe's were constantly calculating and scheming. Keira's lips were plump in a way that hinted at a passionate nature, rather than the work of a cosmetic surgeon's needle. She wanted to be recognized for her efforts, whereas Chloe would do anything to avoid work–including latching on to a wealthy man. If only he'd been in his right mind when he'd met her, not reliant on painkillers and scotch to get him through life without professional cricket. If he hadn't been so desperate to show his father he was the right choice for CEO, he'd never have allowed her steer him into a situation where she could blackmail him. She knew too much, and he had to expend too much energy to keep her from ruining everything, but not for much longer. He'd slipped up with Chloe, and it would not happen again. He would keep his dick safely in his pants.

Or in his own hand.

Aryan stroked his semi-hard-on in time with the insistent beat of the music. Jesus, Keira was a lethal combination. A good girl in a bombshell's body. He wished he could forget everything for a while and seduce her. Forget that she was an actress and that she was here for the money, like most women who passed through his life. Forget his failures, and, if he wasn't careful, that he would lose his chance to save the family business, and himself.

He knew he shouldn't, not with Keira and Zac just outside, but if he could work this urge to get her naked–to see and feel and taste her luscious body–out of his system, he might be more civil. Bracing his forearm on the tiled wall, he closed his eyes and kept stroking his now-rigid cock. He remembered how she'd toyed with him, running her fingers down her neck and cleavage on the plane. Tightening his hand into a fist, he stroked harder and imagined it had been his tongue trailing over her silken skin instead of her fingertips. Hmmm, those breasts… pressed against his chest in the doorway of the jet, her kiss tempting him to drag her inside and fulfill the promise of the chemistry sparking between them.

Diving into his fantasy, he pictured her reclined, limbs splayed, the buttons at the front of her dress undone, her nipples erect and calling for the flick of his tongue. The hem of her skirt high on her thighs, high enough to show she'd come on board without underwear.

He stroked faster, in time with the savage beat of the music. *He would take the seat opposite and watch as she stood, watch as she lifted her skirt to straddle him, her pussy sliding hot and tight down his shaft. Keira, grinding on his cock, arching back, her breasts thrust high…*

Oh yeah. Faster…

In his mind, his cum gushed inside Keira's hot pussy, not against the charcoal tiles of the open shower. The shower *she* would be using.

Fuck.

The pleasure drained from his body, short lived.

What had he been thinking? He should have used Zac's room. He couldn't afford any mistakes this weekend. Even though he had been sober for months and was clear-headed after kicking his dependence on painkillers, it was going to be a challenge. Maybe not as difficult as those first weeks of gambling cold turkey. But he had proven he was strong enough to deny himself the adrenaline rush that was poor substitute for the exhilaration of being in the game, watched by millions.

The past had proven driving at high speed and pursuing forgetfulness with a woman usually led to disaster. He should not still be thinking of Keira, but one release hadn't come close to denting his lust.

He wanted more.

CHAPTER FIVE

"I'M STARVING." Zac rubbed his hands together. "I'm going to call room service and order up whatever the specials are today."

"Count me in." Keira nodded vigorously as Zac picked up the iPad in the kitchen.

"For three then. You're not one of those women who are afraid of carbs, dairy and protein, then?"

"Not at all. And I hear the chefs here are some of the best in the world. There's no way I'm going to pass up an opportunity like this." Keira felt comfortable with Zac, when Aryan wasn't around and he relaxed.

Their conversation hadn't progressed further than their favorite LA restaurants and nightclubs when lunch and a bottle of Krug arrived, minutes before the music from the bedroom switched to something more chilled and Aryan emerged from the bedroom with his suitcase. Dressed in tailored shorts and polo shirt, he looked distracted—and gorgeous. The man could wear a garment bag and look sexy, but it wasn't his fashion sense that drew her attention but the knotted white scar that bisected his kneecap and darted up his inner thigh.

Keira would never forget the day she heard about the accident that ended his sporting career. Eighteen months earlier, the same day she'd traded a walk-in wardrobe and domestic luxury for true freedom. She'd been unpacking her reduced possessions in her tiny West Hollywood apartment while watching old sitcom re-runs when news flashed across the bottom of the screen. The star of the Indian cricket team had totaled a Maserati in Vegas. She'd been shocked, then devastated for him when she'd heard the injury meant he might never play professionally again.

His star never dimmed however, and the adoring public–including Keira–transferred their fascination from elite sportsman to celebrity playboy. No matter what Aryan did, he had seemed larger than life. And here she was sitting across the dining table from him… except now she knew he was a star-sized jerk.

Aryan nodded curtly at his companions and opened his laptop, giving the screen his undivided attention. Zac pushed a plate of food and glass of wine in his direction then made small talk with Keira as they did justice to the luscious array of daily specials. Coconut poached chicken, macadamia crusted swordfish, carrot and coriander glass noodle salad.

Keira wouldn't normally drink in the middle of the day, but she figured it might mellow her nerves and ease the friction between her and her employer. She sipped at her glass of semillon and slanted looks at Aryan, his face hard, a slight frown crinkling the skin between his eyebrows.

As the alcohol and the beautiful surroundings worked their magic, a sense of peace loosened her muscles and she began to relax and feel magnanimous. She should really cut him some slack. She hadn't known about his father, the company, his problems with Chloe. No wonder he was moody.

Looking out at the turquoise water, glimmering with reflections like flashes of diamond lights, she also felt guilty for being paid so much to laze around in luxury, reading magazines and eating exquisite food in the company of the hottest man on earth. She wasn't here for a holiday.

"Shouldn't we do something?" Keira suggested, even though she was loathe to move and disturb her hazy bubble of contentment.

Aryan glanced up, his liquid brown eyes not quite meeting hers. "We could go to the day spa and use the float tanks," he suggested, then looked back at the screen.

"What's a float tank?" Keira looked at Zac, who shrugged and tilted his head at his boss.

"It's a pod half filled with water containing so much salt that you float," Aryan said without lifting his eyes. "It's large enough that you can do so without touching the sides. The pod closes and you can float in total darkness, or leave the light on. They say it's like being back in the womb. It's used relaxation and meditation and for easing the pain of injuries. I have something similar at home for my knee, but mine is a salt pool rather than a tank."

"That sounds nice, but shouldn't we be seen doing fiancé-type things. Isn't that the reason we're here? To be seen." *Just not too closely.*

"You're right." Aryan stood and closed his laptop with an exasperated sigh. "Let's change and go for a swim. Keira, you take the main bedroom. Zac, okay if I use your room?"

"Sure, boss."

In the large change-room off the bedroom, Keira carefully hung her sundress and pulled out her new bikini. In the full-length mirror, she watched herself step into the brief pants, still getting used to the novelty of her first Brazilian wax. She was shocked all over again at the sight of her absolute nakedness. She'd never quite dared to have one before, put off by the thought of the pain, but it hadn't been as bad as she imagined. Neither had she expected the sensual vulnerability.

Slipping the tiny triangle bikini top over her head, her gaze lingered on her nipples, erect with excitement. *You're working Keira,* she reminded herself and tied the top on firmly. *Working for a client who is currently also naked, not far away.* Her thoughts wandered to his room. Was his skin golden-hued everywhere, or lighter on his butt and groin? She wondered where the scar on his leg ended and tried to picture the reality of the hard body she'd felt when he'd pulled her close and kissed her. She imagined the nest of dark curls between his legs, and how they would feel against her newly exposed sex, which had begun to throb with arousal.

Turned on and relaxed from the alcohol buzzing through her system, Keira tied a sarong in Chloe's favorite cool colors around her waist and slipped on flat sandals before stepping back into the living room. Aryan's nether regions were still in her thoughts when she got an eye-full of a whole lot of the rest of him. Wearing brief board shorts and nothing else, Keira's gaze skimmed over his superbly toned chest and abs and came to rest on his groin.

Luckily, when she managed to raise her eyes to his face he was studiously folding and refolding a towel, but Zac was watching her with one eyebrow raised.

"Ready?" Aryan asked and strode to the front door.

Zac grabbed a camera bag and followed.

"You're a photographer?" Keira asked, surprised. With his job as security for a celebrity he would have an uneasy relationship with photographers.

"An amateur. I spend a lot of time checking out the surroundings, and I have the equipment. I hate standing around doing nothing, so rather than just frame compositions in my mind, I record them."

Aryan had one hand on the doorknob and stretched the other out to Keira with a tight smile. "Hold my hand on the way to the pool?"

She held her breath and slipped her hand in his, their fingers naturally curling together. He squeezed lightly, an innocent touch, but as intimate as a kiss.

Outside, the heat caressed her face and arms, the scent of tropical flowers guiding them to an oasis where the resort pool overlooked the sea.

Aryan dropped his towel on a lounge and waited while Keira dropped her sarong onto the lounge next to his, then led her to the beach-like end of the pool. They waded in together and Keira shivered with the delicious contrast of cool water rising up her sun-warmed skin.

Beside her Aryan took a deep breath and exhaled, his shoulders dropping as the tension drained from his posture. He let go of her hand and dove under the water.

Keira launched herself after him, gliding along the surface with a relaxed breaststroke, conscious of the weight of the diamond on her finger as water flowed over her limbs.

Aryan surfaced a few meters in front of her; wet hair plastered to his head, a relaxed smile tugged her forward.

A mischievous urge took hold of her and she scooped a handfull of water at his face.

He blinked, surprise widening his eyes, and his smile grew, forming dimples she hadn't noticed the myriad times she'd seen him in the media. *Was this the Aryan the public never saw?*

Before she could react, he plunged underwater. She swiveled one way then the other, looking for him. His hands brushed up her calves then tightened, tugging her underwater.

She kicked away, surfacing with a laugh, the play reminding her of when she was a child, fooling around in her cousins' pool. She should have had more faith in her stars. It was looking like she and Aryan would get along fine this weekend, after a rocky start. She might even convince him, if not to let her list the job on her acting CV, to at least let her list him as a referee. And as long as there were no issues, there was no reason she shouldn't earn the bonus.

Keira mirrored Aryan as he circled her in the water, their bodies passing close, almost a dance. She was in heaven—the Aries in her exhilarated by the skirmish, her Pisces rising enervated by the water. When his eyes flicked to where Zac crouched in the garden, taking photos of tropical flowers, she lunged at him. Bracing her hands on his shoulders, she lifted herself over him and tried to dunk him underwater.

But his feet were firmly planted on the bottom. He bent his knees, his hands on her waist, guiding her as she dropped down. Time slowed. His face was so close she could see the twinkle in his dark eyes, the moisture on his lashes, the upward tilt at the corners of his full lips. Her body floated down through the water, closing the distance between them, and their mouths were so close she could have brushed his lips with hers. Her breasts nudged his pecs, and when their hips touched, it was obvious that he was turned on. Sinful thoughts filled her head, of them, naked, back in their room...

Closing her eyes, she felt his lips brush hers, softly to start, then he was kissing her, nudging her lips apart with his tongue, deepening their kiss and turning her insides molten.

A tide of lust flowed through her body and yearning subjugated every thought. She needed to feel his chest against her bare nipples, his hard abs against her stomach, his pubic hair against her naked sex as he thrust inside her. In that moment it didn't matter where they were... why they were here... who he was to the world, to her... all she could think of was the driving need to have his mouth and hands all over her, to spend the rest of the day making love to him.

Firm hands gripped her upper arms, pushing her away. She opened her eyes and found Aryan, gasping, holding her at arm's length, shaking his head. Shock at the realization of what she'd done—what she had wanted to do—sobered her like a slap.

Aryan released his hold on her and lunged away, his face tense and closed. "I think that was convincing enough. Maybe you should take a break?" Aryan dove underwater, surfaced and started swimming laps.

Keira glanced around, remembering they were in public. An audience was a good thing in terms of playing her part as Aryan's love interest, but not in the way she was reacting to a man engaged to another woman. She found Zac studiously clicking away on the other side of the garden, his body was tense, as if ready for danger.

With desire still thrumming through her body, she waded out of the pool and sat on the edge of a sun-lounge, welcoming the bite of the sun that evaporated the water from her skin. She laid back and closed her eyes to block out the sight of

Aryan's toned body slicing through the water. But even with her eyes closed she could see him, hear him, taste him on her tongue. *Stop!*

Aryan was engaged, her employer for the weekend. For a short time she'd forgotten why she was here.

Focus on the job Keira.

What would they do if they were just another couple at a resort? What would Aryan and Chloe do? They would go back to their villa, close the door and continue what they'd started in the pool.

All she had to do was act as if that's what they were about to do, without getting sucked back into wanting it to be reality.

A shadow moved between her and the sun, darkening her eyelids. Keira opened her eyes.

As if in answer to her thoughts, Aryan held out his hand and she took it, the slightly calloused roughness of his palm igniting a fire in her veins. Careful to project Chloe while reigning in the lust that surged through her body, she allowed him to help her to stand, then slid her hand from his, trailing her fingertips across his palm. Moving slowly, as if she were anticipating an afternoon of making love, she looked up at Aryan from beneath her lashes, languidly wrapped her sarong around her hips–and prayed for strength.

CHAPTER SIX

KEIRA STEPPED out of the bright sun into the coolness of the villa and waited while Aryan shut the front door behind Zac, who then retired without a word to his suite, leaving them alone.

She turned the ring on her finger, loosened from the cool water.

The walk back had been torture, the warmth of his hand on hers, the creep of desire threatening to overwhelm her senses. *Would he kiss her? And if he did, would she let him?*

No! This was *work*.

But she needn't have worried. When he turned to her, his eyes were cold. "Haven't we already discussed this?"

"What do you mean?" The skin of Keira's face went cold with shock. He was blaming *her*?

"You, acting like we were going to go at it in the pool."

"I was responding to you, and playing my part," Keira said, crossing her arms across her chest to contain what felt like rejection.

"Your part is Chloe. You overstepped."

What the blazes? His mood changes made her dizzy.

"Just like I didn't get instructions for kissing, I didn't get a guidebook for PDAs either."

"Just don't do it again. I'm going to have a shower."

Keira glared daggers at his back as he stalked off to Zac's room. *If I wanted to be bossed around for money, I'd just take my father's.*

When she heard the shower blast to life, Keira stumbled to a chair and sat down. Shaking with frustration, she dropped her head in her hands and berated herself for being so easily riled. How could she have acted so unprofessionally? She was here to play the part of *Aryan's fiancé.*

Shoot! What had she been thinking? Even if he and Chloe had a disagreement, Aryan was engaged. She raked her hands through her hair and clenched her fists. The champagne on the flight and wine with lunch hadn't helped, but it was her reaction to Aryan that made her forget what she was here for—and that he was spoken for.

Poor Chloe. Keira felt like the worst type of bitch. But Aryan was as much to blame as her, with his dimples and his surprising playfulness. And he'd reacted just as much as she had. In fact he'd initiated the kiss. *With his fiancé's body double.*

Keira stood, feeling nauseous. She had to get out of the villa for a while, didn't want to be there when Aryan got out the shower. She retied her sarong as a halter dress and knocked on

Zac's door. "I'm going to take a look at the boutiques," she called out.

The door opened and Zac leant against the frame, camera in hand. "Okay. You have my number. Take your phone and call if you need me."

Keira made her way to the cool shade of the covered shopping arcade, deliberately slowing her steps to a stroll, grateful for the attentive but unobtrusive staff. She glanced at the displays of luxury jewellery and resort-wear, letting the tranquil atmosphere smooth the sharp edges of her frustration, but the tight knot of anger beneath her ribs refused to loosen.

She should have ignored her horoscope, trusted her gut and refused this blasted assignment. There was nothing she could do to change what had happened with Aryan. It was unlikely she could convince him to agree to be a referee for her career now, but she *could* take pride in her work. And do whatever was in her power to make a success of the weekend and earn the bonus Aryan was offering.

To fill in some time until she could trust herself to be civil to him, Keira took her phone out to take some footage of her beautiful surroundings, the sandstone and glass arcade, dancing fountains and the gorgeous mosaics on the floor.

"Chloe." A male voice echoed down the arcade.

Keira tensed and turned around. Had Aryan come after her? To apologise, or berate her for going out without him? She braced herself to play her part, and found him lurking in a dim doorway. Why was he wearing that horrendous bowling shirt and cut-off denim shorts? She looked closer. His face seemed narrower, haggard, his eyes set a touch closer together. It wasn't Aryan at all.

"Ravi Nadar?"

He held a finger to his lips and gestured for her to follow him into the ladies' room.

Darn it. What should she do, avoid him and risk a scene? If she went with him, he would figure out she wasn't Chloe. Although if Ravi was *here*, he must be in on the charade?

Keira sighed and followed him into the pink marble powder room, resigned to find out what he wanted. She had her phone in her hand and Zac's number on speed dial, but her stomach still clenched in alarm when he locked the door behind them.

"Ravi. What are you doing here?" Keira kept her voice light, breathy and girlish, just like the one snippet she'd found of Chloe talking. This would be the true test of her imitation, with Chloe's fiancé's twin brother.

"You can drop the act. I know what you're doing here and what you're being paid for," he said in a voice not that different from his brother's—when Aryan was being obnoxious.

"And what is that?" She didn't like what his tone implied.

"You're being paid to fill in for Chloe," he said and leant back against the vanity, crossing his arms.

Keira stiffened, resisting the urge to unlock the door and walk away. "And…" *And the fact that you're lurking around the ladies' room, being careful not to be seen, is not a good sign.*

"I'd like to offer you more than my brother is paying you to help me instead," Ravi said and scratched at a welt on his forearm.

Keira clenched her fists. What was with these people, thinking she would do anything for cash? At least Zac had armed her with enough knowledge to know not to trust Ravi. And if he knew she wasn't Chloe, it meant he knew enough to damage Aryan's bid for CEO.

And if Ravi knew she wasn't Chloe—even though it wasn't her fault—there would be no bonus, so accepting Ravi's offer would be a good move financially. If she helped Ravi, she might get exposure for her career, but not the kind of fame she wanted.

Keira had no reason to defend Aryan, but the contract she'd signed and her work ethic would keep her mouth shut.

"And how could I help you?" She might not be planning to, but knowledge was the best chance of protecting herself if anything when wrong.

"You're spending time with my brother in the privacy of your villa. You'll see how he spends his time, what he does." Ravi sniffed and rubbed his nose with the back of his hand. "If he's still gambling."

Ah-ha. As she thought, he *was* here about control of NadarTec, but she wasn't going to let on she knew anything about it. He needed her to back him up. "What is it to you?"

"Does it matter? I offered you a lot of money." Ravi pushed himself off the vanity and headed to the door, trying to pretend it wasn't important to him if she agreed or not, but he hesitated before turning the latch.

"It matters because I might be interested in bringing him down a peg or three." *Not by being in cahoots with you though.*

"Okay." He turned and faced her. "If he is still gambling and lying that he's still engaged, I can convince father that I'm the best choice to succeed him as CEO, not Aryan." Ravi resumed scratching the red welt on his arm.

"Wait. What do you mean *'still engaged'*?"

"Oh, he didn't tell you that bit?" Ravi smirked. "He and Chloe broke up."

Fudge. Keira's head spun. *Aryan not engaged.* So that wasn't the reason he'd rejected her physical response to him.

"And if you can get proof he's still gambling, or something worse…"

"Worse? Like what?"

"He and his security guy are very close, closer than one would expect. Close enough to be 'involved'. If Aryan is gay, he may not father any little Nadars, and grandchildren are very important to our father."

"Aryan–gay?" The haze in Keira's mind cleared. He and Zac were very close, intimate even. The way they acted when they were together, so familiar; and the surety Zac had of his position in Aryan's life. Except that Aryan was notorious for the revolving door of women he'd dated…

And judging by Ravi's appearance and behaviour, he was obviously an addict–and grasping at straws.

"Why do you think Chloe broke up with him?" Ravi said with an unpleasant grin, as if reading her mind.

"What about Candice?" Unless the Victoria Secret model had been paid by Aryan as well as the publication for the tell-all interview. *Just as Keira had been paid to come here and play Chloe.*

"Candice has a drug habit she will do *anything* to keep secret, including lie." Ravi said with a shrug.

Keira shivered. What would Ravi do for *his* habit? She would be crazy to trust anything he said, but some of it made sense.

Except what of Aryan's ex-lovers? Even if the story Candice shared with the world was fabricated, Aryan had reacted physically to Keira. So, maybe he was bi-sexual. The only thing she could be certain of was that there was *something* between him and Zac.

But his lover? It would explain why Aryan acted differently with her when Zac was around, why he'd been angry when he responded to her physically and then rejected her so definitively. It would also explain why he needed Keira here to fill in for the absent Chloe if she was no longer in the picture. But surely the truth would come out sooner rather than later.

"What about Chloe? Won't she tell everyone they broke up?"

"No, because it suits her for people to think she's here with Aryan. Thanks to Zac's not so secure email, I know she's shacked up screwing her married agent."

"Oh. Shitake." Zac, head of security, making a slip-up like that? Aryan could afford the best—and if Zac wasn't the best at security, why *did* Aryan have him around? *Because they're lovers.*

"Exactly. The engagement is over, and Aryan needs to keep it quiet for now. Don't look so shocked. This is what happens behind the scenes, love. It's all bullshit." Ravi grimaced.

"Do you hate your brother so much you would ruin him?" What could have happened to make Ravi so bitter?

"No, I don't hate Aryan, just the fact he automatically gets whatever he wants. I was always meant to take over as CEO of NadarTec. Aryan had his career playing cricket. Then when he had to give it up and all of a sudden, he thinks *he* should be CEO? Why should he be named successor, just because he's a few minutes older?" Ravi shrugged and looked away, but not before she caught a flicker of guilt in his expression. "If I have to bring him down to keep what's mine, so be it." Ravi slipped a business card into her hand and turned to unlock the door. "Think of the money," he said, eyes narrowed, before slipping out.

Keira's leant back against the wall, breathing fast. Her crawled to think how far Ravi would go to beat his brother to the prize. Born only minutes apart, the twins might share some traits, but they were very different personalities. At the height of her crush on the Indian cricket star, she'd studied Aryan's horoscope in depth, pleased his May 22 personality showed itself in the determined energy that drove him to be the best at what he loved. In Ravi, the same overreaching ambition seemed to push him to the other extreme. Addiction and resentment combining as a power complex, see-sawing between megalomania and feelings of inferiority.

Twin Geminis. They must have kept their unfortunate parents on their toes.

And now Keira was caught in the middle, her professional integrity at risk. Whatever was happening here could be beneficial or devastating for her career. And it might all come down to how she played her hand.

Even if she wouldn't dream of using any evidence she might find, information was power. In this case, protection against getting sucked into the vortex of lies swirling around her. She needed to keep her head, stick to the script and keep her attraction to Aryan firmly under control.

CHAPTER SEVEN

"ZAC and I thought we might go for a hike. Would you like to join us?" Aryan could have kicked himself for snapping at her, as if had been her fault all he could think of was coaxing more of those sweet little moans of from her throat. The intensity of his reaction to her at the pool had taken him by surprise. He'd been angry at himself for being tempted, when he knew from painful experience that way only lead to danger.

"You boys go ahead, I'm going to take advantage of the private Pilates class," Keira dismissed the invitation with a wave and a frown.

"Are you sure? I hear the view from the look-out is amazing." Aryan said with a smile, trying to convince her. More than anything he needed to keep Keira on-side if this situation had any chance of working.

"I'll need to wash my hair before dinner. If I go with you, I won't have time," she'd said as she saw them out the door, as if eager to see the back of them.

Aryan couldn't blame her after the way he'd taken his frustration out on her. What he wouldn't give to just enjoy a weekend away without the tangle of lies he'd created, all to protect his father's legacy.

"Girls, hey?" Zac joked as they reached the start of the track that would take them past the airstrip and on to the lookout. They strode on in easy silence–except for the chirping of insects–and it quickly became too steep to talk anyway.

Aryan focused on keeping his weight balanced and not favoring his injured leg. The workout was just what he needed to work off some of his frustration. By the time they reached the lookout he felt calmer, and pleasantly fatigued, the sticky heat reminding him of his childhood. He stopped with his hands on his hips while he caught his breath and admired the view: a multitude of small islands scattered across a flat expanse of rich blue as far as he could see, the sun dropping low to meet the horizon.

"You should take it easy on Keira." Zac was bent over to catch his breath, bracing his hands on his knees. He glanced up with a pointed look. "She's into you."

"No... she's not. She's just like... Chloe and Candice. Like... all women."

"Not *all* women, right?" Zac knew how much Aryan respected his mom.

"Right." Aryan sat heavily on a large rock and hung his head to catch his breath and gather his thoughts.

"I'm pretty sure Keira isn't like any of your exes–or Chloe." Zac sat next to him and stretched his long, heavily muscled legs out.

"What makes you say that?" Aryan slanted a sideways look at his friend.

"I didn't mention it before because I didn't think it was important at the time, but when I did the security check on Keira, I found out her parents are mega-loaded."

Aryan sat up. "Really? Who are her parents?"

"I didn't recognize their names, but I've made enquiries."

So, Keira came from a wealthy family too. She did say she wasn't in the acting gig for the money. Maybe they had more in common than he'd thought. "She doesn't behave like an entitled brat," he mused aloud.

"You mean like you?" He joked and dodged the punch Aryan aimed at his arm. "No, she doesn't, does she? She also doesn't act like someone trying to take a ride on your coat-tails either."

Aryan groaned. "God you're lame. Where did you get that expression–from your grandma?"

"You know what I'm saying. She likes you for *you*."

"She may have, until I acted like an ass." Aryan scrubbed his face with his palms, trying to process this new possibility. "What do I do? She drives me insane. I want to shake her one second and kiss her the next. If she's not interested in my money and the only fame she wants is on her own merits, then…"

"Maybe she's perfect for you? She's nothing like Chloe. In fact, she reminds me of a lady called Alaya Nadar."

Aryan had long accepted such a creature did not exist. But if Zac saw the personality similarities between Keira and his mother as well… Aryan stood with his hands on his hips and eyed the distant horizon. "I don't know. And if she is? I need to tell her the truth."

Zac grasped Aryan's shoulder and turned him, so their eyes locked. "You can't. Not yet. There's too much at stake. What if she gets pissed off that you lied to her and talks to your father? Or if you do get together but things go south before the announcement? Think of everything you've done to get this far. It can't all be for nothing. As it is, Ravi is too close to finding out the truth. He's got as far as my personal emails. The red herring I planted won't distract him for long."

"The story about Chloe and her agent?" Aryan smiled and shook his head. He had to admire his brother for being almost as gifted at hacking as Zac himself.

"Yeah. So, my advice? Don't tell Keira anything until you are CEO. And don't sleep with her until you tell her the whole story. She might never forgive you."

"You don't think it's already too late for forgiveness?"

"I think you need to focus on the company first, then go after the girl."

"Sounds easy when you say it like that."

"Just be your charming self. And remember, I have your back." Zac jogged onto the path, and turned his head to call back. "Race you to the shower."

LATER THAT NIGHT, Aryan took Keira's hand as they headed up to the resort for dinner, the still air thick with lingering humidity and the scent of night-flowering blooms. Behind them, Zac's presence loomed like a bulky shadow.

Tense despite Aryan's strong yet gentle fingers interlocked with hers, Keira was hyper-aware of how the two men interacted. She was dying to know how much Ravi had said was true, but justified her curiosity as her constant desire to better understand human motivation, in order to grow as an actor. If the two men were lovers, how must it feel to spend time together in public, but not be able to be a couple, always acting their roles of bodyguard and playboy celebrity in public?

Keira watched them, looking for a meaningful glance, an opportunistic brush of limbs, or an inflection of tenderness in their speech. But Aryan was nothing but charming and attentive to her, as if Zac wasn't sitting at the next table, stony gazed and professional.

"Are you happy to choose off the menu or would you like the kitchen to make something in particular?" Aryan asked as they perused the menu.

"The quail sounds perfect, and the eye fillet, thank you."

"I think I'll have the same. And which wine would you like?"

"The Burgundy."

"A bottle please," he asked the hovering waiter, then looked back at her. Flickering candlelight highlighted the lines of his cheekbones and brow, the murmur of conversation from the distant tables of a scattering of other guests lending them a cocoon of intimacy. It could have been the perfect date.

"So, Keira. What led you to acting?" His voice was low and casual, but Keira was suspicious. His attitude since the hike was so different, as if, in reality, they were two people on a real date, not putting on a show. This was the first time he'd initiated a conversation or shown any interest in her as a person.

Keira shrugged. She was always happy to talk about her love for her work. "Since I can remember, I loved to pretend I was someone else and explore what it would be like to live a different life."

"You weren't happy with your life?" Did he see through her so easily, or was it a lucky guess? Either way it suggested an interest in something other than his own situation. His change in demeanour had her wondering what had happened out on the bushwalk. Whatever had been bothering him at the pool this afternoon had obviously been resolved. *A lover's tiff resolved?*

"Not exactly unhappy, but often bored. I'm an only child and apart from some weekends spent with my cousins, I spent a lot of time alone. I became proficient at entertaining myself. Daydreaming and playacting became a way of life until it became so much a part of who I was I couldn't imagine doing anything else, even when others are determined to steer me on a different path." Keira pressed her lips shut and clenched her jaw, to stop herself waffling about things Aryan probably didn't want to know.

"Someone in your life is pressuring you to do something different?"

He seemed genuinely interested, so Keira explained. "My parents. Even though I've told them acting is my passion, they want me to work in the family company and assumed I would pursue qualifications to suit. I humoured them by getting a Bachelor of Electrical Engineering, but it wasn't enough for them. Dad lost it when I graduated and then announced I still planned to be an actor."

"Electrical Engineering? So, you're beautiful, talented and smart too."

"You sound surprised. You of all people should know, what shows on the outside isn't an indication of what lies underneath." *Even when what people see is a carefully constructed charade.*

"Touché." He lifted his glass in a toast and Keira responded, taking a sip of the wine the waiter had poured while she was busy trying to figure Aryan out.

They settled into a companionable silence to eat, both caught up in their own thoughts until the waiter cleared the entrée plates.

"Engineering is very different to acting." Aryan looked at her over the rim of his wine glass. "How did your parents react?"

"They've cut me off unless I go work in their business." It felt cathartic to be able to share the pain of family discord with someone who had experienced it himself.

"And will you?"

"I might, but not to get access to my trust account. I enjoy tech work, but I love acting. I just want to be free to choose."

Aryan smiled and the warmth of it reached his eyes. "I admire your courage and resolve."

"I believe you should pursue what you love." Keira lifted her chin, challenging him to be honest with her and confide his feelings for Zac. "It's ironic, me wanting out of my parent's business and you wanting to be CEO of yours."

"Since the accident, the career that I love is not an option. I know the family business, but that's not the reason I need to be named successor."

Keira couldn't help but feel for this attractive, complex man. Thanks to her own experience, it was easy for her to empathise with anyone who was forbidden the career they loved. "Why then?"

Aryan hesitated, looking deep into her eyes before he continued. "If my brother gets control of the company, he plans to sell off the automation division, which was the core of the business when my father started the company. Apart from stopping him from breaking my father's heart, robotics is the future of the industry, and key to the ongoing success of NadarTec. If Ravi had his way, he'd sell it off for short term gain, and NadarTec would lose its greatest strength."

Keira softened at his honesty. "Can't you just tell your father?" Any anger she still harboured dissipated. What choice did he have? It couldn't be easy being in mortal combat with his brother to protect his father's business, and the career he loved lost to him. With whatever was going on with Chloe and Zac threatening what he had left.

"Not until I have concrete proof. Zac is working on it, but if he can't and Ravi can influence Dad to name him successor, I won't be able to stop him."

"Zac is more than head of personal security then?"

"Much more," Aryan agreed with a nod and glanced in Zac's direction. "He's also part of the company's cyber security team, and an old boarding school friend."

Cyber security? If Zac was good enough to be employed by one of the largest international tech companies, how did Ravi get into Aryan's email account and find out what Chloe was up to? Unless they'd *let* him get access…

The waiter brought the main course and refilled their glasses. Aryan seemed distracted and Keira studied him as they ate. She felt she understood him a little now. No wonder he and Zac were so close. He seemed to be the only person he could trust.

"Death by Chocolate or tarte Tatin with vanilla bean ice-cream?" Keira mused. The dessert choice was the hardest of the entire menu.

Aryan ordered both. "It might be easier to decide when they get here."

But the indulgence of chocolate looked too rich, and she chose the apple tart. Richly golden with luscious, creamy ice-cream melting over it, it was perfectly complemented by the morsels of chocolate Aryan offered her from his spoon.

"No more please, or I won't be able to walk." Keira waved away another mouthful of chocolate mousse, despite the way Aryan's eyelids lowered seductively every time she took his spoon in her mouth.

Darn it. He shouldn't be looking at her as if he wanted to eat *her* for dessert. And she shouldn't be so eager to get back to the villa, but the thoughtful, relatable Aryan of tonight was so sexy she… Keira stopped that thought dead. She must be crazy for lusting after a man who blew hot and cold, who may or may not be engaged to be married, and who may have a secret lover who was sitting at the next table.

But something had changed. Aryan was acting as if he wanted to seduce her—and Zac was *right there*, watching them.

Aryan folded his napkin and placed it on the table. "I have a plan to work off our indulgence."

"Hmmm, I'm intrigued." Keira's imagination went wild, and she almost melted from the surge of hot lust that shot through her. Yep, she was certifiable.

"I've organised a boat trip for tomorrow. Although, if you'd rather do something else, I can change it. I thought you might like to swim in the ocean while we're here, and I've been told the beach we're going to is worth a visit."

"Sounds great," Keira said, mustering enthusiasm for an innocent day at the beach, rather than the one thing she most wanted in this instant–the one thing that was most off-limits. Aryan Nadar.

As much as his life was open to the public, there was a lot about the man that was a mystery. She didn't trust Ravi at all, but there was definitely more going on here than Aryan or Zac had told her.

If she told him Ravi had approached her, would Aryan come clean with her, or put up his guard again? Whatever he said, she wouldn't know if he was being honest or lying. She had more chance of finding out what was going on by watching and waiting.

Whatever happened tonight once they got back to their villa should shed some light on the true situation.

CHAPTER EIGHT

ARYAN'S LIPS were soft and warm when he brushed them across her cheek, his signature cologne working like an aphrodisiac on her senses, evoking fantasies of soft sheets and naked skin. Until Zac's cough brought her back to the living room.

Aryan stepped away, leaving a void between their bodies.

"Um, we have an urgent matter to discuss?" Zac said from where he leant against the kitchen bench, thick arms crossed over his bulging chest, one eyebrow raised.

"Ah, yes. Sorry, I forgot." Aryan turned back to Keira, and with a chaste kiss on her other cheek, said goodnight. "You should take the bedroom."

"But where will you sleep?" Fuddled with arousal, she glanced around the villa. The lounge was large and comfortable enough, but she couldn't imagine Aryan Nadar sleeping on it.

"Don't worry about me," he said with a smile, then dismissed her with a "sleep well."

"You don't want to use the bathroom?"

"I'll use the one in Zac's room," Aryan said and turned to look out onto the moonlit terrace, waiting for her to leave.

Sick of being kept in the dark and told nothing she could rely on, Keira closed the bedroom door behind her and paused to listen. All she could make out was Aryan's warm, smooth tones and Zac's deeper rumble. She couldn't understand more than the occasional word.

On-edge and frustrated, Keira scrubbed her face clean and slid into the king-sized bed in the new lingerie she'd bought with her wardrobe money. She'd chosen it before she knew the full details of the job, wanting to look the part right down to the powder blue silk camisole, French knickers and matching robe. She huffed and turned onto her side to look out the open sliding door at the moon glinting off the water.

Keira threw off the sheet which had begun to cling to her. *Dammit.* Why did she have to lust after someone she couldn't have, even once? Even with the gentle swish of the waves to lull her, sleep was beyond her reach. Between sexual frustration, and the possibility of what Aryan and Zac might be doing in the other room, there were only two things Keira knew would help and she hadn't brought any sleeping tablets with her.

With a sigh, Keira rolled onto her back and slipped one hand inside her panties, the other under her top. The naked lips of her sex were already slick with arousal and she plunged her fingers into her wetness. With her other hand she squeezed and pinched her nipples until she arched off the bed with pleasure. With thoughts of Aryan in the pool, hard muscles and smooth tanned skin pressed against her in the pool, she climaxed in record time. The muscles of her sex clenched, grasping for his cock to anchor the pleasure in her core. Instead, waves of sensation rippled out from her clit, dissipating through her body, loosening her joints and muscles.

Panting, Keira continued circling her fingers round her swollen clit, craving true release. Imagining it wasn't enough, she wanted him inside her when she came. Throwing off the damp sheets, she settled for a substitute.

On the way to the dressing room she peeled off her cami and knickers and knelt on the soft carpet in front of the overnight bag she'd packed her essentials in. Suspecting the weekend might call for sexual relief, she'd packed emergency assistance. There was enough moonlight to find her dildo without turning on a light and she found it easily, wrapped lovingly in a silk pouch. The flash of her pale breasts in the full-length mirror caught her attention. Turning her body, she looked at herself, her hair a pale halo around her head, lips and nipples flushed dark with arousal. Her gaze dropped to the dildo in her hand and the unfamiliar sight of her bare sex, her labia still moist and engorged from masturbating.

Keira imagined it was Aryan watching and she moved one knee wider, opening her sex so her clit glistened like a pearl. *Take me…*

Inserting two fingers into her mouth, she coated them with saliva, and circled the tips around her clit, tilting her hips to expose more of her sex to the mirror. Picking up the dildo, she ran her two fingers downward and spread her labia. She inserted the tip and watched it disappear as she lowered herself onto it, stroking her clit from the side so she could watch the shaft slide in and out as she rode it.

When the first orgasm ripped through her, Keira was picturing Aryan kneeling before her, his cock deep inside her, his face contorted with lust and pleasure. She took the phallus deeper, her fingers moving faster, driven to exhaust the need that still clawed at her…

She imagined Zac in the doorway, watching … and came like a thunderclap. Shockwaves of pleasure reverberated through her core, making her sob with pleasure.

Boneless and blissful, Keira rolled onto her side on the plush carpet and dropped her head on her forearm.

In her dreams, it was Aryan's cock still inside her.

WHEN KEIRA WOKE LATER–NAKED, cool and a little stiff–she checked the time on her phone. 2am. She closed the app she hadn't used–or needed–that turned her pet cock into a treasure trove of pleasure.

Rising, she rinsed the dildo in the light from the moon streaming in through the bathroom skylight and left it on the vanity to dry. She slipped on her robe, grabbed her phone and poked her head out to scope out the living room. Sex always made her hungry, even solitary sex.

Making sure her phone was switched to silent, she used the flashlight app so she didn't have to turn any lights on.

Stillness greeted her, the gentle lapping of waves from the beach outside the window the only sound. With the beam of light directed toward the floor, she checked the lounge, even the thick rug in front of the coffee table. There was no sign of Aryan in the living room. Despite the fact he was off-limits, disappointment still hollowed her already empty stomach.

Taking a container of sliced fruit from the fridge, she leant against the counter while she fed the beast of her hunger. And noticed Aryan had left his laptop on the dining table. Keira looked at the door to Ryan's suite. It was not completely shut, just closed over.

As shiver of curiosity prickled over her skin. Had Aryan been gambling all those times he'd been online? If Ravi was right and his brother still had a problem, could he be right about the the other stuff?

She held her breath and opened the laptop carefully. She felt like the worst kind of sneak, but if Ravi was wrong about gambling... The screen lit up. She wiggled the mouse and checked the browsing history. Multiple visits to only a few websites. Not gambling–or porn, gay or otherwise–but addiction recovery chat rooms. She was glad for Aryan, and happy Ravi as wrong, about this at least.

She checked the inbox. No emails from Chloe. Keira closed the laptop and looked at the door to Zac's suite.

Pausing outside, she listened for any hint of man-on-man action. Nothing, not even a snore. Carefully lining up her eye up with the crack, Keira tried to find the bed, turned her head from side to side when she couldn't. Too close! Her head pushed the door open. She pulled back, sucking in a breath, but the hinges hadn't made a sound.

Holding her breath, she pushed the door further and yep, there they were. Zac and Aryan in the king size bed, side by side. Aryan on his back with his arm flung above his head, his bare abs stretched and taught, a masterpiece etched in marble. Zac on his front, one arm hanging over the edge of the bed, the other under the pillow, his torso also naked. The rumpled sheets on Zac's side attested substantial activity, enough to be the site of sexual passion.

Keira pushed down a confusing combination of jealousy and arousal and took a bracing breath. They made a beautiful couple. With the moonlight caressing the enticing curves and dips of hard muscle and smooth skin, she could see why Zac felt compelled to capture beauty as a photograph for future enjoyment.

She lifted her phone, turning off the flash function and waiting for the camera to adjust to the dim light. She framed the shot as she imagined Zac would, crouching so she filled the screen with their naked flesh. Beautiful.

Click.

CHAPTER NINE

ARYAN WOKE EARLY, the sun through the open window still gathering strength for the day. Zac was gone, out on his usual early run. Stretching out on the bed, Aryan worked some of the stiffness out of his muscles. It wasn't ideal, sharing a bed with Zac, who slept restlessly and mumbled in his sleep. Not that Aryan blamed him—he would find it difficult to sleep at all if he'd lived through the abusive upbringing Zac once described.

Even sleeping on the very edge of the bed, out of the way of Zac's fists, he'd had too much on his mind to get much sleep. Primarily, the woman sleeping in the other room.

Physically, Keira possessed the stunning looks that also led him to choose Chloe for the initial position. The difference was that Keira was *naturally* beautiful—inside and out—as well as talented and smart. *Shit.* Why couldn't he have met her a few months from now, when he had his life in some kind of order?

How long had it been since he'd met a woman like her, someone he could imagine being a part of his life? Not since he'd been a naïve, rookie cricketer. Not since Candice. He cringed at the memory of how she had played him, then winced at the wrench of physical pain as he swung out of bed, his knee stiffened from disuse. Since he'd weaned himself off painkillers, the only thing that kept him close to pain-free was daily use of his float pool.

He did some stretches and lunges, trying to work out the stiffness in his leg. Despite the constant ache in his knee and occasional numbness in his adductor muscle, he was grateful he'd survived the accident reasonably intact. *Bloody Ravi.* Even after Aryan had covered for him and saved his skin, his twin still did whatever he damn well wanted with no consideration for anyone else. So many regrets… If only he and Ravi hadn't been in Vegas that night, indulging their addictions. If only he hadn't let Ravi drive.

At least that night in Vegas had cured him of his obsession with gambling. If only it hadn't also meant the end of his career, and the beginning of his dependence on painkillers.

If only Ravi had the willpower to beat his addiction too, maybe he would be a reasonable human being. Until then, Aryan had no choice but to do whatever he could to keep his brother from getting his hands on NadarTec.

Ravi had already cost him the career he loved; he wouldn't let him steal his father's last years of happiness too.

His phone beeped. A message from Zac.

Your bro was here, speaking to your 'fiancé'.

What the?

As if he'd conjured him with his thoughts, a picture of Ravi with Keira flashed up on the screen, his hand on her shoulder, standing in front of a mosaic of a big muscly guy coming out of the ocean with a three-pronged fork. The mosaic of Zeus in the arcade leading to the restaurant. *In this resort.*

Aryan's stomach roiled.

Ravi was here, and Keira knew him. *They were planning something together?*

Heat washed over his skin and his chest tightened. She wasn't different at all. She was just like the rest.

And he'd been thinking she might be someone he could care about.

Aryan threw his phone at the ground, as if by shattering the glass he could remove the reality of what he'd seen.

Thank Christ for Zac's advice, or he might have told her everything.

***

ARYAN THREW on a t-shirt and headed out to the kitchen. *Empty.* The door to her bedroom was open.

"Keira?" he called out. What would he say if she answered? *You didn't tell me you knew my selfish, drug addict brother.*

Her bathroom door was ajar. He could hear the shower running. The shower where just yesterday he'd jerked off imagining it was her he was fucking, not his hand. While she was fucking him over. With his brother.

He ran his hand through his hair in frustration–and saw her phone on the bed. Opening it, he spotted Ravi's business card in the pocket.

He turned it on and was surprised he got access without needing a pin. For a spy, she wasn't very careful. He checked her inbox. Nothing from Ravi. *How had they been communicating?*

The front door opened just as the water in the shower stopped.

He put the phone back where he found it and slipped out, looking for Zac. Closing the bedroom door behind him, he followed Zac into the bathroom, closing that door too.

"We need to talk." Aryan sat on the closed toilet seat.

"No sheep, Sherlock," Zac replied as he turned on the shower.

Aryan cringed at Zac's use of one of Keira's quirky expressions.

"I've checked her phone. I don't know what they're up to or how they're communicating, but there are no text messages to or from Ravi."

"Did you check her emails? Facebook messages?" Zac asked as he peeled his wet singlet off and dropped it in the bath.

"No, just SMS."

"Okay. I need to get a look at her phone." Zac turned on the shower and glanced at Aryan. "If you can keep her busy for ten minutes, I'll take a good look."

"Apart from when she's in the shower, she has her phone with her all the time."

"Not if she's swimming." Zac stepped out of his running shorts and under the spray.

"Or in a float tank. She sounded interested when we talked about it before."

"Great idea. Let's meet up afterward and I'll let you know what I find." Zac squirted herbal smelling body wash into his hands.

"Where did you get the photo?" Aryan asked, his hand on the door handle.

"My contact in resort security. He's going to let me know if he sees Ravi again, and if he sees them together."

"Thanks man." Aryan slipped out before Zac started sudsing himself.

"That's why you hired me. Security expert, remember?" Zac called after him.

GOD, he needed caffeine. Aryan paced to the kitchen to put on coffee while Zac finished in the shower. His gut clenched as the bittersweet smell of caffeine hit him. She'd beaten him to it.

"Good morning. How did you sleep?" Keira, her long blond hair in a messy ponytail, glorious face free of makeup, glanced at the doorway with a raised eyebrow and got two more bowls out. She poured some muesli into her bowl, then slid the glass canister across the bench.

"Just great. And you?" Aryan stepped to the island counter and clenched his hands into fists when he saw the short shorts that revealed long, toned legs, and a singlet that left little to his imagination. How could such a gorgeous creature hide such deceit?

"A bit disturbed. Not used to the quiet—or the humidity." She shrugged one sun-kissed shoulder.

"You could use the aircon." Aryan replied through tight lips. He doesn't want to picture Keira, restless in that big bed.

She raised an eyebrow at him. "Someone got out of the wrong side of the bed. I'm aware of the purpose of an air conditioner, but I like the sound of the ocean. It's a nice change from traffic. I could get used to it." Keira held the milk out. "Full cream?"

"Thanks." Aryan took a deep breath and the bottle and poured a generous amount over his generous serve of muesli. It wouldn't do to alert her that he was onto her, but he couldn't find it in him to talk to her like he had last night. Like a potential girlfriend. *Christ, what had he been thinking?*

"What's the plan for this morning. What time do we go out on the boat?"

"Whenever you're ready, but I organized for the boat and lunch around 11. If that time suits and you'd still like to go?"

"Of course. An LA girl like me, pass up the opportunity to laze around on a stretch of sand with no-one but two gorgeous escorts?"

"Just one. Zac will stay on the boat."

"Even better. More sand for us. What would you like to do before then?"

"My knee is giving me trouble. I'm going to use one of the float tanks, care to join me?" Aryan paused at the image of them naked together in one of the float tanks that popped into his mind, and hurriedly added, "not the same one, of course."

"Sure. I'll try almost anything once. What do I need?"

"Nothing once you get there, unless you prefer to wear a swimsuit."

Zac strode into the kitchen, hair damp, dressed in short shorts, a singlet and trainers.

"Are you coming to float as well?" Keira asked him.

He helped himself to a bowl of muesli and Keira poured them all coffee.

"If it is like being back in the womb, I think I'll pass. Thanks for the offer, but I'm going to hit the gym."

———

ARYAN ALWAYS FELT REFRESHED and energized after a float session, but this time he'd had trouble clearing his mind in the inky silence of the tank. He emerged from his float with the legacy of thinking of Keira, naked next door, his balls aching for release and the urge to take himself in hand.

At that moment Keira emerged from her room and she looked so fuck-able, her eyelids half lowered, eyes glistening with what looked frustratingly like desire. Christ, the way her gaze clung to him it was like she'd been thinking of him while she'd been laying next door, naked and with all her senses heightened.

She hadn't tried to hide her attraction to him, and it would be easy to take advantage of her horniness to snatch back some of the power she had taken from him. But he had enough respect for himself—and the respect for women his mother had instilled in him—to resist. He sought out Zac instead, and left Keira to head back to the villa alone.

"It gets worse, mate," Zac said, cooling down from a heavy workout as Aryan did some warm-up lunges next to him. "There's just the one photo but it looks pretty bad man. It's of us in bed together, and it looks like we're naked and have had sex."

"She thinks she can blackmail me with a staged photo?" Damn him for being so gullible. She was a bloody good actor. She'd convinced him she wasn't interested in money.

"It's probably not black-mail she has in mind, if Ravi put her up to it. He'll have something more underhanded in mind."

"Worse than blackmail? Shit."

"Don't panic yet. I checked and she hasn't sent it anywhere. Not even to Ravi. She doesn't have a passcode on her phone, but she has one on her cloud storage. There's no point deleting the photo off her phone if it's in the cloud. She'd know we were onto her and she'd still have the copy. We'll have to work out another way to diffuse this one."

"What do we need to do? Get Ravi off the island?" Aryan lay back on a mat and started doing crunches.

"He might have already gone. He's achieved what he came here for. He's got Keira doing his dirty work."

"Okay, so there must be something we can do?" Aryan grunted as he kept crunching, hoping the increase of blood flow would help him think.

"She's got the photo, and we can't delete it." Zac sat on a press-up bench and scrubbed his hands through his sweat-soaked hair. "We need leverage. Some way of keeping her mouth shut and preventing her from using the photo."

Aryan stopped and lay back on the matt, frowning at Zac. "How would we manage that?"

"I have it!" Zac grinned and clapped his hands on his thighs. "It's the perfect double-header. Blackmail, *and* a way to prove you're into women." He stood, holding out his hand to help Aryan up.

"What's your plan?"

"She's so into you, man. If you encourage her a bit, I bet I can get some footage of you together."

"Tell me you don't mean film us having sex?" Aryan was horrified, even though it made sense. "Blackmail the blackmailer?" It might just work. From what she'd said, her career was everything to her. Or was that just a story she fed him?

"Yep." Zac nodded, but his frown showed he wasn't any happier about his suggestion than Aryan was to consider it.

It felt wrong, but Keira had the ammunition to ruin his chance of saving his father's company. And what Zac was suggesting would arm them with the one thing that would either stop her or ruin her reputation if she refused. If the people who made decisions in the entertainment industry knew she'd screwed her employer, she'd never shake the reputation for familiarity with a casting couch.

"There must be another way," he said, shaking his head as he set up the rowing machine.

"After everything you've already done to be the one named CEO? You do remember what's at stake here. And its not like you are actually engaged."

"But she thinks I am." As if that argument would stop Zac from doing whatever was necessary.

"You could try it on without telling her the engagement is off, but if you think it will give you better odds, tell her you've broken up. Give her the story we planted for Ravi. Actually, if she's been speaking to Ravi, he's probably told her about the email he 'found' about Chloe and her agent getting it on." Zac held up his hand, palm up to stop Aryan interrupting and hurried on. "I know its not exactly ethical, but its perfect for your needs. The footage will prove to the world you're into women, and we use your affair with her to explain why your engagement to Chloe is over—by leaking the photos to the media after you're named CEO." Zac picked up his water bottle and finished the contents, his neck working with the force of his thirst.

Aryan started rowing at warm up speed. Although he was frustrated by his lack of options, he was careful not to stress his injured leg by taking out his frustration in physical movement. If he was honest with himself, it wouldn't be a hardship to seduce Keira. Its not as if he would have to try too hard to convince her, she'd made it clear to him that she was more than willing. And he *had* fantasized about having sex with her since she'd told him what for when they'd first met on the plane. Her beauty had roused him, but her spirit had weakened his defenses. And it had been her choice to play this game, so she couldn't say she didn't deserve the consequences of her duplicity.

It wouldn't surprise him if she was working with Ravi for the benefit of her career, neither could he couldn't blame her for her single-minded ambition. He would have done the same for cricket. As much as he didn't want to have to ruin Keira's career, he would not allow her to help Ravi ruin their father's company either. "Okay, but any photos or footage you take will never be used in the media—only to convince her to back off. It isn't to go public. I couldn't live with myself if I got what I wanted by ruining some one else's life."

"Your call, man. But I don't want to see Ravi win because you've gone soft. Don't forget, if she wasn't in on something with Ravi, we wouldn't need to be talking about damage control."

"I'll organize a romantic dinner outside and you take whatever compromising photo you can get while I try and work out another way to shut her up."

"Good luck with that. Oh, and I had a win on the Ravi front. The company he's made a deal with, on condition he becomes CEO? It's called Future Robotics. We're getting closer to having proof to make him back down."

"I only hope he does–back down. I don't want to have to tell Dad about what he's been up to. It will break his heart. I wish I didn't have to do this either, but Keira has given me no choice."

Zac clapped him on the shoulder and shook his head. "You should have just told him at the time that it was Ravi driving the car, that he was and still is an addict. You would have been the only choice for CEO and we wouldn't have to do any of this."

Focusing on the burn in his muscles, and glorying in the power of his body, Aryan took off at a sprint. Zac was right of course. Aryan had thought he was helping his brother, protecting him. All he'd wanted to do was keep him out of jail, but if he'd let him take the rap, Ravi would have been forced into rehab. Sober and drug-free, Ravi was a different person. They could have worked together to bring NadarTec into the future. Aryan had made the wrong call, and he'd just have to make the best of it.

CHAPTER TEN

KEIRA SHIFTED her weight from foot to foot, her nerves stretched taut as she watched the sleek speedboat glide into the marina and bump to a stop against the jetty. It was torture standing so close to Aryan after the fantasies she'd had in the sensual cocoon of the float tank.

"Nice boat," she said to make conversation. Aryan had been quiet and moody all day. Even his session in the float tank hadn't relaxed him.

"Mmmm. Not bad. A little small, but perfect for a day trip."

Small? Maybe by her parent's standards, but it looked plenty big enough to her.

Zac stepped forward and waited for an athletic man with a tan earned from years in the sun to jump out of the boat and secure it to the jetty, then went on board to security-check the boat and crew.

Keira glanced around. The few people nearby were more interested in their own business. Even so, she slid her hand down Aryan's forearm and clasped it close to her body. *Like a fiancé would.* She told herself it was in case there was a camera or phone aimed at them, but she could no longer resist the need to touch him.

The crew loaded food coolers while the powerful engines idled, throbbing gently as Aryan, Zac and Keira settled on the leather seats on the rear deck. Once the coolers were stowed, the deck-hand cast off and the boat glided away from the jetty.

Once they cleared the shallows, the engines roared and the nose of the boat lifted, a cloud of water spraying out behind them as they sped away from the island.

Keira felt her spirit expand until it felt as she was a part of the wide openness of the ocean and sky. She filled her lungs with salty air and sank, relaxed, back into the seat. It was good to get away from the crowds and pollution of civilisation. Even the small resort felt like an oversized fishbowl.

Surely Aryan's mood would lift out here, with the fresh air and natural beauty of their surroundings, and they could just chill and enjoy the day.

With only the skipper and deckhand, even Zac seemed to relax from his constant on-duty mode. He smiled and joked with Aryan, like best mates out on a fishing trip.

Keira was enjoying exhilaration and feeling of the freedom so much she wished their destination was further away when the boat slowed after barely fifteen minutes.

The skipper anchored close to a pristine beach and killed the engine, the cue for Antonio, the deckhand, to lay out the buffet lunch. Savoury tart, potato and goats cheese salad, pesto chicken and salad wraps, cold frittata, sliced melon and chilled, crisp white wine.

"I ordered a simple meal. Wouldn't want to get swimmer's cramp," Aryan said as he offered a plate for Keira to help herself.

"It's perfect," she said and served herself a selection of everything.

Lunch was finished with a delicate chocolate mousse and crème fraiche strawberry cheesecake. If it weren't for the coffee to finish, Keira wouldn't have been able to resist stretching out on one of the leather seats for a nap.

Aryan stood and stretched, his swim shorts and tight t-shirt leaving little to the imagination, making Keira want to reach out and run her hands over his toned body. "Time for a swim?"

"Yes please," Keira said, unable to resist the enticing pull of the clear, blue water.

Antonio helped them into the tender and Aryan assured the deckhand he was fine to get them to the shore and back.

Once the small boat was nosed onto the shore, Aryan jumped onto the sand and held out his hand for Keira to climb down after him.

"This was an excellent idea. Thank you for organising it," Keira said with a smile as they made their way up the beach, feet sinking into the soft, powdery sand.

"No problem," he muttered, his crankiness taking some of the sparkle off the day.

"That's it. Enough." She stomped to a stop and threw her towel on the sand. "What is going on with you? Have I done something wrong? I thought we were getting along well last night. I thought we might even become friends." The tremble in her bottom lip surprised her. Why was she so upset that he seemed angry with *her*?

He stepped close and lowered his head, so his face was on level with hers. "Yeah, so did I." Taking a deep breath he glanced back at the boat and Zac, who was standing at the back with his arms crossed, watching them. He let out the breath with a whoosh. "Sorry. I'm just under a lot of pressure right now."

He clearly wasn't ready to tell her any more, so she dropped her shorts and strode out into the water. The cool embrace on her sun-warmed skin felt too good to hold on to her resentment. Instead she focused on how lucky she was to be paid to spend time in such a beautiful place and waded further into the delicious water.

There was something irresistible about the beauty of the beach and the radiant blue sky that made her want to shed her bikini and lay her body out like a sacrifice. It was almost too tempting to feel the caress of the water on her nakedness, to cool her body to the point where the sun's heat would feel like a delicious caress over every inch of her skin.

Instead, Keira settled for a quick dip. Once the water reached her ribs and the water depth levelled off, she turned and swam back to the shallows.

When she could feel the sandy bottom with her hands, she rolled onto her back, shoulders out of the water, watching the sun rippling through the wavelets making patterns on her skin, cool water lapping at her nipples through the wet fabric. She closed her eyes, so engrossed in the gentle swish of the waves she didn't hear him swim up to her.

"Is this an invitation?" His voice came from between her legs and she slit open her eyes to see him floating on his stomach in front of her. The man was infuriating. How did he manage to make her want him so badly after he'd acted like a complete ass? Despite herself, she wished they were both naked and that he would crawl his way up her body until...

"It wasn't meant as one. I'm not into grumpy men. And after yesterday at the pool, I got the impression you were being faithful to Chloe." If that didn't get a confession out of him, she didn't know what would.

He rolled over onto his back beside her and gazed out over the water. "Chloe and I had an argument. It was more than an argument. The engagement is off."

Holy moly, *he had come clean with her.* Holey moly, Ravi was right about the engagement. Or the email he hacked was. He'd been wrong about the gambling though...

"Oh. I'm sorry to hear that," Keira said, careful to keep her voice level.

"Are you?" He turned his head so he could study her face.

"I'm sorry she hurt you," Keira said, careful not to give her thoughts and feelings away.

"And I'm sorry I acted like an ass today. I didn't want you to think I hired you to hit on you, but God Keira, you are so gorgeous. It's been torture and the last thing I want to do is cross the line."

She glanced at him, not believing it could be that simple. "And that made you behave like an asshole?"

"Yes, and I'm sorry. I respect that you pulled me up when we first met. Just because I'm paying for your time doesn't mean you owe me anything beyond professional courtesy."

"Well, thanks for clearing that up. And you're right. I'm not for sale." Keira took a deep breath and made her confession, come what may. "But I have to be honest. If you weren't so moody, I might like it if you *didn't* keep your hands to yourself."

"Really?" He looked at her with a slow smile full of smouldering promise.

Keira's stomach turned upside down. She'd just crossed the line herself. If she'd written it in pretty writing on one of her mother's fancy notecards, she couldn't have given him any more of an invitation.

Aryan blinked and his smile faded. "I guess it's a defence mechanism. I meet a lot of women who only want to get close to me for what my money will buy them, or the fame they think they'll get."

"I can understand that." Butterflies erupted in her belly. Aryan's honesty and trust was a potent aphrodisiac, heightened by his proximity, his gorgeous body almost naked beside her.

The realisation that her fantasy might actually become a reality surged through her veins like adrenalin. *He wasn't engaged! And* there was the confidentiality agreement. If this job wasn't going to be her big break, maybe it could be the weekend of her dreams.

"What if I said that I want you too? That whatever happens between us, I'm going into this with my eyes open, aware that it's only for whatever is left of our time here." *Had she just said that out loud?* Oh lord, she had, and she was more excited than a kid at Christmas.

"Sounds good to me. Truce then? I promise I'll be myself, and we'll see where this leads."

Tingles of anticipation rippled out from her abdomen. *He'd apologised… he felt the same attraction she did…* And the reason she was here with Aryan at all, would also protect her reputation. No-one would ever know…

Keira glanced at the boat to see if Zac was watching them. He was, intently, but he seemed relaxed, reclining on the back seat of the boat with his arms outstretched along the cushions. *Huh…*

Aryan floated his hand on the surface until his arm stretched over her, then slowly lowered it to the sand, turning so he was suspended over her.

Keira looked deep into his eyes. He was so close she could see the golden flecks in the deep brown iris, the lust she'd sensed on full display in his expression. She took a shuddering breath, yearning to feel his mouth on hers, his hands on the water-cooled skin of her bare breasts, his erection pressed between her parted thighs.

"Tonight then?" Aryan pushed backward and stood, knee deep in the water, offering her his hand with a smile.

She took it and stood, her body trembling with need. A retreating wavelet sucked the sand from under her feet and she rocked forward unsteadily, her breasts brushing against his chest. Anticipation and desire shot through her body like an electric current, and she licked suddenly dry lips. The sun reflecting off the ocean and white sand was dazzling bright, but Aryan's pupils dilated as he watched the movement of her tongue. *He felt it too, so why was he waiting?*

In an act of defiance, she stepped back, determined she would not be the only one aching for release when they finally got naked. *Tonight.* Keira added a seductive sway to her hips as she walked up the beach to their towels. She *felt* him behind her, stalking her like a lion after a potential mate. She turned and threw him his towel then used hers to dry her belly, up over her ribs, pushing her breasts upward and drying them thoroughly while he watched, mesmerised. *Would he make a move in front of Zac?*

With a muttered curse, he stepped forward and took her in his arms, roughly taking her mouth with his for a deep, hungry kiss. Desire shot from where his tongue danced with hers, charging through her body until it pierced her sex with a sweet burn. Keira melted against him and moaned into his mouth.

"I take that as a yes?" he said with a slow smile. He slowly drew back and passed his towel behind his hips, wrapping it around his waist and bringing her attention to the eager bulge in his swim shorts.

"Oh, yes." Her eyes flicked over his shoulder to where Zac stood on the deck. Watching.

"SHE BOUGHT IT." Aryan sat heavily in the armchair opposite Zac, the sound of Keira in the shower in the room next door a taunting tattoo in his brain.

"So, we're on for tonight?"

Aryan rubbed his hands through his hair, torn between wanting to expose Keira and wanting to protect her. "I can't do it." Even though the evidence proved otherwise, he couldn't believe she was like Chloe and the others. There was an honesty and sincerity about her. It was impossible to picture her sneaking around and blackmailing anyone. Could she really be that good an actor? "No sex."

Zac shook his head, concern creasing his brow. "Shit man, you still care about her, even knowing she's been talking to Ravi. Even after what she did?"

"Yes." Aryan squeezed the bridge of his nose, hoping the pressure would ground his whirling thoughts. "No. I just don't think she should get caught up in the shit storm that is my life." He knew what it felt like to have your face plastered across the media for the wrong reasons. When it was bad, it was as if the world had ended—or you wished it had.

"You know what Ravi is capable of. Even after you took the fall for him crashing that car in Vegas, he went back on his promise to go to rehab. His coke habit ruined your career. Anyone who associates with him deserves what they get."

He hardly recognized his brother now. Yes, the addict Ravi would do or say anything to get what he wanted. But Aryan wouldn't.

"I won't fuck her." Aryan held up his hand to stop the argument he knew was coming. "I will do what I can to get her in a compromising position. Make whatever you can out of it. Be creative, like she did with us." He couldn't let that photo of Zac and him get back to his father, or he would lose the only things he still had to care about. His father's respect for as long as he had left, and the future of NadarTec.

"Okay. I'll do what I can then. I've already organized everything. You'll have dinner at the villa, with her dressed as Keira, not Chloe, otherwise we won't have anything to bargain with."

"Whatever you get, you'll only show her and only to shut her up. No way is the media to get hold of it." The water in the shower turned off. Aryan took a deep breath and stood. He pulled out his phone to take another look at the photos of Keira her agency had sent him. Regret twisted in his gut. He needed her to look like this tonight, like herself, which would make it both easier and more difficult to do what needed to be done. "She wouldn't have brought any of her own clothes. I'll go to the boutique and find something she would normally wear."

He headed for the door with a sense of dread pressing on his shoulders.

Tonight would be the biggest gamble of his life. And the last. Unlike before, he felt no excitement at the risk, even though the stakes were higher than they had ever been.

He was no longer an addict. This time he would not stake everything to win.

KEIRA SPENT what should have been a relaxing couple of hours in the shade of the jasmine-covered terrace *trying* to read, but all she could think about was the coming night. Tossing the book on the coffee table on the way to her room, she decided to use some of her restless energy to prepare for what could be one of the more memorable evenings of her life. She was about to go on a date with man she'd lusted after for years and never expected to meet, let alone have a tryst with.

She hadn't seen Aryan since they'd returned to the villa after the boat trip so she spent the afternoon with growing anticipation as she exfoliated and moisturized her body and her face until she glowed as much on the outside as inside. She applied the light, natural makeup Chloe favored with extra care and styled her hair just so, assuming they would dine at the restaurant before returning to the villa to explore their 'understanding'.

When Keira stepped out of the bathroom, naked except for brief panties and glorying in the freedom of the tropical air, she found an evening dress laid out on the bed.

She stopped and stared at it in confusion. A poolside dress, one piece of fabric to wrap the body, in exquisitely fine silk. But the color! She lifted the fabric to drape against her sun-kissed skin. Blood red, a color Chloe never wore, according to the look-book she'd consulted like a bible since she scored the job. Picking up the note-card, she drank in Aryan's neat handwriting, imagining his lips curving up in a smile as he composed the invitation.

Dear Keira. When you're ready, please join me for dinner on the patio. Off the clock, come as yourself. Aryan.

This was it. Keira slid her arms into the delicate shoe string straps, and wrapped the sensuous fabric over her exfoliated and moisturized skin. Quivering with anticipation of Ayran unwrapping her later, she secured the dress with just the one thin tie and stepped into the gold high-heel sandals. Chloe only wore silver.

She had brought only Chloe-style jewelry with her, so she went without, leaving her décolletage and ears unadorned. On impulse, she opened her handbag and pulled out her go-to lipstick, a deeper red than the dress.

Gripping the gorgeous ring, she twisted and pulled until she'd removed the last trace of the girl she had been pretending to be. She left Chloe's engagement ring on the dresser, then quickly twisted and pinned her long hair into *her* usual French roll, leaving her neck and shoulders bare and exposed. With a last look at herself in the mirror and a deep breath, she turned and walked to the sliding door that led to the terrace, the delicious slide of the silk on her skin a foreshadowing of the caresses she yearned for. It felt surreal to step out onto the terrace as herself, strange to have Aryan turn to smile so completely that his dimple showed - for *her*.

Dressed beautifully in fitted trousers and shirt unbuttoned at the neck, Aryan's skin glowed warm in contrast to the pale lemon of the fine woven fabric. Keira paused and tried to record the moment, the sultry evening, the last traces of day glowing gold and crimson on the horizon, the delicious anticipation, her date. Intelligent, passionate, sexy as hell. If Keira had the power to conjure her perfect man, it would be Aryan.

"I hope you don't mind if we eat here," he said, gesturing smoothly to a candlelit table for two. "It's such a beautiful spot, and we can relax and be ourselves away from the staff and other guests."

"It's perfect," Keira said, placing her hand on his shoulder and kissed his cheek lightly, the impatient desire coiling through her body urging her to skip dinner, to take his hand and lead him inside to her bed. "Thank you for the dress, but I'm confused. Isn't there a chance someone will see us—you with a woman who isn't Chloe?"

"Speaking of the dress. Wow. You look gorgeous." The muscle beneath her hand held a tension that didn't match his warm smile. "It would be worth it even if someone did see us, but don't worry, your bonus is safe—unless you decide to go against the contract and tell people about all this." His voice was jovial but his eyes were sharp as he held her gaze. "I've sent Zac out to make sure no one gets close."

Keira dropped her hand, his reference to the reason they were on the island denting her fantasy. As long as she was under contract, they could never be just a guy and a girl. And they wouldn't be completely alone.

Aryan turned to pour two glasses of champagne and handed her a glass and she could see the weariness in his eyes. Bloody

Ravi. What a piece of work. Keira would do what she could to help make sure he didn't get control.

At least it was in her power to make him forget his worries–if only for a short time.

Aryan placed his hand tentatively on hers, his touch rekindling the barely banked arousal from the afternoon. "Do you forgive me for being difficult to get along with before?"

She turned her hand so their palms met and smiled. "Forgiven."

He picked up her hand and kissed it, the expression in his eyes promising he would make it up to her.

The brush of his warm, soft lips on her knuckles made her belly flip.

Gently releasing her hand, Aryan lifted his glass. "To starting over," his mouth said, but his eyes were saying *to getting naked.*

Keira raised her glass to touch his. "To starting over." She took a sip and worried the rest of the weekend would not be long enough. How difficult would it be to say good-bye, even before the intimacy they would share? "You don't think it–this–is too soon? After the breakup I mean. Or am I your rebound girl?"

Aryan turned to one of the chairs and pulled it out, offering her a seat, a frown dimming the desire from his expression. "Actually, I'm not on the rebound." he paused.

Keira tilted her head, inviting him to continue.

"Chloe was a wanna-be model when I met her. Our engagement was a business arrangement. She agreed to help me convince my father I was settled and in return she would get her big break by being linked with me." Aryan took a deep breath and stood still, his hand tight on the back of the chair.

Keira's heart soared to learn their's hadn't been a love match, but darn it, it was the exact same reason she was here with Aryan this weekend. For her big break. *Was she any better than Chloe?* She paced, too restless to sit.

Poor Aryan, it couldn't be easy, constantly having to assess everyone's motives. The only person he could rely on was Zac. With a start of surprise, Keira realized she wanted to be that for him too. And without Chloe in the picture, maybe there was a chance for more than one night of hot sex. She stopped and turned to face him. "So, you don't love her?"

"I don't even really know her."

"What happened?" she asked, her voice soft. "Why isn't she here? Did she go back on the agreement?"

Aryan looked at her steadily for a minute before staring out into the dark night. "She started an affair with her married agent. I begged her to wait, to put it on hold for a month, told her that we didn't need to go ahead with the wedding, it was enough to keep up the act until after father announced his successor. But she wouldn't wait. I had to get creative. I'm sorry I didn't tell you the truth from the start, but I couldn't risk it. Saving my father's company from Ravi selling it off in pieces is my priority. I need everyone to believe I've settled down and can be trusted to step in as CEO."

Keira reached across and placed her hand on his where it was curled into a fist on the back of the chair. "I understand. I have some experience with family pressure. My father disinherited me because I chose to be an actor. I can't believe she let you down like that. You must be angry?"

"I am, especially as my parents had planned to fly in from India soon to meet her." Aryan ran fingers through his hair, the ensuing untidiness making his seem more human, less god-like.

"I'll marry you." Keira blurted out, his vulnerability touching her deeper than his strength had and making her instinctively want to help him.

Aryan looked appalled, but she resisted the impulse to pull her hand from his.

Ninny. Of course, he wouldn't want to marry a stranger after he'd just taken that gamble and lost. "Pretend to, I mean!" She corrected with an encouraging smile. "To help you get what you deserve. I'll be Chloe and meet your parents."

"You would do that?"

"I would. And pro bono too." Keira winked at Aryan, relieved that she could help in this small way, that she could do something to soothe her own feelings of guilt for even listening to Ravi.

"Thank you. But why?"

"I have a confession to make too. I haven't been entirely honest with you, either." Keira pulled her hand back and fiddled with her bare ring finger.

"Oh?" His eyebrows drew together, his gaze piercing hers as if he was trying to see more than her thoughts.

"Your brother approached me yesterday. He told me the engagement was off."

Keira would have understood if he'd reacted with anger or disappointment, but she didn't expect the look of calm, almost satisfaction, that smoothed Aryan's features. "Ravi knows," he said, a statement, not a question.

"Yes, but he can't prove it," she assured him. "He asked me to help him. He wanted me to get him evidence of a sexual relationship between you and Zac, and proof that you are still gambling."

"He's after anything to convince Dad not to make me CEO. He didn't ask you to tell the media about our arrangement?"

"No, he must know I'm bound by a confidentiality agreement. But I did something I regret. I took a photo of you and Zac in bed together. It's pretty incriminating."

"You did?" Again, more a statement than a question. His glance darted around the garden surrounding the patio, as if he would find Ravi hiding there, listening, taking photos of him with a woman who obviously was not his fiancé.

"I didn't intend to give it to him. I took it because it was a beautiful image of you both. There's only one and I'll delete it. The last thing I want is anyone else seeing it."

"Thank you." Aryan said with a frown, his gaze still darting through the dark.

Keira reached out to him, laying her hand on his cheek, bringing his focus back to her.

"What is it between you and Ravi? Does he not care about your father?"

"The Ravi you met is not a reasonable person. He's a drug addict."

"Oh. I'm sorry." Having met him, she'd suspected as much.

"The addiction amplifies his weaknesses. He may not be the brother I grew up with, but he's still my twin. I'm familiar with how his mind works. He expected to be handed control of the company when our father retired, and he resents there's a chance I may get it instead. He thinks I'm the enemy, that because I was born first, I'm the favorite. He believes that by beating my addictions, I've proven that I'm the stronger, and his only chance to win is by being devious."

Keira wished she could smooth the creases of worry from between his brows. "Maybe you can relax and forget about him for a few hours? He's not on the island anymore. He said he had a boat waiting to take him back to the mainland after he spoke to me."

"Oh. It's not Ravi I'm worried about, it's Zac." Aryan's distraction confirmed that Ravi was right about his relationship status with Zac as well as Chloe.

Zac was out there—was he watching them right now?

Keira dropped her hand to her side. Things were about to get very complicated, but she had made her decision on the beach this afternoon when she accepted Zac as part of the Aryan package. Now she'd found the man behind the celebrity, she suspected her feelings would grow into something more complex than physical desire. It may be that Aryan's affections were already engaged elsewhere, but he was strongly attracted to her, and she'd never met anyone else who could flick the switch of her desire on with a mere glance. Surely a small part of Aryan would be better than nothing. Other men paled in comparison.

Aryan reached for her hand and clasped it in both of his. "Your honesty means everything to me. You know, since I was first singled out as a talent in the team, women have been using me for whatever they could get. I had a feeling you were different. You've just proven you're not like them."

"You're right. I'm not." For the sake of her happiness and his, she would try to share this gorgeous, complex man. "Let me help you."

"Okay. Thank you." He squeezed her hand and his smile warmed his eyes.

Keira's breath stuttered. He might be involved with Zac, but the look in his eyes told her he wanted *her* in his bed. She wasn't playing Chloe now. She was off duty, so she could be herself and enjoy Aryan's company. This had nothing to do with him paying her. Tonight was just *about* her and Aryan—and Zac if he wanted to watch.

"Do you like oysters?" The low, gruff timbre of Aryan's voice made her shiver as if the slightly callused skin of his fingertips were caressing the sensitive skin of her back.

"I do." The prospect of sharing an aphrodisiac with Aryan made her wet with anticipation.

"To our 'engagement'," he said with a devilish smile and lifted his glass to touch hers.

CHAPTER ELEVEN

KEIRA TILTED her head back to take a sip of champagne, and Aryan fought the impulse to rain kisses over the smooth skin of long, delicate neck. *Not now.*

The thought of having access to every inch of her naked skin almost drove him to abandon their dinner, but Zac was out there somewhere with his camera. And now he didn't want Zac to get any incriminating evidence. Aryan wanted to make her make love to Keira until she moaned his name, but not tonight. He would wait until they had privacy—and plenty of time.

The first glass was too easy to drink and gave him a pleasant buzz. Watching Keira tip an oyster into her mouth and lick her lips mesmerized him. He did the same. When she sucked his salty fingers into his mouth, he forgot all about food, his resolution, and Zac.

He moved closer, his gaze locked on her lips, took her face in his palms and kissed her mouth as if he was sipping the nectar of a rare flower. And when Keira kissed him back, he could tell by the languid way her tongue danced with his, her breath quickening and her nipples hardening against his chest… the way her hips ground against his so his cock pressed against the delicious cleft between her legs… the way she moaned deep in her throat… that she wouldn't care if he made love to her right here, for anyone passing to see. For Zac to see. *Shit.*

Zac was out there, in the garden, his lens pointed in their direction, no doubt already snapping away.

Aryan pulled back. He didn't need leverage against Keira anymore, but he couldn't just go and find Zac and tell him to stop.

He stepped away and Keira swayed toward him, but he held her steady with a strong hand on her upper arm. Aryan pulled her seat out a little further, a repentant bow to his head. "Sorry for getting distracted. You're way too sexy. Shall we sit and eat? I believe there is an excellent lobster bisque here somewhere."

She took her seat, looking flushed and confused and so damned sexy he had to distract himself by checking under the silver domes for their entrees.

Aryan sat and ate his soup without registering the rich flavors. It had seemed so simple when he and Zac had hatched the plan months ago, but the tangles just got more complex every day, to the point where he wondered how he would ever unravel them. He wanted to make love to Keira more than almost anything, almost more than saving his family's business, but if he gave in to his craving now, he would miss the chance to come clean and to start an honest relationship with her.

He glanced across Keira and found her soup untouched, a bread roll shredded to scraps on her plate. It was the first time he'd seen her pick at her food.

"Are you okay? Did you get too much sun today?" Aryan poured Keira a glass of water and placed it in front of her, laying his palm on her forehead to check her temperature.

She shook his hand off and stood, her eyes glittering—with lust, not fever.

"I'm so turned on, all I can think about is feeling your hands on my body." Pulling the tie on her wrap dress, she shrugged out of it so she stood before him, naked except for a scrap of fabric concealing her sex, and her sandals. "Or had you forgotten what we discussed on the beach?"

Aryan sprang to his feet, his gaze raking her from neck to toe and back to her face. Blood left his head in a rush his cock surged to attention. Fuck! Why had he chosen a dress that could be discarded with a bloody tug? Groaning, he reached out and gripped her by the waist. Her skin felt smoother than the silk she's just discarded and he yearned to draw her hips close so that her sex was flush with his erection, but instead he lifted her away.

She gasped, her hands flying up to cover her gorgeous breasts. "You've changed your mind? You don't want to?"

The hurt on her face speared his heart. He held his hands out in supplication. "I do, so much, but I'm worried it will ruin everything. We should wait." Those three words felt like the hardest he'd ever had to say. He dropped to a squat and retrieved the puddle of dress from around her gorgeous feet, wishing he could worship her as the goddess he saw her as.

Not yet.

"Don't feel like you need to protect me. I know about Zac."

Aryan looked up in shock and experienced a moment of pure ecstasy at the sight of her long, supple body filling his vision. She knew Zac was out there, yet she'd given him an unmistakable invitation? Aryan stood, leaving her dress on the pavers. "You do?" he said, his eyes searching hers for confirmation.

Keira took a slow step forward that brought he luscious, naked body flush with his. She cupped his jaw in her palms and brought her lips to his ear. "I think it's hot."

With her words and her warm breath in his ear, all rationality fled. His cock pressed almost painfully against the layers that separated him from the heaven her body and her words promised. Mad joy filled him, a surge of rightness he hadn't felt since he'd last sent a ball flying over 100 meters while a world of admirers watched.

If it turned her on to think that Zac was out there and taking photos of them, so be it.

He almost laughed with elation. *Anything to keep my 'fiancé' happy.*

And holy fuck, he *wanted* a record of all the different ways he was going to give her pleasure.

KEIRA'S HANDS bumped with Aryan's as they both sought to free him from his shirt. Pulling it out of his trousers, tearing at it until the buttons pinged at their feet, she bent and took one of his nipples between her lips. He bucked his hips against hers, and she thrilled with triumph. *He was hers… at least for tonight.*

He slipped his shirt off as she unbuckled his belt and unzipped his fly, then he toed out of his loafers and slipped off his trousers. He stopped and stood before her, naked but for his tented boxer shorts, as if checking to make sure she wanted to take the final step to nakedness and carnal pleasure.

Damn, but he was gorgeous—god-like—with or without his clothes. The scar twisting around his thigh from knee to groin did not detract from his beauty but served as a reminder of his passions. Seeing his tawny skin cooled to marble by the moonlight made her yearn to see him in every possible light. She wanted to wake every day to the warmth of his body next to hers, to sleep, spent and sweaty in his arms, every night.

She stepped out of her panties and awareness fluttered over her skin beneath burning intensity of his gaze. When he reached for his trousers and pulled a condom out of the pocket, the absolute proof that he *did* want her, wanted *this*, sent a thrill through her.

She moved close and slid her hands inside his boxers, over his firm butt, pushing the fabric down over his muscled thighs to his knees so he could step out of them. Straightening, she stepped out of her sandals and waited, completely bare, an offering to her god.

Who groaned and moved close, the silken head of his penis nudging her belly as covered her mouth with his. His lips were soft yet demanding, his tongue setting off tremors of desire beneath her skin, making her nipples sensitive to the breeze and the tickle of his chest hairs, engorging her sex and her clit so she throbbed for his touch.

With his mouth and his body, he steered her to the sun lounge and urged her to lie back on the cushion. Hooking one of her legs up as he knelt, he lowered his mouth to her sex. She groaned and bucked her hips as his tongue found her clit. Tilting her head back, she stared up at the velvet blackness of the sky and the diamond shower of stars, abandoning herself to pleasure. With a light, slow, feather touch at first, he teased her, each stroke a little firmer and faster until she writhed beneath his mouth. Registering her need for more, he slipped two fingers into her pussy, hooking up to caress the inside of her where his tongue stroked her clit.

Feeling as if she was about to float away, Keira reached behind her and grasped the back of the chair, lifting her hips high. Pleasure swept away every sense except the feel of his mouth on her sex, her pussy pulsing around his fingers, her body shuddering with release.

Not until the contractions of her pleasure subsided did he stand and roll the condom over his cock. Picking up a cushion from one of the chairs, he held out his hand for her to take and helped her to perch on the top of the rendered wall that divided the paved terrace from the sand.

Spreading her legs, she took hold of his hips, and pulled him close so the tip of his cock nudged her engorged entrance. Wrapping her legs around his butt she pulled him hard against her, burying his shaft deep.

"Fuck," she ground out as he filled her, feeling as if being possessed by him had unlocked some untapped, primitive part of her soul.

Aryan paused for a moment at the unfamiliar profanity, then groaned and thrust deep and hard with a growl of possession.

Keira moaned as he nudged a place deep inside where she had yearned for him. "You feel so good.. so hard."

She rocked her hips to maximize the pleasure of his cock inside her, guiding his hips away and back, demanding he take over the rhythm and velocity. She leant back on her hands and arched her back, giving herself over to the sensations of Aryan's cock stroking her, escalating the warm pleasure, hurtling down the path to delicious release. And it came like the roar of a wildfire, searing her with the intensity of their connection.

Rocking slowly inside her, Aryan urged her to ride her orgasm to its full extent.

Filled with warm bliss, Keira took the base of his penis and guided him out while keeping the condom in place. Releasing him, she stood and indicated the sun lounge with a tilt of her head. "Sit. It's my turn."

ARYAN'S COCK swelled painfully at the sight of his blonde goddess, long legs naked but for her gold high heels, pussy bare so he could plainly see her engorged, glistening labia.

"You are perfection. No woman deserves you as her body double."

Submitting to the force of her hands on his chest, Aryan lay back and got a close up of her pink sex as she swung her leg over him. When she straddled him and lowered herself onto his cock, he had to resist the impulse to thrust. Instead, he groaned and clenched his jaw, hard, as she took the backrest of the chair for support and raised herself, milking him with her tight pussy then pushing down with a forceful determination that blew his mind.

Fuck. It was the sexiest thing he'd ever seen, her breasts heaving as she raised and lowered herself on his shaft as if she was doing low squats at the gym. He couldn't stop his gaze dropping to where his cock slid in and out of her hairless slit, even though he knew it would be the beginning of his end. He leant forward, and with that sight burnt onto his eyelids, took one of her nipples in his mouth, rolling and flicking the tight nub with his tongue as he rolled the other between his fingers, until pleasure made her movements eratic and jerky.

"Fuck," Keira growled in his ear as she clenched around his cock, the sound of that word coming from her usually sweet mouth snapping his tightly held control. Unable to remain still, he thrust into her, abandoning himself to the mindless pleasure of coming inside his woman.

EARLY THE NEXT MORNING, Aryan met up with Zac in the kitchen.

"I see you decided to go the full monty last night." Zac slapped him on the back and pushed his laptop across the counter. "Good work. I have more than we need."

Aryan swiped through the images and scrubbed his fingers through his hair. *Fuck, they were hot.* The actress, perched on the low wall, body arched in ecstasy, the only point of contact where Aryan's cock impaled her. And another… Keira with her knee bent and Aryan's very recognizable face buried in her bare pussy.

The sight of what he and Keira had done together brought the physical memory back with a rush. His cock twitched at the memory of the feel her naked skin against his, her tight pussy clenched around his cock.

"Not the reactions of a woman being fucked by a gay man," Zac said and whistled through his teeth. "Great show, by the way. I had to take myself in hand when you finally finished."

"Too much information, man." Aryan shook his head.

"It's like she posed on purpose."

"She did. She knew you were taking photos."

"How do you know?"

"She told me. She said it was hot, and as she'd already offered to delete the photo of us…"

"How did she find out about me taking photos?"

Aryan cleared his throat and flipped the computer closed. "I have no idea, but we're not using these. And we won't need to hire any more actors."

"What?" Zac thrust his hands on his hips and frowned.

"Keira has offered to pose as my fiancé when my parents come for dinner. Thanks for going above and beyond, man, but I'd appreciated it if you could copy them onto a thumb-drive and delete all other copies." He might not need them anymore, but he would certainly enjoy admiring them whenever he had a spare moment.

"Yeah, no problem. It was no hardship." Zac grinned at him. "And now I can say 'I told you so'. I told you she's perfect for you."

"I just hope she can forgive me when I tell her was never a fiancé for her to fill in for."

CHAPTER TWELVE

THE MOOD in the jet for the flight back to LA was very different from three days earlier. Keira's companions were both quiet but relaxed. If Zac knew what was going on with her and Aryan–whatever 'it' was–he seemed okay with it. She never imagined she would be part of a three-way relationship, but she was willing to give it a go–for Aryan.

When the stewardess had cleared the lunch service, Aryan unbuckled his seatbelt, stood and held his hand out to Keira. She glanced at Zac, who looked at Aryan, nodded and left the cabin, closing the door behind him without a word being exchanged.

Keira placed her hand in his and his touch lit her up like a beacon. Memories of what they'd done last night–and what had followed in the bedroom in the early hours of the morning–rekindled the need that he had thoroughly sated only hours before.

When he led her to the low lounge beneath the cabin windows, she followed him, eager for the chance to feel his lips on hers, on her neck, her breasts… anywhere he wanted. Her desire for him was so intense, there was no room for thoughts of anything apart from his touch. Certainly no room to care if someone walked in on them.

Keira sat beside him, close, so her thigh ran along his, the heat of him radiating through the fine wool of his pants and thin silk of her maxi-dress. Was he going to kiss her here, lay her down and make love to her? Was that why Zac had left?

But Aryan's gorgeous, dark eyes were serious, his lips tensed as if he was about to say something he would rather not. *Pickles, he wasn't going to tell her it was over between them, was he?* That it was over the moment they left the island. Surely, he would wait until *after* she met his parents.

"There's something I need to…" he started to say.

"Please, not now." Keira placed a finger against his lips and got lost in the warm luscious feel of them. His kiss was all she wanted to think about. Whatever it was he wanted to say, she didn't want to hear it. Not yet. She wanted these last few hours to be perfect. When they landed back in LA she would have to go back to the real world of her cramped apartment and her routine of auditions and thrown-together dinners.

Taking her hand, he pressed it against his mouth before entangling his fingers with hers and laying the union in her lap.

Keira stared at their joined hands and told herself she was in a better place than she had been a week ago. Life would be easier now. Thanks to the fee from this job she could be more selective about the roles she applied for. And if the public never suspected it wasn't Chloe at *Cielo en el Sol* this weekend, maybe she'd have a nicer place to live soon too.

Don't think about how impossible this *is.*

She looked up into Aryan's face. At least she could look forward to seeing him when she would play Chloe for his parents.

"Let's just see how things play out. Once you are secure as CEO of NadarTec, we can all sit down and debrief, okay?" She gave him a convincingly bright smile.

"Are you sure?" Aryan frowned but looked relieved.

"You just worry about your work and making this dinner with your parents a success. There's something I'd much rather do than talk for the rest of the flight." Keira slipped her hand over the smooth, warm skin of the back of his neck.

Aryan sighed and closed his eyes as she dug her fingertips into the short hair at his nape, his lips parting as she stood, gathered her skirt and straddled his legs. He half opened his eyes as she settled on his lap and tilted his head back to watch her lips descend. "You'll see the death of me, *Priya*."

Sliding down the lounge, he grasped her by the hips and urged Keira higher on his lap, so her sex brushed his erection.

"A girl can hope," she whispered against his lips, yearning for a perfect world where they could do this every day, until the end of their natural lives.

AS IT TURNED out Keira didn't have to wait long to see Aryan again. He surprised her the night after they returned from Mexico with a knock on her door and the delicious aroma of garlic, melted butter and curry. The sight of him at her doorway was one of the sweetest experiences of her life and she drank in the sight of him, almost forgetting to invite him inside.

"Take-away?" Keira asked, eyeing the paper bags he carried as she stepped aside to let him into her original 1950's kitchen.

"Oh, no. Home made." He grinned and placed the bags on the small Formica dining table, his eyes not leaving her face.

"By you?"

"Of course," he said and glanced around, taking in the tiny space, the living room not much more than a wide hallway leading to the single bedroom.

"Gorgeous *and* domesticated?" Keira asked, squeezing his arm to distract him from her modest home. It was cozy, but so different to what he must be used to. So different from where she'd come from too.

"That's me." Aryan's grin and accompanying wink set off a chain of reactions in Keira's body.

As much as she wished they could skip dinner and use her dining table for something even more delicious, she didn't want to disrespect Aryan's efforts, and it did smell heavenly. She took plates and cutlery out and handed them to Aryan. "Would you set the table? I think I have a bottle of Riesling in the fridge if you'd like a glass?"

"Perfect," he said and made short work of laying the table while she opened the wine.

Keira was tempted to ignore the insistent ringing of her phone, but she'd been hoping to hear from Jude about a sitcom pilot she'd auditioned for the week before. "Sorry, I need to get this."

"Point me to the wine glasses," Aryan said with a smile, taking the bottle from her hands.

"Thank you," Keira said and opened the cupboard where she kept her glasses before grabbing her phone from her bag.

"Jude. You have good news, I hope? It must be something important if you're ringing tonight. Don't you have a *special* date?"

"I do, but this is even more exciting than cocktails with Valtteri. I got a call from Paramount."

"No!" Keira's heart raced and she dropped into her only armchair, suddenly dizzy. "I thought you were calling about the sitcom."

"This is even better. You got the support role in the movie!"

"What?? You don't mean Jutta?" It was the only role she'd read for Paramount.

"I do! They want you in their offices 9am tomorrow. Be ready for a big day. They've already started filming, but they couldn't decide between you and Amber, hence the short notice."

"You mean they chose me over Amber?" Keira couldn't believe it. She was an unknown, and they'd chosen her?

"That's it. I hope you're celebrating tonight." Jude chuckled. "But not too much."

"Oh, I intend to."

"Not too late. Don't want you looking tired tomorrow morning."

"I promise I'll be in bed early." Keira slanted a look at where Aryan had set out covered Pyrex dishes in the center of the table and poured the wine.

He looked back at her expectantly, and grinned.

"Thank you, Jude. I'll speak to you in the morning." Keira stood and dropped her phone on the bench. "I don't believe it." She leant on the bench and dropped her head to focus on breathing, so she didn't pass out.

"You look like you've had important news?" In a moment Aryan was behind her, his body and his breath warm against her. "You're shaking."

Keira turned to him with tears of joy filling her eyes.

"I am… It is. I just got the support role in 'All the Light'. I don't believe it. This is a dream role. I didn't even want to think about hoping I would get it." She shook her head to try to grasp her new reality. *This was her big break.* "Fuck."

Aryan chuckled. "I've only heard you swear once. Does that mean making love to me is as good as getting your dream role?"

Keira threw her arms around his neck and laughed in his chest. "Yes!"

"We should celebrate," he said and handed her the glass he'd brought over. "I think you need this."

Her hand shook as she took the glass and she drank in his beautiful face while she waited for him to pick the other one up.

"To your wonderful career," he said and clinked her glass, his gesture mirroring the pride and enthusiasm in his expression.

Keira took a healthy drink then grinned. Having Aryan here in her tiny apartment at the same time she got the news of her first major screen role made the moment perfect. "Let's eat. I'm starving and this smells heavenly." She pulled out one of the four mismatched chairs and sat as Aryan took a seat opposite.

"Would you dish up? My hands are still shaking."

"It will be my pleasure."

Keira watched as he expertly piled golden rice and vegetarian curry onto both plates and unwrapped a foil package of steaming Naan bread. She picked up her fork, eager to taste Aryan's cooking, the rich aromas grounding her light-headedness.

"Hmmm, this is so good," she said, still savoring the complex tastes of her first mouthful.

"I'm glad to see you're enjoying it. It's good to see a girl with a healthy appetite." He smirked and tucked into his own meal. "And there's plenty more. I brought enough for left-overs."

When they'd finished the first helping, Aryan refilled their glasses and placed his hand over hers, a serious look on his face. "I understand if getting this role means you won't be able to make it to the dinner with my parents."

"Oh, no. I wouldn't miss that for the world." Keira turned her hand in his and squeezed his fingers lightly, hoping the caress would lead to more. She was about to ask him what his plans were for the rest of the night when they were interrupted by the chiming of the doorbell.

"Come in," she sang out, feeling like nothing could spoil this moment, not even an intruder. What kind of robber would come into her modest home, especially when someone built like Aryan was here?

"Keira, that is very unwise," a familiar voice boomed from the doorway. "I brought you up to be smarter than that."

Her father's large but still vigorous frame filled the open doorway, and the kitchen suddenly felt decidedly crowded. "Oh. You have... company." His perceptive look took in the quality of her apartment, her dinner companion and their joined hands in a matter of seconds.

"Father," she said, her body stiffening, ready for conflict. She held on to Aryan's hand when he hinted at pulling away. The joy might be about to drain from her night, but she would not let her father's judgment dictate her actions.

The cheek of the man, telling her she was on her own and then invading her space.

At just on sixty, William Fox was as powerful in person as he was in business. Tall and broad with a full head of steel grey hair, her father often intimidated those he dealt with. But not Keira. Not anymore.

"Keira. Aryan," he nodded a greeting to them both.

"Aryan, this is my father, William Fox." Keira made the introductions without standing. "We were in the middle of dinner. Why didn't you call?"

Aryan gently peeled his hand from Keira's and stood to approach her father with his arm outstretched. "Mr. Fox," he said, and Keira was glad he didn't add *nice to meet you.*

Her father shook his hand and drilled him with an assessing look. Keira knew he was running through his knowledge of the ex-cricketer. *Womanizer, gambler…* engaged. *Shit.*

She stood, ready to volley accusations.

But when he released Aryan's hand and turned his laser gaze on his daughter, his voice was gentle. "I think it's time for us to talk. As you haven't answered my calls, I decided to come in person."

"There is enough here for three, if you'd like to join us," Aryan offered and glanced at Keira with a look of apology.

Keira frowned back at him, which he returned with a serene smile.

"Thank you. I'd love to but Winnie is expecting me," her father said, then turned to his daughter. "Your mother doesn't know I'm here."

"If Mom didn't send you, then why are you here?"

His hand floated up as if he was going to touch her arm, then dropped to his side.

"I want to apologize. It was unfair of me to expect you to give up your dream for mine. I want us to be a family again. I want you to move back home."

Keira glanced at Aryan who had drifted over to her bookshelf to give them some privacy then glared at her father. "How dare you barge in here after you threw me out and tell me what *you* want. I've made my life without you, and there's no way I'm moving back."

Her father took a step toward her his hands out, entreating. "I promise not to pressure you to work with us. I realize now how much you love acting."

"It's a bit late for that, Dad." Was he for real, or had mom guilted him into asking her to come home?

"I just want you to be happy. And safe."

"Thanks for the concern, but I'm going to buy my own place." Keira softened her voice a little at the entreaty on his face. She'd never seen her father look vulnerable before.

"Really? You must be doing well." His forehead creased with unfamiliar uncertainty.

"I am." Tears welled in her eyes at the sweet joy of telling her father she'd made it on her own. "I've just completed a lucrative job and my agent called earlier to let me know I have a support role in Paramount's latest movie, starting tomorrow."

Her father took another step, spreading his arms and inviting her into his embrace, his eyes glittering with an emotion that resembled pride. "That's wonderful, petal. You're a success."

Keira hesitated, yearning for the comfort of her father's embrace, but still angry at him for treating her more like an employee than a daughter.

"Please forgive me?" he entreated with a lowered head and moist eyes.

Keira stepped forward, knowing if they were going to have a chance at being a family again, she would have to meet him halfway. She'd been stubborn and headstrong, and she missed knowing she had her parent's support.

The familiar scent of his pine-scented aftershave and dry-cleaned suit took Keira back to the days before he'd started putting pressure on her to get better grades and study harder. The days when he'd taken her to the movies on weekends, and when she and her mother had gotten dressed up to accompany him to dinner or the theatre. Until he'd become too busy with the business and the only outings he had time for were corporate events that her mom refused to attend.

"Getting the role was the easy bit. Now I have to be a good actor." She smiled against his lapel, the tension of months of estrangement draining from her muscles.

"You'll be brilliant." He gave her a light squeeze and leant back. "Just know that your mom and I are there for you if you need anything. And that we're proud of you, whatever you do."

"Thank you, Dad. That means a lot to me." Keira smiled up at him, feeling more settled and ready to tackle the biggest day of her career.

"I'd better get home; your mom will be worried." He lifted a hand to her face and gently stroked her cheek before dropping his hand. "Will you come over for dinner soon? Tell us how it's going at the studio?"

"I'll call once I've settled in and know my schedule."

Her father released her and strode to the living room to shake Aryan's hand. "Nice to meet you. I was sorry to hear about your accident. It was a blow to world cricket."

"Thank you. I hope to meet you again, and Mrs. Fox, under less rushed circumstances."

Keira paused with her hand on the front doorknob. "You won't tell anyone you saw Aryan here, will you?"

Her father kissed her cheek. "I don't know what's going on, but I trust your judgment. I won't say a word."

CHAPTER THIRTEEN

ARYAN'S MALIBU home was barely visible from where the driver stopped to let Keira out, only the warm glow through the shrubs hinted that a residence was to be found amidst the verdant garden.

Adopting a loping walk, Keira followed the path lit by lights at ground level, and tried to submerge herself into Chloe's persona. She inhaled deep breaths of salty air and focused on the nearby murmur of the ocean to calm her nerves, but failed to banish the anxiety that had settled as a weight on her chest. Even though the engagement was a ruse, she couldn't help dreading Aryan's parent's disapproval of her for not being a suitable match–for not being Indian.

Aryan greeted her at the door, gorgeous as ever in a bespoke suit and crisp white shirt, open at the collar. He ushered her inside, past a large man dressed in a tailored suit standing with his back to the polished concrete wall, his hands behind his back, still as a statue. Momentarily, Keira wondered where Zac was, until Aryan leant in to kiss her on both cheeks.

His enticingly familiar scent took her back to their weekend in Mexico, of sultry nights and bare skin, until she channeled her mind to the job at hand. To convince Mr and Mrs Nadar she was Chloe Thompson.

Aryan's relaxed posture from their last meeting was gone, but the look of desire in his eyes confirmed that the floor length, navy halter-neck she'd decided on after spending her break combing the costume storage of Paramount was an acceptable compromise between classy and sensual.

Picking up her hand, he thumbed the engagement ring and looked deep into her eyes. "Tonight won't be what you're expecting. I apologize that I don't have time to explain. I just hope you'll forgive me."

"I'm sure your parents aren't that bad," she attempted to joke while resisting the urge to scratch an itchy spot on her scalp. She'd had to have her hair cut for her new role and borrowed a wig from the studio that was as close to Chloe's style as she could find. "Don't worry, I won't slip up. I've been rehearsing." Keira gave him a smile that quivered despite her brave words. What was Aryan apologizing for? Would his parents use some kind of torture akin to water-boarding to interview her for the position of future daughter-in-law?

Against the eventuality that they grilled her about her background, she'd carefully fabricated a story to go with the little she knew about Chloe, and rehearsed it until she almost believed she *was* Aryan's fiancé. She'd tried to Google Chloe Thompson, but nothing had come up except her link to Aryan. Hoping his parents didn't have access to personal information she didn't, she'd made up a fictional suburban story for the girl who had worked at Walmart whilst studying to be a teacher, until being discovered by a talent agent who was shopping in the store she worked in. Keira told herself it was acting and not lying, but under the circumstances it was a hard-sell.

Aryan gently squeezed her hand and led her over a seamless granite floor into a living room that was larger than her entire apartment. The double-storey room overlooked a romantically lit tropical garden and a large expanse of night sky, through an entire wall made up of large glass sheets.

Keira adopted Chloe's sweet-as-pie smile at the middle-aged Indian couple who sat on the low lounge with a view of the garden. They stood, his mother smoothing the front of her tailored trousers, his father pulling on his shirt cuffs. Keira smothered her surprise and berated herself for expecting traditional Indian clothes.

Aryan cleared his throat, the only hint that he was less than confident, his voice otherwise clear and strong. "Keira, I'd like you to meet my parents, Manish and Alaya Nadar."

Keira stiffened and resisted the urge to stare at Aryan. *Keira? What the fig?*

"Very pleased to meet you." Keira stepped forward and took their hands in turn, bowing her head respectfully and hoping they hadn't noticed the slip-up.

"Abbu, Ammu, may I introduce Keira Fox," Aryan said, putting emphasis on her name before turning to her with a mouthed *sorry*.

Manish looked confused and opened his mouth to say something, but Alaya beat him to it. "Aryan why don't you pour us all an aperitif?"

"Yes. Of course." He seemed relieved to have something to do other than confront the questioning look from his parents. But Keira wasn't so lucky. She tried not to fiddle with the wig as she avoided their searching looks, watching Aryan fumble for glasses in the vintage liquor cabinet.

Keira had never seen Aryan look flustered, but somehow he managed to be sexy even when awkward. *What the hell was he playing at, using her name instead of Chloe's?*

Aryan handed each of them a small glass of Pernod and they touched glasses to his toast. "To family," he said and tipped his head back, draining his glass.

Manish was the first to speak after a brief sip of his drink. "I thought your fiancé's name was Chloe," he asked, looking perplexed.

"Father, I'm sorry, I need to come clean with you. I know this could jeopardize my chance at being named your successor," Aryan paused and took a deep breath before continuing, "but there never was a fiancé. Chloe was the name of a model I hired to pretend to be my fiancé."

Keira nearly dropped her glass, her fingers nerveless, the liqueur like glue in her suddenly dry mouth. "What? So, Chloe never worked at Walmart?" Keira couldn't stop herself blurting out the one question to solidify amongst her whirling thoughts.

"Chloe Thompson doesn't exist…"

"Then who is this?" his father interrupted.

"Please, let me finish. Chloe Novak is a model just moved here from Croatia. I hired her to pretend to be my fiancé until after your successor is announced—to convince you that I've settled down." Aryan put his glass down on the coffee table and adjusted the collar of his shirt. "But she decided she wanted more than the fee we'd agreed upon."

"Again, I ask, who is this?" his father demanded, gesturing Keira with an elegant arc of his hand.

"Keira is an actor I hired because she superficially resembles Chloe Novak. And I've fallen in love with her." Aryan's words tumbled out of his mouth.

He couldn't have shocked Keira more. Chloe was a model he hired. *Chloe* Thompson *did not exist. There was no fiancé at all.*

"I am disappointed in you Aryan. To lie to us like this." His mother shook her head.

Aryan bowed his head beneath her disapproval but his posture didn't bend. "I'm sorry that I deceived you, but it was for good reason. We have bigger problems than a fake engagement, but I won't lie anymore. It's time you knew the truth."

Alaya turned to Keira with a frown. "Keira, you may prefer to wait for us in the dining room."

"I would like Keira to stay. I want her to know everything." Aryan lifted his chin high as if daring his parents to object.

Keira blinked, too stunned to move even if she wanted to.

"Tell me then. What are these bigger problems?" Despite her delicate appearance, Alaya's anger was formidable. "What could be worse than lying to your mother?"

"I'm sorry to tell you this, *Ammu,* but Ravi has been scheming to get control of the company and sell off the automation arm of NadarTec. He is a drug addict and not fit to head the company."

"And you are worthy of the position because you have given up gambling and beaten your dependence on painkillers?" Manish demanded.

"Yes. And I've been learning every aspect of the business, which is how I discovered Ravi's scheme."

"And you have proof of this scheme?" His father raised his eyebrows.

"Nothing concrete."

"We do." Alaya said with a raised eyebrow.

"You already know." Aryan looked as stunned as Keira felt. She felt like she was onset a real-life soap opera.

He stood unmoving and watched his mother cross the room and take him by the forearm. "We know about Ravi's plan to sell off part of the company. We also know about his drug problem. He has promised to get clean."

"He told you all of this?"

A knock sounded at the door and Manish nodded at the security guy to open it.

"We have known for months that he was negotiating with a number of rival companies to sell shares in our robotics operation. When we arrived yesterday we confronted him about it. If he'd succeeded, he planned to sell 49% of NadarTec. He knew that with the speed of growth in industrial robotics he wasn't capable of future-proofing the company without outside help."

"He could have talked to me. We could have worked out a way forward together." Aryan shook his head. "Stubborn…"

"I couldn't," Ravi's voice echoed from the direction of the entry hall. "How could I ask you to back me after I ruined your career… your life?"

Alaya brushed Ravi's shoulder as he walked past her and stopped facing his twin. Seeing them together, the disparity

Keira had noticed on the island was glaringly obvious. Ravi seemed a shrunken and faded version of Aryan, his skin colorless and slack, his body ravaged by his addiction.

"Ravi admitted he was driving the car when you were injured," Alaya said, her sad eyes leaving Ravi to focus on Aryan. "You should have told us."

"I was trying to protect you." Aryan said, exasperated, his hands outstretched to his brother.

"I know that now." Ravi reached out and took one of Aryan's hands, as if in supplication.

"But you didn't tell our parents that the engagement to Chloe was off? You saw the email. You saw me with Keira on the island." Aryan frowned in confusion.

"No, I didn't tell them. I knew you would tell them yourself when you saw them. We are brothers. When Keira didn't contact me, I knew she had told you what I'd asked her to do. Its one of the things I always resented about you, the way those close to you will do anything for you. It gave me a lot to think about. You know how to get the best people for the job and inspire loyalty, people like Zac and Keira. I realized you are the best candidate for CEO. But I want to help, to be involved, if you'll have me."

"Ravi, will you stay for dinner?" Alaya interjected. "We can talk more."

"I have a car waiting to take me to Promises. We should wait until I'm better."

Aryan stepped forward and pulled Ravi against his chest for a hug. "I'm glad you'll be close by." Ravi bowed his head on his brother's shoulder, and Aryan patted him on the back. "Be healthy brother. Get better and come and help me make our parents proud."

Alaya walked Ravi to the door and returned looking thoughtful. "I realize you did all this out of love for your brother and your father. Apart from this engagement business, we are proud of you, son. But there can be no more lies."

"I agree. No more lies," Aryan said and hugged his mother.

"We will speak more about the future later—after we have eaten." Manish said and glanced at Keira. "Let us get to know this girl you say you love, even though you have just recently met." He lowered his head respectfully and gestured for Keira to walk with him. The dining room overlooked a small interior pool surrounded by a lush garden oasis. Aryan and his mother followed behind and a discreet waiter seated them and poured water and wine.

"I prepared something traditionally American to celebrate," Aryan said as the waiter served succulent roast turkey with all the trimmings.

"I'm glad you still find time to cook." Alaya smiled fondly at her son, then turned to Keira. "You have tasted Aryan's cooking?"

Keira blushed, remembering the night they finished the rest of Aryan's delicious curry cold, naked in her small double bed. "I have. He's a very good cook." She resisted looking at Aryan, knowing she would turn beet-red if she saw the memory of pleasure in his expression.

"He learnt from his *dadu*—his grandfather," Alaya said, her voice soft with affection.

"I thought you might like a traditional American meal," Aryan said and Keira was grateful to him for moving the focus back to himself.

Dinner passed by in a blur of questions from his parents about her real family and her childhood. At first it was difficult to abandon the persona she'd carefully prepared and psyched herself into, but she gradually relaxed with their genuine interest to tell them about Keira Fox. She told them about being an only child of very busy parents, of weekends spent with her cousins, about her fledgling career as an actor despite the pressure to join her family's business.

"It seems harsh, but I'm sure they have your best interests at heart," Alaya said with an understanding smile. "Sometimes parents must be hard on their children, so they can identify for themselves what it is they truly want from their lives." She reached out and grasped Aryan's hand with a pointed but loving look.

He glanced back at her with understanding.

Once the dishes which had recently held delicious home-made apple pie were cleared, Alaya folded her napkin with an air of having settled something.

"Thank you, that was lovely. You are an excellent cook, darling. And it was lovely to meet you Keira. I can see by the way you look at my son you have strong feelings for him also. We would be pleased to see more of you in the future." She shifted her compelling gaze to her husband. "It is time Manish."

He smiled and nodded encouragement.

Aryan frowned and Keira hoped it wasn't bad news about his father's health.

"As you know, due to my failing health I have decided to step back from the running of the business. Son, you have proven yourself worthy to take control. But we have decided to delay making any announcements regarding the future of the company your mother started until Ravi finishes rehab."

"Mother started?" Aryan turned to stare at Alaya. "NadarTec is *your* company?"

"It is. It was not acceptable when I was your age for a woman, especially an Indian woman, to be head of a company. Your father posed as figurehead and we ran NadarTec together. I know you have the intelligence and ambition to take our place—with the right people advising you. We intend to name you acting CEO, until Ravi is well and we can make some permanent decisions, while I oversee the growth of our automation branch. Ravi is right, to ensure the future success of the business we need outside help. Industrial robotics is the future of our company and we need a strong partner to make it happen. I have narrowed down a short list of possibilities, but we will discuss that another time." Alaya stood and the rest of the party following her lead. "Your father needs to rest now."

"Let me know when you'd like to meet, and I'll re-organise my schedule if needed." Aryan walked his parents to the door, Keira trailing behind.

"No need, I'll work around your commitments. Manish and I will be basing ourselves here until we officially retire." She kissed Aryan and held him at arm's length, looking fondly into his face. "As much as we would like to see you settled, now that I know the engagement was a charade, I will admit I am glad you are not rushing into marriage to prove your worthiness. I will leave it to you to deal with announcing the end of your engagement and your new relationship."

She turned to Keira and reached for her hand. "Keira, it was very noble of you to offer to help Aryan. I trust my intuition when it comes to people and you seem like a good girl. One day we might be fortunate to welcome you into our family in reality."

AFTER HIS PARENTS LEFT, Keira and Aryan made their way back through to the dining room and stood at the window looking out into the garden. They each had a lot to process, and the peace of trickling water helped to clear Keira's mind. She stepped out of her shoes and peeled off her wig. The refreshing touch of the cool tiles beneath her feet and breeze on her damp scalp helped, and she inhaled a deep breath, absently watching the water from the small waterfall flow into what must the float pool Aryan had told her about.

"That was interesting," she said with a chuckle.

"I'm sorry I didn't have a chance to explain before. I didn't realize myself I was going to do confess like that until I saw you dressed as Chloe again. I wanted my parents to meet *you*..." Aryan turned and lay his hand on her upper arm, urging her to face him. His gaze ran over her face and took in her hair.

"Even though I now look like another fictional character?" Keira asked and ran her hand over her now shoulder length hair, bleached pale blond for her role as Jutta. "I didn't think your parents would notice a wig, but in the end, it didn't matter."

"I like the new look. And no matter what you change about your appearance for a role, it will always be *you*. Keira Fox is an actress, and soon the world will know it too."

"I am glad I met your parents properly, even though it wasn't the ideal way to be introduced." Keira placed her palms on his chest and rested her weight on her forearms. "And it's a relief to be able to shed Chloe's ghost."

"Keira, I am so sorry I didn't tell you earlier Chloe Thompson doesn't exist."

"You tried to tell me, didn't you? On the plane?" She shrugged and glanced at the beautiful ring that never was an engagement ring. "You know, it's strange, but I'm kind of glad you lied about her. It means you weren't really engaged. Doesn't it?" She looked up at him hopefully.

"It does. I've never had a real fiancé."

"So… Bunny?" she joked to distract him from the thoughts that were making him frown.

Aryan chuckled. "I thought it was funny at the time."

"You didn't look amused–at the time. But I like it. Bunny." She smirked at him.

"So do I–when you say it." He grinned back.

Her smile faded and she slipped the ring off, offering it to Aryan in her palm. "I guess we won't be needing this anymore."

Looking intently into her eyes, he didn't move to take it from her. "Not now, but I hope you'll wear it–or one like it–one day."

"Slow down, tiger," she said, even though her heart swelled at the thought of being Aryan's wife. "Let's see how things pan out first. And what about Zac?" She took his hand and dropped the ring into his palm. He might want a future with her in this moment, but it didn't mean he was emotionally unencumbered.

Aryan closed his fist around the ring and shrugged. "It's nice of you to be concerned for him, but he still has a job whether I end up being CEO or not."

"That's not what I mean. Wouldn't he be upset if we got married?"

"Not at all. I expect he'd be very happy for us."

"Where is Zac by the way? I hope he's not unwell?" The security guy had left with Mr and Mrs Nadar's and was obviously in their employ.

"He's taken some time off to visit his family."

"Hmm, so it's just the two of us tonight." Keira slid her arms around his neck and pressed her body against his. Now the pressure was off, and they were alone, the night stretched promisingly ahead of them.

He slid his hands up her back and dropped his head to rub her cheek with his. "My home is secure, and I'm capable of protecting us both if that's what you're worried about."

Aryan pressed a kiss to her bare shoulder and Keira shivered as desire raced over her skin.

"Not exactly, but with you doing that and the house to ourselves, I can't remember what it was I *was* thinking about."

"Good. I only want you to think about this," he said and pulled her closer, stopping any conversation with a deep kiss.

Keira lost herself in the feel of his lips on hers, his tongue sliding between her lips, his body pressing her against the glass window… until the waiter who served the meal called out that he was leaving.

Aryan stepped back, ruffled, and followed the waiter to lock the door after him. On his way back to Keira, he pulled a thick book from a drawer in the buffet. She nearly melted from the heat in his dark gaze as he handed it to her.

"It's not exactly an appropriate un-engagement present, but I printed these for you before I deleted all the files. It was a very memorable night. I thought you might enjoy a memento."

Keira took the book and flipped open the cover, stunned at the photograph she found there. Her in a red silk dress, on the terrace of the Mexican villa, Aryan kissing her…

She flipped the page and gasped. A photograph of her dress open, naked except for her panties, Aryan studying her with heavy lidded eyes.

With the feel of him behind her, his warm breath of her neck, Keira flipped through the pages, her breath quickening with arousal at the progression of their lovemaking in images.

The images were artistic, and *hot*. How had someone gotten close enough to take them? Zac was supposed to keep everyone away. "What are these?"

"Something to remember our weekend by." With his lips on her neck Keira found it difficult to focus her train of thought.

"Where did you get these?" she choked out, aroused and panicked at the same time. What if these got out? They wouldn't hurt Aryan now, but they might damage *her* fledgling career.

"What do you mean? You said you knew Zac was taking them." Aryan lifted his head from where he'd been feathering kisses along her shoulder.

"Noooo." Keira turned and thrust the book at his chest. "What's going on?"

"Zac was in the garden that night, taking photos. You knew… didn't you? You said it was hot." He put the album on the lamp table as if it stung his flesh.

"Ah, no..." Keira took a deep breath and clenched her fists. Then, the memory of what she fantasized about filling her with shame. She'd been turned on at the time imagining Zac was watching them make love.

"Oh shit." Aryan scrubbed his fingers through the hair at the base of his skull. "I'm so sorry. I'm sure I heard you… I must have misunderstood. Oh god. Can you forgive me? I'll burn them right now…" he turned to reach for the album.

"No," Keira said and gripped his wrist, not wanting the stirringly beautiful images to be destroyed. She would be a hypocrite to let him think she hadn't been more than okay with Zac watching them. And the photos were good, and sexy… "They *are* very hot," she conceded. "And I can see how you misunderstood. At the time I was telling you I was happy for Zac to watch." So he'd had his camera with him. She understood the urge to record beauty, sensuality. She'd done the same herself.

"Oh," Aryan managed, obviously speechless at her turn-around.

It was all such a mess…

Before he found words, Keira hurried on. "Maybe we should start fresh. It worked well last time…" She grinned and held out her hand for him to shake. "Aryan Nadar, let me introduce myself. I'm Keira Fox."

He took her hand and squeezed gently, sending a jolt of arousal through her body.

"It's a pleasure to meet you, Keira Fox." The way he said her name, along with the residual arousal from seeing image of their past lovemaking, made her knees weak.

She licked suddenly dry lips. "And you, Aryan," her voice hitched at the look of hunger in his eyes.

"Is it too early in our acquaintance to kiss you?" he asked in a low, husky voice.

"I think that is an excellent way to get to know each other," she said and slid her palms up his chest and behind his neck, pressing her breasts against his chest.

'Rewards beyond expectation' her horoscope had promised the day she'd made the decision that led her here. Keira felt like she'd been rewarded beyond even the stars' expectations.

CHAPTER FOURTEEN

KEIRA HAD BEEN tense since she'd woken at 4am on the morning of her meeting at Paramount. Nervous about her first time as a support actress on a big-budget movie, anxious to make a good impression on set while focusing on learning all she could about the industry she had been so desperate to be a part of, she hadn't stopped to take a deep breath all week. But the warm sensuality of Aryan's mouth on hers made her forget it all, even the apprehension at meeting his parents, unlocking her muscles so she melted in his arms. Filled with a bliss she had never experienced, she smoothed her palms down his chest, over his abs. The rest of the night stretched ahead of them, they were alone. No parents, no Zac…

Zac. Darn it. There was something very important they still needed to discuss.

Keira placed her palms against his chest and made some space between them. Aryan opened his eyes, lips parted, pupils huge, his expression questioning.

"Wait. Before, you misunderstood what I meant. I need you to know that I'm aware of your relationship with Zac. I'm okay with it, even though I'd rather you were completely unattached."

Aryan's expression of curiosity turned to confusion. "Me and Zac? *Lovers?*" He shook his head with a frown. "No. We've been friends since school, then he came to work for me. That's all."

"Are you saying you're not in a sexual relationship with Zac?"

"I'm not and have never been. You thought we were gay?" Aryan asked with an amused grin.

"Not initially…" Keira said, glad he wasn't angry.

"Until Ravi suggested it was the case?"

"Shivers, yes." Keira paused and thought back to the 'evidence' that had convinced her they were in a relationship. The actions and reactions that had everything to do with the secret they'd been keeping. The real secret. That Aryan hadn't broken up with Chloe, that there never was an engagement. "I'm so sorry!"

"I can't say I blame you." Aryan shrugged and placed his hands gently on her hips. "Zac and I are closer than friends, we've been through a lot. He's the one person I know I can trust."

"Hopefully there's another person now." Keira smiled and then the enormity of it sunk in. "So, I don't have to share you with anyone? Not Chloe, not Zac?" Keira felt light-headed again. Sometimes life was full of very pleasant surprises.

Aryan lowered his head and his lips brushed her ear. "I'm all yours."

She shivered in his arms. "And that's your float pool?" she whispered.

"It is, would you like to try it?" His lips resumed their exploration of her neck, his fingers playing her ribs like a delicate instrument.

Keira shivered, remembering the seductive feeling of being naked and weightless. "I'd love to."

He trailed his fingers beneath the curve her breast, down her inner arm and took her hand, guiding her into his private indoor garden room. One side was unglazed and let in the faint scent of the ocean and the chirping of night insects.

"I almost feel like we're back at *Cielo en el Sol*. What did Benedict call it? Heaven."

"Mmm. It feels like heaven with you here. I don't suppose you have a swimsuit with you?"

"I don't. But I went in the tank naked." Keira raised an eyebrow and smirked, untying her the top of her halter neck dress as she turned her back to Aryan. "Unzip me?"

The feel of his fingertip tracing from her nape down her spine sent shivers over her entire body. *Sugar,* she couldn't wait to get wet and naked with this man. *Her* man. And then it hit her. *He'd told his parents he loved her.* And after lying to them about Chloe, he wouldn't have said it unless he was certain of his feelings.

Keira turned as he finished unzipping her. The fabric slid down her body, leaving her naked. "You love me?"

Aryan raised his palms to cup her jaw and smiled, eyes soft with admiration, desire, love. "I do." He tilted his head to indicate the dark tiled pool, and waiting water, barely disturbed by the faint breeze. "Shall we?"

"Only if you're naked too."

While she watched, the man who loved her toed out of his shoes, pulled off his socks, unbuttoned his shirt and stepped out of his trousers. And, as he stepped out of his boxers, Keira slipped off her panties, and they stood, naked before each other.

"Do you have any cuts or wounds you want to keep the salt out of? I have some pawpaw cream."

"Hmm, I remember thinking when I got in the tank, I could find a better use for it than keeping the salt out of a wound." Keira held out her hand, palm up and Aryan handed her a tube.

"And what was that?' he asked, his voice husky.

While he watched, she squirted out a generous amount and reached between her legs.

Aryan's cock jerked as he watched her spread the cream around her entrance. "From now on I'll get a hard-on whenever I use it."

"Hmm, I wish I could be here whenever *that* happens," Keira said, admiring his cock, thrusting very enthusiastically in her direction. She reached out and slid her fingers through his and led him to the steps and into the pool.

As they sank to their knees in the shallow water, the buoyancy of the high salt-content invited her to lay back.

"Close your eyes," Aryan urged, and she complied, trusting him implicitly.

Warm water lapped at her scalp as she floated, weightless. His lips and fingers trailed paths of fire over her mouth, down her neck, over her breasts. At the touch of his tongue on her nipple, she arched into him, stretching her stomach to his trailing fingers, opening her legs for his touch.

"I have an idea."

Keira heard his words through a haze of arousal and gently sloshing water.

"Whatever it is—yes," she panted her reply.

"I use these to strengthen my knees." Opening her palms one at a time, he placed a rope in each hand. "There are ropes attached to the side of the pool. You have the handles in your hands."

With his hands on her hips, he steered her gently through the water, so her legs were parted either side of his hips.

She looked up at him and watched as he sat back on the shallow step, his cock floating on the surface.

Aryan guided her into position so her feet rested on the tiled edge of the pool either side of him, his cock nudging her entrance. "You're in control now," he said.

A thrill of power shot through Keira's body and her sex clenched in anticipation. This was even better than what she'd fantasized about in the float tank in Mexico.

Aryan kept his hands on her hips, stabilizing her keeping his hands on Keira's hips to stabilize her as she tried out the logistics. Pulling on the handles, she bent her knees, and gasped at the feel of his cock nudging inside. She straightened her legs, enjoying the pressure of his cock moving against the wall of her pussy. Bending her knees again, deeper and pulling harder on the ropes pressed his cock deeper inside her. By alternatively pulling on the rope and bending her knees then straightening her legs, she found a rhythm that built pleasure without rushing to completion, the lube counteracting the friction of their wet flesh.

When the plateau of pleasure tipped over onto the slippery slope to climax, Keira couldn't resist increasing the pace and force, taking Aryan's cock deep and hard inside.

But it wasn't enough. She needed to feel his chest pressed against hers, to taste his kiss and share his breath. Dropping the handles, she reached for his hands and he pulled her up onto his lap, where she rode him hard and fast until they both gasped with the force of their shared orgasm.

Afterwards, Keira and Aryan drifted side by side in the water, with the sound of their slowing heartbeats and breath echoing in their ears. Keira rolled onto her side and reached down to trace the scar on his thigh with gentle fingers. She loved his scars as much as his beauty. It was his flaws that made him who he was, a damaged, perfect man.

She loved him.

As if he read her mind, Aryan turned in the water to face her.

"I'm in love with you, too," she said as he floated into his embrace. "Bunny."

the end

SKYCLAD

A SECOND CHANCE, BEST FRIEND'S
BROTHER ROMANCE

Skyclad (ˈskaɪˌklæd) - Adjective
(poetic or paganism) Nude, naked, especially outdoors. Having
no covering; bare; exposed.

Naturist (**ney**-cher-ist) - Noun
A person who goes naked in designated areas; a nudist.
A person who worships nature or natural objects.

CHAPTER ONE

PERTH, Western Australia

Last summer…

Beneath the unforgiving glare of the studio lights, Alexandra Roye struggled through the final story of the show, her heart hammering madly in her chest.

What was she doing here? Coming back to work had been a terrible idea. Despite her conservative blouse and tidy chignon, she knew she was being judged by the audience as the worst type of woman. *Homewrecker.*

"…and its good night from me," she said with a practiced smile at the camera, trying not to think of the faceless sea of humanity watching her. For the first time since those first months as weather girl for Perth's most popular news network, she felt exposed. Naked.

Experience and repetition had thickened her skin, but now, after nearly nine years in front of the camera, she was more than exposed. Most of those people watching – her viewers – had *actually* seen her naked.

Finally, the Monday edition of the *Daily Wrap* was done. In a hurry to escape, she stood and strode away from her desk, her pencil skirt and high buttoned shirt clutching her like a straitjacket.

She avoided looking at the camera guys she'd known for years, even though she knew they would be studiously avoiding looking *her* in the eye. Making for the main passage and access to the stairs, she cursed the five-inch heels that made the climb to her workplace sanctuary too slow, her gait unnaturally awkward.

It felt like an age before she pushed through the heavy door beyond the fourth floor and burst out onto the roof, where the weight of the scandal lifted slightly with the vastness of the evening sky. She sucked in cool fresh air and strode to the edge of the roof, feeling a little less suffocated.

Her gaze slid down the windowless outer wall of the studio, where she spent too much of her life and energy, then skimmed the sprawling bitumen carpark and kaleidoscope of cars, picking out her mother's red Mercedes and her father's black Jag.

Of course, they were still working. The studio was more of a home than their Dalkeith mansion.

In an effort to dispel the weight of their disappointment, Alexandra rolled her shoulders and lifted her gaze to sweep the horizon. The sun was setting in a flare of orange and lilac over the ocean, but her attention was greedy for the distant tapestry of darkening green bushland. It was bittersweet torture to be trapped in the prison of her choices when what she *really* needed was almost within reach. If only she had the courage to grasp for it.

She yearned to be out there, to draw comfort from the leaf-littered soil, or to walk barefoot on the sand, feel the connection to the pulse of life. She needed the sense of belonging that was such a fleeting but necessary part of her soul, dreaded being swallowed up again by the dead block of concrete that broadcast her failures to the community.

Her gaze narrowed on trees blurred by tears and shadowed by approaching night.

I can't do this anymore.

This was no life. It had to end.

CHAPTER TWO

SUNSHINE COAST, Queensland, Australia

Three months later, Saturday 11am…

THE COMFORTING WHOOSH of waves caressing the sand, the laughter of children and chattering of their parents dropped away the moment Alex Roye glimpsed the apparition from her past. Her breath caught in her chest as her gaze locked on the man who had wandered up to the market stall next to hers. *What was he doing* here, *so far from Perth?*

Oblivious to her panic, his gaze scanned the tea paraphernalia on the next table, task focused, like a man on a mission.

Would he stop at her stall? Would he recognise her? Alex's grip tightened on the mobile ATM machine in her hand.

"Are you okay?" Corinne leaned close and asked in a low voice, breaking her trance.

Alex sucked in a breath and smiled at her friend, who had called in to say hello an hour earlier and, on finding her frantically trying to serve and re-stock her table, stayed to help.

Remembering that she was in the middle of a transaction, Alex glanced down to tear off the receipt and hand it with the last hand-decorated paper bag to the girl who had just purchased a pair of amber earrings.

"Would you be a love and grab some more gift bags from under the table?" she asked Corinne, who obliged with a smile. And then her world stopped as Jamie Ainsworth stepped up to her stall and looked straight at her.

His blue eyes widened with recognition as they locked on hers. "Alexandra?"

In the unguarded face of the now-grown man towering over her, Alex glimpsed the happy, easy-going teenager she'd once known. And felt a faint echo of the attraction they'd shared twelve years ago reverberate through her body.

Then he blinked and his face emptied of expression.

"Jamie," she choked out, cold prickles of regret tingling across her face. Remembering the coping mechanisms Dr Ingle had taught her, Alex breathed deep, absorbing calm from the salt-scented air.

"James?" Corinne said with surprise as she popped up with a handful of recycled paper bags and noticed their newest customer. "You know Alex?"

"Knew," he countered in a low, flat voice. "Nice to see you Corinne."

It was so long ago now, but what did she expect, when she'd broken off contact with his family so suddenly, at the worst possible time?

"Yes, it's been a long time," Alex agreed and dug her toes into the grass beneath her bare feet, taking comfort from her connection with the warm earth to lessen the sickening memory of the twisted car wreck in which her best friend had died.

"Oh, I see." Corinne glanced at Alex, who frowned and narrowed her eyes in response. "Um, I can look after the stall for a while if you two want to catch-up."

"No need." Jamie said and turned as if to walk away.

"Are you looking for something in particular? A gift for May?" Alex said quickly to stop him. She had the feeling he would do everything in his power to make sure their paths never crossed again if she let him walk out of her life now. She didn't know what she was hoping for, but now that she'd seen him again, she yearned for *something*…

"Yes. A gift for Mum for her birthday." Jamie addressed the table and shoved his hands in the front pockets of his jeans.

Friday would be the first of May. *May day.* Funny how she still remembered it every year. Most likely because May and Cameron Ainsworth had been more like family than her own self-absorbed TV celebrity parents.

She'd lost more than her best friend the day Bec had died.

Alex picked up a pendant, the copper and blue abalone shell crafted into an abstract butterfly design. "This would be lovely with her blue eyes and dark hair."

"Her hair is mostly grey now." Jamie's full, wide lips thinned, and the crease between his eyebrows deepened. He pulled his wallet out of the back pocket of his jeans. "But she would love it."

"And these are a gift from me." Alex slipped the matching pair of earrings into a bag while Corinne processed the payment for the pendant. "You don't have to tell her that," she drew a shaky breath, "that they're from me, I mean." Alex knew a pair of earrings, no matter how much love and passion went into creating them, could never make up for being out of touch all this time.

She held out the bag to him, willing her hand not to shake as she waited for him to take it, and tried not to let him see how overwhelmed she felt. The teenage boy she'd known and cared for had matured into an impressively built and handsome man. A stranger who looked at her as if they'd not shared every weekend for a year on a labour of love with his father and sister. Those days spent fixing up Bec's first car, when she'd felt like part of a real family, had been some of the best times of her life.

"Thanks." Jamie was careful to avoid contact when he took the bag. "Good-bye," he said with finality. With a slight softening of his expression, he nodded at Corinne. "See you at work."

Then he was gone.

Alex yearned to follow him with more than her eyes as he melted into the crowd, but she remained rooted to the earth. She watched his progress instead, the sun bright on his dark blond hair, until he turned between two stalls and out of her line of sight.

Alex sighed, deflated. Before Jamie arrived, she'd been buoyant with the record sales she'd made, having already sold most of her back-up stock. Now he'd gone, the weight of her past pressed down on her. *Why had she thought she could make a new start?*

"So, you know Jamie?" Alex asked, not daring to look at Corinne in case her friend saw the longing in her face. There was no point broadcasting her affection for a man who obviously hated her.

"Sure do. He works for local council too."

Summer Shire Council, where Alex first met Corinne at the customer service desk when she'd registered her home business.

"But more importantly, how is it that *you* know the gorgeous James? It's common knowledge that he's a loner, much to the frustration of the girls at work, and you only moved here a few months ago."

"I knew him when I was growing up in Perth. Jamie's sister was my best friend at school."

"James is from Perth too? I didn't know that, or that he has a sister."

"Bec died when we were both seventeen," Alex said in a flat voice, numb with a pain that always hovered just below the surface. "I knew his family moved away after the accident, but I didn't realise they'd come here."

What were the chances they'd wash up on the same stretch of Queensland beach?

"Oh. I'm so sorry. It must have been difficult, seeing James like that." Corinne's brow creased with sympathy as she took a brooch in the shape of a bird's wing from a customer and wrapped it in tissue. "You didn't stay in contact with them?"

"No." Alex dug her toes deeper into the earth. "Her parents tried to stay in touch, but it was too painful. And then I lost track of where they were."

It had taken years of therapy to come to terms with the grief of losing Bec, while her guilt had prevented her finding comfort with the only people who understood her pain. She'd been responsible for her best friend's death, and the self-blame she had worked so hard to overcome suddenly bloomed like one of those fetid flowers that erupt overnight then quickly shrivel into a stinking mess.

"Will you contact them now you know where they are?" Corinne gave the bag and cash change to a teenage girl with a friendly smile.

"I don't know, when I have time, I guess I will. I'm going to be crazy busy this week making more jewellery, if sales are going to be anything like today." Maybe she would finally break even and prove that she could make a life out of being creative. But if she was going to succeed, she needed to re-stock, quickly, and thinking about Jamie, Bec and their parents wasn't conducive to getting in 'the zone'.

Only one thing was guaranteed to work – and for that she needed to be alone.

SUNDAY 4PM...

A gust of wind through the open French doors of her studio stirred the tips of Alexandra's hair, tickling the bare skin of her back. Her nipples puckered in the sudden chill.

A storm was coming.

Using a jeweller's hammer to put the finishing touches on the second of two beaten copper earrings in the shape of feathers, she ignored the urgency niggling at the back of her mind, focussing instead on the unrestricted path of creativity that came with the freedom of being unfettered by clothing.

With her studio open to the weather and the birds congregating in her backyard a reminder of the expanse of national park beyond her back fence, she felt as close to nature as was possible whilst being inside. Naked and exposed to the elements, there was nothing to hamper communication with her muse. The spirit that fed her inspiration danced in delight as the creativity flowed unrestricted through Alex, unhampered by society's expectations.

These moments of ecstasy had been missing from her old life, moments that made the difference between merely existing and living in joy. Now she'd experienced it, nothing would take it from her again.

Alex had just attached the first hook to the copper feather when the doorbell rang. It took a moment for the meaning of the sound to reach her, she was so deeply in the zone. She contemplated ignoring it, loathe to lose the connection even for a few minutes, but the voice of reason broke through – there may have been a severe weather warning. She'd had enough experience of devastating weather to be cautious and knew the kindly old widower next door felt protective of her, a young woman living alone.

"Just a minute," she called out and placed the earring and pliers down on her workbench. Reaching for the light robe on the hook by the door, Alex sighed with annoyance as she covered her nakedness.

She opened the door and sucked in a breath when her eyes encountered not Reg's wrinkled and age-spotted face, but a well-muscled chest in a fitted blue t-shirt. *Jamie!* Her gaze travelled upward, over his sculpted jaw, tight with tension and shadowed with a weekend growth of beard. The generous, smiling mouth she remembered so well was almost unrecognisable, with lips thinned – *in disapproval?*

Why was he here? Why seek her out at home, if he was going to judge her and act like they didn't have a history of respect and affection? Whatever it was they had been – friends? potential lovers? – there was no trace of it when she raised her gaze to meet his, coldly blue and distant as the day before.

"Jamie." Had she summoned him here by dreaming of him last night? His presence had haunted her, following her from bed until she'd found her flow state by throwing herself into making as many pieces as she could.

"May I come in?" Despite the lack of expression on Jamie's face, Alex knew him well enough to sense the strong emotion he was holding in check in the way he held his shoulders.

"What are you doing here?" Alex asked, wary.

"I need some answers," he said with a raised eyebrow.

"Answers for what?" She kept her voice and face expressionless while her heart thumped wildly in her chest. *How much did he know?* "And how did you get my address?"

"I ran into Corinne at the supermarket and when she seemed to know our history, I told her I wanted to give you some of Bec's belongings. Don't blame her. She offered to pass them on to you herself, but I convinced her you would be happy for me to visit."

"Well, normally I would be, but I'm working." *But that wasn't true, was it?* She doubted she could be at peace in his presence again. Jamie was a threat to the sanctuary she'd carefully created after the scandal that had convinced her to leave her home, her job and her parents. She didn't want to think about the way his presence made her hyperaware of her nakedness and the slide of silk against her skin, or long for the way he'd once made her feel.

"It should only take a minute." He indicated the notebooks he held wedged against his hip.

Alex stepped back to let him in, even though she knew that his visit was bad news. As he stepped past her, her hands itched to learn the texture of his stubbled cheeks and the smooth skin of his biceps. Instead she kept them busy tightening the tie on her robe.

Closing the door behind Jamie, Alex followed him into her open workshop and waited while he completed his study of what had been a living room when she'd bought the 'renovator's delight' two months earlier. Her first modification had been to pull up the brown and orange carpet, polish the concrete floor and convert the space into a large, open studio. The rest of the house would have to wait until her business started making money. Not even a kitchen that had seen its best days five decades ago would entice her to touch the trust fund her parents had set up for her.

Jamie walked over to the stainless-steel workbench, held up by industrial strength brackets, that ran the length of two exposed brick walls and placed the notebooks down on the only empty space available.

"I thought you might like to have Bec's sketchbooks. I remember the two of you huddled over them every chance you got." He nodded to the part of the work bench scattered with the steel shapes she'd cut last week and turned to face her. "You make more than jewellery?"

With the growing popularity of her market stall, she'd temporarily abandoned her attempt to create a piece larger and more tangible than a pendant or pair of earrings. But her plan to create a large frame and attach shaped metal plates as an abstract representation of a bird's sleek feathered body constantly called to her.

"I'm trying." She hadn't quite got her design right, no matter how often or thoroughly she shed her clothes and courted her muse. Maybe she just wasn't cut out to be a sculptor. The welding wasn't the problem – she'd had that covered since the summer they'd all worked on Bec's car. The summer after they graduated, before they went off to study – Bec, fine art and Alex, engineering drafting – with the goal to start their own business. They'd planned to meet on weekends and start practising in the workshop in Bec and Jamie's Dad's shed. But Bec never made it to uni, and after Alex finished her study, the qualification – and her dreams – seemed useless. So, she'd taken the easy road and gone to work as an intern at the studio where her parents worked.

"TV presenting didn't work out for you?" Jamie's abrupt question snapped her out of her thoughts.

Alex froze, her muscles locking in place. *Shit. Had he heard what happened, all the way over here?* Ice water trickled down her spine at the possibility that Jamie kept in touch with his friends from Perth. After 'the scandal', Alex had moved as far away as she could without leaving the country, relying on the isolation of her old home to keep her past where it belonged, separated by hundreds of kilometres of desert and mostly deserted countryside. But it seemed the nightmare had followed her, appearing at her door in the form of the only man she could have loved.

"It did for a while. But after eight years, being recognised on the street got a bit old." Especially when she became better known for a certain sordid photograph that went viral, rather than her ability to inform anxious viewers about drought, floods and tropical cyclones.

"So, what made you move over here, so far from your parents?" The way he narrowed his eyes and crossed his arms across his chest told Alex he didn't buy her excuse and wasn't going to let it go.

She tore her eyes away from the shapely pecs bulging beneath his t-shirt and gathered her hair in her hands, twisting it over her shoulder as anxiety tightened her throat. He was ruining her mojo and she needed to get rid of him or practicing her grounding exercises, or even getting naked, wouldn't get her back in the zone. And she needed to get more work done tonight. "I wanted a new start, far away from painful memories." If he wanted to hear her confession or excuses, he was going to be disappointed. She'd firmly closed the door on that chapter of her past. Telling him why she'd chosen this particular stretch of the east coast might satisfy him, though. "That holiday, when I came here with your family, was the happiest time of my life."

Jamie nodded and unfolded his arms. "I guess we ended up here for the same reason then. My parents couldn't live with the constant reminders of losing Becca. They decided to move away, not long after she died. I think here they can feel close to her without being constantly reminded of her death. They were renting a place nearby when the house they used to hire for holidays came up for sale. They've been there almost ten years now."

So, she'd been living a couple of suburbs away from Bec's parents for the last few months without realising. She shook her head and crossed her arms. "So now we're all caught up, I have a lot of work to do."

CHAPTER THREE

JAMIE FOUGHT DOWN AN INAPPROPRIATE LAUGH. "WORK?" he asked as his gaze travelled over Alex's robe. He tried not to notice the outline of her erect nipples and forced his eyes back to her face. But he couldn't erase the sight of the silhouette of her body, the setting sun through the French doors behind her showing through the thin fabric of her robe, making it translucent.

She must have been about to step in the shower when he'd arrived. He caught his breath at the sudden desire to unwrap her, to touch and taste her silken skin… *Don't go there.*

"Jamie, please. Can we just leave the past where it belongs?" she asked in a tortured whisper. Even frowning and defensive and with her eyes troubled, the sight of her knocked the air from his lungs. The pretty girl he'd often sketched in secret had matured into a stunning woman. He hadn't picked up a pencil and paper for pleasure since he'd given in to his father and turned his talents to commercial engineering, but the sight of Alex made his fingers itch to do so now.

Jamie directed his train of thought back to the reason he'd come to see the girl who had been such an integral part of his teenage years. He'd once hoped she would be as much a part of his future too, until she'd turned her back on his family when they'd needed her most.

"I'm only here because something doesn't add up about Bec's accident. I've been thinking about it for years."

"I don't want to talk about that night." Her words were sharp as a slap.

Jamie ran his fingers through his hair and massaged the back of his neck, frustrated with himself. *Shit.* He should have thought this through, not barged into her home and put her on the defensive. He should have called her and asked her to meet him.

"Please Alex. I need to know." When she didn't protest further, he pushed on. "You said a rabbit ran out in front of her car, and Becca applied the brakes too hard as she swerved, which made the car roll. The police didn't question it because you were an eyewitness and the body of the rabbit was there, but I went to the scene not long after. The only skid marks in the area didn't look fresh." He placed his hands on his hips, searching her face for a reaction that would confirm his suspicion. The Alex he'd known before was honest and open, but she had acted like a stranger after the accident. It was the change in her more than the circumstances of the crash that had made him suspect he was to blame.

"Is there something you're hiding from me?"

Alex took a step backward and leant against the bench, crossing her arms. "What I told the police is exactly what happened. I won't discuss it again."

"Okay, so if that's the case, why did you break contact with me?" Even though it has been years since she'd broken his heart, he couldn't stop his voice catching.

"It had nothing to do with you." She lowered her head and her voice, but not before he saw a glimpse of agony in her eyes. Was her pain for the loss of her best friend, even after all these years, or was there another reason? What was she hiding? Not knowing if it was his fault was worse than knowing for sure.

"I deserve an answer Alex." At least if he knew he was responsible for his sister's death, he could be content knowing he deserved the punishment he put himself through every day. He'd lived with the guilt so long, it had become part of his reality, but seeing Alex now, made his self-imposed isolation suddenly unbearable.

When he'd seen her yesterday at the market the shocking reminder of his loss and guilt had drowned out all else, but then he'd started to wonder if this was his chance to finally get the answers that even now kept him up at night.

If she wouldn't speak the words, maybe she would show him the truth. He stepped forward and cupped her face in his hands, his gaze drilling into her liquid brown eyes. Couldn't she see he needed to know?

"Please. Tell me what really happened." All the pain from the last twelve years was distilled in those words, and the rawness of his plea nearly broke him.

"I can't." The expression in her eyes begged him to understand.

But he couldn't. What was the point of hiding the truth now? Frustrated that she would withhold the verdict of his guilt or innocence, he lowered his face to hers. All she had to do was open that beautiful mouth and say the words 'the brakes failed', but her lips stayed stubbornly closed.

If he could get her to just open her mouth, maybe the truth would come spilling out. But no, even though every atom of his being yearned for her, the memory of her sweetness still clear as the day they'd acknowledged their feelings for each other, it would be wrong to kiss her.

He took a deep breath and lifted his head, but before he could distance himself from temptation, her hands were on his shoulders and she'd pulled herself on tiptoes. The shock when her lips found his washed away every reason why they should not.

Years of built-up longing flooded through his body. For a moment there was nothing but the roar of his blood racing as the girl he still dreamt of pressed against him, her familiar yet unfamiliar mouth on his, sparking a blaze that had grown – not diminished – with years of being denied. The one kiss they'd shared years ago had been worse than none. It had ruined him for every kiss he'd experienced since. The feel of her tongue against his now was even more intense than he remembered, turning his blood to liquid fire and his body to a needy beast.

But it was wrong. They couldn't do this. Not now, maybe not ever.

He pulled away while he was still able. The taste of her intoxicated him, taking him back to the innocent days when they'd had a bright future to look forward to.

Summoning every ounce of self-control, he released her arms. "I'm sorry." He stepped away. "I shouldn't have."

Alex pressed her hand to her mouth, her eyes filling with tears.

Shit. He glanced away from the fresh pain he'd inflicted, down to where she resumed twisting the life out of her hair. One side of her robe had slipped, revealing bare skin and the curve of her breast.

Christ. His body roared with the need to find out if she *was* completely naked beneath the robe, to explore her sweet body with his hands and his mouth, to show her how much he worshipped her. Even now.

"I should leave." Frustrated with her stubbornness and his body's response, he turned and strode to the door. The meeting had not gone at all as he expected. He had expected her to offer him a coffee and a reasonable conversation. She would admit she'd been wrong to not tell him earlier and assure him it was a simple mistake, he'd been young and inexperienced and if it weren't for the rabbit he would have found his error and rectified it. That it was just bad luck. He would have understood if she'd slapped him and placed the blame firmly on his shoulders. He could live with that. But he could no longer live with not knowing.

ALEX JERKED at the sound of the front door slamming, then sank to her knees on the jute rug as the thrill of their kiss drained out of her, leaving her with an unsatisfied hunger for the man who'd reminded her what desire felt like.

In the years since she'd last seen him, she'd convinced herself her infatuation for Jamie had been a teenage crush, but the way her heart had pounded when they'd kissed twelve years ago was nothing compared to what they'd just shared, as man and woman. She raised trembling fingers to her lips, reliving the sensation of his mouth on hers. Their teenage kiss had been a revelation, but chaste compared to the passion he'd just unlocked with his lips and the touch of his body.

She knew now what she had suspected back then – she and Jamie shared a connection that went deeper than any she had experienced. The realisation, considering the insurmountable lie between them, was more devastating than when she had believed she would never see him again.

When she'd left her old life behind, Alex had thought she could escape the mess she'd made of her life and start fresh. But maybe the only way to be free was to confess her biggest mistake. If she was strong enough.

Slipping her hand inside her robe, Alex found the line of scar tissue and traced the knotted flesh beneath her breast, where a broken rib had punctured her skin. The scar, the daily physical reminder of her weakness and her strength – and her salvation. She'd first visited the naturist club on advice from her psychiatrist to confront the memories that haunted her. With the group Alex had discovered the philosophy that she hadn't realised had been missing in her life, and an acceptance she craved. The absence of the trappings of financial or social standing fostered a rare and precious equality, and finally Alex had felt free to be herself. She wasn't the only one with scars and imperfections on display.

And it had been so much more than that. Communing with nature had given her a connection to her muse, clearer than she'd ever experienced, and of the monthly group activities, creating art from found objects had reconnected her with her creativity. She had found herself with the help of like-minded acquaintances, and although she hadn't yet been able to trust enough to allow friendships to grow, the belonging and acceptance she'd received from the group had allowed her to begin to heal.

Cold wind gusted through the open French doors bringing her back to the present. Alex shivered and stood to shut out the rain that spattered the polished concrete floor, but the sight of the old red toolbox stopped her. Instead, she reached under the bottom shelf of her workbench and pulled out the metal box covered with the names of bands from the last decade, written in Nikko pen by two teenage girls.

She sat back, the coarse fibres of the rug scratching her thighs through her robe. Holding her breath, she opened the lid for the first time since she'd hidden the box – close enough for comfort but out of sight. Thanks to Jamie, the monster was out, maybe airing her memories would appease it?

With cool wind tugging at her hair and tears flowing over her cheeks, Alex reacquainted herself with each sketch and magazine clipping before clutching them in her left hand. Pictures of places she and Bec had planned to visit, the buildings and sculptures which had fired their creative passion. They'd wanted to travel, to see those structures in person, view them from all angles, feel their presence, walk around them, study the play of light on their surfaces.

Beneath the paper, at the bottom of the box, lay the lump of black plastic that had caused so much grief. An old mobile phone, smaller than a modern one but thick, almost unidentifiable compared to a modern smartphone, the plastic case split open where it had crashed against a rock. Bec's parents had given it to her as a birthday present, making her promise to turn it off whenever she was driving.

Jamie had seen there were no marks on the road to show Bec hadn't applied the brakes – because she'd been looking at her phone and not the road. She hadn't seen the rabbit until Alex had squealed, and then she'd over-reacted, wrenching the wheel to avoid hitting it, so hard she'd thrown the car into a deadly roll.

Sniffling and drained in the wake of ebbing emotion, Alex packed everything back inside the box and closed the lid, then stood and navigated the now-wet floor to close the doors. Outside, lightning flickered in the bruised grey sky, the treetops swaying in the growing storm. With little hope she'd make anything else worth selling that night, she turned toward the bathroom with plans for a bracing shower, when the sketchbooks Jamie left behind caught her eye.

The familiar manila covers, covered in patterns doodled by her best friend, were the repository of their shared dreams. Approaching cautiously, she flipped open the cover of the top book.

Bec had always been the creative one, her sketches loose and full of energy. Slipped between the pages were Alex's translations of the sparse and confident lines, her technical drawings to make Bec's design something tangible. What a team they would have made, if only their youthful dreams hadn't been smashed on the rocks beside a remote road.

One sketch in particular seemed more vibrant than the rest. A kingfisher caught in flight as it emerged from the water, a golden perch clutched in its beak. Notes in Alex's handwriting decorated the edges of the page. Tracing the lines of the bird with a fingertip, Alex remembered the day Bec had sketched the bird in class, when they should have been concentrating on algebra. Bec knew how much Alex loved birds, but this was one of her best so far. They'd thrown around ideas of how they would create the kingfisher on a large scale, with a frame of metal rods and the shell made up of individual plates of metal, painted in the colours of a kingfisher.

Her gaze locked on the signature at the bottom corner of the page, an 'a' and a 'b' distinct yet intertwined. *One day*, they had vowed, they would build the kingfisher, using the skills they'd learnt from Bec's father while doing up her car in the back yard.

Alex still used those skills, every day but on a smaller scale, when she shaped and soldered delicate pieces of jewellery. In fact, with the hindsight of experience, she would have suggested steel plates to represent the feathers of the kingfisher, using heat oxidising to colour them shades of blue and bronze and turquoise. Colours perfect for a kingfisher.

In fact, the design would be perfect for the local water festival. Alex felt Bec's hand in this – their sketchbooks coming back to her and the reunion with Jamie – now, when there was an opportunity for Alex to honour their dream. Building their kingfisher would be the perfect way to honour her friend's memory.

Slipping the notepads in a drawer, Alex carried the kingfisher drawing to the kitchen table where she'd left the local paper. She flipped through the pages until she found the article about 'Halcyon Days', the water festival council planned for the first weekend in June. The local artist, who'd been contracted to create the sculpture to commemorate the inaugural event, had pulled out. They were calling for last minute tenders to be submitted by the end of the week.

Excitement bubbled through her, making her giddy. It was as if fate were guiding her. Halcyon was the name for the bird in Greek legends generally associated with the family of bird species *Alcedinidae* – or kingfishers. *This was it.* If she could win this job it would be her opportunity to honour her best friend and celebrate the beginning of her life as an artist. She tore the clipping out of the paper and reached for the phone to dial Corinne.

The girl she'd met over the customer service desk at council had been her rock in those first difficult months of finding her feet in her new home. As planning officer Corinne had patiently explained the process of registering a home business then generously offered to meet Alex on her lunch break to help fill out any parts of the application she was unsure of. Alex suspected it wasn't a practice encouraged by her employer, but when she got to know Corinne as a friend, she realised that the Brit empathised with her situation, having recently made a new start in a foreign place herself.

"Hi Alex, did James contact you?" Corinne asked, her tone beneath her Geordie accent cautious.

"Yeah, he just left."

"I hope it was okay…"

"No problem. But I'm calling about something else. A favour."

"Of course. Name it."

"Will you help me fill out a tender application? It's for the sculpture for the water festival."

"Sure. You'll need to register a business name though."

"Okay. I'll jump online now. Are you free tomorrow after work?"

"Sure. 6pm?"

"I'll bring Thai. And Riesling."

"Say no more. You've got a deal!"

Alex flipped open her laptop and searched 'business name registration'.

Her fingers hovered over the keyboard. *Name of business entity…*

She paused only a moment, then typed in *Skyclad*. It was perfect, hinting at Alex's love for all things winged, but most importantly, not many people would know its true meaning – *naked in nature* – or link it to the source of her creativity.

CHAPTER FOUR

ALEX PULLED up in the carpark down the road from the house where they'd spent that memorable two weeks before all their lives had changed so dramatically. She'd arrived half an hour before she was expected so she had time to steel herself to see the couple who had been such an important part of her childhood, her second family. Anxiety tightened its hold on her throat at the thought of facing them after twelve years of no contact.

Had Jamie told his parents about the scandal that had made her flee her life in Perth? Would his parents treat her differently, would they believe the rumours? The message May left on her phone didn't give that impression, her voice friendly and optimistic. She'd sounded just as Alex remembered. Like warm hugs and laughter.

"Alexandra! James told us you've moved here too. It's my birthday darling, please come and have dinner with us. No need to call back unless you can't make it, or if you need the address. I'll see you Friday."

Alex had called back as soon as she'd heard the voice message, not to say she couldn't make it, but to ask if May would like to celebrate at a restaurant, or if she could bring Thai or Indian take-away to save her cooking on her birthday.

"Oh no, but thank you love. You know it is one of my greatest joys to cook for my family. And that includes you. Jamie told you where we're living? Do you remember the address?"

"Thank you, I do." When Alex first moved from Perth, the holiday house and nearby beach she remembered from her sixteenth summer had called to her. She'd found the address and driven by, giving in to the need to reminisce, not realising May and Cameron lived there.

At the time, she'd told herself it would only be the once, but in the months since her first indulgence, whenever the loneliness became too much, she found herself sitting in her car in the car-park between the house and the beach, watching the waves roll in.

The sand beneath her feet, still warm from the day's sunshine, and the damp breeze off the ocean on her skin helped to calm her anxiety, but also reminded her of those joyous days of youth, of freedom and belonging. For an only child with mostly absent parents, being with her best friend's family day and night had been a glimpse of heaven. Warm summer days spent with Bec, walking down to the beach and swimming all day. The sun kissing her skin while she imagined Jamie's caresses, nights spent fantasising about being cradled in his arms in the room next to hers. Wishing he would notice how her body had filled out, that he would look at her and not all the pretty girls in bikinis. Watching him at every opportunity, fascinated by his newly tanned and muscled body. Laying on the beach, propped on her elbows trying to pick him out amongst the other boys surfing.

How Bec had teased her when she'd noticed how distracted Alex was – and the reason why. Oh, what she would give for Bec's teasing now…

Finally, on the last day of their holiday, she'd noticed Jamie looking at her in a different way – as an adult. As a woman. After they returned to Perth, it had been months of torture before he finally kissed her a week before Bec's accident. She only saw him a few times after that – at the hospital, at the police station, at the funeral.

So many years without him in her life, and she hardly recognised the Alex he'd known. She only glimpsed her when immersed in creativity – or connected with nature as she was now.

Alex took a deep breath of the salty air that blew her loose hair across her face, as ready as she would ever be. Whether they knew the reason she'd left Perth or not, it was time for her to be brave and face the family she'd let down and lied to twelve years ago.

Turning, she headed back to her car and drove the short distance to the Ainsworth's home.

Alex took a bracing breath and walked up the path through the once bare garden now planted with May's favourite roses and camellias. Gripping the chilled bottle of wine tight in her trembling fingers, she paused at the front door, a homecoming and penance rolled into one knot of stubborn anxiety, her chest tight and aching as if it were packed with cement. Jamie would be there, distant and suspicious beneath a polite mask he would wear for his parent's sake. Alex couldn't blame him.

Her knock was answered instantly, as if May had been waiting just inside the door.

Bec's father, Cameron, stood nervously smoothing the front of his short-sleeved shirt, then hurried over with a warm smile to kiss Alex on the cheek.

The kind, beaming faces of the couple who had been more approachable than her own parents started to break up the cement shell around her heart. She almost cried with relief, as the years melted away and she relaxed into their unconditional hugs.

"Happy birthday," she said and handed May the bottle of champagne.

"Ooh, lovely. Thank you." May turned to her husband. "Honey, would you open this so we can celebrate our reunion?"

May slipped her hand through Alex's arm and together they followed Cameron into the living room, where the old holiday house decor had been replaced by pale wood furniture and neutral colours. Jamie unfolded himself from a deep armchair with a frown.

"Mum. You didn't tell me you'd invited Alex."

"No, but it's a lovely surprise, isn't it James? You don't think I would miss the opportunity to invite Alexandra to share my birthday celebration once I found out the reason you'd dug out Rebecca's old sketch books?"

"Surprise," Alex joked with a tentative smile at Jamie, who crossed the room to give her a distant kiss on the cheek.

"Now, what have you been doing with yourself?" Cameron asked, handing her a glass of champagne.

"I worked at the station with mum and dad. I was the weather presenter for about eight years."

"And how are your parents?" May piped in.

"Fine. Focused on their careers as always. Dad is still hosting the morning show, and Mum has stepped off camera to produce." Alex swallowed the sharp stab of guilt. It was only by the support of their loyal viewers that her parents were able to hold onto their jobs following the shake-up at the station and the inquiry into Charles King, the station boss. It was bad enough people assumed she'd got the job as weather presenter through her parents – which she had, but that had only made her more determined to do her job to perfection – but she'd earned her hard-won promotion to anchor. Despite people thinking it had been payment in return for sexual favours for her boss.

"Happy birthday, Mum," Jamie lifted his glass for a toast, and they all clinked glasses to drink in May's honour.

"Why don't we sit down, dinner is ready if you are," May suggested and Jamie led the way through what used to be a very small dining room. With the entire back wall gone, the room opened into an enclosed patio.

"I love what you've done with the place," Alex said, admiring the floating wooden floor and bi-fold doors opening out onto the back yard.

"Yes, all Jamie's idea. You should see the house he designed and built, on the other side of the bay." May raised an eyebrow at Jamie who smiled tightly and held out a chair for Alex to sit opposite Cameron. He said nothing and followed May to the kitchen to help bring in a large casserole dish, a platter of roasted vegetables and basket of bread.

"And what brings you to this side of the country?" Cameron asked as he past her the basket of bread rolls.

Alex relaxed a little more, his inquiring look confirming the scandal hadn't reached them. Even if Jamie knew her true motivation for leaving Perth, it didn't seem as if he'd told his parents.

"Work life balance. The entertainment business and everything that goes with it doesn't leave much time or energy for creativity." Alex smiled ruefully as May and Jamie took their seats. Working in the entertainment industry left no room for privacy either. "I'm looking forward to being creative and anonymous now I've extricated myself." If she kept a low-profile maybe being a naturist wouldn't be an issue as it had in Perth where anyone who watched local TV in Perth had known who she was and gave the accusers the ammunition to ruin her when they discovered her lifestyle choice.

"Yes, you were always so talented, but a sea-change? Couldn't you have done that in Perth?" Cameron asked with a frown. "Not so far from your family?"

"I wanted to make a fresh start." Alex hedged, his innocent question a bit too incisive. She would have to be even more cautious, now she knew Bec's parents were in the same community. Would they understand her lifestyle choice if they knew, or see it as an eccentricity someone from a privileged and wealthy background would indulge? Exactly the impression she tried to avoid.

"And we are so glad you did! It will be wonderful having you close by again." May leaned over and squeezed her arm before helping herself to the casserole after everyone else had served themselves. It was so much like the old days that it was hard to ignore Bec's missing seat.

"So, you moved to sunny Queensland to follow your dream." Cameron piped up.

"A market stall selling jewellery." Jamie shook his head.

"Jamie!" May chastised him.

"Sorry. I meant no offense." Jamie lifted his hands in a gesture of surrender. "You are talented, and your work is very good, but you're not charging what it's worth."

"Initially it was more important to me that I do something creative that I love. Once I'm established, I plan to expand the scope of my work," Alex answered defensively. "And my fees."

Jamie looked at her intently, as if he were reading the true message beneath her words. *Creativity was the reward, not the tool.*

"Alexandra isn't here for business advice, love." May turned to Alex, her hand skimming over the pendant and earrings Jamie had given her for her birthday. "These are beautiful. I'll treasure them even more because you made them."

Praise from the woman who had always found the time to soothe her fears and uncertainties, who had shown her an understanding her distant parents had not provided. The warmth of May's regard turned to scalding shame when Alex thought how she'd repaid her with dishonesty. She'd kept the truth from them all this time, and they still welcomed her after so many years of silence.

I don't deserve to be welcomed into their home, back into their hearts. At least Jamie sees me for what I am—the worst kind of friend.

"I'm so glad you like them." Alex replied with a tight smile. "And Jamie is right. I still need to learn marketing and everything else needed to run a successful business."

"That will come. The product is the most important aspect and I can see the workmanship is top class. It surpasses anything I taught you." Cameron said, beaming with pride.

Alex flushed with pleasure at the compliment. He used to look like that whenever Bec got top marks in art class or won an award.

"So, you're still welding after all this time?" Cameron continued.

"Only on a small scale, mostly soldering, although I have been thinking about tackling something larger." Corinne had hinted she was about to get some good news, but Alex didn't want to say anything until she knew for sure. If she won the tender to create Bec's kingfisher, she would surprise them with a dedication to their daughter when it was finished.

"Excellent! I'm very glad to hear your talent won't be wasted. But what's stopping you from jumping into a larger project?" Cameron asked, his tone encouraging.

"I have the skills to create and install large sculpture, but not design it." Except in the case of the kingfisher, where the design was already done. In fact, now she had three sketchbooks full of her friend's designs, she had plenty of inspiration and material to fulfil the dream she and Bec had created together.

"If you need any equipment, dad still has all his gear in the garage," Jamie offered, then dipped his head as if he hadn't meant to speak.

"Good thinking. Any time you need it, you're welcome to use it here or I can drop it—or anything else you need to use—over to your place," Cameron said with a smile and a nod, as if it was decided.

"Thank you. That's very kind of you. Eventually I'd like to buy the equipment I need, but I might take you up on that offer in the meantime. You don't happen to have a pipe-bender, do you?"

"Matter of fact, I do. Any time you need it, you're welcome to use it here or I can drop it, or anything else you need to use, to your place."

"Thank you. I might be in touch about that soon." Alex glanced at Jamie who was focused on the delicious chicken casserole on the plate in front of him. She remembered him being enthusiastically involved in dinner-time conversations, if not overly chatty, but tonight he was quiet, verging on morose. Was it because she was there, or was this what losing a sister did to a man?

"So, Jamie. What do you for council?" Alex asked.

"I'm in construction. At the moment I'm working on the new Council building near the river."

"James is an engineer." May said with a proud smile.

Alex looked at Jamie, surprised.

He lifted his eyes slowly to hers. For a moment, she thought she saw a spark, a remnant of the flame that had driven his dreams. Was he was also remembering that night when she felt they were on the verge of something spectacular, the night when they'd sat on the beach not far from here, in a group of kids around a bonfire?

That night… it had felt like it was just the two of them, with the sound of the ocean whispering to them as it caressed the sand; the endless possibilities embodied by the expanse of starlit sky above them; the light of the flames reflecting in his eyes as he'd confided his dream to her. His dream to study fine art and learn the techniques of the masters so he could spend his life creating beauty.

The spark in Jamie's eyes flickered and died and he looked back at his plate.

So, he'd put his dreams aside too.

He'd followed his father's wishes, his father's dream, rather than his own.

CHAPTER FIVE

ONSITE, Botanic gardens

Alex shrugged her shoulders beneath the heavy fabric of her overalls, a trickle of sweat snaking over bare skin, humid air stifling under her welding mask.

Just a week ago she had learned she had won the tender for the water festival, and after borrowing tools from Cameron, begun construction on the metal frame that would form the framework of Bec's kingfisher. It wasn't until the metal frame had disappeared around the corner on the back of the truck on its way to the botanical gardens that the logistics of working on-site occurred to her. She would have to wear heavy safety clothing at all times. How would she connect with her muse?

When she'd created the technical drawings in the privacy of her studio, the final sculpture had been clear in her mind's eye, each plate heat-tinted in subtle hues of gold, copper, blue, turquoise and indigo, to emulate the yellow breast and iridescent blue-green wings of the kingfisher. Now, restricted by her overalls and full-face mask, and working near the public entrance of the gardens, she was struggling to get in the zone. It was crucial that she find a way if she was going to finish in time and have a chance of bringing her and Bec's dream to fruition.

As she bent to select another plate, her scalp prickled. She was becoming accustomed to being watched by curious passers-by wandering through the gardens, but the work boots that appeared in the strip of ground visible through the narrow lens of her mask announced a rare visitor *inside* the cyclone fence.

She turned her head and glanced up at the vague outline of the man. All she could tell was that he was tall, built like rugby forward and wearing a hard-hat. Alex cursed under her breath. *The council inspector.*

Before straightening to greet him, Alex reached to turn the gas off, but a hand waving in front of the valve wheel prevented her.

"No need to stop." He yelled to be heard through her earmuffs. "I'm from Summer Council. I'll just take a quick look and be on my way. I can see you're behind."

Alex's grip tightened on the handle of the welding torch. *Like I need to be reminded.*

She nodded, but the inspector had already turned away and was looking up at the skeletal head of the bird; the most challenging part of the piece, still to be completed. A gust of wind cleared the sulphurous welding fumes and wafted his after-shave in her direction. The scent was slightly familiar – warm, woodsy – but pre-occupied as she was with filling her plates per day quota and struggling to communicate with her muse, she couldn't place it.

Picking up a green-tinted plate, the colour of a forest waterhole, Alex clamped it in place, all the while aware of the man walking away from her with his arm outstretched, his hand tracing the line of the wing. He moved in close to inspect the welds, as if looking for a fault.

The heat inside her mask intensified. It was his job to ensure the installation was safe for a public place – even though it would be surrounded by a lagoon of shallow water when it was finished – but she wasn't accustomed to having the quality of her work questioned.

She flipped down the shade and pulled the trigger, concentrating on the glowing arc of her weld, the only light as the welding shade auto adjusted. As soon as she was satisfied the plate was secure, Alex pushed up the shade to select another, her gaze catching on something—someone—at the edge of her vision.

The inspector was standing behind her, safety goggles on. He'd been looking over her shoulder, checking her technique.

Alex turned the flame off, her rising anger at his attitude making her handshake. She removed her earmuffs and straightened, pulling off the welder's mask and turning to face him.

Jamie!

They both stepped back in shock.

"Alex? What are you doing here?"

"Jamie." Alex put a gloved hand to her chest. "What are *you* doing here? You said you worked as an engineer for council."

"That's right, and that involves inspecting public works. You didn't tell me you were tendering for this, although I should have known when I saw the business name." He waved his hand at the structure that barely held the promise of eventually representing a bird. "I could have helped you. It looks like you're going to struggle to make the opening ceremony."

Any creativity she'd managed to channel evaporated and her stomach clenched with dread.

Grateful for the breeze on her damp face and hands, she sucked in deep breaths, the rest of her body crying out for freedom, for the kiss of fresh air. She needed to get out of the sweat suit and let her body breathe. "You're right, the timeframe is very tight. I've been working as late as I can and starting as soon as its light. I'm doing this for Bec, and I didn't want your parents to know until it's finished. I want to invite them to the launch."

"Oh." His lashes dropped, shielding his eyes but not before Alex had seen them soften.

"Mum and Dad would love that. And I'm sure you parents would, too?" He frowned.

"You never did know my parents very well, did you?"

"I guess not. You look like you could do with a break. Walk with me? I'm sure we can work out a way to get it finished on time."

"Okay. Thanks." Maybe she just needed to take more breaks and walk through the garden. Nature, the water and the birds would ground and refresh her and feed her productivity.

"So, tell me, what's the problem?"

She studied his face. Could she trust him enough to confide in him? Could she afford not to, if there was a chance he could help? Her chance to succeed in a business she loved in return for baring her soul. Until recently only her fellow naturists had known the truth. Even if he didn't empathise, surely the history they shared would keep her secret safe?

Alex took a deep breath and braced for the leap of faith. "I need to be naked to be creative."

"What do you mean?" Jamie frowned, uncertainty creasing his eyes.

"I need to be unrestricted by clothing to properly connect with my creativity."

"So that's why you're struggling with productivity?" He glanced over at her overalls then continued for a few steps in silence, before stopping in the shade of a tree. "Is that why you were wearing just a robe the day I came to your house?"

Alex leant back against the trunk, the texture of the bark and the solidness of the tree against her back giving her confidence. "Yes. I'm a naturist. I was part of a group in Perth, but I haven't plucked up the courage to approach the local group."

"The ones that use the bay in the national park for nude sunbaking?"

"Yes, the 'A-Bay' group. I want you to know, it's more than getting an all over suntan. It's a way of life. And don't look at me like that. It's not sexual. It might look like it from the outside, but it is definitely not. The opposite if anything. It's about connecting with yourself – with your natural spirit, and without the trappings of financial situation and social class, everyone is equal. The acceptance was liberating, and the group helped to fill a little of the void Bec's death left in my life."

"I'm glad for you," Jamie said and leant his shoulder against the tree beside hers, his tone sad yet encouraging. "I might have an idea that could help. I'll show you if you're interested."

Alex sagged back against the tree, relieved he seemed to understand. "Okay," she agreed, cautious, not daring to imagine what he was about to suggest.

"There's a gardener's cottage in the gardens that won't be used until after winter. I can leave the key with you. You can store your things there and take a break whenever you need— in complete privacy." His cheeks flushed at the inference of how she might use that privacy.

"Will you show me?"

Jamie nodded and pushed away from the tree. He led her along a gravel path between overhanging Lilly Pillies to a small brick building completely enclosed by a tall wooden fence, except for a solid wooden door. Inside it was more welcoming, with plenty of windows letting in natural light from the yard outside where large terracotta pots of different sizes and shapes were stacked. The building was perfectly positioned to take advantage of the winter sun while being insulated against the winter heat.

"A local artist has been using the cottage to hold weekly life-drawing classes, but without heating it was getting a little cold for the model to sit for so long." Jamie looked seventeen again when he blushed.

That would explain the platform in the centre of the room, around two metres across and built the same shape as the hexagonal room. With the front door closed the cosy interior was serene and very private, separated from the expanse of public garden outside by a high fence, while the natural light flooding in through the windows on four of the six walls was perfect for drawing or painting. She could see why Jamie thought it perfect for her to use as a sanctuary until she finished her sculpture.

He did *understand.*

Alex pointed up at the swathes of fabric hanging from the centre of the ceiling to each wall, giving the room a slight tent-feel. "Did the artist add the Bedouin tent touches?"

"Yes, she's quite the bohemian apparently," he said over his shoulder as he opened one of the sash windows.

A family of finches trilled amongst the grass seed and the tinkling of a fountain on the other side of the fence floated in.

At the sound of rustling amongst the pots, Alex stepped close to the window and found a large olive green and black striped lizard staring back at her, as if he planned to challenge her over the territory.

"Oh, that's William, the local water dragon. His harem is scattered around the gardens. He won't bite if you leave him to have the run of the place."

Alex breathed in the scent of jasmine and magnolia and felt her muscles loosen in relief. The cottage would be the perfect retreat for when she came up against a creative brick wall. And with a place to reset, she was confident she would finish her sculpture in time.

There was a basic kitchenette with a kettle, bar fridge and microwave. In fact, if there'd been a bed she would have been tempted to move in until Bec's kingfisher was finished.

"Thank you – this is perfect." She stepped forward with a rush of gratitude and lifted her arms to give Jamie a hug, but he stepped away.

A shutter went down over his expression of friendliness and understanding.

Alex wrapped her arms around herself to contain the surge of hurt and disappointment. She'd expected too much. If it wasn't for his offer to help, she would have cursed her decision to confide in him.

"Whatever needs to be done," he said with a shrug and turned to the door. "The opening of the festival can't be delayed."

BY THE NEXT AFTERNOON, Alex had finished welding the last of the metal plates she'd allocated for installation that day and was standing back to admire the completed wing when Jamie pulled up in his work truck.

"Two visits in two days. To what do I owe the pleasure?" she asked with a cautious smile. He'd made it clear their relationship was purely professional.

"I wondered if I could ask a favour?"

Alex's heartbeat accelerated. "Nothing wrong with your parents is there?"

"No, they're fighting fit as usual. In fact, Mum keeps asking me when you're coming for dinner again. I told her you were busy with a commission and that you'd contact them as soon as you have time."

"Thank you." Even though she'd had little time for anything but work and sleep, it hadn't stopped Alex wishing she could spend more time with May and Cameron. And wishing things were as they had been between her and Jamie. "Speaking of which, I've organised an invitation for them to the opening of the water festival. Will you convince them to come?"

"I can do that. The reason I stopped by was to ask your opinion on something."

"Sure. Shoot." Alex cocked her head at him, curious as to what he could possibly need her advice on.

"It's the building I'm working on for the new council offices. I hoped you might have some suggestions on how we can make a necessary and functional feature a bit more decorative. I'll need to show you if you have time. It's not far away."

"Sure." She grabbed her satchel with her sketchbook and rulers and pencils and her car keys so she could head home once he dropped her back.

After climbing into the passenger seat of his ute, Alex pulled the door closed and was immediately wrapped in the embrace of his cologne. She turned her head slightly to watch him slide behind the wheel, his large frame and presence filling the cab. Transfixed by the economy of his movements, she watched as he closed the door and start the engine. The muscles in his thigh tensed and bunched as he pressed the clutch, the muscles of his forearm rippling beneath a shower of hairs sparking gold in the late afternoon light as he changed gear. She turned away from the sight of his large, strong hands and glanced out the window.

When he pulled to a stop and cut the engine, Alex jumped out quickly, worried she wouldn't be able to keep her hands to herself much longer. She hurried after him as he strode to the three-storey building with Hebel cladding.

"So, what's the issue?" Alex asked his broad back.

Jamie stopped and placed his hands on his hips and looked up at the rather stark looking building, the pale walls glowing in the late afternoon sun. "This is going to be headquarters for development and planning and needs to represent the shire's philosophy, which is closely tied with nature and sustainability. In order to use minimal energy for cooling in summer or heating in winter, we need to shade this wall, but in a way the sun can penetrate for warming in winter. It would be an advantage if it looked good as well."

"And if it was decorated to represent the shire philosophy?"

"That would be a lot to ask," Jamie replied, his voice cautiously hopeful.

"It would." Alex looked up at the wall, then walked around to view it from different angles. "But it might be possible. Do you have the plans?"

"They're inside. Do you want to take a look at them?"

"I would. I have an idea." Alex nodded.

Jamie unlocked a discreet door – a staff or delivery entrance by the placement at the back of the building.

She followed him inside, where the floors were still exposed concrete slab, the walls a web of steel framework and the space littered with tools and the detritus of construction. Upstairs was more finished, the walls plastered and the ceiling lined, the smell of fresh paint tingling in her nostrils. It was still very much a worksite, with plastic sheets hanging from the ceiling, plastic chairs and a couple of work benches scattered around.

Jamie motioned to where the plans were laid out on one of the benches.

Bending over them, Alex flicked through until she found the elevation drawings, braced herself with her hands either side and leant over to study the exterior of the building. She pulled out her sketchbook, ruler and pencil from her satchel and glanced up at him. How would she manage this?

"Umm, I need to…" she started, and glanced down at her overalls.

Realising her dilemma, Jamie backed slowly toward the door, rubbing his hand across the back of his neck. "I should leave. You know, so you can get in the zone?"

"I'll need to ask you some questions as I work. Maybe we could move a trestle behind one of these plastic sheets?" They were splattered with paint and almost opaque. Looking around, she pointed to one of the sheets hanging parallel to an outer wall made up mostly of windows. Bracing her hands under one end of the bench, Jamie lifted the other and they shuffled behind the plastic sheet.

From her side of the screen, Alex watched Jamie turn and look out the window. She was acutely aware of him being so close as she peeled off her overalls. She was naked beneath the heavy, stifling fabric and the sudden feel of the cool air on her skin was like diving into a refreshing pool, her awareness a full body experience rather than just in her mind. If only she could think and feel this clearly all the time. She stretched luxuriantly, arms over her head and inhaled deeply, studying the blurred outline of Jamie. His presence, a ghostly shape through the plastic, was outlined by the light, which was just beginning to fade, adding a delicious spark of hyper-awareness to her skin that was foreign to her creative process. She felt vividly alive and free at the same time.

Turning to the drawing, she picked up a pencil and pulled a blank sheet of paper in front of her. "The outer walls are clad with Hebel?" she asked, trying to sound professional and not distracted by his proximity.

Jamie cleared his throat. "It is."

"And the windows are all double glazed?"

"They are."

"Good. So any decoration we create on the west wall needs to be at a particular angle, so the wall is shaded from the intensity of the summer sun from midday on, but the negative space of the design allows it to shine through during winter to help warm the building. In-between seasons the wall would receive filtered light. We just need to angle the metal screen exactly right."

Unpacking her gear, Alex focused on the kiss of cool air on her skin, and ruled up the side view of the screen, using a protractor to indicate the angle needed to block the afternoon summer sun. Next, she ruled up the elevation of the west wall in the proportions indicated on the plan. As the imagery of a wetland sketched itself in her mind, Jamie faded to a comforting presence.

Her mind was so caught up with the drawing in front of her, she was immediately able to see how to get it to work. Her spirit soared and her hand flew, the design drawing itself on the paper. Freehand for the first time, she designed – a wetland scene with local waterbirds, clumps of local swamp grasses and shrubs creating the spaces where the light would come through.

Her chest expanded with elation and a new feeling.

She was designing, not just drafting.

CHAPTER SIX

"ALMOST FINISHED," Alex called out and Jamie heard the last scratches of her pencil on the paper then the sound of it dropping to the bench. "Would you like me to take this home and draw it to scale?"

"Only if you want to. Council has a draftsperson who can do it, if you'd prefer to focus on your sculpture?"

"Of course. Yes, that makes sense."

From the sound of rustling fabric, amplified in the silence of the empty building, it was too easy to picture her stepping back into her overalls. He'd been surprised when she'd stepped behind the screen and he'd only heard her remove the one layer of clothing, now it was impossible not to see her in his imagination – long slim legs sliding inside the coarse fabric, the overalls gliding upward over her thighs, her stomach, ribs, breasts and arms…

He took in a deep breath, grateful he hadn't figured out she was naked beneath her overalls any earlier, or he wouldn't have been able to think clearly enough to realise the gardener's cottage would help her dilemma. He also wouldn't have dared to ask her to come here with him alone.

It had been hell standing there, trying to get his brain to focus on her questions and not the nakedness of the woman who had been the star of his teenage wet dreams. Even then it hadn't been merely a physical craving, but a need to be close to her, to live a meaningful life together. For twelve years, he had existed in two dimensions. He'd thought it was the loss of his sister, but now that Alex was back, he knew it was also the loss of the woman who owned his heart.

But she was not for him. If she knew what his negligence had done, she would hate him. For Bec's death. For nearly killing her too.

At that moment, Alex pulled back the plastic and stepped out, hesitating with the roll of paper in her hands and a triumphant, joyous look on her face. She looked more beautiful than ever.

Shit. As if it wasn't hard enough to be close to her.

Jamie glanced away. After standing so close while she was naked, it was as if his desire had given him x-ray vision. He didn't know how he would manage to concentrate on the road when he drove her back to her car.

At the touch of her hand on his shoulder, he started and stepped away, facing the window.

"You're different," she whispered in the quiet building. "I see glimpses of the Jamie I used to know, but most of the time he's hiding. What happened?"

"I lost my sister."

"It's more than that."

Was he so transparent? He tried so hard to hide what he was, did everything so thoroughly, triple checking everything, but it wasn't enough.

He didn't let anyone get too close, in case they noticed. But of course, he couldn't keep Alex at the same distance. She'd known him *before*.

He sighed and hunched his shoulders. Nothing he did now could reverse the one huge mistake he'd made. He couldn't stand the torment anymore. He would never deserve Alex. If he confessed, she wouldn't want anything to do with him, but at least he would know for sure if he was to blame. At least he could finish doing his penance and try to move on with the rest of his life.

"I rushed connecting the brakes on Becca's car." Jamie snapped his mouth shut, even though the incriminating words were out.

"What do you mean?"

"The day of the accident. I think Becca crashed because the brakes didn't work properly. Because she took the car out before I tested them." Even though his eyes filled with tears, somehow saying it out loud eased the weight pressing down on his shoulders.

Alex stared at him and shook her head. "No."

"I know what happened, Alex. I just want to hear it from you. Tell me it was my fault."

Alex blanched and shook her head again, her eyes wide with shock. "Take me home. Not to my car. I'll get it tomorrow," she said then turned and walked away.

As he followed her from the building, the cold silence that stretched between them made Jamie feel sick. He deserved her hatred, but it still hurt.

She was silent on the drive to her house, frowning out the window at the darkening streets, then jumping out before he turned off the engine.

Jamie waited in the car, not sure if he was meant to follow or leave. He thumped his fist on the steering wheel as he watched her hurry up the path. *Had he lost her forever with his confession?*

At the front door she hesitated for a moment, and then turned and beckoned him with a wave of her hand.

He took a deep breath and followed her. At least she was giving him the chance to talk about it. He closed the front door and found her kneeling on the polished concrete floor, dragging a toolbox out from beneath a shelf.

What was she doing? Pulling out a gun to make him pay for his mistake?

He almost wished she would.

When she stood and turned to face him, she held a small black object in her hand, but she held it out and offered it to him. An ancient mobile phone, the case chipped and cracked, smashed at one corner.

He took the battered piece of plastic and noticed the Motorola badge. His instinct was to drop it when he recognised it as the phone he'd helped his parents buy for his sister's last birthday. *Why did Alex have it? Why was it in this state?*

"It wasn't the brakes." There was no infection in her flat voice. "They worked fine—when she finally used them."

Jamie felt dizzy as images of what might have happened flashed through his mind. "What do you mean?" he asked, dreading the words that would confirm his suspicion.

Alex nodded to the phone in his hand. "That happened in the crash."

He looked down at the twisted plastic in his hand and the reality hit him like a cresting wave, smashing down on his head with an icy blast. He staggered to the bench and put the phone down, bowing his head and struggling for breath. "It was… in the car? Mum thought Becca must have lost it… before."

"She hadn't lost it. She was *using* it."

"While she was driving?" He spun to face Alex, his heart pounding in his ears as he waited for her answer. The answer he dreaded but would also set him free.

"Yes. It flew out the window when the car rolled," she answered, her face pale, her hands twisting her hair into a tight rope. "I picked it up before the police came. At the time, I thought it was better if your parents and the police didn't know she was breaking the law."

The sudden relief was overwhelming. Despite the shock of the revelation, he felt suddenly buoyant. Now he could finally grieve as a brother, not a murderer.

It wasn't his fault.

His stomach churned and the ground dropped away from beneath his feet. Alex had deliberately kept the truth from him. Because of her he'd spent twelve years blaming himself. Twelve years without joy and no hope of happiness. She'd abandoned him and let him believe he was to blame for his sister's death. How could she do something that cruel and selfish?

"How could you do this to my family, to me? We loved you." The coldness in his voice sounded unfamiliar to his own ears.

"I didn't know you thought it was your fault!" Alex held out her hands, as if to offer him comfort but too scared to touch him. "Shit Jamie, I was seventeen. I'd promised them I would make sure she didn't use the phone while she was driving."

"I've been punishing myself for twelve years, thinking I was responsible for Bec's death." He shook his head in disbelief. "I thought you cared about me."

"I did − I do. So much." Her eyes pleading, lips trembling, Alex took a step toward him, reaching for him.

"Don't touch me." He stepped sideways to avoid her and strode out the door. He couldn't bear to look at his childhood sweetheart and see the woman she'd become. The liar she'd become.

HE DROVE AIMLESSLY, unable go home, not with this revelation turning his brain into a faulty electrical circuit and filling his stomach with acid.

It wasn't his fault Becca was dead.

Alex had been in the car with his sister when she'd crashed. Knowing Becca's stubbornness, even Alex wouldn't have been able to stop her using the phone if she was determined to, but she should have told him and his parents. She could have helped them understand what had really happened.

When he stopped driving, he found himself parked outside his parents' house. He needed the comfort of family right now, he needed to be with his parents now that he knew he was free from blame.

With light steps and a heavy heart, he knocked on the front door and let himself in. He found his Mum in the kitchen, always her favourite room of any house they'd lived in.

"What a lovely surprise." She wrapped her arms around his middle.

He leant down to give her a proper hug. For the first time in twelve years, he let himself take comfort in her love. "You should stay for dinner. The roast is big enough and I can put some extra potatoes and vegies on."

"Thank you, but please don't trouble yourself, Mum. I came by because there's something I need to tell you both."

"Well, your dad should be home soon. He's been down at the Men's Shed this afternoon." She chuckled and the sound broke through his numbness. His mother's innate happiness, despite losing a child, was embodied in her laugh. For the first time in so long, her joy touched him and a little of the tightness in his chest released.

"He always comes home with a healthy appetite after gossiping all day. Why don't you put on the kettle love and we'll have a coffee while we wait for him?"

Moving as if through neck-deep water, Jamie filled the kettle, flicked the switch and got the cups out. He might be able to be around his parents now without the weight of guilt, but he still had his feelings for Alex to deal with. When his auto pilot failed, he stopped, staring blankly out in the dark back garden through the kitchen window, until May shooed him away and finished making the coffee.

Unaware of his movements, Jamie sat down at the kitchen table, absently staring at the old shoe box in front of him. The lid was off, and a jumble of old letters spilled out. The address on the top envelope was their old one in Perth and he recognised Alex's writing from the sketchbooks he'd pulled out for her the other day.

Mum took the seat opposite and set down the two cups of coffee with a frown of concern.

"There's something troubling you. Are you okay James?"

"Not really."

"It looks like you have something important to share."

Jamie looked away from the hopeful, knowing look in her eye. Of course, she knew how he'd felt about Alex, she would have noticed the way he'd tried not to look at her at dinner the other night.

"I'm so happy that we've all reconnected with Alexandra. She was such a sweet girl and she's grown into a lovely young woman; don't you think?"

Jamie took a swig of the coffee, welcoming the burn on his lips and tongue. He wished he wasn't about to wipe that happiness from his mum's life, wasn't about to dig up the old grief and taint his parents' affection for the girl they loved like a second daughter. If it weren't for all the mess about Becca's death, Alex might have been their daughter by marriage.

"She never missed one of our birthdays, you know? Not Rebecca's, yours, mine or your dad's. Even after we moved, Bev next door sent a package of our mail over every few months. I wrote back to Alex you know. She must have moved, but her cards kept coming though. I wondered if sending them was some kind of therapy that helped her to heal."

She nodded at the box and Jamie looked at the open Mother's Day card on top. *To May from Alexandra.* And a letter.

"You should read it."

James looked up at his mother, who nodded encouragement, then back to the letter. He unfolded it with stiff fingers.

You were like a mother to me...

I've lost my best friend, and the family I loved more than my own...

I wish it was me who died...

Bec had so much talent and so many people who loved her...

Jamie's stomach clenched and he couldn't keep reading the words she hadn't been able to say to them in person, her heart exposed on a sheet of old foolscap paper. Alex had lost as much as they all had. Her best friend, the family who meant more to her than her own, her dreams. Her guilt at what happened so deep she'd wished she could trade her life for Becca's. He understood her now, and that understanding was like a balm to his simmering anger at her. It wasn't her fault he'd chosen to blame himself.

She may not have stopped Becca using the phone as she'd promised, but she'd had to live with that. It must have eaten her up inside. He was sure she would have spent all these years blaming herself, just as he had. All for no reason. It was Becca's error of judgement – his sister's mistake alone.

The full truth hit him like a kick in the gut. He needed to tell her, to make her see that she was not to blame any more than he was.

"The poor girl. Those negligent parents of hers. And then the scandal. Any wonder she moved fair across the country to escape it all."

"What scandal?"

AFTER STRUGGLING through the morning trying not to dwell on how badly she'd handled the situation with Jamie, Alex took a break at the cottage. Sitting on a folded blanket by the open window, she absorbed energy from the fresh air as sunlight bathed her bare legs. William made his lunch of small grasshoppers in the grass while she ate leftover lamb and cous cous. The sound of her phone ringing broke into the peace, and she blinked with surprise when Jamie's name came up on the screen.

"Do you know the old dam off Blackman's Road?" he asked, sounding as tired as she felt.

"Sure," Alex asked carefully. "Why?"

"Meet me there? At 5 o'clock?"

Alex drove to the disused quarry, her fingers drumming nervously on the steering wheel of her functional station wagon. What could Jamie want to see her for, and why would he ask her to meet him somewhere so isolated? No doubt he hated her for her part in his sister's death, and he'd been furious that her silence had reinforced his own self-blame.

Did he want revenge? She wouldn't blame him if he did, in fact she'd welcome it. Her attempt to be free of her past had failed. She would never escape it.

When Alex arrived, Jamie's work truck was already parked at the end of the track. Dreading his anger but compelled to be close to him, she made her way to where he stood at the lip of the dam, facing away from her.

She glanced around, but there was nothing here to draw comfort or strength from, no nature or beauty to be soothed by. Even the sky was grey and featureless.

If this was to be some kind of retribution, she was ready. She shrugged and continued toward him, devouring every inch of him as she approached, from the top of his dark blond, wind-swept hair to his work boots. His physique may have changed since she'd known him in Perth, but he was still achingly familiar and dear to her.

"You have the heart of a romantic," Alex joked to cover her unease. The scarred and bereft location dragged at her soul.

Jamie turned with a frown of concern and held out the shattered phone.

Alex braced herself for his anger.

"It's up to you, but I think you should toss it, and stop blaming yourself for Becca's death."

Alex looked at him, unable to form words. *Had she misheard him?*

His eyes locked on hers, Jamie continued. "She was stubborn as an ox. Nothing you could have said except threatening to stop being her friend would have dissuaded her from using that bloody phone whenever she wanted to." He reached for her hands, placing the phone in her palm and cradled her hands in his. Closing her fingers over it, he caressed her gently with his thumb. "And you loved her too much to ever say anything to jeopardise your friendship. You loved her as much as we did."

Alex looked down at the green tinged water. Could she do it? Could she let go of the one thing that represented her most painful mistake, and let go of the guilt?

"Council is going to bulldoze all this soon and plant native tress. It will be a thriving, clean place soon. I've taken the battery and circuit-board out, so it's just plastic and glass. Not as bad as some of the crap already in there. I thought throwing it away would give us both closure."

"Closure?"

"I forgive you Alex. But you need to forgive yourself.

Closure was something Alex thought she'd never have. She had been willing to take her mistake to her grave, but here was an opportunity to take the first step toward a life with forgiveness.

With a bracing, deep breath, she pulled her arm back and threw the shell of the phone with all her strength.

Shoulder to shoulder, she and Jamie watched the black plastic fly through the air and drop into the water.

The small splash unlocked Alex's tears and a sob rose in her chest.

Instantly, Jamie gathered her against his chest.

The feel of his warmth encircling her, the arms she'd dreamt of but never believed she would feel again, unlocked the hope for the future she'd given up on the day she'd knelt at her dead friend's side. Every muscle in her body loosened and she would have fallen to her knees with the relief of it if Jamie hadn't been holding her tight. But it wasn't over yet. He'd forgiven her, but what sort of future di they have? And since reconnecting with his parents, she was determined to have them in her life again. She would have to tell them too.

Not daring to embrace him for fear she would never let go, Alex slid her arms between them and wrapped them around her ribs. He loosened his hold, so his hands rested on her shoulders.

He knew what she'd done, and he was still talking to her, still touching her. Was there a chance she and Jamie could start fresh, now they'd aired their guilt? There was so much history between and behind them... could that be a good thing? With the chemistry that still existed between them – had in fact become more potent now they were adults – they might have a future together.

If there was any chance for a future for them unless she admitted everything.

"Can I tell you why I moved away from Perth?" She scrubbed at the tears wetting her cheeks and stepped back, needing the distance to gather her thoughts.

"Sure." He said and slid his hands into his trouser pockets.

"There was more to it than wanting to be here."

"I'm all ears."

"There was a man." Alex gathered her hair in to a chunk and twisted it over her shoulder.

"Hmmm."

"Not in that way," she said quickly. "He joined the naturist group I belonged to in Perth. He was creepy, staring at me, trying to get close, not in the innocent way the group would tolerate. His attention became more insistent and when I rejected him, told him there was no chance, he stopped coming to the activities and meetings. I thought it was over. But apparently he got his sister to join up." Alex tugged at the rope of hair until her scalp ached. Even thinking about the slimeball made her feel sick.

"She took photos of me at one of the outings and photoshopped me into a photo of Charles King – the network boss – on a recent holiday on his yacht. It looked like I was there with him, naked. It looked like I was the reason for his divorce." She searched Jamie's face for a sign he'd heard the rumours, but he just looked back at her with no evidence of judgement.

"It was just after my promotion from weather girl to anchor. Of course, no matter what I said everyone believed that we'd been having an affair, that I was the reason his marriage broke up and sleeping with him was how I got the promotion. It almost ruined Mum and Dad's careers and reputation. The only thing I could do to help them was to leave." Alex shrugged. "Once I got here, I realised I should have left years ago."

"So that's why you haven't contacted the local naturists?" Jamie asked, a thoughtful look on his face.

"I've been too nervous to. But also because of the scar."

"From the accident?" He frowned.

"It's pretty ugly. I need to feel comfortable and trust anyone I show. I've always felt as if it's a mark of my failure."

"Do you think it might be easier now? Now that you've admitted to hiding the phone?"

"I think it will be – once I tell your parents I failed them."

"Um. They already know." Jamie said then hurried on. "Sorry Alex, I told them. It makes no difference to them – a rabbit or being distracted by her phone – she's gone. They don't blame you. They know what Bec was like, even more so than you do."

"Oh." Alex reeled with shock and the ground suddenly felt unstable beneath her feet. She'd thought she'd been taking the confessions step by step, but in reality, all her secrets had been laid bare. "Wow. It's hard to grasp, after carrying that for so long. I was sure I'd take it to my grave."

"Would you have preferred to tell them yourself?"

"I don't know." Alex flicked her hair back over her shoulder and looked up at the sky, bright blue and just darkening to dusk, a colour so like Jamie's eyes. "No. I'm glad you did. It must have been hard. Thank you."

"It wasn't easy, even though at the time I was angry with you. The truth is, I just wanted it all out in the open. I told them I thought I'd made a mistake with the brakes too, but Dad said he checked them when he checked the drive shaft just before he lowered it off the hoist. If we'd all discussed our fears at the time, we could have saved twelve years of blaming ourselves."

Alex stood up straight, her breath filling her chest without a trace of tightness. "You're right. No more secrets or hiding. And I will join the local group soon, as soon as I finish Bec's kingfisher." She smiled. In this place of devastation that promised renewal, everything had changed. Her future held more than creative fulfilment, now she had the chance for the belonging she craved.

Jamie cared.

He understood that her creativity was reliant on her connection with nature.

He accepted what and who she was.

It was so much more than she dared hope for, but did he still care for her?

WHEN ALEX TOOK a break for lunch the next day, she'd already caught up from her less than productive day the day before. Checking her phone, she found an SMS with a link to the A-Bay naturists. And a text message from Jamie.

If it helps, I can go along with you the first time

I didn't realise you were interested in naturism

I'd never thought about it until you mentioned it. It sounds liberating. I'll give most things a go once. If you can handle seeing your best friend's brother naked?

Oh, you have no idea! *Thank you I'll let you know*

Even with Jamie's support, Alex wasn't sure she could take that first step. Getting naked in front of complete strangers after what happened in Perth? Even though naturists shared a philosophy based on respect and equality, how did she know she could trust them? Was she really ready to take the risk?

Also, I have a contact interested in coming up to the festival to look at your kingfisher. He is after something similar for the entrance of a sustainable housing development opening in two months.

Alex let out a squeal of excitement, startling William who scuttled beneath the fence.

It was only a show of interest, but this was how the ball started rolling. And she knew Bec's kingfisher would impress anyone who was in the market for an outdoor nature-related sculpture.

The profit from the kingfisher was going to be modest, because she'd desperately wanted to win the tender, but she would be able charge a lot more in future. All it would take now was positive word of mouth and her business would grow. She could finish renovating her house. And even though she wasn't confident she could design anything commercially viable on her own, she had a multitude of designs she and Bec had worked on together until she *was* confident. Alex hoped there would be more opportunities to keep her friend's spirit alive.

Before she could back out, she sent the A-Bay naturists a message saying she was in a group previously, had had a bad experience, would it be possible to meet in a social situation initially.

We have a group dinner at Angelo's next week. You're welcome to join us.

CHAPTER SEVEN

WHEN SHE SLIPPED on her sky-blue sheath dress and twisted her dark hair up into a messy bun, the artist, Alex Roye, transformed into Alexandra, director of Skyclad. She'd thought she'd left being the centre of attention behind – but this was different. Tonight was in recognition of her artistic talents. She wasn't just a mouthpiece, presenting a weather forecast or other people's stories. She would be representing her business, a business she hoped would be her future.

Alex arrived at the gardens early, wanting to savour the exquisite feeling of excitement and pride. Even though her new home was located in the sub-tropics, the night was unseasonably warm and balmy for a late-autumn night. The perfect temperature for the invitation-only opening of the annual Halcyon Days Water Festival, and the unveiling of her sculpture.

Underwater lights placed around the lagoon flared upward to illuminate the opaque sheet draping her sculpture. The grassed area in front, where a large crowd mingled, was lit by fairy lights, and surrounding trees lit with up-lights. Waiters wove through the revellers with trays of drinks and delicious smelling finger food.

She was speaking with Bec's parents when she spotted her friend Corinne picking her way over the grassed area in super-high heels. After Alex introduced them, May and Cameron excused themselves and went to find the table of refreshments.

"I had a peek before they covered her up. Wow! She looks amazing!" Corinne squeezed Alex's arm and handed her a glass of champagne.

"Thanks. For a while there I wondered if I'd finish on time, with that rain we had on Monday."

"Well you did, and she's magnificent." Corinne held out her ipad and handed Alex the stylus. "I'm here in a professional capacity until you sign off – and then we celebrate!"

She signed her signature under Corinne's, confirming the commission was complete.

"To Skyclad," they toasted and drank, the delicious bubbles tickling Alex's nose.

The faint burn as the liquid hit her empty stomach didn't help her nervousness over the unveiling of her first large sculpture, or the unease that Jamie hadn't arrived. She wanted him here when she dedicated the sculpture to her best friend in her speech. What if Jamie missed it? Was he even coming? Had she been wrong about the growing closeness between them?

He'd encouraged her to join the naturist group and even offered to go with her, to hold her hand. He was helping her get contacts so she could get her business established. Surely these things suggested that he wanted her to stay in Summer Shire – she hoped it was, so they had a chance to finish what they'd started twelve years earlier.

Maybe she was wrong.

Had the scandal with her boss in Perth put him off? Or maybe he would always see her as his little sister's friend.

Alex took a deep breath and pulled her shoulders back. Yes, she was disappointed, but she wouldn't let anyone sour the sweetness of this moment she'd worked so hard for.

"I'd better go and let the Mayor know she's up." Corinne gave Alex a hug of encouragement. "You'll be straight after. Go up there and tell everyone how talented you are."

Alex made her way closer to the temporary stage and tried not to fidget while the mayor explained the significance of the water festival, acknowledged the traditional owners of the land, and talked about the local flora and fauna, indigenous to the area they called home. Excitement buzzed through her when she saw two event staff take position, ready to pull the veil off her creation.

Then she was stepping onto the stage, just as the mayor signalled for the unveiling.

"Please join me in congratulating the talented artist who created what will be the symbol for our annual water festival, Alex from Skyclad."

Buoyant, Alex accepted congratulations from the mayor, and the microphone.

The crowd 'oohed' and applauded as the sheet slid off and her majestic kingfisher emerged from the newly-filled lagoon, its shimmering wings outspread as it launched itself from the water, its catch of golden perch held triumphantly aloft. The subtly hued plates reflected light at different angles, some glimmering iridescent as they would in the sun, the ones in the shade deeper in colour.

The response warmed Alex all the way through and she glowed with pleasure. This sweet acknowledgement of her creativity was what had been missing from her life.

As the applause peaked, her eyes caught on Jamie, pushing his way to the front of the crowd. The beaming smile he gave her sent her heart soaring, as high and free as the birds she adored. Like Bec's kingfisher. He had come, and that smile told her she hadn't been wrong.

"Thank you," Alex said to the crowd when the clapping petered out. "I'm so glad you like my representation of the *Alcedinidae*, our local kingfisher, and for welcoming me as a new resident to the shire." Her eyes locked on Jamie's and the crowd melted away. It was just the two of them, in the presence of nature on a fine winter's night in the sub-tropics, honouring the girl they had both loved.

"It was the dream of myself and my best friend, Bec, to create sculptures such as this. Tragically she lost her life at the age of seventeen and I have created our kingfisher on a sketch I recently re-discovered – one of her many beautiful designs." The crowd materialised again, and Alex sought out May and Cameron standing on the edge of the crowd. The look of joy and wonder on their faces filled her with a warmth and peacefulness that made her spirit take flight like the kingfisher she'd created. She would always be proud of this lasting and tangible reminder of Bec's talent, in the place where Bec had been so happy. Her gaze was drawn back to Jamie's and Alex didn't try to contain the fullness of her smile. "I would like to dedicate this sculpture to my friend, Rebecca Ainsworth."

Alex handed the microphone back to the mayor and bowed with tears of joy clouding her eyes at the surge of applause and whistles.

For you, my beautiful friend.

As she graciously accepted the crowd's applause, a playful idea to make Jamie pay for his tardiness rose out of her bubbling joy. Stepping away from the stage, she sought out Jamie, admiring the way his dark-blond hair curled away from the strong lines of his face.

As if sensing her attention, he turned and looked directly at her. Without taking his eyes off Alex, he finished his conversation and strode over to meet her. The intent way he focused on her, the way his eyes communicated his desire, told her he saw her as more than his little sister's best friend.

Alex slid her arm through his and steered him away from the crowd. "I'm feeling a little overwhelmed. Will you come with me to get some fresh air?"

"Of course, lead the way. Are you feeling okay?"

"Perfectly fine. I just wanted to celebrate in nature, and I thought we might be able to see the moon reflecting off the lake."

"Look who's being a romantic now."

"Do you have a problem with that?" Alex asked as they passed through a grove of eucalypts.

"Not at all," Jamie said in a low voice as Alex slowed to a stop by the shore, the spot where she'd often paused on her way to the gardener's cottage. No one would find them here.

He stopped beside her and breathed in deep. "I can see why you're so fond of nature. Somehow it cleanses your soul."

Happy she had the right position, Alex turned to him. She just needed to keep him occupied for three or four minutes, then she would have her sweet revenge for his tardiness.

Lowering his head, Jamie brushed gentle lips over hers, then pulled away, teasing.

Every part of Alex wanted to follow his lips, to feel his mouth on hers, but he'd teased her enough tonight. It was time for her to have the upper hand. Alex held still, waiting for him to come to her, ready to run.

When he kissed her again, he didn't pull away, but moved his lips against hers, his tongue urging her lips apart.

Alex moaned and melted in his arms. She'd underestimated her physical response to him, his touch like an accelerant, igniting a blaze that flared and radiated where their bodies met. When he cupped her breast through the fabric, she arched back, searching for more contact with his large palm, her pelvis thrust against his. All thoughts evaporated with the surge of need that flashed through her. The click of the sprinkler popping up didn't register through the fog of desire, or the hiss of the sprinkler starting, the first indication her plan was about to explode into fruition.

The first shaft of cold water jerked Alex to her back to reality, but it was too late to avoid the deluge that soaked them both. They gasped in unison, dragged out of their lust, and hand in hand, staggered across the grass. Out of range of the sprinkler, they stopped, panting, and looked at each other, hair and clothing plastered to their bodies.

Mirth rose like helium in her chest, escaping as giggles as Jamie threw his head back and laughed to the star-speckled sky.

She didn't care that her plan had backfired. Taking his hand in a firm grip, Alex pulled Jamie toward the cottage. In the glow of the security light, Alex fumbled the key from her clutch, steadying her shivering hand enough to unlock the door.

She stepped inside – and gasped at what she found in the room she'd come to regard as her sanctuary. Cocktail jazz played low and fairy lights gave the interior a warm glow, illuminating a padded platform covered in throw cushions in the centre of the room. An ice-bucket and a couple of champagne glasses sat on the lunch table.

Jamie had planned to bring her here. This is where he'd been when before he came to the unveiling. Why he'd arrived late.

Alex turned to glance at Jamie over her shoulder, his gesture warming her deep inside, hope fanning the flames of her hunger for him.

"I love what you've done with the place," she said with a grin.

"I thought we could celebrate with a Bedouin supper." Jamie's voice was low and rough as he pressed his cold, solid body against her back and placed his hands on her shoulders.

Warmth bloomed where he touched her and set her heart fluttering. "And what dies a Bedouin supper contain, may I ask?" Alex asked in a husky whisper.

"Something very similar to an antipasto plate ordered from Jen's deli I believe." His chuckle vibrated against her back.

Alex shivered and turned with a smile on her lips. She looked up into his eyes, crinkled at the corners and sparkling with mirth. Reaching between them, she tugged at the knot of his wet tie. "I'm still full of the delicious finger food they were served *before you arrived*. And I think we should get some of these wet clothes off you," she said, loosening the tie.

When the knot was loose enough, Jamie lifted it over his head and hung it on the handle of her welding trolley. "Gladly, but what about yours?" he asked with a crooked smile.

"It's silk. It's ruined, but it is virtually drip-dry." Her damp dress left little to the imagination, and Jamie's gaze raked her from eyes to lips, lingering on her erect nipples and lower, to the small triangular shadow visible through the fabric.

She stepped close, and helped him shrug out of his wet jacket, turning to hang it over the back of a chair.

Jamie stepped forward to stand with Alex in the pool of light. She felt cocooned by his closeness, surrounded by acres of dark garden just outside the walls of their sanctuary. Out of the breeze and warmed by the sun all day, the temperature inside the cottage eased their shivering. "Can I interest you in a glass of Champagne? Or a dance?" He held out his hand and she placed her palm in his, her other hand on his chest and stepped into his embrace.

"Dancing might warm us up," Alex said and followed his body as he swayed slowly to the music.

"Your kingfisher is magnificent. We are lucky to have your talent, and my parents are very glad you moved here too."

"And what about Jamie Ainsworth?"

"Can't you tell how happy I am you're here?" The heat in his gaze made it clear he wanted her, but she had to be sure.

"Are you sure?"

"I've never been more sure about anything in my life." The catch in his voice would have been enough, but his earnest expression convinced her.

Struggling to draw enough breath, Alex gasped with the intensity of her need to feel more of him, to have his lips on hers, his hands on her body. Pressing closer, her pelvis nudged his. Her heart leapt with anticipation to find he was as aroused as she was. Need coiled through her lower abdomen, winding tight into to a throbbing need that pulsed through her sex. Pressing her mouth to his, she steered him backward.

"Me too. Lie down," she said as she lifted her lips from his to pull her hem around her thighs and straddle his hips. Seeking his mouth again, thirsty for his kisses, she pressed her sex against his erection and unbuttoned his shirt with urgent fingers. She needed him naked, wanted him bare for her.

Alex pushed his shirt open and gripped his shoulders, squeezing the solid muscle, assuring herself he really was here. She had wanted this for so long, and here he was, the man she dreamt of, beneath her, between her thighs. She groaned and pressed herself against him, seeking and gathering the hot desire that ignited where they touched.

His big hands around her waist anchored her to him as she dragged her palms over the mounds of his pecs, fingers circling and pinching his nipples until he arched beneath her.

"Alex," he gasped and lifted his head, seeking her mouth.

"Not yet. I want to see you. "Moving down his body until she reached his belt, she unbuckled and unzipped, then travelled lower to pull off his shoes and socks.

"Come here, goddess," he commanded in a husky voice, and this time she gladly obeyed, kissing her way up his toned abdomen, over his pecs and up his neck to his jaw.

"My turn, minx," he growled, and rolled her onto her back before she reached his mouth.

Those big, now-warm hands travelled over her ribs, tickling and teasing their way to her breasts. She arched against him, offering herself to his caress and he answered with his fingertips, teasing and plucking her nipples until she squirmed against him. The throbbing in her sex intensified so she was breathless with desperation to feel him inside her.

Reaching down, she shimmied her dress up until she could feel the soft fabric of his trousers against her calves, her knees, her inner thighs.

Alex took his face in her hands and she imagined the scrape of light stubble against tenderer skin that that on her palms. "I want to feel you inside me," she gasped and nudged her pelvis against his. "Do you know how long I've dreamt of this, thinking it could never be?"

"Then I was dreaming the same dream," he breathed against her neck and reached down, sucking in a breath when he found her sans underwear. "I should have known you would be naked underneath," he growled.

"You should have," she said, then moaned as he parted her with gentle fingers, a shiver of pleasure travelling over her body.

Jamie lifted his hips and without moments Alex had divested him of both trousers and boxers, freeing his eager cock to nudge her thigh, reminding her of the condom she'd put in her evening bag, hoping this was how the night would end. "Wait," she panted and lifted to her elbows.

"Looking for this?" he asked and pulled a condom packet from the cushion behind her head. "I was being optimistic." Jamie tore the packet open with his teeth and a grin and Alex fell back onto the cushions, heart clenched at the sight of the smile she thought she'd lost forever.

CHAPTER EIGHT

DAMN, the woman felt like heaven in his hands. The way her flesh and her body moved against him wove a spell on his soul. Jamie knew that once he entered her, he would be well and truly lost, but he didn't care. He didn't need his heart or his soul if he couldn't have her. If she didn't want him after this, at least he would have this one night.

And if it might be only once, he wanted to do it her way. Bared. They had to lose all their clothes.

He put the condom beside her hip and knelt back to shrug off his shirt, his skin warming where her eyes caressed him.

He stood and stepped out of his trousers and boxers, his cock jerking with impatience as her gaze devoured him like a warm mouth. Fuck, he wanted to see her naked. He wanted her to feel free and uninhibited.

But when he knelt between her knees and ran his hands over her hips, pushing her now-dry dress upward, her hands gripped his, stopping the movement.

"Is there something wrong?" he asked, confused.

"My scar."

"Oh." He would have pulled his hands away, but her grip stopped him.

"It's not so much that it's ugly, I didn't think that would bother you, but…"

"You're worried it will remind me, that it will spoil this. That her ghost will be here with us."

"Yes." Of course, he understood. She released his hands.

He placed his forearms either side of her face and looked into her eyes, their noses inches apart.

"You know, Bec used to talk all the time about what it would be like if her best friend was my wife. It was her deepest wish that the two people she loved most would find happiness together. I always let her think it was her dream, but I think she instinctively knew it was my dream too. We can heal each other, now we've found each other again. Will you let me show you?"

"Yes." Alex smiled shyly and pulled the hem up, baring her sex, her abdomen, her ribs. Her eyes urged him to look.

He moved away enough so she could pull the dress over her head, her breasts thrust upward, the exposed puncture wound and twisted scar glowing pale in the light.

He hadn't known she'd been so badly hurt in the accident and the realisation had the effect she'd feared. The horror of the day crashed over him, knocking the breath from his lungs and deflating his desire.

She reached for his hand and moved his fingers to the healed wound.

He held his breath and touched the knotted flesh tentatively. The skin there was warm and pliable, although not as soft as the rest of her. But she didn't flinch. With growing confidence, he traced the scar, then cupped his palm over it as if he could take away the memory of that horrific day by covering it with his own flawless flesh.

"Does it bother you?" she asked.

He looked into her worried eyes. "No. I'm glad I've seen it. I'm so sorry this happened to you. It must have taken months to recover."

"I don't really remember the physical pain. All I could think of was that I wasn't conscious when Bec died. I wasn't there for her. I didn't get to say good-bye." A tear snaked down her cheek and Jamie wiped it with his fingertip. "When I came to, she had already passed away. The only thing I could do was protect her from her mistake."

"She knew you loved her. And she will always be with us, in our hearts." He said and cupped her cheek. "Would you like me to take you home?"

Alex took his hand and placed it on her breast.

Desire returned with a vengeance but he hesitated, needing to be sure she still wanted him.

"Kiss me?" she asked with a searching look.

And he did, gently at first. When she responded, wrapping her arm around him and nudging his tongue with hers, he groaned and kissed her harder, his cock nudging her thigh.

"Make love with me?" she breathed when their lips parted.

He dropped his forehead to hers and looked into her eyes. "I thought you'd never ask."

Holding his breath, he rolled on the condom and paused, the head of his cock nudging at her entrance.

"Don't tease," she sighed, her hands gripping his butt as she lifted her hips, begging him to claim her.

With his last clear thought, he thanked fate for bringing them back together and plunged into her warm depths. Stunned at the feel of her tight pussy gripping him, at finally experiencing the fantasy he'd tried – unsuccessfully – not to entertain, he paused, buried fully in the heat of her.

"Don't stop," she growled.

He obeyed, pulling out so he could plunge deep again.

"Jamie," she sobbed and shuddered beneath him, her fingers digging into his flesh and stealing his control.

"Alex," he sighed and kissed the wetness from her cheeks as he moved slowly, rhythmically, making love to her with every muscle and fibre of his being, hoping to hell this wasn't the only time, but determined to savour every moment in case it was. Each time he paused, buried so fully her wet heat clasped him to the balls, he thought they couldn't get any closer, but each time he moved inside her, the feeling that their edges were melding continued to grow until he experienced her pleasure as his own.

And it was bringing him undone.

Each torturously slow thrust was a battle between the instinct to surrender to ecstasy and not wanting it to end. With her every hum and moan of pleasure against his neck, his will melted and his pace quickened.

And when she called his name and clenched around him, he was lost, her pleasure becoming his as her body stiffened with climax and together, they rode the waves of bliss.

•   •   •

JAMIE WOKE as dawn lightened the sky in a wash of pale pinks and orange. He traced his fingertips lightly down Alex's arm as her eyelids fluttered open. Her expression was soft and warm as her lips had been only hours before and he yearned to feel them against his again.

"You are so beautiful," he said, and shifted his weight onto his elbow so he could look down and better appreciate her high cheekbones and luscious mouth, her tawny hair spilling around her face. "I wish I could paint you."

A chorus of magpie song cut through the air and reminded Jamie there would be crowds of festival goers flooding into the gardens at 10am.

"We should probably get out of here, unless you want to do the walk of shame through half the residents of Summer shire?"

"Shit! I completely forgot." Alex jumped up, her slim body twisting as she searched through her work gear and pulled out a pair of overalls. "There will be council staff setting up soon. They must not see us together." She stepped into the overalls and zipped them up before bending to search the ground for something other than her high heels to put on. Finding her spare pair of work boots under the table, she sat and pulled them onto her bare feet.

"You're worried people will assume we just spent the night together?" Jamie asked.

She paused at the hurt tone of his voice. She'd forgotten everything last night while she was in his arms, but now it all came back in an instant of clarity. Her business, her reputation, his parents. It could all go horribly wrong, like it had in Perth, but this time she would deserve the rumours if people found out.

"Yes. I'm a council contractor, and in a roundabout way you're my boss. You inspected and approved my work, goddamn it." Alex said, getting agitated.

"Okay. Calm down. I parked in the bus drop-off zone, in the opposite direction from the main carpark. You leave first and take some of your equipment – tell anyone who asks you came to collect it for another project you're working on. I'll wait for a while before I leave and if I see anyone, I'll tell them I drank too much and left my car here last night. That I've come back to pick it up."

"Okay." Alex turned and took his face in her hands to lean in and kiss him hard on the mouth. "Thank you for understanding."

"I know this is awkward for you after what happened in Perth." He stroked her cheek with the back of his fingers and looked deep into her eyes. "Don't worry, I'll make sure you don't get any more council contracts," he said, and winked.

Alex rewarded him with a deep-throated laugh. He still knew how to ease her fears.

"And don't forget, we have the meeting with Ian at 11am," he reminded her.

In the excitement of the launch and what came after, Alex had completely forgotten the meeting they'd set up with one of Jamie's colleagues who worked in the private sector. Ian McKinlay wanted to speak to her about a large sculpture for the entry of a new eco estate.

"I'll meet you at *Coffee Been*?" Alex collected her evening bag, heels and ruined dress, and dropped them into the bag she used to carry her tools. Lifting it, she turned to smile at Jamie.

"I'll be there." Jamie caught her hand before she got to the door. "Can we do this again?"

A wave of joy washed over her. *It wasn't just one night. He wanted more.*

"I'd love to. But somewhere more comfortable next time."

The image she carried with her through the morning was Jamie, gloriously naked, searching for his shirt and trousers.

———

JAMIE AND IAN had already arrived and ordered brunch by the time Alex hurried into the café. Taking a seat in the chair Jamie pulled out, she gratefully accepted the coffee and eggs benedict he'd ordered for her.

"I'm famished." She smiled and blushed as she recalled how she'd worked up her appetite and why she hadn't had time for breakfast.

Jamie ignored the look. "Ian McKinlay, this is Alexandra, owner of Skyclad. As you know, her magnificent sculpture of a kingfisher was unveiled at the opening of council's inaugural water festival at the botanic gardens just last night."

"A pleasure to meet you, Alexandra. I drove past on the way here and it certainly is impressive. I'm looking forward to taking a closer look after brunch. Your style of work looks ideal for our development and I hope you'll agree to work with us."

"Did you have anything particular in mind?"

"Well, we will be preserving the nearby wetlands and native Wallum, so the committee had hoped to do something to reflect the endemic wildlife, which strongly features bird life. I hear that is your speciality."

"It is, and I have visited the area you're talking about. I noticed there was a particular species of waterhen specific to that area."

Alex opened her napkin and pulled a pen out of her bag and began to sketch a purple swamp hen in flight, its long thin legs dangling at a recognisable angle. The lines flowed from her pen and Alex was surprised at how the strategic positioning of a few crucial lines could perfectly capture the bird's characteristics.

She glanced up at Jamie with an excited inhale. She'd never felt this surge of creativity without being naked, and the possibilities of creative freedom blew her mind.

Jamie seemed just as excited; his raised brows hidden beneath the dishevelled flop of his blond hair. With a grin, she went back to her sketch.

Ian's shadow fell on her face as he leant to look. "That looks perfect. I can tell you are the right person for the job. Can you do three sketches with accompanying technical drawings and material quantities and costs? Then we can put the three options to the committee."

"Of course. I'll do some research on local birdlife and get the drawings and quotes to you by the end of the week."

"Alex," a familiar voice called from the counter. Corinne walked over, smiling broadly, until she noticed Ian and stopped in her tracks, her smile disappearing. "What the hell are you doing here?"

"You two know each other?" Alex asked, trying to imagine a connection between an out-of-town property developer and her recently naturalised friend.

"Ian is Gerald's brother," Corinne said, folding her arms.

"Gerald, as in your fiancé?" Alex asked when the pieces fell into place. Corinne had moved from Northern England with her fiancé, only to have him leave her for an Australian girl he'd met at work. Having tied up her old life in the UK and found a good job and a place to live, she'd decided to stay.

"That's right."

Ian stood and gave Corinne an apologetic smile. "Hey, it's great to see you. Is there any chance we could talk? Privately."

"It looks like you're busy," she replied, her voice cold.

Ian glanced at Alex and Jamie. "I'm sold. I'd just like to look at the kingfisher, and then I think we can continue by email?"

"I can take Ian to show him your sculpture," Corinne said, her voice tight.

"Are you sure?" Alex looked at her friend searchingly and noticed the pinkness of her cheeks.

"I don't mind," Corinne said and looked pointedly between Alex and Jamie. "It looks like you two have plenty else to occupy your day…"

"Actually, I need to go grab some gear from the cottage," Alex said and stood too.

Jamie walked her to her car. "I'd offer to help you move your gear, but Dad mentioned he's already organised to come by with his trailer and I know it means a lot to him to be able to help in any way."

"I have a lot to thank your family for." Alex sighed at the feel of the breeze dancing in her hair. "Your dad's a great guy, but he's not perfect, is he?"

"You mean my decision to study engineering instead of fine art?"

Alex nodded and stopped on the footpath beside her car.

Jamie shrugged. "None of us are perfect, are we?"

"No, but we all have the choice to follow our dream – or someone else's."

"Speaking from experience?"

"Definitely,' she replied and leant back against her car.

"And look at you now. About to launch yourself as successful outdoor sculptor." Jamie took a deep breath and leant against the car beside her. "I admit my decision to become and engineer was my way of atoning for my guilt over Becca's death, for the pain I'd caused. But I am glad I took that path. With hindsight, it was a better career move than being an artist, and financially it has allowed me to build a good life, to build the home of my dreams. And there's still plenty of time to explore my artistic side."

"I'm glad, and you're right. You could take night classes. We could do some work together… after the water festival." Alex trailed off.

"I'd like that. And speaking of being artistic, what was with the sketch in there? I thought you said you can't design. Not with clothes on." Jamie raised his eyebrow and he looked so cute Alex that she had to fight the urge to kiss him right there on the street.

"I can't. Even when I'm naked and in the zone, I can't draw like that. It was as if I was possessed." Alex shook her head with a smile of wonder. "Something has changed."

"Maybe it's because you've been possessed by me," Jamie said with a grin.

"I'm sure that's what it is." Alex chuckled. "Maybe my muse is as attracted to you as I am." She grew serious as a powerful realisation stuck her. "I don't need to be naked anymore to connect with her."

"It might have something to do with forgiving yourself for what happened when Becca died." Jamie lifted his hand toward her face as if he was about to brush her hair behind her hair, then pulled back, glancing left and right.

"You might be right. Whatever the reason, I think it's the perfect excuse to spend more time with you." Alex felt bad that her insecurity was the cause of Jamie curbing his affection. Not for much longer. As soon as this contract with council was finished, they could be open about their relationship – whatever it turned out to be. "You could be my business mascot."

"That works for me. The more time I get to spend with you the better."

"Shall we start with lunch tomorrow? My place?" Alex couldn't wait to get him alone again, but she needed to work on her presentation for Ian after she got her gear from the gardener's cottage.

"Then maybe we could go to the closing ceremony together tomorrow night? There'll be a barbecue and fireworks," Jamie added hopefully.

"Sounds great," Alex said, but thought they could create more impressive fireworks alone.

CHAPTER NINE

ALEX LAY her sketchpad on her lap and closed her eyes. She was getting impatient.

The fabric of her singlet dress was more distracting than being naked had ever been, considering her lack of underwear – her only nod to prior creative requirements. The soft cotton teased her nipples whenever she moved her arm to draw, and tickled her pubic hair whenever she shifted in the beanbag. The building arousal made her think of Jamie, and she wished he was there already.

After Cameron had helped her move her gear home from the gardener's cottage, Alex took some time to work on her new project. Although she would hardly call it work – sitting on her beanbag in the studio, savouring the afternoon sun streaming through the open French doors and listening to the birds calling to each other. She'd picked out eight different species she could recognise, and two she couldn't place – yet.

The session had been surprisingly constructive, and a pile of sketches lay beside her on the floor. It seemed Jamie was right. By forgiving herself for her part in Bec's death, she no longer needed to seduce her muse with naked skin. Despite being constantly distracted by memories of their night together in the gardener's cottage, Alex had already completed some impressive proposals for her presentation to Ian. It was a relief to know she wouldn't always need Bec's sketchbook for ideas. She wasn't going to assume her current communication with her muse would continue to be so productive, but in the case of this project, the client could choose between their collaborative designs and Alex's new ideas.

When Jamie arrived for lunch, they made salad sandwiches and ate at her kitchen table, flicking through magazines and the Sunday paper. It felt so easy between them now, so much so that she picked up her pencil and created her best design yet – an Eastern Great Egret – while Jamie washed the dishes. Despite the temptation to watch the muscles of his shoulders and back ripple beneath his t-shirt as he moved, she focused on the lines she was making on her sketchpad until it was finished.

Finished with the dishes, Jamie flicked the tea-towel over his shoulder and came around behind her, whistling through his teeth in appreciation. "You just keep getting better," his voice rumbled next to her ear, before feathering kisses down the side of her neck.

"Hmm, and I'm starting to think your presence might become counter-productive," Alex said with a shudder of pleasure and dropped her pencil. How could she think straight, let alone draw, if he was going to distract her with kisses? And when he traced the outer edge of her ear with his tongue, then sucked her lobe, she lost the ability to think about anything but getting him naked.

"I promise to keep my hands to myself when you need to work," he said and pulled away.

"Good thing I've finished then." Standing, she turned in his arms, and the tie that was on the back of her chair slid to the ground. She bent to pick up the twisted water-damaged fabric, deliberately allowing him a glimpse down the front of her dress.

Jamie's eyes darkened with desire.

"I'm afraid the silk is ruined," she said and draped it around her neck, sliding the soft fabric enticingly between her aroused nipples. "I tried ironing it...".

"It looks much better on you." Jamie took hold of each side of the tie and started to tie it.

"Your dad pretended he didn't see it when he helped me move my gear back home," she smirked at him. "But I'm sure he recognised it was yours."

"Looks like we've been found out. I'll get the fifth-degree next time I see them."

"I'd love to be a fly on the wall."

"Maybe you should come with me. Share the joy."

"Is that the equivalent to inviting me home to meet your parents?" She raised an eyebrow at him and glanced down at the crookedly tied silk. "Lucky you don't wear a tie often. Did no-one show you how to tie one?"

"It's definitely not my strong suit. But you know what is?" he said, his voice husky as he reached for her. "Inspections. Would you like a demonstration?" He stepped close and bent his head towards hers.

Alex stepped back with a saucy smile. "I would, but not just yet, inspector. I have other plans for you."

"I can hardly wait. What would you like me to do, boss?"

"I'm assuming you came prepared with at least one condom. Where is it?"

"In my front pocket."

She looked down at the front of his trousers with a raised eyebrow and traced the outline of his erection with a featherlight touch before dipping deep into his left pocket. "It's not in here," she said after a very thorough search.

"The… other pocket." He groaned as she thrust her hand into the right pocket, behind the bundle of condom packets to caress the length of his cock through the fabric, before pulling the packets out. "Good, this should do for a couple of hours." The feel of his hard length reminded her of how good he'd made her feel when he'd caressed her – inside and out. She could hardly wait to feel him inside her again.

"Alex, you're killing me. Tell me what you need," Jamie pleaded.

"You." Alex said in a low voice and grasped his hands, looking up into his face. "Promise you won't storm out on me this time?" She looked deep into his eyes. "The last two times you've been here, you left in rather a hurry."

"I promise I'll stay as long as you want me," Jamie promised with a sexy smile. "Unless you have any other nasty surprises for me?" He added, with a hint of insecurity.

"No more skeletons," she assured him, pushing away the niggling feeling that until the festival was over, their relationship was something she needed to hide.

"But just in case, I think I'll ensure you can't leave until I'm done with you." With a wink and eager fingers, she unbuckled his belt, unzipped his trousers and stood back, overwhelmed with desire and not trusting herself not to rip something. "I want you to finish undressing." She leant against the back of a chair, trying to slow her breathing and heartbeat. She caressed the tie between her breasts, imagining the silk was his skin, as she watched him shuck out of his shoes and socks.

His gaze remained locked on hers, passion smouldering and his movements purposeful. Stepping out of his trousers, then his boxer briefs, he straightened in front of her, arms at his sides, while she admired the beauty of his form. Solid and strong, not an ounce of fat.

At the sight of him, and the eager angle of his cock, Alex was impatient to take him up against the wall, on her work bench, on the floor. But stronger than her hunger to have him, was the desire to savour the sparking heat between them.

"Take a seat, inspector," she commanded through a suddenly tight throat, as she lifted a chair for him to sit.

He sat, obediently, but with a grin, and she walked behind him. "Hands behind your back." She removed the tie from her neck, untied it and bound his hands before returning to stand in front of him, so close that their knees were almost touching.

"Alex. You're killing me."

With a smile of satisfaction, she bent forward and placed her palms on her thighs. The neck gaped open, exposing her nipples to his gaze. Straightening, she gathered her dress, so the hem grazed her calves then her thighs, and collecting the fabric until it gathered at her hips, revealed her sex to him.

"Let me tell you *my* little secret." She paused with a wicked grin. Two could play that game. "I'm a naturist."

"And what does that mean?" he asked, playing along.

"As Walt Whitman said, *'Never before did I get so close to Nature; never before did she come so close to me... Nature was naked, and I was also…"* She recited the words, as she stepped forward to straddle his thighs until her sex almost brushed his penis.

His arms jerked against their binding, his expression speaking of the urge to take hold of her hips and bury his erection in her wet heat. "You're not naked now," he choked out as she tore the condom wrapper in front of his face.

"No, but I'm in control." She smiled and rolled the sheath over his penis.

His head dropped back, his eyes falling closed as a look of sheer ecstasy washed his face.

"Head up, inspector. Look at me."

Lifting his head, Jamie locked his eyes on hers. The need she saw there, and his submission, melted any thought of teasing him.

With a sigh of satisfaction, she lowered herself onto his erection, burying him deep, then lifting off him, slow and smooth. Dropping the hem of her dress, she grasped the chair behind his shoulders as an anchor, and used his cock for her pleasure, riding him hard and fast, then slow and deep. *She didn't want this to end, ever.*

She experienced his pleasure through his expressions, and saw his effort to delay his climax.

The surly inspector under her control. Seeing his struggle intensify triggered the aching need building in her pelvis expand to overflow. Slowing the rhythm of her hips as her orgasm unfurled around his cock, Alex gave in to the sensations flooding her body, riding the waves of pleasure for as long as possible as his hips bucked beneath her.

When she had caught her breath, she kissed him deeply, and stood, looking down into his face, so dear to her. The face of the man she loved, the man who had bared his soul and his weakness to her.

Her thighs either side of his, she pulled the dress over her head with a sigh of relief, revealing her nakedness, her scar close to his face. Discarding the dress on the floor, she stepped away from him, and circled the chair to untie his hands and return to face him.

Standing, he reached for her, his fingers seeking the dip of her waist, the curve of her hips, the bumps of her ribs and the knotted scar. "*You* are a work of art." He took the tie from her hand. "My turn."

"What do you have in mind?" she asked, nervous of relinquishing control. But this was Jamie. She trusted him.

"May I put this over your eyes?"

She jerked with alarm. She couldn't make herself any more vulnerable than being naked and sightless. But he'd trusted her, put himself at her mercy, she would do the same for him.

Taking a deep breath, she nodded, and excitement flared at the uncertainty of what he planned for her.

He stepped behind her and dropped the tie in front of her face. "Close your eyes."

Alex obeyed and she felt the gentle caress of silk on her eyelids, his warm hands smoothing the fabric over her cheeks before he tied the blindfold behind her head.

"Stand," he said and held her hand as he led her to her studio. She stopped when he did, and he took her other hand and supported her as she reclined onto her beanbag.

Naked and sightless, her senses were on high alert. She felt him hovering over her, not quite touching her, but she could feel the warmth of his body. The brush of his lips, teasing hers, gently. The smell of him, delicious, his cologne, her arousal on his skin. His tongue teasing, her mouth opening… then he was gone.

"Don't stop," she whispered, straining to listen, trying to work out what he was doing.

Confused by a furtive rustling, she was tempted to take the silk from her eyes when a damp touch slid across her belly.

What was that?

Another stroke and her flesh shivered. *A paintbrush.* She had become his canvas. He was using her brushes and acrylics to paint his desire on her skin. With each stroke of his brush, the pressure and direction always varying, she visualised a different colour. Sunny yellow, sensual red, green, blue…

Jamie painted his message over her belly and ribs, over the mounds of her breasts, teasing her nipples with light fast strokes, deepening and slowing, circling and teasing, until she cried out in frustration. "Jamie, fuck me. Please."

A chuckle. "Soon, goddess. Be patient, you're not done yet."

Finally, when she could stand it no more, she gripped his wrist, pulled the brush out of his hand and dropped it to the floor. She held her breath. How and where would he touch her now that his instrument of torture was gone?

Relief came with his hot mouth on her sex, and she arched into the caress. She sighed with satisfaction and pressed herself against his tongue. He rewarded her until she shivered with approaching ecstasy. Just as his brush did with her nipple, his tongue circled and flicked her clit, and all the colours he painted on her skin burst behind her eyelids as her sex pulsed with orgasm.

When the waves of pleasure receded, she heard and felt him climb up her body, his cock sliding easily inside her as he took her mouth in a hungry kiss. He buried himself deep, thrusting hard and determined and Alex writhed beneath him, urging him deeper.

When his thrusts became erratic, she reached up to pull the silk from her eyes so she could witness his climax.

"I love you," Jamie breathed in her ear as he cradled her head in his hands.

She opened her lips to reply, but the words "I love you, too," seemed to lodge in her chest as pleasure exploded between them.

THE BEANBAG PROVING TOO small for two exhausted adults, Alex led Jamie to her bedroom where they spent the rest of the afternoon dozing in each other's arms.

"I could get used to this," Jamie said as he stretched out, his golden chest hairs glinting in the late afternoon sun streaming through her open window.

"Sleeping with a council contractor?" She teased and lightly bit one of his nipples, making him curl toward her and groan with pleasure.

"No, making love to you Friday night, brunch with you on Saturday, making love Sunday afternoon… then Sunday night. *Oomph!*"

Alex wacked him lightly across the middle with a pillow. "Assuming privileges already?"

"Not at all, just hopeful." He smiled and ran his fingers down her arm, making her skin pebble.

"Hope is a good thing, but right now we'd better have a shower and get dressed. Don't forget we'll be expected at the festival barbecue and fireworks."

"Or we could just stay here…"

His fingers were making a very good argument for his case, but before they managed to convince her she slipped out of his grasp.

Skipping into the bathroom, she turned the taps on in the shower, knowing she would have to wait for the hot water to come through. This would be the next room she'd renovate. She'd been about to convert the heating to gas when she'd run out of money.

Alex smiled and looked in the mirror. She couldn't remember being so happy, not since Bec's death. She almost looked like a different person. Ever since the day at the dam, when they buried the cause of Bec's death, she'd felt lighter, freer. And she'd noticed changes in Jamie too. Each day he seemed more and more like the Jamie she used to know. It wasn't just his relaxed appearance, but the re-emergence of his sense of humour. The carefree teenager she had a crush on had matured, and with that maturity, Alex found him even easier to love.

Just before she stepped into the shower, Alex glanced down at her painted body in the mirror, at the scar he'd caressed and the body he had loved. She paused, stunned by the beauty Jamie had created on her flesh. He was good. Very good.

In her reflection, she traced overlapping leaves and curling vines over her stomach and breasts, her gaze coming to rest on the lotus bloom he'd painted around her navel.

The final layer of guilt tore and dropped away. Jamie had helped her forgive herself for Bec's death and to realise her dream of living a creative life, but she'd also helped him to re-connect with his dream.

THE FESTIVAL'S evening entertainments were well underway when Alex and Jamie arrived at the entrance to the botanic gardens. As they approached her kingfisher, Alex stopped and stared at her achievement in awe.

She had built this beautiful creature. She'd created this monument to Bec, with nothing but her own two hands and her friend's sketch for inspiration.

Jamie moved away before they reached the manned entry point for the festival, so there was no chance of their hands brushing. It felt like a rejection, after all they'd shared recently. Even though she knew he was doing it for her, it felt like more than just physical distance.

When the crowd thickened and they were forced closer, the reasons she'd tried to hide their relationship no longer made sense. She'd uprooted her life over what happened at the studio in Perth – for the better, as it turned out – but she would not let other peoples' opinions dictate how she lived her life anymore. Jamie deserved more than that, and so did she. They had nothing to be ashamed of.

As they approached a group of people she recognised as council staff, Alex slipped her arm through Jamie's and pressed close to his side.

"What are you doing?" he whispered loudly out the side of his mouth.

"I don't want to hide how we feel. I had the contract for the sculpture before we hooked up, and I did bloody good work. I have nothing to hide, and everything to be proud of."

Jamie stopped and turned to her, with a concerned look. "Are you sure?"

"I'm positive. I love you," she said and raised up on her toes, resting her hands on his shoulders and pressing her lips to his. Jamie sucked in a surprised breath and instinctively opened his lips, welcoming her tongue in a slow dance of passion and promise as he slid his arms around her back. Sliding her hands behind his neck, she pulled him closer still, and the joy and freedom of the intimate caress surpassed any kiss they'd ever shared, as if by broadcasting their feelings to the world, they had opened the gates of trust.

Alex pressed herself against him. She never wanted it to end, wanted to feel this close to Jamie always, but with commendable effort, she pulled her lips from his and stood smiling idiotically up at Jamie's stunned expression. "Wow."

"Yeah. Wow." Jamie said, sounding as awed as she felt.

"So, I guess that means we're officially a couple now?" Alex asked, her voice husky with emotion.

"I guess we are." He replied with a wide, contagious smile.

"I'm glad we sorted that out, because here come your parents."

CHAPTER TEN

THE NEXT WEEKEND, Jamie invited Alex for a picnic, texting her the location only an hour before they were due to meet. When she pulled up to the address, it wasn't a park as she'd expected, but a rammed-earth beach house located on the opposite side of the bay from his parents' home.

Jamie's house.

He answered a moment after she knocked on the timber panelled front door.

"I thought we were having a picnic," she said, handing Jamie a chilled bottle of wine.

"We are. Come on in." With a smile tinged with youthful excitement, he opened the door wider, inviting her inside with a preview of clean lines and open spaces.

Alex followed him through the foyer into a large open-plan living area which, through its perfect proportions and clever angles, complemented but didn't detract from the stunning view. Sea and sky spread before them through the enormous bi-fold doors that filled the entire east wall. Even from this distance, she recognised the beach across the bay where they'd spent that memorable summer.

Pausing at the open wall where inside met nature, Alex thought she could happily stare all day at the blue ocean and pristine sand that stretched beyond the dunes, if it weren't for the distraction of the gorgeous man beside her.

Even the spacious bedroom with a plain yet sumptuous bed and a view as stunning as the living room couldn't compete with Jamie, who leant against a minimalist dresser, his hands in the front pockets of his jeans, his casual shirt unbuttoned just enough to see the tanned curve of the top of his pecs.

"It's beautiful," she said, breathless with awe of him and his home. "You've created something beautiful."

An inherent sense of peace imbued the stunning yet comfortable home he'd created, proof that even though he'd compromised his dream of being a fine artist, he'd made creativity an integral part of his life. Warm satisfaction filled Alex with the knowledge Jamie had found an outlet for his artistic talents after all.

When he led her outside to the deck, she turned and raise done eyebrow at him. Close to the table set for two, a pair of easels were set up with paper, and a small table between them with palettes, brushes and paint.

"For later," Jamie said mysteriously.

"I'm intrigued," Alex replied with an encouraging smile, unsure if she was more excited at the prospect of sharing the joy of painting with Jamie, or disappointed that doing so would delay their inevitable lovemaking.

"Please, sit. I'll bring lunch out," he said and pulled out a deck chair for her before he strode inside.

The meal and wine he served her was light and delicately flavoured, perfect for a beach-side picnic.

"Thank you for a very tasty lunch," Alex said as they shared a fruit plate and dark chocolate mousse. It was so great sitting out on the deck together, so close to nature, in the home he'd created. In love, with their secrets and fears exposed and put to rest, and so much to look forward to…

"It was my pleasure. A pleasure I hope to enjoy much more often," he said as he placed a black velvet bag on the table next to her plate.

Alex inhaled sharply, her eyes widening as she studied Jamie's face for confirmation of the contents. He looked back at her, the muscles of his face tense but with an otherwise closed expression – he was nervous.

Could it be? The moment she'd dreamt of as a girl, and not dared to hope for as an adult?

Alex picked up the bag, weighing the contents and trying to restrain the joy that threatened to overwhelm her. Except rings usually came in velvet boxes, not bags. She loosened the opening, slid her fingers inside and pulled out the flat metal object. *A key.*

Alex glanced up and found Jamie looking at her expectantly.

"Will you move in with me?" He paused then hurried on. "I understand if you want to keep your own place as well, your studio, but I want to share this with you. To have meals together – and share a bed. We could create a beautiful life together."

Alex didn't need to think about it. "Yes!" she cried as she leant over to take his face in her hands and kiss him soundly, her heart beating wildly. It was exactly what she wanted too.

"And if I asked you another question would your answer be the same?" Jamie held her hand gently in his while he leant away from her to reach for something on the seat beside him. He straightened and offered his other hand to Alex, a small, square object cradled in his outstretched palm. His eyes, serious but warm with emotion, searched hers.

She glanced down at the red velvet box. Her mouth went dry at the thought of the question she hoped was about to ask.

"When I was seventeen, I thought you were the one for me," he said and squeezed her hand. "Now I *know* that you are. I never stopped thinking about you, never stopped regretting that I lost you. If I'd known you felt the same I would have come to find you, but maybe it wasn't the right time until now. Maybe we needed to learn the hard lessons to appreciate how lucky we are that we ever met."

Oh god, he was going to propose! Alex was breathless with anticipation, and giddy with the thought of spending every day with Jamie for the rest of her life. Not so long ago she'd believed she would never see him again.

"Well, goddess, what do you think?" Jamie asked with a slightly unsteady smile. "I love you Alex Roye. Will you marry me?"

Alex could only nod, her vision blurring with tears of joy. It was all she could have hoped for when he'd asked her to move in, but now he was asking to be with her forever. The reality surpassed her most precious hope.

Jamie knelt and kissed her knuckles. "Is that a yes?" He flipped the box open and Alex blinked at the gorgeous ring. A gorgeous, vibrant diamond standing proud, supported by interlocking wings decorated with trails of tiny diamonds.

Alex leant forward and cradled his face in her hands. "Yes! I want all of that too." she said and kissed him.

Jamie pulled back before it got too passionate. Standing, he urged her to her feet and slid the engagement ring onto her finger. "Alexandra Ainsworth?"

The band fitted her finger perfectly and already she couldn't imagine ever taking it off. "Yes! I can't wait to be Mrs. Ainsworth!"

And then he kissed her until they were both breathless.

Alex pulled back and looked up into her fiancé's beautiful face. She giggled at his dazed expression.

"I can't believe after all this time, all that has happened, we've ended up together." He shook his head with a bewildered grin.

A warm breeze brushed her bare arms and for a moment Alex felt as if they were being watched. She glanced around quickly but no-one was there. No-one living. But she sensed her friend's presence in the garden with them, in the sweet scent of the flowering wattle and the afternoon birdsong drifting on the breeze. She felt her joy at the happiness they had come so close to losing forever. "Bec would be ecstatic."

"Almost as thrilled as mum and dad will be when we tell them," he chuckled and gathered her into his arms for a hug.

"I can't wait to see their faces." Alex rested her cheek against his warm chest, imagining their reaction, and everything in her world settled into place. May and Cameron, the parents she had once daydreamed were her own, would be family. She couldn't speak for the pure emotion that was almost too much to contain at the thought of their joyful welcome, of being part of a proper, loving family.

Turning her head, she kissed the warm skin at the base of Jamie's neck to ground herself before looking up at him. The hungry look she found in his eyes suggested lunch wasn't over just yet. "Well actually I can," she giggled. There was plenty of time to break the news to Jamie's parents. Much later.

"So, tell me, what is the art equipment for?" she asked and raised an eyebrow at him.

"I thought you'd never ask. As well as making me deliriously happy, you've inspired me. I thought I'd pick up where I left off, if you'll be patient with me. You weren't the only one who felt eclipsed by Becca's creative genius. I used to hide my drawings because I knew our parents would see them as inferior, and then I stopped altogether."

"I'd like to see your work." Alex said, intrigued to know what he had chosen for his subjects and whether he'd favoured a realistic or abstract style.

"Nothing survived, but I'm keen to start again. Although I should warn you; I'm going to be very rusty." He paused and brushed a loose tendril of hair behind her ear. "Will you paint with a novice like me?"

A flashback of the garden of delights he had painted on her naked flesh came to mind and her body flushed with remembered pleasure. If that was rusty, she couldn't wait to see what he would create with practice. And the beauty and pleasure they would create together.

"I would love to, but I should warn you, I do my best work when I'm naked."

"That's why we're having a picnic in my *private* garden." Jamie grinned and slipped off his t-shirt. With a raised eyebrow, he unbuttoned his shorts. Stepping out of them, he stood before her, completely naked, his toned, tanned body glowing in the sun.

"It's going to be difficult to concentrate," Alex said and pulled her sundress over her head, her body and her love revealed to him. With the sun and her fiancé's gaze caressing her nakedness and her scars, she breathed in the salty fresh air and dropped her dress on a chair. In that moment, standing bare, she finally had everything she needed to create the fulfilling and happy life she had once dreamt of. Love. Respect. Belonging. Friends and family. A career she loved. And Jamie.

Who took a long, deep breath and held out his hand to her. "You are the most beautiful thing in my world. May I paint you?" Jamie said.

"On me?"

"Not today, although I'd certainly love to repeat that very pleasurable exercise very soon."

Alex shivered with anticipation and gave him a sultry smile. "Hmm. I'll look forward to it."

The end

Thank you for reading!
If you enjoyed *Girls On Film*, help other readers find it too and consider leaving a review wherever you purchased the book.

Keep up to date with my news and receive regular freebies by
subscribing to my newsletter

Or my blog:
www.josiebaker.exposed

ABOUT THE AUTHOR

- romance with an erotic twist -

Josie is a lover of beauty and all things sensual. Her stories are inspired by everyday experiences and often by the people she meets.

"Daisy, Chained" won the 2018 RWA Spicy Bites award for Erotic Romance, short fiction and appears in the Spicy Bites Anthology "Chained".
Josie's story "Esther Jones and the Temple of the Moon" appears in the RWA 2019 Spicy Bites Anthology "Masks".

For more about Josie and her books,
visit josiebaker.exposed

Would you like to hear about new releases, special offers and freebies? Sign up for Josie's monthly newsletter

ALSO BY JOSIE BAKER

Love, Lust & Nipple Clamps

Inspired by Anaïs Nin's 'Little Birds', Josie's collection of sensual short stories explores many fascinating facets of female desire and sensuality.

Each story will take you on an erotic journey...

watch as Gwen sheds her puritanical fiance and delves into an illicit sex club where voyeurism is the only entry requirement...

visit a penthouse apartment in Paris where reality exceeds Lilianne's most uninhibited fantasies...

and experience a connection that transcends physical boundaries.

Become a voyeur and join Josie as she delves into the worlds of exhibitionism, dominance & submission, self pleasure, sex with a stranger and ménage à trois.

Contains re-edited short stories, previously published in four editions of 'Peep Shows' plus additional novelette 'Penetration'.

"Josie Baker writes erotic stories that trigger some serious fantasy. Her voice is contemporary, capturing rich and sensual moods expressed in clear and exotic prose. The creative and enticing themes stay with you long after the story ends. A pure pleasure to read." Elsa Holland, Author of The Velvet Basement Series